Angry shrieks of disruptor fire filled the air.

Julian Bashir didn't know who'd shot first—it might have been Sakonna, but it could just as easily have been Kitsom or Cole—but within seconds of Cole's order to attack, Bashir and Sarina were in the thick of the assault, laying down suppressing fire as they charged down the scout ship's ramp. They reached the deck and split up, Bashir to the right and Sarina to the left, to get out of the way of Webb's handheld cannon.

The Breen in the docking bay stood frozen as the barrage of disruptor blasts erupted from the hold of the *Králik*. Most of the technicians and engineers fell or were launched backward as the fusillade slammed into them. All those who stood between the Section 31 team and the sealed blast doors that led to the station's interior were downed within moments.

Bashir turned, crouched, and snapped off a flurry of shots at another group of Breen. He felled two in quick succession, then had to dive for cover behind one of the *Králik*'s landing struts, to dodge an incoming salvo from a Breen trooper in a guard post on an upper deck overlooking the docking bay. Before Bashir could recover his bearings to retaliate, Sakonna drew out the trooper with harassing fire, and Kitsom finished him with a precision head shot.

Then came the thunder.

More Stories of

SECTION 31

Cloak
S. D. Perry

Rogue
Andy Mangels and Michael A. Martin

Abyss
David Weddle and Jeffrey Lang

Shadow
Dean Wesley Smith and Kristine Kathryn Rusch

STAR TREK®
SECTION 31

DISAVOWED

DAVID MACK

Based on *Star Trek*
created by Gene Roddenberry
and
Star Trek: Deep Space Nine®
created by Rick Berman & Michael Piller

POCKET BOOKS
New York London Toronto Sydney New Delhi Ikkuna Station

Pocket Books
A Division of Simon & Schuster, Inc.
1230 Avenue of the Americas
New York, NY 10020

This book is a work of fiction. Any references to historical events, real people, or real places are used fictitiously. Other names, characters, places, and events are products of the author's imagination, and any resemblance to actual events or places or persons, living or dead, is entirely coincidental.

First Pocket Books paperback edition November 2014

POCKET and colophon are registered trademarks of Simon & Schuster, Inc.

For information about special discounts for bulk purchases, please contact Simon & Schuster Special Sales at 1-866-506-1949 or business@simonandschuster.com.

The Simon & Schuster Speakers Bureau can bring authors to your live event. For more information or to book an event, contact the Simon & Schuster Speakers Bureau at 1-866-248-3049 or visit our website at www.simonspeakers.com.

Cover art by Tim Bradstreet
Cover design by Alan Dingman

Manufactured in the United States of America

10 9 8 7 6 5 4 3 2 1

ISBN 978-1-4767-5308-9
ISBN 978-1-4767-5313-3 (ebook)

Dedicated to Ira Steven Behr,
who conceived of Section 31,
and to Bradley Thompson and David Weddle,
who brought it to life

Historian's Note

This story takes place in January 2386, a few months after newly elected Federation president Kellessar zh'Tarash pardoned Doctor Julian Bashir for the actions he undertook to save the Andorian people from extinction (*Star Trek: The Fall*, Book III: *A Ceremony of Losses*). Events in the alternate universe occur approximately seven years after the founding of the Galactic Commonwealth by former members of the ultimately victorious Terran Rebellion (*Star Trek Mirror Universe: Rise Like Lions*).

The true way to be deceived is to think oneself more knowing than others.

—François de La Rochefoucauld, *Maxims*

DISAVOWED

One

All that stood between Thot Tran and salvation was unrequited love and the edge of the universe.

In recent years his scientific career had been marred by one failure after another. Despite grievous setbacks, he had retained his position as the director of the Special Research Division, one of the loftiest posts in the Breen Confederacy, but one more failure would be the end of him. Domo Pran, the leader of the Confederacy, had made that grim fact abundantly clear. Now Tran's entire career hinged upon proving a mad hypothesis before Pran's patience expired.

To make matters worse, his only hope of success lay in the eccentric genius of his Tzenkethi collaborator, Choska Ves Fel-AA. The humanoid outworlder was strangely beautiful to Tran's eyes. Lithe and silver skinned, Choska was blessed with coppery tresses that fell past her elegant shoulders, and the irises of her ovoid eyes glittered like gold. Upon first meeting her, Tran had shaken her delicate hand—and even through his uniform's insulated glove his flesh had prickled from an electric tingle. Though he'd been warned ahead of time that Tzenkethi could impart such an effect upon contact, he had been unprepared for the thrill it had given him. Every detail of Choska's being was rapturous. Her voice was melodic, like the ringing of chimes incapable of striking a false note. Her movements were grace incarnate. Even her most outlandish ideas and outrageous theories possessed a strange elegance.

Tran's life and career both hung by a slender thread, and all he could think about was the fact that, against all reason, he had fallen in love with an alien who would never love him back.

Not that he hadn't set limits. When Choska had suggested they convert their shared laboratory space aboard Ikkuna Station into a gravity envelope enclosure, so that all its surfaces— the walls and ceiling, as well as the deck—could be utilized as operational space, Tran had invoked his privilege as project's director to keep their lab securely on the floor. After all, Ikkuna Station had been built by, and was run by, the Breen, just inside Confederate space, and converting the bulkheads and over- heads to serve the same functions as the deck would have been quite tedious and time-consuming. Which had made it all the more shameful, in his opinion, that for a moment he actually had considered granting her request before he'd vetoed it.

Since then, her already inscrutable façade had become impenetrable, hardened against his searching gaze by what he could only presume was resentment. The only discourse that passed between them now was the cold, dry jargon of the laboratory.

Choska spoke without shifting her eyes from the master console in front of her. "The generator is at full power. Mem- brane penetration anticipated in twenty seconds."

"Noted. Increase power to the threshold stabilizer on my mark."

The beguiling Tzenkethi physicist adjusted the settings. "Ready."

Their shared project was plagued by so many variables, so many unknown factors, that Tran had no idea if his proposal would work when translated from theory to practical applica- tion. All he could do was hope that the unrealized potential he had seen in the Tzenkethi's designs for an artificial wormhole generator had not been misguided—or, worse, a delusion.

The latter scenario was all too real a possibility for him to ignore. He had been the chief architect of the Confederacy's recent failed plan to salvage from Federation space a wormhole-propulsion starship that hailed from an alternate universe. That botched mission had squandered billions of *sakto*, not to mention many lives and several years of research and development. The operation had imploded just shy of success, making its collapse a bitter pill for Tran to swallow. He had been certain the new domo, Pran, would have him killed as an example to others.

Instead, Pran had allowed Tran to retain his post as the director of the Special Research Division, and he had even authorized a substantial budget for Tran's project to seek out a passage to the alternate universe. Tran had proposed the project to Pran as a means of salvaging some value from their lost investment in the recovery of the wormhole ship, which he was certain had originated in a close parallel dimension, a nearby quantum reality much like the one they inhabited. Although there were decades of theoretical research supporting parallel universes, many Breen scientists continued to scoff at the notion such realms could possibly exist in anything resembling stable configurations.

Tran was gambling his last measure of credibility on proving them wrong.

To do it, he needed the artificial wormhole generator developed by the Tzenkethi. It had not lived up to their expectations when it was first deployed a few years earlier. It had depended upon the existing subspatial geometry of the Bajoran wormhole to give it shape, and it had proved disastrously vulnerable to sabotage and attack. Regardless, it had constituted a major scientific breakthrough—one that Tran now intended to exploit to its fullest advantage.

He switched the master console's main display to an exterior view focused on the generator's projection zone. "Initiate phase shift. Start at point zero three and increase slowly."

"Starting." Choska entered more commands on the console. She stopped when an alert flashed beneath her fingertips. "We're picking up severe gravimetric distortion."

"That's expected. Keep increasing the phase shift. I'll stabilize the threshold." On the viewscreen, a broad swath of space trembled. Subsonic vibrations traveled through the deck beneath Tran's booted feet. Steady tremors from Ikkuna Station's antimatter generator shook his bones, a tangible manifestation of excitement. "We're almost there. Get ready to launch the recon ship."

Choska remained all business. "Recon One at standby."

Then it happened. All of Tran's predictions came true.

Space-time ripped itself apart outside Ikkuna Station, and a rift in the invisible barrier between quantum realities was revealed. It was a wound in the skin of the universe. Brutishly cut, its edges glowed with energies beyond measure or definition. The ragged, irregular aperture dilated, revealing another cosmos: one populated by the same stars, all at once entirely familiar and yet undeniably foreign.

The Breen scientist gathered data from his sensor panel. "The quantum signature matches the ship we found on Tirana Three. That's definitely its universe of origin. Launch the recon ship."

"It's away. Crossing the threshold now."

Tran knew his teary-eyed, hopeful gaze was safe behind his snout-shaped mask—the ubiquitous identity-erasing uniform of Breen society. And if his voice should quaver with emotion, he could trust his mask's vocoder to strip it bare and garble it into meaningless machine-speak. *How can I ever reveal myself to Choska while I remain a prisoner in my own flesh? How can I show her that I'm more than just a cog in the Confederacy's machine when I can't even tell her my real name?*

His maudlin reflections were banished as the rift contracted without warning, shredding the reconnaissance vessel into a cloud of sparking debris. He activated a review of the sensor logs even as he vented his frustration at Choska. "What happened?"

"As I warned, the passage between quantum universes is intrinsically unstable. Based on sensor readings from the moment of collapse, I would postulate that ambient energy emissions from the reconnaissance vessel destabilized the throat of the wormhole between the universes."

"Fortunate, then, that the reconnaissance vessel was an automated ship with no crew."

"Yes, that was a prudent precaution on your part, Thot Tran." Choska adjusted some settings on her side of the master console. "It will take several days to analyze the data and devise a plan for shielding vessels that need to pass through the quantum rift."

Tran knew of no politic way to explain to Choska that they might not have that much time. Domo Pran was eager for results—and he had made it understood that any failure to deliver them would be met with the harshest of punishments. "Do whatever you can to expedite your analysis, Doctor. The sooner we complete this phase of the project, the better."

"I will do my best." She downloaded the sensor data to a padd and left the control center—most likely to review the results in the privacy of her office.

Tran watched her leave, knowing he should start his own independent review of the failed recon deployment. But all he could think about was escaping through the rift, with Choska at his side—and cursing the Confederacy, the Typhon Pact, and the Tzenkethi Coalition as he and the magnificent object of his affections left them all behind.

Two

Few environments had ever mesmerized Julian Bashir to the same degree as the interior of Laenishul. The sprawling, multilevel restaurant was situated more than a hundred meters below Andor's storm-tossed East La'Vor Sea. It was sheltered beneath a hemisphere of transparent aluminum that stood more than forty meters tall at its apex. An external layer of light-amplifying crystal extended the visibility and clarity of the restaurant's view of the surrounding ocean realm.

Laenishul's floors also were composed of the same see-through metal, enabling its patrons to gaze into a yawning aquatic abyss beneath the restaurant. The deep chasm was lit from far below by bioluminescent algae and other self-illuminating life-forms. Inside the dome's pressurized oasis, hovering orbs cast dim amber light on each table. Faint glowing lines etched into the floor marked the pathways that connected the various seating areas, their staircases and lift platforms, the kitchen and back offices, and the refresher facilities.

Access to the restaurant was limited to a single turbolift from its hovering outpost above the surface. In calm weather, the platform was quite stable; shuttlecraft and other small personal vehicles came and went, picking up and discharging passengers in a well-choreographed dance. During the region's rougher seasons, the platform retracted the turbolift umbilical from the restaurant and served instead as a transporter signal relay, to help coordinate traffic from the capital as well as from ships in orbit.

One detail of Laenishul struck Bashir as ironic. Because the undersea bistro had been financed in part by the New Imperial Andorian Aquarium, its menu was devoid of seafood. Not even replicated versions of thalassic victuals were to be found on its extensive bill of fare.

He put down his menu and looked across the table at his inamorata, Sarina Douglas. "Does it seem odd to you that I have a sudden hankering for sashimi?"

"Not at all." The slender, late-thirtyish blonde continued to peruse her menu. "Men always want what they can't have."

He took her playful verbal jab in stride. "I think it's a generally *human* failing."

She skewered him with a narrowed stare. "Really? You think you can trump my sexism with your racism? Color me appalled, Julian." She resumed her study of the menu. "Normally, a filet mignon would sound good to me, but I've yet to find a place on this planet that can cook one properly." An elegantly arched eyebrow telegraphed her query. "What're you having?"

"Some kind of midlife crisis, I suspect."

"Well, make sure you get a salad with that. It'll help your digestion."

Bashir was about to parry her bon mot with a cutting quip, but he swallowed his retort when he saw the Andorian maître d' escort their dinner guest across the dining room to their table. He caught Sarina's eye and directed her with a subtle lift of his chin to look to her right.

She glanced quickly—just long enough to recognize the stylishly dressed, fair-skinned, dark-haired woman approaching them as Ozla Graniv, an award-winning journalist for the Trill-based newsmagazine *Seeker*. Graniv appeared to be in her early forties, but Bashir recalled from a bio he'd read that she was actually in her early fifties. She had a square chin, prominent cheekbones, thick eyebrows, and a piercing stare behind which burned the light of a fierce intellect. Graniv thanked the maître d' quietly and dismissed him with a nod. As he turned away, the journalist sat down with Bashir and Sarina and met their apprehensive stares with a smile. "Thanks for agreeing to talk with me. I know you haven't been keen on granting interviews since your return to civilian life." She nodded at the menu Bashir held. "What're you having?"

"Second thoughts."

"I see." She averted her eyes and brushed a stray lock of hair behind her right ear, revealing her species' trademark pale brown spots, which ran in a narrow band from her temple, past her ear, and down the side of her neck under her collar. She adopted an air of humility and looked Bashir in the eye. "Say the word, and I'll go."

He was about to accept Graniv's gracious offer of a painless exit when Sarina put her hand on top of his. She gave him a reassuring look. "It'll be all right, Julian."

Bashir calmed his frazzled nerves and nodded. "All right. Let's get on with it."

"Thank you." Graniv took a small recording device from her pocket, switched it on, and set it on the table. "For the record, this is Ozla Graniv, interviewing Doctor Julian Bashir on Andor. Today is January seventh, 2386. It's a pleasure to meet you, Doctor."

"Likewise."

She rested her arms on the table and leaned forward. "Just to set your mind at ease, I'm not here to make you rehash the actions you took on Bajor, or here on Andor, to deliver your cure for the Andorian fertility crisis. All of that is a matter of record, thanks to the redacted but still enlightening transcripts of your Starfleet court-martial."

"I'm glad to hear that, but I feel compelled to correct you already. The retroviral gene therapy I brought to the Andorian people was not, strictly speaking, my creation. Most of the research and work had been done by Professor Marthrossi zh'Thiin and Thirishar ch'Thane before I became involved. In fact, I'd say the work was ninety-nine-point-five percent done before I was asked to pitch in. I'd also had considerable help from several prominent medical scientists, and my mission would have failed if not for the courage of civilian pilot Emerson Harris, who gave his life to make sure both I and the cure reached Andor."

Sarina let slip a low *harrumph*. "So much for not rehashing your actions."

Graniv ignored her and pushed on with the interview. "What I'm more interested in, Doctor, is your life after the court-martial. The Federation government tried to downplay the importance of your pardon by President zh'Tarash and the strings her administration pulled to have your Starfleet discharge amended from dishonorable to honorable. Can you tell me—"

"Excuse me." A young Andorian *shen* stepped up to the table from behind Graniv. "I'm sorry to interrupt, but I just wanted to say thank you, Doctor." She pressed Bashir's left hand between her blue palms, lifted it, and kissed his fingertips. "My name is Jessala sh'Lero, and my bond group and I are expecting our first child thanks to your miracle cure."

"You're very welcome." Bashir tried to withdraw his hand. The *shen* tightened her grip.

"May Uzaveh the Infinite and Mother Stars watch over you, all the days of your life."

He pulled back a bit harder than he would have liked and freed his hand. "Too kind."

The overwrought *shen* continued to utter blessings and

thanks as the maître d' and a pair of servers ushered her out of the dining room and into the turbolift. Graniv watched the retreating spectacle with a glimmer of cynical amusement. "Does that happen a lot?"

"Not too often." Bashir shrugged. "Ten, maybe twelve times a day. But only when I make the mistake of leaving my house." He took a sip of his Altair water. "You were saying?"

"I was going to ask what your life as a civilian has been like since the pardon, but I think I just saw all I need to know."

Bashir and Sarina traded weary, knowing looks. She answered for him. "Not entirely. For all the Andorians who want to kiss Julian's hand, there are more than a few who'd love to cave in his skull with a brick for tampering with the purity of the Andorian genome."

That revelation surprised Graniv. She looked at Bashir. "Is that true?"

"As my old pal Vic Fontaine would say, 'Andor is a tough room.'"

The journalist nodded, then turned her attention toward Sarina. "It's my understanding that you resigned from Starfleet after Doctor Bashir's court-martial."

Sarina looked and sounded defensive. "That's right."

"Can you tell me what your billet was before you resigned?"

"I was the senior deputy chief of security aboard Starbase Deep Space Nine."

"So you *weren't* acting as an operative for Starfleet Intelligence while on DS Nine?"

Graniv's penetrating gaze met its match in Sarina's serene poker face. "No."

"Have you ever served in that capacity?"

Sarina remained unfazed. "No comment."

"What about your current civilian employment? Is it correct that you're now assigned to the Andor office of the Federation Security Agency?"

A thin, taut smile played across Sarina's face as the unanswered question hung between her and Graniv. Bashir knew that smile was not an expression of amusement but a warning sign. He set aside his menu, pushed back his chair, and stood. "Forgive us, Ms. Graniv, but we're late for an appointment. Perhaps we could continue this another time."

Graniv stood as Sarina got up to make her exit with Bashir. The Trill stepped into Bashir's path. "I just have one last question, Doctor. Do you miss your life in Starfleet?"

He frowned, unable to conceal the emptiness he still felt when he thought of all that he'd given up in order to do what needed to be done. He ushered Sarina past Graniv as he answered her question in a low and somber voice. "More than you will ever know."

Three

The Alternate Universe

The aft hatch of the command deck opened with a soft hiss, turning the head of Honored Elder Taran'atar. The Jem'Hadar acknowledged the arrival of his superior, the Vorta known as Eris, with a nod. "We have dropped back to sublight and are approaching the Idran wormhole."

The violet-eyed commander stopped at Taran'atar's side. They were a study in contrasts. He was tall, broadly muscled, and protected by a thick, scaly gray hide studded with chitinous spikes, a genetic inheritance that likely had evolved to thwart would-be predators. She was delicate of frame, with soft pale skin and a tall crown of tightly curled raven hair. Her long ears hugged the sides of her head and followed the elegant line of her jaw.

Compared to a Jem'Hadar, Eris might have appeared to be helpless. Taran'atar knew better. He had seen her wield telekinetic powers—a rare and special gift from the Founders—to devastating effect on unwary foes. But her true strength lay in her mantle of authority. She was a Vorta; that meant she controlled the ship's daily ration of ketracel-white, which ensured the obedience of her legion of Jem'Hadar soldiers. Even though Taran'atar himself had no need of the white—a genetic anomaly even more rare than Eris's psionic talent—he accepted it from her every day with gratitude, as an example to his soldiers.

This was the order of things, as the Founders had willed it.

Eris lowered her holographic eyepiece into place. "Have our escorts arrived?"

"Yes. All support ships are in position, awaiting final orders." He tapped the side of his eyepiece's headset, initiating a transfer of his tactical overlay to Eris's eyepiece.

A subdued smile brightened her face. "Well done, First." She studied the mission plan. "Battle Cruiser 815 will take the point position as our fleet enters the wormhole. Battle Cruisers 674 and 918 will flank Carrier Vessel 181. We'll follow the carrier. Attack Vessels 319 and 560 will defend our flanks. The rest of the battle group will follow us in standard formation."

Taran'atar reviewed his commander's deployment strategy in his holographic eyepiece. "Permission to make a recommendation."

"Granted."

"I suggest Battleship 432 and its escorts stay behind to guard our side of the wormhole."

Eris furrowed her brow. "For what reason?"

"Long-range sensors have detected Ascendant battle groups in adjacent sectors."

She grimaced at the unwelcome news. "Is there reason to think they've detected us?"

"Not yet. But now that our fleet is assembled, we risk our presence being noted."

Her voice dropped to a tense whisper. "We can't let the Ascendants find the wormhole. Not until our mission on the other side is complete."

"Battleship 432 and its combat group can deploy in a patrol pattern to mask the wormhole's coordinates after we move the rest of the fleet to the Alpha Quadrant. If it encounters the Ascendants, it will do so away from the mouth of the wormhole."

His advice mollified Eris, though only to a small degree. "Very well. See it done."

"As you command." He used a nearby panel to amend the deployment plan and then transmitted it to the other ships in the fleet. Within moments he verified confirmation codes from all the ships. He turned back toward Eris. "All orders confirmed."

"Thank you, First. I'll let her know we're ready." Eris moved aft so she could have some privacy while speaking to the ship's most important passenger: a Founder.

In all of Taran'atar's thirty-two years of life—which, to the best of his knowledge, made him the oldest Jem'Hadar who had ever lived—he had never seen a Founder. Through countless military campaigns and decades of deep-space exploration, his only companions had been his fellow Jem'Hadar and their Vorta commanders. On more than a thousand worlds he had met hundreds of intelligent species, most of whom he'd helped bring under the control of the Dominion and its reclusive godlike masters, but until a few days earlier, he had never had reason to think he was ever in the same star system as a Founder, much less on the same starship. Knowing he had been entrusted with the sacred duty of safeguarding a Founder's life had filled him with a measure of pride he'd not felt in decades—not since his long-ago promotion to First.

He set his holographic eyepiece for an external view. The other ships of the fleet circled like raptors. They slipped past one another in graceful turns as they moved into their assigned positions for the journey through the wormhole to the Alpha Quadrant—a jump of more than sixty thousand light-years, to a distant and largely unexplored region of the galaxy. To date, only Eris and Taran'atar's vessel, Battleship 774, had ventured to the far side of the subspace anomaly. For years, they alone had gathered vital intelligence about that far-off quadrant. In recognition of their initiative, they had been rewarded with the honor of escorting a Founder to the Alpha Quadrant on what promised to be a historic mission.

Eris returned to Taran'atar's side. "She's coming."

Taran'atar raised his voice to fill the bridge. "Attention!" The crew turned from their posts to face him and held themselves ramrod straight, their arms pressed to their sides, their chins raised with pride. A moment later the aft hatch slid open. A feminine humanoid entered. Her mien was soft and without detail. The most prominent features of her visage were her deep eye sockets, narrow lips, and high forehead. Her face was framed by a pulled-tight helmet of flaxen hair. Only her head and hands were bare. From the neck down she was covered by a modest garment of loose-fitting beige cloth, and she wore simple footwear.

Eris stepped forward to greet the nondescript alien woman. The Vorta shut her eyes and bowed her head as she spoke. "We are honored to receive you, Founder."

Taran'atar's eyes widened. *So this is a Founder.* All his life he had wondered what it would be like to look upon the face of one of his gods. Now she stood before him, and he found himself perplexed. The Founder was almost a cipher, an approximation of a humanoid without definition. Regardless, Taran'atar knew on an instinctual level that she was who Eris had proclaimed her to be. If not for the genetic programming that compelled him to remain alert at all times, he would have bowed to her, just as Eris had done.

The Founder picked up a command headset, put it on, and lowered the holographic eyepiece. "Everything has been made ready?"

Eris kept her head bowed to show deference, but lifted it just enough to look upon her divine leader. "Yes, Founder. Honored Elder Taran'atar has seen to the details."

A pleased nod. "Excellent." The Founder raised the eyepiece and faced Taran'atar—showing her back to Eris in the process. "I'm well pleased with you, First."

He remained silent because she had not asked him a question, nor had she instructed him to speak. Instead, he stood at attention and betrayed no sign that the Founder's unflinching stare felt as if it were drilling into the darkest corners of his being.

She stole a look over her shoulder at Eris, then fixed her eyes on Taran'atar. "I've paid close attention to you ever since you discovered this wormhole nearly five years ago. Your work has set the stage for what I expect will be the next great chapter in the history of the Dominion. But I wonder, Taran'atar— are you prepared to play the role I have in mind for you?"

"I live to serve the Founders in all things."

She sighed with mild disappointment. "Of that, I have no doubt."

Taran'atar had no idea what else he could have said. It was a truth into which he had been born and with which he would die. It was inescapable.

The Founder left him and returned to Eris's side. "It's time."

Eris nodded to Taran'atar, who barked curt orders at his men, setting them and the rest of the fleet in motion. Through his eyepiece, he watched the wormhole explode into being from the emptiness of space, a swiftly unfolding blossom of blue fire and white light. When everyone was, at last, in position, he used his headset to open a subspace channel to the rest of the fleet.

"All vessels, this is Battleship 774. Proceed into the wormhole."

Tensions were high aboard the wormhole jaunt ship *Enterprise*. Captain Jean-Luc Picard felt his crew's rising tide of anxiety as he walked from his quarters to the turbolift. In the past few weeks, the almost palpable sense of dread had gone from mild to severe, and Picard hadn't needed the empathic talents of his half-Betazoid security chief Deanna Troi to tell him why. There was one thing that had everyone aboard on edge, one thing driving an endless march of rumors.

The Dominion.

Nothing like a dose of the unknown to stir up people's fears. He fought to keep his own doubts and concerns buried as deeply as possible. *The crew needs to be able to believe in me, now more than ever.* That was just one of many essential lessons Picard had learned during the past nine years he had spent commanding the *Enterprise*, on missions that had run the gamut from exploration to peacekeeping and everything in between.

The turbolift doors opened, and he stepped in. Troi was already inside the lift car. Her dark hair was knotted in a loose ponytail. She smiled at him. "Good morning, Jean-Luc."

"Deanna." He had tried for years to get her to address him as "Captain" while they were on the ship, but their years of informality prior to their recruitment by Memory Omega had forged habits too hard to break. She had, at least, taught herself to address him by rank when they were on the bridge. It was a minor concession, but a hard life marked by arbitrary cruelties and heartbreaking losses had taught Picard to be thankful for even life's smallest victories.

Troi turned a sly, sideways look in his direction. "The crew knows something's up."

"Do they? And how, pray tell, do they know?"

The diminutive security chief struck a deceptively de-mure pose. "Apparently, our first officer had the engineering department up all night fine-tuning everything from the jaunt drive to the waste reclamators. It seems to have created the impression that we're heading into danger."

Picard was at a loss. Commander K'Ehleyr was a superb

executive officer, and after serving with the half-human, half-Klingon woman for nearly a decade, Picard had come to think of her as indispensable. Her passionate approach to command served as a welcome balance to Picard's more cerebral style of leadership, but her relentless pursuit of perfection—from both herself and the crew—had, on a few occasions, done more harm than good. Picard hoped this would not prove to be one of those times.

The turbolift doors opened with a whisper of sound, followed by the low susurrus of muted conversations and computer feedback tones that defined the ambience of the *Enterprise*'s bridge. K'Ehleyr noted Picard and Troi's arrival. The tall woman stood from the command chair. "Good morning, sir. We jaunted into the Bajor system at oh seven twenty. We're currently holding station approximately one million kilometers from the Denorios Belt."

Picard settled into the center seat. "Any activity from the wormhole?"

"Not yet, sir. We're keeping watch."

At the forward duty stations were the regular Alpha Shift personnel: the Tellarite operations officer, Lieutenant Trag chim Pog, and the female Vulcan flight controller, Lieutenant Tolaris. Behind Picard, Troi relieved Ensign th'Fesh, a young Andorian *thaan* who manned the security and tactical station overnight during Gamma Shift. Troi reviewed the reports on her console and keyed in a few commands. "Captain, you have an update from Memory Omega."

"On my panel." As soon as he'd spoken the command, the communiqué appeared on the small touch screen mounted beside his command chair. He activated the biometric security scan, which checked his genetic profile, retinal pattern, voiceprint, and quantum signature—all in a matter of nanoseconds. From his perspective, it was over as soon as it began.

The encrypted message from the secret benefactors of the Galactic Commonwealth opened on his screen.

He made a quick perusal of its contents and closed it.

K'Ehleyr had learned to read his moods at a glance. "Bad news?"

"Let's just say it was far from encouraging." He dropped his voice to a more confidential volume. "Fifteen jaunt ships are standing by to reinforce us if this goes badly."

"If this goes sideways, fifteen ships won't begin to stanch the bleeding."

"Trust me, Number One—I'm well aware of that fact."

An alert beeped on Pog's console. The yellow-furred Tellarite turned and looked back at Picard and K'Ehleyr, his solid-black eyes wide beneath fear-arched brows. "Tetryon surge inside the Denorios Belt. I think the wormhole is—" The image on the main viewscreen finished his thought with a brilliant tableau of swirling light and glowing ionized gases. A chasm in space-time unfurled itself, a vortex of cold fire born of forces Picard couldn't begin to fathom.

A fleet of Jem'Hadar ships surged up and out of the wormhole, cruising in a solid battle formation on an intercept course for Bajor—and the *Enterprise*.

It's begun.

Picard knew the attention of the Commonwealth—and the rest of the Alpha Quadrant—would be trained upon this moment, waiting for the shape of the future to be revealed. He took a calming breath and prepared himself to face the inevitable. He stood, smoothed the front of his black uniform, and forced his face into a semblance of courage.

"Lieutenant Commander Troi. . . . Open hailing frequencies."

Four

There was peace in submersion. Beneath the surface of his heated patio swimming pool, Bashir neared the end of his ninth consecutive fifteen-meter underwater lap. He had taken to swimming laps first for the cardiovascular value of the full-body workout, but he had come to revel in his late-night swims for their solitude. His aquatic retreat refracted light and muffled sound, rendering the surface world into impressionistic blurs. It was as close as he could come to shutting out the world without removing himself from it.

Knowing these escapes were temporary and fleeting made them feel that much more precious. Privacy had become a commodity in short supply now that he was a celebrity—famous in most quarters of Andor, infamous nearly everywhere else. Even if he had wanted to fade into obscurity, that was no longer a possibility. All he could do now was keep a low profile and hope that the public's notoriously short attention span would soon latch on to some new shiny object du jour and allow him to slip away, into the fog of the forgotten.

His outstretched hand found the wall of the pool. He tucked and curled through a flip-turn, determined to swim one more length underwater before coming up for air.

One hundred fifty meters of submerged swimming was an impressive feat for a human being, though far from unprecedented. Centuries earlier, before the advent of genetically augmented humans, the Earth record for a man swimming underwater without equipment had been 186 meters. A handful of twenty-fourth-century human men had pushed that record to 219 meters. Bashir had no illusions about his own athletic prowess. At the age of forty-four he was still very much in his prime, but he knew that he couldn't last much beyond 160 meters underwater, and he had come close enough to death on several occasions that he no longer had a young man's desire to flirt with its dark embrace.

The end of the pool shimmered into sight. Through the watery veil it resembled a mirage, but its glassy tiles were smooth and cool to the touch as his hand made contact. He exhaled what was left of the breath in his lungs, crowning himself with bubbles as he surfaced.

His face met the brisk night air. It was high summer in Sheras, on the western shore of the La'Vor Sea, but the frigid Andorian climate compelled Bashir to paraphrase an old human aphorism: *The coldest winter I ever spent was a summer on Andor.* He gasped, sending up a plume of vapor, then drew a long and much-needed breath as he wiped the chlorinated water from his eyes. Then he saw the man standing on the deck in front of him.

Bashir recognized his uninvited visitor at once. "Cole."

"You flatter me, Doctor. After all this time, I wasn't sure you'd remember me."

The middle-aged human looked just as he had the first time they had met, nine years earlier. He was of medium height and build, with dark hair cropped close to his handsome, symmetrical head. His eyes were the same arresting hue of emerald, and he was still clean shaven. Like his peers in the nefarious secret organization known as Section 31, he was garbed in a leathery black uniform.

Everything about Cole—from his grooming and attire to his steady and confrontational posture—put Bashir on edge. He eyed the older man with suspicion. "As I recall, the first time we met you dosed me with an aerosolized psychotropic drug. What's tonight's trick? Spiking the water I swim in?"

"Nothing so gauche. I'd like to think we're past the need for such tactics, wouldn't you?"

Bashir climbed onto the wood-planked deck that ringed the pool and nodded toward his towel, which was draped over a chair behind Cole. "Do you mind?"

Cole handed Bashir the towel. "You're looking well."

Bashir dried himself. "What do you want?"

"Manners, Doctor. There's no need for such rudeness."

"Oh, really? The last time we met, you sent me on a manhunt into the Badlands, to fix one of *your* mistakes. If memory serves, that 'simple assignment' became a bloodbath. To be blunt, Mister Cole, your presence conjures less than cordial memories."

The accusations drew a thin smile of mild embarrassment from Cole. "Touché."

Bashir lifted his thick gray cotton robe from a hook on the privacy wall of mortared stones that surrounded the deck. "It's late. Do us both a favor and get to the point."

The agent crossed his arms. "As you wish. There's a situation developing that will very likely require a response from the organization. Because of the specific details of this crisis, I think you're uniquely qualified to be of help."

"Not interested." Bashir tied his robe shut.

"You haven't heard the details yet."

"I don't need to. I was opposed to everything your organization represents when we met nine years ago, and I find it—and you—just as offensive now."

A mirthless smirk hinted at Cole's growing ire. "What aspect of our remit offends you? The part where we save innocent lives? Or the one where we defend the Federation?"

"I object to your utter lack of accountability. You act without legal authority, oversight, ethics, or humanity. You're a cancer infecting the Federation, an infection I'd gladly excise."

Cole shrugged. "I guess it's true. You can't please everyone."

Bashir took a step toward Cole, intending to confront him, but halted as the agent uncrossed his arms and let his hands fall to his sides, open and tensed to act. Subtle shifts in the older man's balance and posture signaled that he was ready to defend himself, and that he would likely prove to be a merciless opponent in hand-to-hand combat. Sensing that he was out of his league against a trained killer such as Cole, Bashir backed off just enough to signal he had no intention of pressing an attack. "Joke all you like; I find nothing funny about what you are."

"What I am, Doctor, is *effective*. Something you ceased to be the moment you let yourself get drummed out of Starfleet." He pivoted from his hips, making a show of looking around with disdain at the luxury residence Bashir now shared with Sarina. "You can't tell me *this* is your idea of a meaningful life?"

"Actually, I'm planning on opening a private practice here on Andor."

The agent let out a short, derisive chortle. "Of course you are."

"Meaning what?"

"Where else can you go? As I understand it, Andor's the only planet that'll give you a license to practice medicine these days." He held up a hand to forestall Bashir's rebuttal. "Yes, I know Federation law says other member worlds have to recognize your license—full faith and credit, and so on. But without a Federation-issued license, you'd have to retake your board exams on every world you visit before you could practice there. Sounds inconvenient to me."

Anger began to show through Bashir's carefully crafted mask of indifference. "If all you have left to offer are insults, feel free to do your disappearing trick anytime now."

"I'm not trying to pick a fight with you, Doctor. All I'm saying is, I understand how . . . *unfulfilling* your current circumstances must feel. Until now, you'd spent your entire adult life either in Starfleet or at its academy, preparing for your medical career. Now the admiralty's cast you aside for no better reason than you caused them some embarrassment, by doing what they should have had the courage to do in the first place. You've devoted your life to others, to serving the Federation and the ideals for which it stands. Are you really going to spend the rest of your life on the outside looking in, just because Starfleet says so? Come work with us, and you can still serve the Federation—where, when, and how you're most needed."

Bashir moved beneath the heat lamps, under the trellis in front of the sliding glass doors that led to the top floor of his and Sarina's hilltop villa. He looked back at Cole and shook his head. "I see what you're trying to do. It won't work. Appealing to my wounded pride isn't nearly enough to make me abandon my principles, no matter how patriotic you try to make it sound."

"What if I told you the Breen are looking for a way to reach the alternate universe? The one you visited back in 2370 with your pal Kira Nerys."

That news snared Bashir's attention. "Why would the Breen want to go there?"

"To steal advanced technology. The Terran Rebellion you helped inspire won its revolution a few years ago, with a little help from some folks a lot like us. Unfortunately for them, their success has painted a target on their backs—and the Breen are taking aim."

It was a troubling scenario, but Bashir knew better than to take Section 31 at its word. "How do I know you're telling me the truth? What proof do you have?"

"Nothing solid. Not yet, anyway. For now, we have to rely on educated guesswork."

"I see. More smoke and mirrors. The same old story." He walked toward the glass doors, which parted in response to his approach. Warm air billowed out of the villa and washed over him. "Sorry, but I won't sell my soul in the name of 'guesswork.'"

Cole still sounded confident. "So if I bring you solid evidence, you're in?"

Bashir stopped and looked back at Cole. "I didn't say that."

"You didn't have to." A sinister smile deepened the creases of the agent's weathered face. "I'll be in touch, Doctor. Good night."

Bright colors washed over Cole from crown to sole. He flickered and pixelated for an instant, and then he vanished like a dream lost at the moment of awakening.

Bashir gazed upon the empty space left behind by the interactive hologram of Cole. For all his protests, he had been expecting a visit from Section 31 for some time. The only surprise had been the organization's decision to use Cole as their messenger.

He stepped away from the doors. They slid closed, leaving Bashir to regard the dark outline of his reflection on their tinted glass. *So far, my infiltration of Thirty-one is going exactly as Sarina and I planned.* He frowned at his shadow self. *That can't be a good sign.*

Sarina Douglas knew whom she would find waiting for her when she reached the Kathela Falls Bridge. The long, narrow walkway, which passed behind the falls' roaring wall of water, was deserted except for the Vulcan woman who had summoned her. Though Sarina was not prone to acrophobia, she avoided looking down through the transparent aluminum walkway plates at the vertiginous drop to the falls' indigo lake, more than three kilometers below.

She stopped beside L'Haan, who stared at the curtain of falling water. The Section 31 handler's voice was low and dispassionate, yet tinged with notes of accusation. "You said he would cooperate. That he would be receptive to our overtures."

"If you had been the ones to liberate him from the black site prison—"

"That wasn't an option." The bangs of L'Haan's Cleopatra-cut black hair stayed in place even as she turned and tilted her head in a birdlike pose. "Why did he refuse our invitation?"

"From what I heard, he made his reasons clear to your man Cole."

"I'm not interested in his naïve rationale. I want your explanation for this setback. You assured me that once he was out of Starfleet, he'd be ready to join us. What happened?"

Sarina faced L'Haan, deliberately leaning in to encroach on the older woman's personal space. "You want to know what happened? The *pardon* is what happened. We were supposed to approach him when he had no other options—no career, no home, no allies left in Starfleet. But you let the Andorians spring him from prison. Then zh'Tarash gave him a clean slate, and the Andorians gave him a new medical license. He doesn't need us now."

"You didn't account for those possibilities?"

"No, and neither did you. Because when we started this, there was no way we could've known the sitting president pro tem would turn out to be a war criminal with a stolen identity. Or that his chief of staff would end up in prison. Or that Andor would get fast-tracked back into the Federation. Or that an Andorian would win a surprise victory in the presidential election—and end up granting a full pardon to the man who saved her species from extinction."

L'Haan backed away from Sarina and turned her eyes back toward the water. "When one frames the situation in those terms, the paradigm shift becomes easier to understand." She tapped her right index finger against the bridge's railing. "We need him for this mission."

"I can bring him into the organization."

"How?"

"Exactly as you predicted four years ago. The key to Bashir is his sense of romance. He loves me. There's nothing he won't do for me. If I ask him to join us, he will."

It was a bold suggestion, and a dangerous one. Sarina knew it was necessary to expedite Julian's infiltration into Section 31, but she had to make sure the organization didn't suspect her true motives, or Julian's.

As she'd expected, L'Haan met the notion with a dubious glare. "Do you think it's wise to risk abandoning your cover? Revealing yourself to him as one of our agents might sabotage all your efforts to secure his affections."

She shook her head. "Not a chance. I know how to control him now. He'll be upset at first. He'll resist, and he'll argue. He might even try to turn me. But in the end he'll decide I matter more to him than his hatred for Section Thirty-one."

The Vulcan considered Sarina's argument, then gave a grudging nod. "Very well. But this has to work, Agent Douglas. If he betrays you to Starfleet, we'll have to eliminate you both."

"I understand—but that's not going to happen. Trust me:
I can deliver Bashir."

"When?"

"Midnight tomorrow."

"See that you do." L'Haan retreated into the icy shadows
without offering Sarina so much as a token gesture of valediction.

Alone on the bridge, Sarina watched the plunging water
vanish into the misty depths far beneath her feet, and she
remembered that according to Andorian legends, Kathela
Falls was where star-crossed lovers came to take their own
lives. Then she reflected upon the disastrous course she had
just set for herself and Julian, and wondered whether L'Haan
had understood the cultural significance of the place she had
chosen for this fateful meeting.

She stared into the blue gloom where the falls met the
lake, and she faced the bitter truth. *No turning back now.
We're already over the edge—and there's nowhere left to go
but down.*

Five

The Alternate Universe

Kersil Regon waited on the shore. Kilometers away, in the middle of the shallow lake, stood a twisted mountain of metallic wreckage and broken thermoconcrete—the shattered remains of the once proud floating city known as Stratos. At home on Cardassia Prime, Regon had grown up surrounded by monuments to victory and success. Not until she had come here, to the now abandoned protectorate world of Ardana, had she ever seen a shrine to failure.

She was tempted to read too much into the fate of the dead metropolis. It had been felled years earlier by renegades acting on behalf of the Terran Rebellion. Her poetical nature wanted to extract a metaphor from the city's tragic end, but she dismissed the urge. It had been destroyed because its incompetent Klingon half-breed intendant, B'Elanna Torres, had been too foolish to see the threat of the rebellion for what it was, and too weak to defend herself from it.

Regon's mood turned maudlin. *No one can save us from ourselves.*

Footsteps crunched on the rocky ground behind her. Approaching with long strides and heavy steps was Kort, a Klingon whose assignment at Imperial Intelligence was the same as Regon's had once been at the now disbanded Obsidian Order. He had donned drab civilian clothing for their meeting, just as she had done.

They met, clasped each other's forearms, then came together in a brief embrace. Kort bared his jagged teeth in a broad grin. "It's been too long, dear Regon."

They parted, and she gave him an approving nod. "You're looking well, Kort."

"All an illusion, I assure you."

Up close, she saw that the furrows in Kort's weathered face had deepened beyond what could be blamed on time's relentless passage. His angular features had become care-worn.

Despite her curiosity, she elected not to pry into his personal life. Instead, she turned her eyes toward the broken peaks of Mount Stratos and steered their conversation toward business. "Thank you for coming. I know it can't have been easy for you to get away."

"No more challenging than it must have been for you." He took in the bleak landscape with a disappointed frown. "We used to own all of this. Now we're trespassers here."

She was suspicious of his seemingly innocent choice of pronoun. "I presume when you say 'we' used to own all of this, you mean the Alliance—not merely the Klingon Empire."

He feigned offense. "Naturally." A teasing smile dispelled his charade. "You and I might not agree which of our peoples deserved to be the dominant partner in the Alliance, but we've always agreed they were stronger together than separately."

"True. That's why I contacted you." She crossed her arms against a cold wind that gusted over them and rippled the surface of the lake. "Ever since the armistice, Damar has done his best to erase the Obsidian Order from existence, but many of its members remain. And they don't look kindly upon his détente with the rebels, or their new common-wealth."

A chortle masquerading as a cough rolled inside Kort's barrel chest. "I'm sure his support of the Oralian Way hasn't won him much love from the old guard, either."

"Your gift for understatement is rarely seen in Klingons."

"A consequence of circumstance. Regent Duras has been vexing the High Council and the high command of the Defense Force with his talk of restoring the ancient codes of honor. It seems no one ever told him 'Kahless' is just a name. He treats it like a magical totem."

"I confess I'm torn when it comes to your regent. On the one hand, I despise him for appeasing the rebels by recognizing their government. On the other, he has been quite generous to Cardassia in its time of need."

Kort gathered a mouthful of spit with a great wet rasp, then spat on the ground between himself and Regon. "Curse him and his charity. The strong should not coddle the weak."

His implied insult made a murderous chill course through Regon's veins. She reined in her urge to draw the blade hidden beneath her sleeve and slash the Klingon's throat. "Save your venom for the real enemy, Kort. Cardassia's clandestine services have been neutered, but those of us who still know how to do our jobs have learned something worth sharing. That is, if you and your allies at Imperial Intelligence are interested in restoring the balance of power."

"I belong to a shadow section that stands ready to act." His eyes narrowed beneath their shaggy brows. "What have your people learned?"

Regon wondered how much Kort knew. It was possible he was fishing with a naked hook, hoping to reel in some morsel of actionable intel while giving up nothing of value in return. Or he might pretend to do so, soliciting help from her and then withholding his own. Despite the many times they had saved each other's lives in previous decades, she still found it hard to trust him, now that they both were desperate for leverage.

Faced with no better alternative, she chose to put her trust in her old brother spy. "Our sensor posts have been tracking the Commonwealth's fleet. They're usually hopping all over the place, sometimes so fast we can barely keep up with them. But over the past week they've been oddly static. As if they're waiting for something. Something significant."

The Klingon digested that news with a pensive grunt. "Interesting. One of our scout ships reported yesterday that a small fleet of alien vessels arrived through the Bajoran wormhole."

"An alien fleet? From the Gamma Quadrant?"

"So it seems. We're still trying to decrypt their comms with the jaunt ship that was sent to meet them. All we know so far is that the newcomers hail from what they call the Dominion."

The pieces of the puzzle aligned in Regon's imagination. "That must be what has the Commonwealth fleet on alert. They're all standing by in case they need to go to war."

"Wishful thinking, dear Regon. And not a shred of proof to support it." He grinned. "You haven't changed a bit."

"Maybe not. But we'll both need to change if you want to come with me."

"Why? Where will you be going?"

"To Bajor. The only way to know what's really happening there is to put ourselves in the thick of it. And to do that"— she stroked his cheek—"we'll have to be able to fit in."

Kort winced at her implication. "Cosmetic surgery? Tell me you aren't serious."

"Unfortunately, I am. But look on the bright side." She leaned close to him and breathed a coquettish whisper into his ear. "For once, we won't be able to tell which of us is the prettier."

The thoroughfares of Erebus Station coursed with activity. Director Saavik moved along the edges of the crowd. The elderly Vulcan woman passed one docked jaunt ship after another. Steady currents of young men and women, hailing from a variety of species, moved on and off the vessels. Some were members of the ships' crews; others were engineers and mechanics who were involved in preparing the Commonwealth's next fleet for launch in a few weeks.

Saavik remembered the early years of Erebus Station, when it had been all but deserted, an automated shipyard programmed to first build itself and then to construct the wormhole-drive jaunt ships that had changed the fate of the galaxy by giving the Terran Rebellion an unassailable advantage over the now defunct Klingon-Cardassian Alliance. The station's vast interior spaces had echoed with emptiness, and its arresting view of the entirety of the Milky Way galaxy's elliptical spiral, as seen from more than two hundred thousand light-years away, had gone unappreciated. As jealously as Saavik guarded her scant hours of quiet solitude, she preferred to see Erebus Station alive with the hustle and bustle of daily activity.

Except when it interrupted her train of thought.

"Director Saavik? Excuse me! Director Saavik!"

The urgency of Sherlas Rokaath's plea for attention stopped Saavik in the middle of the station's central concourse. She watched the young Zakdorn wend his way through the floodcrush of pedestrian traffic. His struggle to catch up to her reminded Saavik of a fish fighting a river's current to return to its ancestral spawning waters. By the time he reached her side, he was more than a bit winded. He bent forward and grabbed his knees. A moment later he held up one hand, a pleading gesture for patience. "Sorry. I've been looking everywhere for you."

"You should have paged me."

"We tried, Director. Several times."

Saavik concealed her fleeting mild embarrassment. Age was starting to take its toll on her, in ways both crude and subtle. One of her body's more insidious betrayals had been the slow degradation of her hearing. "My apologies, Rokaath. I will have my aural implant adjusted. Now—what do you need to tell me?"

He held out a padd. "The QR sensors detected a dimensional breach."

She took the padd from him. "An incursion from the other universe?" She skimmed the report, expecting the worst. Most of the previous crossovers from the other universe had occurred in the Bajor system—the one locale in which neither Memory Omega nor the Galactic Commonwealth could afford a disruption at this critical juncture. When she saw the coordinates of the breach, she was surprised. "It occurred inside Breen space?"

"Just barely." Rokaath reached over and touched an icon on the padd's screen to call up a map of the sector around the anomaly. "It happened within less than a light-year of the Commonwealth's neutral zone."

"Most unusual." Saavik turned and walked at a brisker pace than she had before.

Rokaath hurried after her. "What do you think it means?"

"I have insufficient data to draw a conclusion." She turned a corner and quick-stepped toward a nearby bank of turbolifts that would take her to the station's subspace transporter facility. "Come with me. We need to return to Omega Prime."

She led him into an open lift pod. As soon as the doors

closed, she spoke her destination for the computer to hear:
"Subspace transport." The lift pod sped away without any
discernible sensation of movement; only the flashing of lit
panels on the bulkheads and a steady hum of electromagnetic
drivers signaled their rapid passage to the station's core.

The pod's doors opened on a long passageway. Saavik and
Rokaath exited the lift. Despite his youth and longer legs, he
had to exert himself to keep pace with her, and he sounded
out of breath as he spoke. "Do you think the Breen know
about the incursion?"

Saavik tapped the padd and called up a tactical report.
"Unlikely. We've detected no changes in their fleet deployments since the breach."

"That's good."

"Not necessarily. It might suggest the Breen caused the
event."

The Zakdorn's ridged, gray face scrunched with doubt. "I
don't see how they could have. They have no ships or stations
anywhere near those coordinates."

"Then that *is* good news." She turned right, and a tall pair
of doors parted ahead of her. Rokaath followed her inside a
cavernous, silo-shaped compartment. Three curved banks
of glossy companels ringed an elevated platform, which was
accessible by short stairs between the control stations. White-
jacketed technicians hailing from several species manned the
various posts. One of them, a dignified-looking graybeard of
a Tellarite, cracked a broad smile at Saavik. "Good morning,
Director."

"Hello, Doctor Treg. Please set coordinates for Omega
Prime."

"Yes, Director." He nodded at his colleagues, who translated the order into action.

Saavik and Rokaath ascended the nearest flight of steps to

the platform. They stood at arm's length from each other in the center of the dais.

Treg checked the master console, which stood apart from the others. "Coordinates locked, coils charged." He looked up at Saavik. "Ready on your mark."

"Energize."

The Tellarite scientist activated the subspace transporter. The oppressive force of the annular confinement beam seized hold of Saavik. It was an unpleasant feature of the system, but a necessary one to prevent mishaps during the dematerialization sequence. Next came a brilliant flash of white light that prompted Saavik's inner eyelid to blink shut for her own protection, just as those of her ancestors would have done against the glare of Vulcan's fierce desert sun.

The blinding flare abated. Saavik and Rokaath stood in a chamber identical to the one they had left on Erebus Station, but this one was located in the secret headquarters of Memory Omega, which was sequestered deep inside an enormous asteroid in the Zeta Serpentis system.

Looking back at her from this room's master control panel was its Andorian supervisor. The tall, gaunt-faced *thaan* greeted Saavik with a small nod. "Welcome back, Director."

"Thank you, Arrithar. Inform the observation lab that I'll be down to see them directly."

"Yes, ma'am."

She led Rokaath off the platform and out of the room. They crossed the corridor and stepped into the lift. Saavik ordered the computer, "Observation lab." The lift hummed into motion, hurtling swiftly deeper into the core of Zeta Serpentis.

Rokaath grew anxious. "We need to secure the breach site as soon as we can."

"We need all the jaunt ships standing by in case something goes wrong at Bajor."

"*All* of them? We can't spare even one? What if someone's crossing over?"

His presumption vexed her to no end. "So far there's no evidence of any crossing. You yourself told me we've detected no ships in that vicinity. No, this doesn't merit a jaunt ship. Not yet, anyway. We'll investigate through subtler means."

"And if further action is required?"

"Let's not get ahead of ourselves." The lift stopped, the doors opened. She led him to a checkpoint area secured by a variety of biometric scanners. "Saavik, authorization one nine alpha sierra seven kilo blue."

As she crossed the room, devices she couldn't even see confirmed her genetic profile; others verified her retinal pattern and voiceprint. One checked the distribution of her body mass while a related system analyzed her kinetic profile. By the time she reached the reinforced blast door on the far side of the room, it moved aside to grant her ingress to one of Memory Omega's most closely guarded tactical secrets: the observation lab.

It was a small octagonal chamber just twelve meters across, and fewer than four meters from floor to ceiling. Its perimeter was packed with the fastest, most powerful computers Memory Omega possessed—all linked to the bizarre machine in the center of the room.

The bulk of the contraption was a free-floating gyroscope with a harness seat, all encased in two interlocking hemispheres of transparent aluminum. Welded to the harness seat's frame, in a position optimized for viewing by its occupant, was a curve-cornered, rectangular frame of gray metal with a width-to-height ratio of 2.35:1. The frame was curved forward on both sides into a 120-degree arc.

Its inner sphere was enveloped by a larger one, also composed of transparent aluminum. Repulsor emitters lined the interior surface of the outer sphere and generated a steady field of uniformly distributed energy that kept the inner sphere suspended in place while also permitting it to pitch, yaw, and rotate freely on all three axes. Precisely ten centimeters of empty space separated the two hollow orbs.

Outside the spheres, four massive robotic arms—two mounted in the floor, two anchored in the ceiling—stood ready to seize the hemispheres when it came time to part them, whether for routine maintenance or to facilitate the comings and goings of its operators.

Inside the machine, strapped into the harness seat, was one of Memory Omega's most skilled operators of the quantum window: a doe-eyed young human woman named Jesi Mullins. Her long dark hair was gathered into a utilitarian bun behind her head. Perspiration shimmered on her forehead as she guided the gyroscope back to equilibrium and a gentle stop.

Monitoring her progress from a control station a few meters away from the machine was the project's current supervisor, Doctor Tsemiar. The lanky Efrosian wore his long white hair loose and wild, and his snowy mustache drooped and curled upward again with incomparable élan. Only the slightest hint of crow's-feet beside his pale blue eyes betrayed his imminent slide into middle age. He noted Saavik and Rokaath's arrival with raised eyebrows. "Well, this is a pleasant surprise."

"It shouldn't be. I told Arrithar to advise you I was coming."

"And so he did. I merely sought to soften the rough edges of our day with a bit—"

"We need to use the machine." Her interruption sounded

more brusque out loud than she had intended, but she knew that Tsemiar could prattle on endlessly unless one curtailed his verbosity. She handed Rokaath the padd and pointed him toward the control panel. "Mister Rokaath will program the new coordinates."

Mullins shot a desperate look at Tsemiar. "Doc? I've been strapped in for almost six hours. I need a break."

Tsemiar's eyes brimmed with pathos as he looked to Saavik for mercy. "I agree with her, Director. We should bring in a fresh operator."

"No. This is a priority assignment. I need your best—and that's her."

The soft-spoken scientist demurred with a slight bow of his head. "As you wish."

Mullins breathed an angry sigh that resonated inside the spheres. "Thanks a lot, Doc."

Rokaath keyed in the coordinates of the breach, and then he looked at Saavik. "Which frequency? Ours or theirs?"

"Start with ours. If something made it through, we need to know immediately. If not, we can shift our investigation to their side and see what they're up to over there."

Rokaath tuned the machine. Countless times over the past century, Saavik had seen Memory Omega's brightest minds use the quantum window to spy on a seemingly infinite variety of parallel universes—not for the sake of contact, or to discover the true extent of the multiverse. They had done it for two reasons only: to identify potential threats to their universe and neutralize them before they manifested, and to discover the greatest technologies of thousands of other realities—and steal them for Memory Omega.

The image of deep space appeared inside the holographic frame of the quantum window. Mullins rotated the gyroscope and let it free-tumble as she searched the interstellar void for any sign of an interloper from the most troublesome parallel universe of all—their closest quantum neighbor, whose previous incursions had altered the course of this universe's destiny. The computer superimposed semitransparent, real-time telemetry and sensor data over the image while she worked.

Rokaath handed off the control panel to Tsemiar and returned to Saavik's side. He sounded worried. "What if our friends from the other side are up to their old tricks again?"

"Then we might need to teach them the same lesson we taught the Alliance: that they cross us at their peril."

Six

Every meeting was different. It was for security reasons, they had told Sarina, and once the methods were explained to her, she had understood. A major part of the rationale was to avoid creating anything that might be interpreted as a pattern, by whoever might be observing an agent. The result was that she never knew until the very last moment what to expect of her next meeting with Ilirra Deel, her Starfleet Intelligence liaison.

Sarina's instructions came in the form of anonymous personal advertisements placed in various daily periodicals. Sometimes, if it was unclear where she would be when the message was sent, a global or interplanetary publication was used. At times when her location was relatively stable, such as her current residence on Andor, local media were used instead.

A complex set of ciphers governed the code. Different keywords were used to identify a coded message depending upon the date and the day of the week. Thanks to Sarina's genetically enhanced eidetic memory, it had been easy for her to memorize the patterns.

Most often, the message was concealed in whatever section of the personals existed for "missed connections" or "casual encounters." They were always phrased in the past tense, as if to imply the paths of strangers had crossed and one of them was reaching out in the desperate hope of reconnecting. Sarina often wondered whether anyone who placed or browsed such ads ever found the person they'd sought, or recognized themselves in someone else's plea for contact. She doubted it. All she needed from the coded ads meant for her was a place and a time, and some hint as to what disguise Deel would be using to conceal their sub rosa meeting.

When Sarina needed to set the meeting—as was the case on this occasion—she used her own version of the cipher, one in which she posed as a male Bolian with a speech impediment seeking a second chance to make a first impression on some fetching beauty or other. On such occasions, Sarina dictated the specifics of Deel's disguise. To amuse herself, she had taken to imposing the most absurd details she could think of—much to the Betazoid woman's dismay.

Left to her own devices, Deel chose pedestrian cover identities, personas she could easily slip into and out of on a moment's notice: a prim Vulcan woman with a penchant for midnight blue apparel; an auburn-haired, blue-eyed Trill student whose allergies to most ophthalmic medications and ocular implants forced her to correct her vision with old-fashioned glasses; or, when she was feeling lazy, she would simply wear blue contact lenses to cover her solid-black irises and don a blond wig to pose as a human.

For today's meeting, Sarina had been determined to make Deel work a bit harder.

Sarina was the first to arrive at the meeting site in New Therin Park. It was only a short walk from the Federation Security Agency's office tower in Lor'Vela, which had been appointed the new capital of Andor after the Borg invasion leveled the previous capital nearly five years earlier. She found a bench in the middle of the park, near one of the natural hot springs that sustained the lush green oasis, and pretended to read from a padd.

The bench across from hers was empty. Because it was early, just past dawn, there were few people in the park other than herself and a few joggers, plus a small multispecies group practicing tai chi on the south lawn.

A few minutes later, Deel arrived, disguised as Sarina had directed. Every exposed bit of Deel's flesh had been painted the dark green of an Orion, and she wore a copper-hued wig that contrasted sharply with the rich emerald color of her eyes. Completing the portrait of a woman out of her element, she was decked out in an uncomfortable-looking latex bodysuit accessorized with thigh-high boots and an extra-short imitation leather jacket.

Deel made a point of avoiding eye contact with Sarina, who nonetheless felt the Betazoid's resentment radiating toward her like the heat of a bonfire. Then she heard her liaison's viperous telepathic voice inside her head.

<<*I'll get you for this.*>>

Even though Sarina had no native telepathic ability, she had been trained by Deel to serve as an active receiver for psionic contact. Deel did most of the work; she had been born a gifted telepath, even by Betazoid standards. Now, after years of working together at Starfleet Intelligence, they had grown quite adept at sharing their thoughts.

Sarina focused her mind to reply, as Deel had taught her during her first months of training as an agent. *Don't be so dramatic. You look great.*

<<*I look like a damned socialator.*>>

Socialator was a Betazoid euphemism for *prostitute.* As much as Sarina wanted to laugh at her friend's expense, she concentrated on keeping her face slack and emotionless, and her eyes on her padd, as she projected her thoughts back at Deel. *You're too smart to be a socialator. Now, if you're done feeling sorry for yourself—*

<<*Do you have any idea how long it takes to put this makeup on? I ought to kill you.*>>

All in due time, Ilirra. They made contact with Julian last night.

That revelation added focus and intensity to Deel's mental voice. <<*What happened?*>>

It was Cole. He all but rolled out the red carpet for him.

Across the path, Deel looked one way and then the other, as if searching for her absent connection, but her thoughts remained focused on Sarina. <<*What did Julian tell him?*>>

He played hard to get, like we planned.

<<*Make sure he doesn't resist too much.*>> Deel feigned a disappointed sigh and stuffed her hands in her jacket's pockets. <<*We don't know how many overtures Thirty-one is likely to make. If this is the last time they reach out to him, we can't afford to let this opportunity slip away. We need you both on the inside to make the plan work.*>>

Sarina tapped on the screen of her padd. *I'm aware of that. But the Andorians crapped on the plan when they sprang him from jail, and zh'Tarash flushed what was left of it when she pardoned him. If Julian accepts Thirty-one's invitation without a good reason, they'll know something's up. If you want me to get him inside, I'll need to give him a better cover story.*

<<*Give him any legend you like, as long as it works.*>>

We've already got one worked out. If it flies, I should have him inside Thirty-one by tomorrow morning.

<<*And if it crashes and burns?*>>

Sarina stood, tucked her padd inside her handbag, and walked away.

Then it's been nice working with you, Ilirra.

Bashir's enhanced hearing picked up the sound of Sarina's footsteps while she was still outside their villa's front door, crossing the walkway from the landing platform where they parked their personal transport pods. By the time she opened the front

door, he had prepared himself for the scene they had planned
the night before, under the cover of their sensor-jamming,
synthetically produced cone of forced privacy. Everything
they had worked toward for the past three years, all he had
sacrificed in the name of conscience and duty, would be forfeit
unless they played their roles perfectly in the next few minutes.

It took all his willpower to remain calm and keep his
heart rate and breathing slow. If Section 31 was spying on
him and Sarina—and he was sure they were—then they
would be monitoring his vital signs for any sign of deceit or
duplicity. He couldn't afford to give them a single reason to
doubt him or Sarina. That meant he needed to remain aware
of every aspect of his feigned physical and mental states. He
needed to lie so persuasively that even he believed his own
falsehoods. He needed to own this charade so deeply that it
became his new truth.

But, for now, he had to appear calm. He sipped his
chamomile tea and set the cup on its saucer. Then he called
out over his shoulder, "How was your day?"

Sarina drifted into the room, well submerged into her
role as a woman struggling under the burden of a terrible secret. She subtly wrung her hands as she sat beside him on the
sofa. Her averted eyes and taut posture made her a portrait of
guilt and apprehension.

He regarded her with tender concern. "Is something
wrong?"

She took her time mustering her faux courage. "There's
something I need to tell you."

"All right. I'm listening."

She stalled with a sharp draw of breath. "It won't be easy
for you to hear."

That was his cue to turn his affectionate worry into the
first inkling of dread. "What is it?" He touched her shoulder,

as if he thought he needed physical contact to draw her out. "No matter what it is, you can trust me."

"That's the problem, Julian. What I'm saying is . . . *you* can't trust *me*. Or you shouldn't have. I—" Her voice caught, and tears shimmered in her eyes. "I've been lying to you."

He pulled back his hand. "About what?" As he leaned forward to reestablish eye contact with her, she turned away. "What's this about?" Bashir darkened his countenance with jealous anger. "Is there someone else? . . . There is, isn't there? Who is it?"

She shook her head. "No, no. It's not— I mean, you—" She hid her face in her hands, slowed her breathing, and looked up at him with sorrow-reddened eyes. "It's not that."

Impatience put an edge on his voice. "What is it, then?"

Sarina stood and paced away from the sofa. She stopped to gaze out the broad picture window. The apparition of her reflection looked back at him from its surface, while beyond it the low urban nightscape of Sherlas glittered in the distance beneath an indigo sky.

"I'm not who you think I am, Julian."

He did his best to sound confused. "What are you talking about?"

"Last year . . . when I accessed the Meta-Genome data for you. I didn't get it through my contacts in Starfleet Intelligence."

Now it was Bashir's turn to stand. He took a hesitant step toward her. "What are you saying? Where did it come from? How did you get it?"

"I used my real contacts—inside Section Thirty-one."

He froze and concentrated on making his mind draw a blank and his face go pale. A hard swallow left his jaw tight enough for him to mutter with convincing horror, "You did what?"

She squeezed her eyes shut for a moment. Then she opened them and turned to face him. "I'm one of them, Julian. I'm part of the organization."

Bashir let her "confession" take a few seconds to sink in. His outward expression shifted from shock to dismay, and then from fury to despair, all in less than half a minute. He turned away from her and stumbled back to the sofa. As his knees met its edge, he pivoted and collapsed onto it, sprawled like a beached invertebrate. "How? Why?"

"It was the only logical choice, Julian. Do you remember when Starfleet asked me and the others to help analyze their war-game scenarios against the Dominion?"

He didn't react, though he did recall the first time he had met her, many years earlier, during the war. Back then Sarina had been practically catatonic, a victim of a genetic resequencing gone wrong. Her neural pathways had been accelerated almost beyond the ability of science to measure, but her sensory inputs hadn't been upgraded to match. Consequently, all her mental processes had fallen out of sync, leaving her trapped in her own mind, her thoughts racing ahead of her perceptions, her body lagging behind her will to action.

However, he had found her locked-in syndrome almost endearing when compared to the behavior of her fellow patients: Jack's violent mania, Lauren's predatory sexual advances, and Patrick's childlike naïveté. They all were products of genetic augmentation gone wrong. There was little that Bashir or modern medicine could do for most of them, but Bashir had been able to correct Sarina's synaptic asynchronization. Since then, she had in many ways become his equal in her intellectual development—and, in some ways, she had far exceeded even his impressive abilities. In the process, she had become the woman he had waited his entire life to find: one who could not only keep up with him but also challenge him to better himself.

Now he had to convince whoever was watching and listening to them that she had crushed all his dreams for their future together. He stayed quiet and let Sarina take the spotlight.

She kneeled beside him. "Remember when we analyzed the threats facing the Federation? It looked hopeless. And if the facts we'd been given were true, it would have been hopeless. But we didn't know the Federation had another line of defense, one that its enemies rarely see: *Thirty-one*." He rolled away from her, but she grabbed his shoulder and pulled him back, forced him to look her in the eye. "We live in a hostile universe, Julian. There are powers we can scarcely imagine that would like nothing better than to see us erased from creation. The organization exists to keep that wolf from the Federation's door."

He shook his head. "No. You can't tell me you believe their lies."

"Lies, truth. You act like those are absolutes, but they're not. One person's truth is another's lie. The only absolutes in the cosmos are life and death. Existence and oblivion."

"No, there has to be more than that. Or else nothing we do matters."

She pressed her palm to his cheek. "You mean morals, Julian? Can you still be that innocent, after all the horrors you've seen? After all the blood you've shed?"

He got up and retreated from her, tripping over furniture and his own feet as he backpedaled toward the kitchen. "I don't even know who you are. You betrayed me."

She wore a disappointed frown. "No, I'm trying to save you. I'm still the same person I was yesterday. The same person you thought I was. Nothing is different between us."

"How can you say that? It's *all* different! This changes *everything*!"

"Like what? It doesn't change the fact that I love you. And I think that if you look into your heart, and if you're honest with yourself . . . you'll see that you still love me."

He trembled with unchained fury. Tears brimmed in his eyes. "If you loved me, you wouldn't have lied to me." He slammed the side of his fist against the counter. "All this time!" He pointed an accusatory finger at her. "Wait! How long? When did this start?" His bark became a roar. "*When did you join them?*"

"They recruited me a month before I joined Starfleet Intelligence. In fact, I applied to SI because the organization asked me to. They wanted someone like me on the inside." Somehow, she made her cheeks flush on cue. "And they told me to seduce you into the organization."

Losing himself in the role, he let her words knock him back half a step, as if he'd been gut-punched. His voice trembled. "So that's all this has been, since the beginning. Just a sham, all of it. You . . . me . . . the mission to Salavat . . . everything since then. Just one big lie."

"Not everything. When I first joined, they didn't even want you. They'd given up on you. They thought you'd never see reason, that you'd never understand why the Federation needs them. But I convinced them you could still be an asset. That you could learn to see clearly."

He recoiled with ersatz offense. "*Learn to see clearly*? Are you mad?"

"Julian, you're not just smart—you're a goddamned genius. You know as well as I do that for all its noble talk, the Federation would be little more than the galaxy's punching bag if it didn't have someone to do the dirty work. Someone willing to make the hard decisions."

"That's why it has an elected council and a president, and why they appoint intelligence services to protect the interests of the Federation. Thirty-one has no charter, no oversight—"

"And a near-perfect track record of safeguarding the Federation from all threats, foreign and domestic, for nearly two hundred and thirty years." She moved into the kitchen and cornered him. "It doesn't exist to run the government, Julian. It doesn't dictate how people live their lives. Most of the time, it stays hands-off, out of the picture. It's only when someone or something comes along that threatens the safety of the Federation that it takes action." She gently grasped his arms and stared at him until he looked into her eyes. "I know you, Julian. And Cole was right—you won't be happy living on the sidelines. You joined Starfleet so you could be on the frontier, exploring and making a difference. You'll never be satisfied with your life unless you know you're being of service." Her hands traveled up his arms, over his shoulders and neck, to the sides of his face. "We all need to serve something greater than ourselves, Julian. Even when that something turns its back on us." Her face inched closer to his. "The organization is offering you a chance to go on serving the Federation. To live a life worthy of your potential. You should take it . . . Join me, Julian."

He bowed his forehead against hers. "You're asking me to serve something I hate."

"No, I'm asking you to go on serving the Federation. The organization is just a tool." She embraced him and whispered into his ear. "If we become part of it, we can change it. We can try to guide it. You say the organization has no conscience. We can become its conscience. We both need to be part of something that matters, and the organization needs us to steer it in the right direction. I can't do it alone, Julian. I need you. Come with me."

He kissed her, doing his best to believe she was still acting and not in fact trying to pull him down into the ethical morass of Section 31. Their lips parted, and tears fell from his eyes. "I won't do it for the Federation. And I don't give a damn about saving Thirty-one's soul." He kissed her again, then gently lifted her chin so she could meet his gaze. "But I'll do it for you."

The trio stood bathed in the blue flicker of the holovid. L'Haan appeared impassive as she watched the recording of Bashir and Douglas's dramatic confrontation, which Cole had recorded less than an hour earlier. Their peer, Vasily Zeitsev, cocked one eyebrow with critical disdain as he watched the playback. He looked many years older than either L'Haan or Cole, though the Vulcan woman was at least a few decades Zeitsev's senior. But where she still enjoyed the trappings of youth, he had given himself over to the gray shades of antiquity.

Suspended in the air before them, Douglas's confession sounded to Cole like a moment out of a bad daily serial: *"I'm one of them, Julian. I'm part of the organization."*

He shook his head. "She's the worst actor I've ever seen. It's a wonder she isn't dead."

L'Haan, who bore direct responsibility for managing Douglas as an asset, remained cool as she absorbed the indirect criticism. "Not Miss Douglas's best performance, to be certain."

The recorded scene continued, and Zeitsev crossed his arms. "She's wooden, and he's overselling it. Can anyone tell me why we wanted to recruit them in the first place?"

His derogatory query drew a shrug from Cole. "They did all right on Salavat."

"Salavat was sloppy." Zeitsev turned a scathing eye toward

Cole. "They completed the mission, but they were identified by the Breen Intelligence Directorate, and she got captured."

Cole was unwilling to let his superior's hypocrisy go unchallenged. "So did Sloan."

"Different situation." Zeitsev held up a hand. "Hang on, I like this part."

They stopped talking and watched the next few seconds of Bashir and Douglas's face-off. In the hologram, Douglas put on her most earnest expression. *"We live in a hostile universe, Julian. There are powers we can scarcely imagine that would like nothing better than to see us erased from creation. The organization exists to keep that wolf from the Federation's door."*

Bashir protested, but his words were drowned out by Zeitsev's derisive laughter. "She tries so hard. It's sad, really. I *want* to believe her. There's nothing I'd like more than to think such a brilliantly engineered creature was one of our true believers . . . What a shame."

A dull pall of boredom settled on L'Haan's elegant features. "We've known she was a double agent from the beginning. I fail to grasp why we have let her come as far as she has."

"Keep your friends close," Cole said, knowing his compatriots would by reflex fill in the second half of the ancient aphorism: *and keep your enemies closer.*

Zeitsev nodded. "True." He squinted at the holovid. "What I wouldn't give to send these two to some acting workshops. What's she doing there? Is that some method-acting bullshit?"

L'Haan mimicked Zeitsev's expression. "Perhaps. Though her style seems rooted more in the techniques of Strasberg than Stanislavsky. With some elements of Deltan realism mixed in."

"You're both full of shit," Cole said. "She's just hamming it up."

The Vulcan wore her disappointment openly. "I should have made her spend more time studying improvisation."

The supervisor waved off L'Haan's lament with a callused hand. "It's not your fault. She was never meant to be a long-term asset. There was no point teaching her all our secrets. She'd only have used them against us." His eyes narrowed as he turned his focus toward Cole. "She might still be dangerous. Are you sure you know what you're doing?"

"Positive." He scrutinized the subliminal details of Bashir's and Douglas's performances, the microexpressions and hidden verbal tics that betrayed their words as hollow lies. "In fact, if they're to be of any use to us at all, we need to let them embed themselves even more deeply than they already have. After all, if we try to freeze them out, they might realize we're on to them." He chuckled softly at their ham-fisted attempt at deception. "The key from this point forward is to keep them both on short leashes. We need to compartmentalize all intel they receive and make sure all their perceptions are filtered through our lenses."

With a motion of her hand, L'Haan paused the playback of the holovid as Bashir and Douglas leaned their foreheads together. "I renew my objection. I think we will have more success manipulating them separately than together."

"I disagree," Cole said. "When I tried to run Bashir on Sindorin nine years ago, he nearly went off the reservation. If Salavat showed us anything, it's that both of them are easier to control when they think the other is in danger. Keeping them together serves our purposes."

Zeitsev nodded in assent. "I agree." He staved off L'Haan's protest with a raised hand. "I understand your concern. Having two double agents on one op is a risk. But Cole's right. We can use them to keep each other in line. And in case you've forgotten, L'Haan, the success of our mission in the alternate universe entirely depends upon Bashir's participation."

"I have not forgotten."

Cole harrumphed. "Good, because it's too late to rewrite the mission profile."

The older man mirrored L'Haan's disapproving countenance. "You'd best be certain about this, Cole. I'm putting you in charge of the next phase of the operation. It's up to you to make sure Bashir and Douglas play their parts—and end their turns on the stage, as planned."

"I assure you, sir. One way or another . . . this mission will be their curtain call."

Seven

The Alternate Universe

There was no room for error. All the officers on the bridge of the *Enterprise* understood the need for precision. Every word, every action would be scrutinized, and a single mistake would carry dire consequences for the lives of billions. No one on the bridge was more aware than its commanding officer of the stakes confronting the ship and its crew. Captain Picard felt his responsibilities weigh upon his shoulders like a lead apron. Its burden made him reluctant to stand from his command chair as the ship's chronometer counted down to the fateful moment.

On his right, his first officer looked up at him, her mien both apprehensive and meant to encourage. K'Ehleyr shared his anxiety about the Dominion, but her training as a field operative for Memory Omega, coupled with her years as his executive officer on the *Enterprise*, gave her a measure of calm and poise in the face of what might prove to be a calamitous turning point in history's long arc.

Standing above and behind Picard's left shoulder, manning the tactical console, was his other trusted adviser. Deanna Troi had been Picard's traveling companion for many years; they had entrusted their lives to each other long before they had sworn to serve as soldiers and explorers—and also, apparently, diplomats—for the Galactic Commonwealth. There was no one else whose counsel carried as much weight with Picard. He glanced in her direction, and her calm smile reassured him that everything would be all right, that all he needed to do was stand and soldier on, and Fate would take care of itself.

The chronometer beneath the main viewscreen reached 0900. It was time.

Picard stood tall and smoothed the front of his black uniform tunic. "Commander Troi, hail them. Commander K'Ehleyr, relay my command screen to the main viewer, left one-third."

Troi keyed in the commands. "Opening hailing frequencies." A moment later she touched the small, inconspicuous earpiece she wore while on bridge duty. "They're responding."

On the left third of the forward viewscreen, the text that Picard had been studying for the past several days was superimposed over the image of the fleet of Jem'Hadar warships that the *Enterprise* had met in the Bajor system. Picard swallowed his apprehensions. "On-screen."

The daunting spectacle of the Dominion battle group was replaced by the unsettling image of one of the Dominion's revered Founders. She was humanoid, pale, and vaguely feminine in her carriage and aspect. Her chestnut hair was taut against her skull.

To her left stood a Jem'Hadar who was intimidating even by the fearsome standards of his genetically engineered super-soldier brothers-in-arms. On the Founder's right stood a creature Picard had come to recognize as a Vorta; this one was lovely, young, and female, and went by the appellation Eris.

The Founder acknowledged Picard with an almost imperceptible bow, a forward lean of just a few degrees. *"Greetings."*

Protocol was of paramount importance now. Picard resisted the urge to extemporize and forced himself to follow what he had been told was the negotiated script for this encounter. He read the words from the side of the screen while doing his best to maintain steady eye contact with the Founder, despite the unnerving quality of her presence.

"Greetings. I am Captain Jean-Luc Picard, command-ing officer of the free starship *Enterprise*. On behalf of the Galactic Commonwealth, I welcome you and your entourage in peace, and greet you as honored guests to our quadrant of the galaxy."

The Founder's reply was just as stilted as Picard's saluta-tion, which he supposed meant she was reading from the preapproved script, just as he had been.

"Thank you, Captain Picard. On behalf of the Founders, the Dominion, and my traveling companions, I accept your gracious welcome in the selfsame spirit of peace. May this first official visit prove beneficial to both our peoples."

The script recommended a slight bow by Picard at that juncture, and he did as it directed. Then he straightened and put on a slight smile—one warm enough to be ingratiating but not so exaggerated as to call itself into question. "It is my duty and pleasure to confirm that you and a contingent of your choosing are invited to follow us to Bajor, the fourth planet of this system. On its surface you will be welcomed and offered accommodations meeting your previously stated requirements. After a brief interlude, you will be invited to a private audience with our elected head of state, Chairman Michael Eddington of the Commonwealth Assembly."

The Founder copied Picard's well-practiced smile with unnerving precision. *"Thank you, Captain. We are honored to receive your gracious invitation, and I look forward to meeting with Chairman Eddington. My trusted lieutenants, Commander Eris of the Vorta, and Honored Elder Taran'atar of the Jem'Hadar, will stand ready to receive your approved flight plan and issue such orders as are necessary to follow your vessel to orbit of Bajor. There we will await final authorization from the planetary authorities to initiate our transport to the surface."*

"Very good." Picard turned his head and nodded at Troi, who entered commands into her panel, as rehearsed. "We are transmitting the flight plan to your vessel now. In a few moments we will come about on a new heading. At that time, please follow us to Bajor. Once we've all made orbit, final transport coordinates will be sent to our vessel by Bajor Planetary Operations Command, and we will relay those co-ordinates to you."

A curt half nod from the Founder. *"We understand, Captain. Thank you."*

The transmission ended abruptly, returning the image of the Jem'Hadar battle fleet to the *Enterprise*'s main viewscreen. Picard sighed with relief. The exchange had ended on cue without any major gaffes by either party. So far, he had fulfilled his duty by not misspeaking the Commonwealth into an accidental war. He turned away from the viewscreen and looked at K'Ehleyr. "Commander, set course for Bajor, quarter impulse."

"Aye, sir." K'Ehleyr issued curt orders to the helmsman and navigator, who pivoted the ship back the way it had come, toward the Bajoran homeworld. Then the half-Klingon woman fired off a quick smile at Picard. "Nicely done, sir."

"Thank you, Number One." He sank back into his command chair. "Now all we have to do is lead those ships into orbit. After that, if someone starts a war by mistake, it'll be Chairman Eddington's fault."

Chairman Michael Eddington stared dumbfounded at the array of cutlery set at each place along the banquet table. He had no idea why any meal should require a person to use three forks and two spoons, all of varying sizes, not to mention two knives, three glasses, and a teacup of bone china so delicate that he was certain his would crumble at the slightest touch of his hand.

No one in the Galactic Commonwealth had ever hosted an official reception for a visiting foreign head of state. A few persons ensconced within the fledgling interstellar government had once or twice acted as servants, attending the dignitaries at affairs of the now-defunct Klingon-Cardassian Alliance, but none of them had ever been privileged to coordinate such an event. Forced to improvise on nearly every detail of the formal soiree, the catering staff had delivered a state dinner marked by equal measures of pomp and paranoia.

The senior delegates of the Commonwealth Assembly gathered around the lanky, fair-haired Eddington. To his left, Kellerasana zh'Faila of Andor—"Sana," to her friends—stood with Min Zife of Bolarus. Both the Andorian *zhen* and the Bolian man had bedecked themselves in off-white finery that contrasted with their blue complexions. Zife's skin tone was a few shades darker than zh'Faila's. Seeing them together, Eddington thought of cobalt and cornflower.

Behind the chairman's right shoulder stood the Assembly's other two senior delegates, who were also its most frequently opposed verbal sparring partners: Bera chim Gleer of Tellar and Sevok of Vulcan. Despite their proclivity for debate inside the Assembly chamber, the Tellarite and the Vulcan were inseparable friends outside it. Tonight, Gleer had draped his lean frame in green and gray; Sevok wore the humble, simple garb of his people, a dark brown hooded cassock cinched at the waist by a long, rough, unbleached rope knotted at each end.

Gleer picked up one of the forks. "What's with the gardening tools?"

Zh'Faila almost swatted Gleer's four-fingered hand. "Put that down!"

He wrinkled his snout at her. "Relax. I'm not going to *steal* it."

"No one said that," Zife protested, as if he feared a diplomatic incident were unfolding.

Sevok unfolded his clasped hands to gesture at the fork in Gleer's hand. "Her advice is sound, Bera. A strict protocol governs events such as this one. Even the smallest item out of place can be taken as an intentional slight and undermine years of diplomatic groundwork."

Eddington rested his hand on Gleer's shoulder in what he hoped would be seen as a congenial gesture. "Please, Bera. Listen to Sevok and put the fork down before you start a war."

A low snort escaped Gleer's flared nostrils. "Fine." He returned the fork to its place on the table. "I still think any meal that needs this much hardware isn't worth eating."

A fanfare sounded from outside the banquet hall and put an end to the discussion of flatware, much to Eddington's relief. He and the others took their places.

The delegates lined up by seniority on either side of the red carpet that started just inside the hall's gargantuan double doors and ran down the broad aisle in the center of the room. Interspersed among the elected representatives were high-ranking commanders from Starfleet, the Commonwealth's defense and exploration agency.

Behind the lines of people in dress uniforms and crisply tailored formal wear, dozens of large circular tables awaited them and their guests from the far side of the galaxy. A minor legion of servers stood along the room's back wall, all of them attentive and waiting for their cue to begin serving the dinner, one exquisite course at a time.

The towering doors swung inward. The Dominion contingent entered.

At the head of the long procession was the Founder who, as far as Eddington had been able to determine, had no proper name as he understood it. She was simply the individual selected by her race, the Changelings, to speak on behalf of the Dominion. He was unnerved by her oddly undefined face. Blank of detail or expression, her visage reminded Eddington of an artist's mannequin, or an unfinished sculpture.

A male Vorta, slight of build but with keen eyes, trailed the Founder by just over a pace, behind her right shoulder. Opposite the Vorta walked a grizzled, scarred Jem'Hadar. As per the negotiated terms of the summit, no one had come to the reception bearing arms, but one look at the company of Jem'Hadar filing into the banquet room convinced Eddington that the Dominion's soldiers were more than capable of killing them all bare-handed, and perhaps even blindfolded. He swallowed hard. *All the more reason to make sure this meeting goes well.*

The Founder stopped at arm's length in front of Eddington. "Mister Chairman."

"Madam Founder. Welcome to the Galactic Commonwealth." He gestured to the delegates who stood closest behind him, on either side of the red carpet. "Allow me to present the senior members of our governing assembly." He introduced zh'Faila, Gleer, Sevok, and Zife in turn. The Founder acknowledged each of them with the slightest bow of her head.

Then it was her turn to speak. She gestured first to the Vorta. "Allow me to present my senior diplomatic counselor, Weyoun."

Her aide-de-camp clasped Eddington's outstretched hand in both of his. The Vorta flashed the most obsequious grin the chairman had ever seen. "A pleasure to meet you, Chairman Eddington. I expect this conference to usher in great things for both our peoples."

Eddington extracted his hand from Weyoun's grip. "Very nice to meet you, sir."

When he turned toward the Founder, he stood confronted instead by her imposing Jem'Hadar escort. For a moment, Eddington thought he saw a glimmer of mirth on the Founder's smooth face, but if he did, it passed without comment. She folded her hands at her waist. "This is Taran'atar, the Jem'Hadar First and Honored Elder who discovered our terminus of the wormhole. He is the oldest and most accomplished Jem'Hadar who has ever lived."

At the risk of having his hand crushed, Eddington extended it to Taran'atar. "Welcome."

The Jem'Hadar looked at Eddington's hand but made no move to accept the gesture until the Founder urged him in a low voice. "Taran'atar." As soon as she spoke his name, he took Eddington's hand in a firm but respectful grip and shook it once before letting it go.

Grateful to have escaped unscathed from his first encounter with a Jem'Hadar, Eddington took a half step back and smiled at the Founder. "Now that the pleasantries have been observed, why don't we all take our seats and—"

"That won't be necessary," the Founder cut in.

Her stern rebuff made Eddington self-conscious. "I don't understand."

Weyoun shot an imploring look at his head of state. "Founder?" He waited until she nodded her assent, and then he looked at Eddington as he continued. "Perhaps it would help, Mister Chairman, if you explained why there are so many places set at these tables."

Confused glances passed among the Commonwealth delegates as Eddington replied to Weyoun. "So that we can all sit and dine together. It's a chance for us to get to know one another in a social setting before we start discussing the terms of our treaty and trade agreement."

The Founder exuded disappointment as she shook her head. "So predictable. It's been so long since we've dealt with solids who weren't already socialized by contact with the Dominion, that we've forgotten how"—she let her disdainful gaze pass over the elaborately set tables—"*quaint* your customs can be."

Eddington was not ready to give up so easily. "Perhaps you could indulge us this once."

"Quite impossible, I'm afraid. My species does not ingest organic matter for sustenance."

"And your entourage?"

Taran'atar spoke with pride. "Jem'Hadar require no nourishment other than the white."

That left Weyoun, who shrugged and hid behind his fawning half smile. "Vorta have almost no sense of taste. I'm afraid my own palate is limited to *kava* nuts and rippleberries."

Behind his back, Eddington heard Gleer quip under his breath to the other delegates, "Well, *this* was time and effort well spent."

The chairman shot a quick skunk-eye glare over his shoulder at the delegates, quashing any nascent replies to the Tellarite's off-the-cuff snark. He softened his aspect when he faced the Founder again. "Might I suggest we retire to a more private location, then?"

She approved with a tilted half nod. "A capital idea, Mister Chairman." Her manner turned cold and steely as she spoke to Taran'atar. "Deploy your men. Secure the perimeter."

A single gesture from Taran'atar was all it took to snap the

Jem'Hadar into action. They moved swiftly, their every action precise and rehearsed. The rear half of the formation turned about and left the way they had come. The rest divided into squads of five and left through the room's various exits. Some headed outside to establish a cordon around the ground floor of the Elemspur Monastery; others ascended to its upper levels to keep watch from above.

Eddington led the Founder, Taran'atar, and Weyoun out of the banquet hall through its rear exit. Mystified expressions traveled across the faces of the delegates and Starfleet officers who watched them depart. In accordance with instructions Eddington had given to his peers before their arrival on Bajor, zh'Faila and Sevok fell in behind them.

The group traversed a long hallway to a flower-filled solarium that, despite its seeming fragility, had been hardened with force fields into one of the safest sites on the surface of Bajor. A small round table awaited them in the middle of the circular, high-ceilinged room, whose transparent aluminum walls looked out upon a meticulously sculpted garden. Eddington took the seat that put his back to the garden's hedge maze and motioned for the others to sit as well. The Founder sat opposite him, while Taran'atar and Weyoun remained standing behind her.

Emulating their visitors, Sevok and zh'Faila eschewed their planned seats to stand behind Eddington, offering him their silent support.

The chairman met the Founder's unblinking stare. "To business, then."

"Agreed." Her eyes narrowed, as if she were sizing him up to devour him whole. "Let's not waste time being coy. What does your Commonwealth ask of the Dominion?"

"Freedom to explore the Gamma Quadrant. A fair trade agreement for the importing and exporting of goods. An immigration policy. An extradition treaty. And full diplomatic relations."

His request was met by a low, cynical huff. "Your political agenda is even more ambitious than your dinner plans."

"We're prepared to offer the same privileges that we seek. Your people would be welcome to travel in both directions through the wormhole, explore this quadrant of the galaxy, engage in—"

The Founder halted him with a raised hand. "It's not your terms that trouble us. Many within the Great Link harbor concerns about negotiating binding treaties with a state born so recently of revolution. The Dominion has persevered for more than two thousand of your years, while your Commonwealth has barely been weaned from its violent mother."

Weyoun cleared his throat as a preamble to butting in. "What's more, your choice of a parliamentary representative democracy as your system of government seems . . . untenable."

"I will concede it is the worst form of government," Eddington said, "except, of course, all those others that preceded it."

His attempt at levity was met by hard, unyielding stares. The Founder looked at Weyoun. "Give him our list of requested concessions."

The Vorta reached inside his loose, flowing robe and pulled out a small electronic device that was similar to a padd. He offered it to Eddington, who deflected it with a small gesture into the hands of Sevok. The Vulcan accepted the padd without comment, and then he and Weyoun returned to their places, facing each other with naked suspicion.

The Founder collected herself. "Take as much time as you require to review our proposal. When you are ready to resume our discussion, send word to Weyoun." She stood, so

Eddington got up, as well. The Founder nodded once at the chairman and his colleagues, and then she turned and walked out of the solarium, followed by Taran'atar and Weyoun.

Sevok perused the information on the padd, then cocked one eyebrow. "Their list of demands is . . . substantial."

"Of course it is," zh'Faila said. "Once again, politics is merely war by other means."

Eddington feared there might be more truth in the *zhen*'s complaint than she realized. "Sevok, review their demands and let me know which points seem the most negotiable. Sana, get word to Picard on the *Enterprise* and Saavik at Omega Prime. If this all goes to hell, they might need to be ready for anything—up to and including full-scale war."

Eight

"Come in. Sit down." Thot Tran ushered the Spetzkar company's command team inside Ikkuna Station's small auditorium. The six Breen elite commandos entered single-file and descended the ramp to the center row, where they settled into alternating seats. Tran admired their efficiency. Without hesitation or discussion, they had occupied the acoustic sweet spot of the tiered theater.

Tran walked past them to the front of the auditorium and took his place on its low stage beside Choska, who held the remote control for the holographic projector system. He reduced the volume of his vocoder for the sake of discretion. "All set?"

The Tzenkethi scientist nodded and stepped to one side of the stage, while Tran moved away to the other side. He cued Choska with a nod, and then he addressed the commandos as the holovid appeared in midair between him and his colleague.

"Thot Trom, by order of Domo Pran, and with the full consent of the *thotaru*, I am dispatching you and your company on a special assignment." He gestured at the image of the dimensional rift projected over the stage. "You will command the fast-attack cruiser *Tajny* through an engineered breach into a close parallel universe."

Choska stepped forward. "Thot Tran proved that this parallel quantum universe was the origin of a starship we discovered crashed in Federation space last year." Sensor images and schematics of the wrecked vessel were added to the holovid. "Based on its engine design and other elements, he deduced that this ship possessed a wormhole-based propulsion system."

The commandos leaned back and regarded one another with sly head turns, but none said anything, so Tran pushed on with the briefing. "The tactical value of such a propulsion system cannot be overstated. Not only would it enable us to project force anywhere in the galaxy at a moment's notice, we could do so without warning. We would be free to strike at any target, at any time, without exposing ourselves to counterattack." That drew approving nods.

Trom leaned forward. "Did we salvage the ship?"

"We tried." Recounting the greatest failure of his career pained Tran, so he made his best effort to minimize the appearance of catastrophe. "Despite the sacrifice of many assets, we were unable to recover the wormhole drive from the surface of Tirana Three before it was destroyed by the Starfleet vessel *Enterprise*. Also, because of sensor-impeding compounds in the planet's surface, our scans of the derelict were incomplete, and insufficient to replicate the drive system."

Choska highlighted the dimensional rift in the holovid. "That brings us to now." She called up an image of the *Tajny*, a narrow, dartlike starship. "Your ship has been equipped with a Romulan-made cloaking device. As soon as you've reached the alternate universe, you will engage the cloak and proceed to the next phase of your operation."

Tran moved to center stage. "Your orders are simple, but accomplishing them will not be. You are directed to locate, intercept, board, and capture a wormhole-drive starship and pilot it safely back to this universe so that we may reverse-engineer its technology."

The Spetzkar commander sat quietly for a moment. "What's our exfiltration strategy for the captured vessel? Does this rift of yours work in both directions?"

"It should," Choska said. "Theoretically."

"Have you made successful crossings in both directions?"

Tran called up the project's flight logs. "We have. Just over six hours ago, we piloted an unmanned recon vessel through the rift. After it completed a series of programmed long-range scans, it returned through the rift on autopilot, undamaged and with actionable intelligence."

Trom absorbed the report with a sage nod. "All right. How much do we know about these wormhole ships? If we're to capture one, we'll need a full tactical profile."

"We've prepared one," said the radiant Choska. "It's available on the station's comnet. I urge you and all your troops to review it before you deploy."

"We will. I guarantee it."

Crin, the Spetzkar second-in-command, asked, "What time do we ship out?"

"Tomorrow morning," Tran said. "You and your company have sixteen hours to load the *Tajny* and finish your combat prep. We've updated your navcomp software and the comm encryptions, but it'll be up to your team to vet the tactical grid and the drive reactors."

Trom stood, stepped into the aisle, and faced his command team. "All right, you heard him. Crin, muster the company in the *Tajny*'s main hold in one hour. Karn, supervise the weapons check. Solt, I want a full report on the warp and impulse systems in three hours. Rem, make sure all hands download and review the tactical profile before we ship out."

The other commandos sprang to their feet and filed out of the auditorium at a quick step. Thot Trom followed them out. The door slid closed after him, leaving Tran alone on the stage with Choska. She turned off the holovid. "I think that went quite well."

"It went as well as could reasonably be expected." He tried

to purge his thoughts of the memory of Tirana III and the calamity it became.

Choska remained inexplicably optimistic. "Cheer up, Tran. All we have to do is get the Spetzkar through the rift and then guide them back again. The rest is up to them now."

"I know," Tran said. "That's what worries me."

Morning came all too soon. Trom strode onto the command deck of the *Tajny* and was pleased to see everyone at their assigned posts, making final preparations for their mission to the alternate universe. Second officer Rem stood beside Karn at the tactical console, where they conferred in subdued tones. Yoab sat at the flight control station directly in front of the command chair. The flight-status indicators that Trom could see as he took his place in the center seat showed all systems fully operational.

First Officer Crin entered from the port-side turbolift and crossed the deck to stand beside him. "All hands aboard and accounted for, sir. The ship is ready for service."

"Well done, Crin." Trom used the panel beside his chair to open an internal comm channel to the *Tajny*'s engineering deck. "Solt. Status report."

"All systems nominal, sir. Ready to launch."

"Good. Look sharp down there. The lab rats say we might be in for some chop."

Solt sounded confident. *"Can't be any rougher than the beating we took on Mazlas."*

"We'll know in a few minutes. Command out." Trom closed the channel and looked up at Crin. "Signal the station and tell Thot Tran we're ready to depart."

"Yes, sir." Crin stepped away to the communications panel and sent the message. Several seconds passed while the first officer awaited a reply from the station. Then he raised the volume on his vocoder to address the entire bridge crew. "Thot Tran confirms he is ready to open the rift. He requests that we depart and move the ship to position one."

"Acknowledged," Trom said, knowing Crin would relay his confirmation to Tran. "Yoab, detach umbilicals, seal exterior hatches, and back us away from the station."

Yoab entered commands at the helm. "Moorings cleared. We are free to navigate." The edges of Ikkuna Station drifted beyond the frame of the forward viewscreen as the ship maneuvered to its designated starting position. The starfield outside slowed to a crawl, then settled into a static view. Yoab throttled back the impulse drive to standby. "Holding at position one. Ready for full impulse on your mark, sir."

"Good work, helm. Karn, charge the shields and stand by for final nutation settings from Doctor Choska." Trom sat back and did his best to project quiet confidence. There was nothing more for him or his crew to do until they received the order to proceed. All the pressure was now on Tran and his Tzenkethi partner to open a stable passage to the alternate universe.

Trom held out little hope of a prompt departure. *Given how timid the lab rats are, maybe I should return to my quarters until they—*

His train of thought derailed as a band of crimson fire tore an uneven scar across the face of the cosmos on the forward viewscreen. Within moments the wound in spacetime ripped itself wide open and became an amoeba-shaped pocket of emptiness, a portal into a formless void. Then another gash formed inside that alien darkness and pulled itself apart, opening a window on another universe. Trom stared at the spectacle for several moments before recalling his orders.

"Rem, full-spectrum sensor sweep. Yoab, confirm the coordinates on the far side of the rift. Karn, verify the nutation settings from Thot Tran and compare them against the energy emissions at either end of the rift, as well as the null space between portals." Trom opened an internal comm channel. "All decks, this is the commander. Secure for dimensional crossing and stand by. Command out." He pointed his mask's empty snout at Karn. "Anything?"

"The nutation settings are coming over now." Karn entered new data at the tactical console. "They check out. Simulations look stable. Energy levels are within rated norms."

Yoab reviewed the new intel on the navigation console. "Coordinates on the far side of the rift appear to be coterminous with those of our universe. The quantum signature of the other universe is a match for the one in the mission profile, and for the ship found on Tirana Three."

"Excellent." Trom swiveled his chair toward Crin. "Let me talk to Thot Tran."

Crin punched in a command on the communications panel. "Channel open."

"*Tajny* to Thot Tran. Are we clear to proceed?"

Muffled conversation filtered over the comm channel before the scientist replied. "*A few moments, please. We need to make sure both ends of the rift are in phase.*"

Rem turned away from his post. "Sir, we're picking up signs of debris on the far side of the rift. It looks like the wreck of the recon ship Tran lost a couple of days ago."

"Does it pose a navigational hazard for our trip through the rift?"

"Maybe. I recommend we adjust our flight plan and deflector configuration."

This was the kind of petty complication for which Trom had no patience today, but it had to be addressed. "Coordinate with Yoab and Karn—and be quick about it."

"Yes, sir."

The trio of Spetzkar hurried through a series of improvised changes to their flight plan as Tran's voice returned via the overhead speakers. *"Rift apertures are stable. Proceed."*

"Acknowledged. We are navigating into the rift." Trom leaned forward, eager to meet this bold new mission head-on. "Helm, take us into the rift, one-tenth impulse."

"Ahead one-tenth."

The crew tried to pretend they all were paying attention to nothing but their own consoles, but Trom knew they all were stealing long looks at the main screen as the *Tajny* ventured through the first aperture, into the null space of the rift—each of them no doubt eager to see what it would look like to be outside of normal space-time, even if only for a moment.

Then everything turned to fear and fire. Horrific wails of stressed metal resounded inside the ship, and alarms cried out from every panel. The primary lighting system faltered and failed, leaving the command deck lit by the staccato flickers of malfunctioning companels. All of Trom's men barked out reports. They overlapped one another and reduced the moment to pure chaos. Trom turned his vocoder's volume to maximum and cut through the clamor with a distorted bellow: "*Quiet!*" He pointed at Karn. "Report!"

"Shields failed as soon as we hit the void! We're losing power."

Trom bolted from his chair to the flight-control station and loomed over Yoab. "Increase power! Divert emergency batteries to the inertial dampeners!"

Crin called out, "Sir! Thot Tran says to turn back!"

Then came a panicked shout from Rem. "Don't do it, sir! The rift is destabilizing behind us, and it's converging on us!"

Trom pointed at Rem. "Aft view, on-screen!" He turned to see the aperture behind the *Tajny* fold inward upon itself—and on them. That was all he needed to know. He slapped a gloved hand on Yoab's shoulder. "Full impulse! We need to reach the other side before the rift closes!" The deck pitched and heaved as he struggled back to his chair, staggering like a drunkard. On the main viewscreen, the far end of the rift was contracting; its angry red wound stitched itself shut. Trom fell back into his seat and clutched one armrest for support while he used a control panel on the other to open an internal comm channel. "All decks! This is the commander! Brace for—"

His last order was lost in the din as the far aperture of the rift snapped shut on the *Tajny*, and everything Trom knew turned to darkness and thunder.

Nine

The Alternate Universe

Consciousness returned to Trom in painful fits and starts. Deep aches suffused his limbs, and even the smallest shifts of his weight made him aware of the blunt-force trauma that had racked his torso. The holovisor inside his mask was dark. He knew he wasn't blind because he saw brief glints of light through some of the cracks in his helmet. To test the vocoder, he cleared his throat. The speaker embedded in the snout of his mask spat out staticky noise.

He heard the shuffling of boots on a starship deck. Then he was greeted by the vocoder-parsed voice of the company's surgeon, Doctor Nev. "Are you all right, sir?"

Trom waved his hand in front of his mask. "Holovisor's broken."

"We know. It's dark on the outside, too."

Trom nodded. When operating correctly, a holovisor emitted bright green light over its exterior sensors. This light was engineered to be invisible from inside the helmet; as far as Trom had been able to determine, the exterior light's only function was to prevent others from perceiving even the slightest clue to the species of the individual inside a Breen suit. This, Trom had long ago deduced, was how equality was enforced when administered by a committee: with brute force and identity-crushing mandatory anonymity. He kept his criticisms of the social order to himself, of course. To mention them aloud was tantamount to branding oneself a traitor.

Better to suffer in silence, he reminded himself.

He pointed at his mask. "How long to get it fixed?"

"Solt has a damage-control team making the rounds. I'll—wait, here's one now." He lifted his voice to draw the mechanic's attention. "Over here! The commander's visor is out!"

Running steps and the clatter of tools reassured Trom that something was being done to address his dilemma. He felt bumps and prods against his head as the mechanic fixed his helmet. Meanwhile, with or without his eyesight, he had a job to do. "Crin!"

The first officer replied from a short distance away. "Yes, sir."

"Damage and casualty reports."

More footfalls. Based on the ambience and the echoes off the bulkheads, Trom knew he was still on the *Tajny*'s command deck. He heard the abrasion of fabric and the subtle interplay of armored plates as Crin squatted beside him. "No fatalities. Multiple injuries, most of them in engineering. The medics report all hands will be ambulatory within the hour."

"And the ship?"

"Not nearly so resilient as her crew. We're in an uncontrolled spin. Impulse and warp drive are off-line. Tactical grid is overloaded, so no weapons, shields, or cloak. Backup computer core and life support are operating on emergency battery power. Hull breaches in the aft sections of Decks Fifteen and Sixteen."

"Communications?"

"Rem says the subspace transceiver is intact. He's trying to raise Ikkuna Station."

A flicker of pixels teased Trom with a ghostly afterimage of the scene around him. The mechanic tinkering with his helmet gave something a few more pokes and twists. "Hang on, sir. This should just about—"

Trom's holovisor switched on, its wraparound view rendered in crisp detail and full color. He nodded and clapped his hand on the mechanic's shoulder. "Nice work."

"Thank you, sir." The mechanic gathered his tools and hurried off to his next task. Trom stood and assessed the situation on the command deck. Ruptured plasma relays in the overhead rained intermittent sparks on the crew working beneath them. The forward viewscreen was dark. So were most of the duty stations. Adding insult to injury, his command chair was now ever so slightly crooked atop its pedestal. His sense of pride wanted to prioritize its repair. How could he be expected to command a company of Spetzkar while sitting tilted to the right?

The more pragmatic side of his nature prevailed. *I'll just have to lead while standing.* He turned to face Crin. "Are the EVA pods working?"

"Yes, sir."

"Tell Solt to have operators for those pods standing by. As soon as we recover impulse power and helm control, we'll maneuver back to the wreckage of that recon ship Tran and Choska lost yesterday. Then we'll deploy the pods and use them to salvage anything we can from the debris. Tell them I want everything—hull plates, wiring, spare parts, all of it."

Rem pivoted away from the communications post. "I have Ikkuna Station."

Trom moved to stand beside Rem. "Patch me in." Crin joined them while Rem opened the channel on the dedicated speaker at his console. A nod from Rem was Trom's cue. "Ikkuna Station, this is Thot Trom. Do you read me?"

Thot Tran answered, *"Affirmative. Go ahead, Commander."*

"You first. What the hell just happened to my ship? You said the rift was stable."

"It was, until your ship tried to cross it."

"You have a keen grasp of the obvious. Can you explain *why* the rift destabilized?"

Choska responded, *"Our current hypothesis is that the more intense energy signature of the* Tajny, *coupled with a feedback loop created by its shields, triggered an uncontrolled collapse of the apertures toward the highest energy point in the null space between them—specifically, your vessel's warp core."*

The beast of Trom's anger threatened to slip its reins. He tightened his grip on his temper before he continued. "I thought the adjustments to our shield frequency nutation were supposed to prevent that. Or did I misunderstand?"

After an awkward pause, Tran pushed on as if Trom's question hadn't been asked. *"What is the status of your ship and crew?"*

"Serviceable."

"Can you elaborate?"

Trom nodded at Rem, who transmitted a quick data burst on the channel's subfrequency. "I'm sending you our damage and casualty reports. We expect to recover attitude control within the next five minutes. After that, we'll initiate salvage operations, followed by full repairs."

"Understood. The micro-rift we're using for this comm signal will close in a few minutes. It will be at least another day before we can reopen the rift to facilitate your return."

"That won't be necessary. Once the ship is repaired, we'll be continuing the mission."

Choska sounded concerned. *"Are you certain that's feasible, Commander?"*

"Positive. You sent us here to steal a wormhole ship. That's what we'll do. All we need from you is a stable rift in place when we get back. But once we have your ship, if we jump back here only to find this thing closed, I'll make you both wish you were never born. Understood?"

His warning seemed to have the desired effect on Tran. *"I*

assure you, *Thot Trom, when you return, the rift will be open, and it will be stable—and we'll have corrected the flaw in the shield nutation frequency. You have my word.*"

"Your word? How nice. I feel better already." He closed the channel with a tap on the console, then stalked back to his off-kilter command chair. *Damn the lab rats and their promises.* He sank into the chair and lamented his shattered command deck. *They'll be the death of us all.*

Omega Prime's senior staff looked up as Sherlas Rokaath barged into the conference room. Most of the faces around the table registered surprise or annoyance at the Zakdorn. Saavik regarded him without emotion as he looked at her, his alarm evident in his gray eyes.

He held up a padd. "Forgive the intrusion, Director. I have urgent news."

She motioned him toward the far end of the conference table, opposite her. "Proceed."

With a few taps on his padd, Rokaath called up a star chart on the full-wall display behind him. "We've had another cross-dimensional breach, at the same coordinates we detected yesterday." He used his padd to emphasize different details and produce new information on the wall display as he continued. "This was no accidental event, and it was not produced by natural phenomena. We've monitored this sector since the previous event, and we've detected signs of persistent disruption. Based on the energy levels involved, we deduced that someone or something was working to facilitate a high-mass transfer from the close parallel universe to our own. Specifically"—the image of a starship appeared on the display—"a warship capable of carrying more than a hundred personnel."

The senior staff sat forward, their faces taut with concern.

Most worried of all, if the furrowing of his shaggy brow was any indication, was Kol jav Megh. The sable-maned Tellarite logistician squinted his black eyes at the image on the wall. "Is that a Breen ship?"

"We think so." Rokaath highlighted small details of the image. "There are some minor deviations from known Breen ship classes, but the general configuration is consistent with their design aesthetic. Its quantum signature confirms it originated in the other universe."

Veen, the director of extradimensional surveillance, stared in dismay at the image. "We had no idea the Breen were developing this kind of technology, in that universe or any other." The round-faced Bolian clasped his beefy hands over his bald pate. "Where did they *get* it?"

An answer came from Inglis Arkell, the head of Memory Omega's scientific research division. "Look at the gravimetric deformations that define the rift's mouth." The dark-haired Trill woman keyed in commands from her interface at the table and overlaid a wire frame of the cross-dimensional rift's invisible subspace geometry. "That was made by a Tzenkethi-designed wormhole generator, one modified to breach dimensional membranes."

"That makes sense," said Dannis Palancir, the director of counterintelligence. "In their universe, the Breen and the Tzenkethi are members of a military and economic alliance known as the Typhon Pact. It's analogous to their membership in our universe's Taurus Pact, except theirs also includes the Romulans and the Kinshaya."

Fallanooran th'Sirris, Omega's chief military strategist, twitched his antennae as he spoke. "Never mind the alt-history. If this was a deliberate incursion, what are the Breen after?"

Rokaath shrugged. "No idea. We've picked up some limited comms between the ship and something on the other side, but we haven't been able to break their encryption yet. We could be looking at a scout, an explorer—"

"Or an invasion," interrupted Ruxin Ejor, Omega's political liaison to the Galactic Commonwealth. The young Bajoran was the newest member of the senior staff. The others tolerated his habitual pessimism for only one reason: his dire predictions frequently proved to be prescient. Today he directed his ire at th'Sirris. "We have most of the Commonwealth's forces standing by for a showdown with the Dominion. You think it's a coincidence that this"—he searched for a word and was frustrated not to find it—"*whatever* this is, showed up *now*?"

"Correlation is not evidence of causation," Arkell interjected.

Ruxin remained irate. "This isn't some science experiment, Inglis. This is the real world. When two events coincide in a way that can get you killed, odds are it's not a fluke, it's by design." He aimed his pointed stare at th'Sirris. "So what're you prepared to do about it?"

Saavik chose that moment to intercede. "He will do nothing until I order it, Mister Ruxin." She turned attention back toward Rokaath. "Is Observer Mullins continuing to monitor the intruder's actions?"

The Zakdorn looked abashed. "Negative. Intense gravimetric distortion caused by the breach disrupted our ability to focus the quantum window on those coordinates. The only way to track the intruder would be to dispatch a jaunt ship to intercept it."

That turned Saavik back toward Megh. "What ships are ready to launch?"

The Tellarite lifted his bushy eyebrows. "None of them."

His protest drew a dubious glare from th'Sirris. "Nonsense. You have four ships waiting to leave Erebus Station. Merge their flight-test crews for one mission and have them investigate."

"Leave the logistics to me, Falla." Megh became apologetic as he turned toward Saavik. "Even if we united all the test-flight personnel, we'd barely have a skeleton crew for one ship."

"That might be enough," Saavik said.

Rokaath leaned in to object. "I disagree, Director. Megh is right to be concerned about deploying an understaffed jaunt ship. If these intruders are hostile, sending an untested, under-strength crew to deal with them might prove disastrous."

Saavik was unmoved by their protests. "It is not my inten-tion to send them on a combat mission, Sherlas. Their orders will be to intercept, observe, and gather intelligence. Nothing more. Even a skeleton crew can execute such a limited mis-sion profile. Who can we send?"

Megh picked up his padd and reviewed his files with a frown. "The *ShiKahr*."

"Very well. Send me a list of candidates for the command crew, and have the ship ready to jump to the breach coordi-nates as soon as possible."

The Tellarite bowed his head. "Yes, Director."

"Everyone else," Saavik said, "task your divisions with learn-ing all they can about this incursion. I want preliminary reports by tomorrow morning, with response protocols. Until we know more, treat this as an unplanned first-contact scenario."

Ruxin met her order with wary cynicism. "And if the visi-tors turn out to be hostile?"

Rokaath gave voice to the unpleasant truth everyone in the room already knew. "Then we'll need to be prepared to face new wars on two fronts instead of just one."

Ten

"Wake up, Doctor."

Cole's voice jolted Bashir from a fitful sleep. He sat up in bed. "Computer: lights."

Sarina tumbled out of bed into a defensive crouch as the room's wall-mounted lights came up slowly, dispelling the darkness. They faced the black-clad Section 31 operative, who stood at the foot of their bed. His hands were clasped behind his back, and his relaxed but confrontational body language projected an air of smug superiority. "Sorry if I startled you."

Bashir scowled. "No you're not." He and Sarina had expected this visit, but their anticipation hadn't made Cole's intrusion any less unwelcome in the wee hours of the morning. "Why can't you use the comm or ring the door chime like a normal person?"

"My way has more finesse."

"I think we have differing definitions of that word."

A dismissive wave. "I didn't come to talk semantics. The situation I mentioned during my last visit is evolving." Cole picked up Bashir's bathrobe from the foot of the bed and tossed it to him. "You weren't interested in a hypothetical threat to Federation security. Now we have a confirmed threat. Are you ready to listen now?"

"That depends. Are you ready to stop talking in circles?"

"Do you recall the artificial wormhole technology the Tzenkethi developed?"

Bashir nodded as he got up and donned his robe. "The one they tried to use at Bajor?"

"That's the one. The Breen repurposed it to open a portal to the alternate universe. Nine hours ago, they sent a fast-attack cruiser manned by an entire company of their elite Spetzkar commandos through a rift they created from an interstellar science station on our border."

Sarina slipped into her own bathrobe without taking her eyes off of Cole. "Why would the Breen launch a military operation into another universe?"

"To capture something they failed to acquire here. Last year, the Breen executed a massive disinformation campaign against the Federation. They burned countless assets, including one of their top secret intelligence programs, all so they could steal the wreckage of a single starship that crashed on a planet under Federation control."

Cole held up a short, slim metallic cylinder, which Bashir presumed the agent must have had hidden in his palm or up his sleeve. He used it to project a hologram in the air between himself and Bashir and Sarina. A grainy, indistinct sensor image appeared—the faintly visible outline of a starship's fractured hull. "These scans of the downed vessel on Tirana Three were made by the *Enterprise*-E, moments before they fragged the entire site to prevent the Breen from escaping with a partial salvage of the wreck."

Sarina and Bashir edged closer to the projection. Her eyes were wide, her mouth agape. "What makes this worth so much trouble and effort?"

"Intel from the alternate universe indicates this is something known as a jaunt ship. It generates its own artificial wormholes and is capable of making instantaneous jumps across almost any distance within the galaxy, and across vast reaches of the void outside it. This is what enabled the Terran Rebellion to prevail against its oppressors."

Imagining the possible applications of such a technology,

Bashir understood why Section 31 was treating its potential acquisition by the Breen as a crisis. "A fleet of ships with drives like these could project force anywhere in the galaxy, without warning."

"Never mind the fleet, Doctor. All one would need to do is use these wormholes to bombard distant planets with a hail of photon torpedoes. Attacks could drop in beneath an enemy's defenses and glass their planets before they knew what was happening." He switched off the hologram. "If the Breen capture one of those ships and reverse-engineer it, they could wipe the Federation and its allies off the map in a matter of weeks. From a tactical standpoint, they'd become invincible."

It was a sobering prospect, one that compelled Bashir to grasp at alternative readings of the evidence. "Are you certain the salvage operation and this latest mission to the alternate universe are related?"

"All the evidence points to it. Less than three weeks after the Breen operation on Tirana Three failed, they started pouring resources into their dimensional-rift project on Ikkuna Station. And the same scientist who ran the Tirana Three op is in charge of this one: Thot Tran."

Sarina stood close against Bashir's back while keeping her focus on Cole. "Cut to the chase. The organization has plenty of operatives. Why do you need Julian?"

"Actually, we want *both* of you for this mission. And I should think the reasons would be obvious. You two are the only Federation agents who have ever successfully infiltrated the Breen military. Based on your debriefings, it's clear you've both retained a moderate fluency in the written Breen language, and your familiarity with their customs and body language would be invaluable for covert operations inside their territory. Add to this, Doctor, the fact that you are one of the few people to survive a visit to the alternate universe, and you should understand why your name is at the top of our list."

"The experience you've cited qualifies me to advise your agents, not to be one."

Cole reacted with a wry smirk. "Your performance on Salavat suggests otherwise."

Bashir waved off the comparison. "Not an experience I'd care to repeat."

"No one's asking you to. I understand you had misgivings after the fact, especially with regard to what turned out to be civilians employed at the shipyard. This mission is something completely different. You'd be up against a vastly superior force of elite military troops. There won't be any innocents in the crosshairs this time."

"Am I supposed to take your word for it? Forgive me if I find you less than trustworthy."

A pained smile. "Fair enough. If you want to limit your role to that of an adviser, so be it. But your counsel will be needed in the field, and you will be required to carry a weapon, for the protection of your teammates if not for yourself."

"I still haven't agreed to go."

"Now who's playing games, Doctor? I know you're going; she knows you're going; and so do you."

"What makes you so sure?"

It felt to Bashir like Cole was looking right through his brave façade into his soul. "Because I know you better than you know yourself. You're going to go because you can't *not* go." He glanced at Sarina, then met Bashir's stare. "Get dressed, but don't bother packing bags. We're traveling light."

"What about my medkit?"

"Leave it. From now on, Doctor, whatever you need, you'll get from us."

Eleven

The Alternate Universe

"Captain, we'll be exiting the wormhole in five seconds."

Hanalarell sh'Pherron, the captain of the free starship *ShiKahr*, acknowledged her flight control officer's report with the slightest of nods and a renewed focus on the bridge's main viewscreen. The blue chaos of the artificial wormhole raced past, a swirling blur so bright that it almost hurt to look at it. The Andorian *shen* squinted against the glare. Then it vanished, a curtain of energy abruptly pulled aside to reveal the familiar starry darkness of normal space. Nothing looked amiss, but sh'Pherron knew how deceiving appearances could be. She swiveled her command chair toward her chief of security. "Any sign of our cross-dimensional visitors?"

Ensign Riaow checked the readouts on her tactical console. "Negative, Captain."

"Run another sweep. Omega wouldn't have sent us here for no reason." She rotated her chair forward again. The vista pictured on the holographic main screen was empty and serene. "Helm, are we sure we're in the right place?"

"Positive, sir." Lieutenant Zareth superimposed the *ShiKahr*'s coordinates on the viewscreen image. "We came out of jaunt precisely on target."

The ship's Vulcan first officer stepped away from his sensor console and moved to sh'Pherron's side for a consultation at a discreet volume. "Captain, regardless of our knowledge of the Breen in this universe, we have no way of knowing the capabilities of a Breen vessel from the other universe. I recommend we proceed with the utmost caution."

"I agree, Turak. Reconfigure the sensor array for a wide-area tachyon sweep."

"That will take approximately ten hours to prepare, Captain."

"Then you'd best get started, Commander. In the meantime, run all available sensor protocols for detecting cloaked vessels." Turak nodded his understanding and returned to his post while sh'Pherron doled out further orders to the crew. "Mister Zareth, program a search pattern. Start in a tight radius around the reported position of the dimensional breach, and extend the search area gradually."

"Aye, sir." The Chelon plotted the ship's course with the broad, scaly digits of his huge leathery extremities, which resembled hands in only the most general sense.

How can he work the helm with those stumps? It was a mystery sh'Pherron decided was better left unsolved. "Commander Turak, contact Memory Omega. Confirm that we've arrived, and that we've begun the search. Ensign Riaow, proceed on the assumption that we're hunting a cloaked vessel. Take us to Yellow Alert, charge shields, and set all weapons to ready standby."

Her officers confirmed her orders quickly and set themselves to work. Despite the vast emptiness of space pictured on the viewscreen, sh'Pherron refused to relax her guard. *I played it fast and loose at Alzoc Prime, and I nearly got my crew killed. I won't make that mistake again.*

Some youthful spark of optimism deep within her wanted to believe this was all just a fool's errand—that there was nothing to be found in this sector of the void except trace gases and stray neutrinos. But the hard-edged survivor instinct that had sustained her through a childhood yoked in slavery, an adolescence spent in rebellion, and a young adult-hood mired in war told her there was someone else out here with her and her crew. Someone lurking unseen in the dark-ness, watching the *ShiKahr*. To what end sh'Pherron didn't know, but she was determined not to call off the hunt until she found her prey—and learned for herself what its motives really were.

It was difficult for Trom to read the mood of his crew—just one more reason for him to resent and despise the snout masks they all were forced to wear as core elements of the Breen social costume. Further complicating the matter was the tendency of Breen vocoders to strip emotional cues from one's voice, rendering all conversations in the same flat me-chanical monotone. It made it hard for Trom to gauge when morale might be waning and in need of reinforcement.

Then there were the moments when no mask could hide his troops' dismay.

Yoab stared at the overhead. His voice was hushed. "They're hunting us."

"No need to whisper," Trom said. "They can't hear you through vacuum."

The Spetzkar pilot clenched his fists and continued star-ing upward, as if he could see through the *Tajny*'s bulkheads and across space to the enemy ship, which at this range would be invisible to the naked eye. "They're executing a search pat-tern. They're looking for us."

"Which is exactly what we want them to do." Trom clasped one gloved hand onto the pilot's shoulder. "Stay sharp, Yoab. This is all part of the plan."

The pilot nodded. Satisfied that Yoab was calm and focused, Trom walked back to his command chair, only to see his second-in-command, Crin, beckon him to the aft engineering station. Trom made a point of not hurrying; he walked calmly to Crin's side. "What is it?"

"Our cloaking device is barely functional." He pointed at a few screens of data above the console. "It's leaking dangerous radiation into our lower decks, and one tachyon sweep at less than half a light-year will leave us completely exposed."

Trom considered his options. He hated all of them. With a jab of his thumb, he opened a channel to main engineering. "Command to engine room. Status report."

Solt's voice crackled over the intraship channel. *"Repairs continuing, sir."*

"Do we have weapons or shields yet?"

"Not for six hours, at least." The chief engineer sent up a screen of estimated repair times for the ship's compromised systems. *"Unless you want to shut off life support and propulsion in the interim, in which case we can have shields in two hours and weapons in four."*

In spite of all the times Trom had heard engineers try to be funny, he had never once found their unique brand of droll sarcasm amusing. "Maintain life support and propulsion for now. Prioritize tactical repairs and keep me apprised of your progress. Command out." He closed the channel before the engineer could sneak in another retort.

Rem joined him and Crin at the sensor console. "The vessel that's hunting us is definitely a wormhole ship. It's just what we came for."

Crin nodded at the screens of damage-repair estimates. "Unfortunately, their timing couldn't be worse. If our intel about their armament is correct, they could shred us right now."

"We'll take her down soon enough," Trom said. "But not until we're ready." He turned away from Crin and Rem to snap orders across the command deck. "Yoab, set evasion pattern *mara* and take us as far from the wormhole ship as possible, one-quarter impulse."

"Yes, sir."

Trom turned back toward Crin and Rem. "Now isn't the time to force a confrontation. But when our repairs are complete, we'll strike—and make that ship ours before its crew has the slightest idea what's happened."

Twelve

Bashir emerged from the transporter beam almost as soon as he had realized the process had begun. The dematerialization sequence had engaged in silence, and the rematerialization protocol ended the same way. A faint ephemeral flash was all that had marked his and Sarina's transition from their villa on Andor to wherever Section 31 had just taken them.

Cole stood a couple of meters from the transporter platform and regarded Bashir and Sarina with an inscrutable expression. Next to him was a trim Vulcan woman whose prominent bangs and stern countenance matched Sarina's description of her handler, L'Haan.

She said with cool disdain, "We took the liberty of deactivating your phaser, Doctor."

He reached reflexively for the phaser holstered on his hip. A quick inspection verified the weapon had been neutralized. Bashir threw a sour look at his hosts. "What's wrong? Don't you trust me?"

Cole seemed amused. "Just as much as you trust us."

The agent's cynical honesty coaxed a crooked smirk from Bashir. He stepped down off the platform, and Sarina followed.

L'Haan intercepted them. She lifted a small tricorder-like device and scanned them. A few seconds later, she switched off the scanner and stepped back beside Cole. "They're clean."

Cole kept his eyes on Bashir as he answered his cohort. "Just as I said." He gestured toward the door to his left. "Shall we?"

Bashir sneaked a glance at Sarina, who reassured him with a furtive nod. He flashed an insincere smile at Cole. "By all means."

Cole moved toward the door, which slid open ahead of him with a muted swish. Bashir and Sarina followed him out of the transporter room, and L'Haan trailed them into the gradually curving corridor. The passageway was wide enough for three people to walk abreast, and its overhead was high, nearly three meters. Aside from some white numerical markings on thick black placards mounted on the walls beside the doors the quartet passed, there was no signage to indicate what might lie behind any of the closed portals. Adding to the monotony, the walls, floor, and ceiling were all the same shade of dark gray.

"I don't recognize this class of ship," Bashir said.

A sly backward glance from Cole. "Who said we're on a ship?"

The agent's denial had no effect on Bashir's conclusion. "Spartan surroundings. The ambient hum of life-support systems. A high-frequency buzz of plasma conduits. Air filtered to the point of being practically antiseptic. The millisecond delay in resistance from artificial gravity. All of which suggests we're either on a starship or a space station."

From behind came L'Haan's cool reply. "So why assume it's a ship?"

"The ultrasonic vibrations caused by a sudden jump to high warp speed. I didn't hear it, but I felt it, roughly five and a half seconds after Sarina and I beamed aboard."

Cole aimed a knowing smirk back at L'Haan. "I told you he was good."

"I remain unimpressed." She met Bashir's glance. "Any space-service veteran could have made that deduction with such a wealth of information at hand."

Bashir felt compelled to mock her arrogant dismissal. "O,

ye of little faith." He and Sarina followed Cole into a turbolift. After L'Haan stepped in with them, the doors closed.

Cole commanded the lift into motion. "Deck Four, Section Two." There was a slight lurch of momentum as the lift car accelerated upward, and then all sensation of movement abated as the passenger car's inertial dampeners kicked in. An awkward silence settled over the group.

There was no point trying to gauge the car's movement, Bashir decided. It was too well insulated, both inertially and acoustically, for even his enhanced hearing to derive any useful clues as to how far they were traveling, their velocity, or their direction. He turned his head and lifted his brow to catch Cole's attention. "What's our destination?"

"You heard me direct the lift car."

"No, I meant, where is the ship headed? Where are you taking us?"

His inquiry seemed to exasperate Cole. "You're new to the organization, Doctor. In time you'll learn not to ask those kinds of questions. When there's something you need to know, you'll be told. Assume all unspoken details are irrelevant."

"That seems . . . inefficient."

"It's called compartmentalization, and it's a big part of why the organization has persisted and remained operational for as long as it has."

"How long is that?" Another inquisitive arch of Bashir's eyebrow drew a scowl from Cole. Bashir accepted the silent rebuke with a frown and a nod. "I see. Need to know. Right."

Cole and L'Haan volleyed peculiar looks. After a moment, he sighed. "We don't mean to quash your enthusiasm, Doctor. The organization is excited to welcome you into its ranks. But you'll need to adapt to our way of doing things if this relationship is to go smoothly."

It was Bashir's turn to affect an arch tone. "I never said I was joining you."

"Self-deception is a terrible thing, Doctor. I suggest you accept the new status quo."

Bashir remained resolute. "I agreed only to act as an adviser. Nothing more."

L'Haan's voice was low and cold. "You say that now. But when you see what we have to offer, I think you'll reconsider. Few have ever come so far only to turn back."

Her colleague reached out and pressed a reassuring hand onto Bashir's shoulder. "She's right. Like it or not, you're one of us now. And your life will never be the same again."

As the turbolift came to a halt, Bashir mused that Cole's promise might be the first truthful statement he had ever heard from a Section 31 operative. "So then . . . what now?"

"Now?" The turbolift doors opened, and Cole ushered Bashir and Sarina into another dim gray corridor. "Now we show you how the universe *really* works."

Induction into "the organization," as Cole referred to it, took less time than Bashir had expected. Unlike his initial acquisition of a Starfleet security clearance, Section 31 hadn't needed him to provide voiceprints for analysis, retinal patterns or fingerprints for scanning, or any other form of biometric confirmation of his identity. Apparently, they had already appropriated all that data from Starfleet's records, along with copies of his recent transporter patterns.

As intimidating as they were, he had to respect their efficiency and thoroughness.

Despite having told Bashir and Sarina not to pack bags, Cole had grudgingly consented to beam up a single duffel for each of them. Bashir inspected the contents of his bag in the quarters he shared with Sarina and found that most of his personal effects had arrived intact. Only a few items had been confiscated: his medical tricorder, his phaser, and a compact holographic scanner he had hidden inside a hypospray canister in his medkit satchel.

The organization's message was clear: they knew all his tricks, including the ones he hadn't even thought of yet. *So much for hoping to capitalize on one of their mistakes.*

Unexpected was what they had left for him, on the bed.

One of their trademark black leather uniforms.

Bashir had been reluctant to pick it up. He had wanted to reject any gift from this self-appointed cabal of lawless agents, but none more so than their uniform. Everything about the jacket, from its styling to the flat darkness of its material, projected hostility. These were the colors of his enemy. Even knowing he had come here to infiltrate them, he hesitated to put it on.

Sarina watched him as he stood in front of the mirror, wearing the sleek black trousers but still holding the jacket in front of himself. "It's time, Julian."

He looked at her reflection, hoping he could think of some reason to refuse to cooperate. None came. He wished he could put on his old Starfleet uniform and flaunt it like some kind of magic charm against this garment of violence, but he'd forfeited that privilege.

This is what has to happen.

He looked his mirror image in the eye as he donned the black jacket and secured it shut over the dark gray T-shirt that hugged his lean torso.

All at once, he felt the change in his carriage. It was a subtle thing: a lift of his chin, a narrowing of his eyes, a straightening of his back. It came with wearing a uniform. After more than two decades in Starfleet, he thought it likely this was how his subconscious would react to knowing he was dressed in *any* uniform. It filled him with a sense of purpose, a renewed concept of identity and power. It was not the vestment of his youth, but seeing himself in Section 31's black garb filled his soul with the same intangible reward: *pride*.

I hate everything they stand for. But I miss being part of something so badly that wearing even this evil skin feels better than roaming the galaxy as a civilian.

He took a breath and quieted the chaos of protest from his conscience. Then he turned away from the mirror to face Sarina. She stood before him, also attired in the subtly textured black leather pants and jacket of the organization. Before this evening, Bashir had never seen Sarina in the Section 31 uniform. He found the sight of her bedecked in the form-fitting leather both exciting and alarming. He swallowed his desire and steeled himself for what was to come.

"I'm ready. Let's go."

Cole stood waiting for them in the corridor outside. "Right on time. If there's one quality the organization appreciates, it's punctuality." He started walking. "This way, please."

They followed him into a turbolift. The ride to Deck Ten was brief. He led them through some more generic gray passageways and through a parting pair of double doors into a briefing room. Three other agents were seated on the far side of the table.

Cole made curt introductions as he motioned Bashir and Sarina toward adjacent empty seats on the near side of the long oval table. "Everyone, meet agents Julian Bashir and Sarina Douglas." He let Bashir and Sarina sit down, and then he continued. "Doctor, Agent Douglas, allow me to present the rest of our team." He gestured at the other agents as he spoke, starting with the Vulcan woman at the far left. "This is Agent Sakonna. We recruited her from what was left of the Maquis after the Dominion War started. Her specialty is infiltration." In the middle was a thirtyish man who appeared to be human; he had light brown hair, a square jaw, and a boyish mien. "This is David Webb. His specialties are munitions and close-quarter combat." The third and last agent looking across the table was another young male human with a thin face, dark hair, and a steely gaze. "Agent Ken Kitsom is also trained in close-quarter battle, as well as counterintelligence ops."

The trio of agents greeted Bashir and Douglas with nods but no words. Just looking at Kitsom and Webb, Bashir could sense both men were trained, remorseless killers.

Sakonna, however, shed her aloof persona almost instantly. "It really is you," she said to Bashir. "I have great respect for your actions on Andor, Doctor—and for the sacrifices you made as a result. Your moral calculus was both logical and exemplary in its bravery."

He was caught off guard by such effusive praise from a Vulcan. "Um . . . thank you."

Cole sat down on Bashir's right. "Let's get to business, please." Using an interface on the tabletop, Cole called up a series of reports that recapped what Bashir and Sarina already knew about the operation: that the Breen had launched a mission to the alternate universe to steal a wormhole-drive jaunt ship. Bashir surmised the recap was being provided for the benefit of Sakonna, Webb, and Kitsom, whose keen attention to the briefing suggested it was new to them. Bashir and Sarina's interest perked up as Cole moved past the basics into new intelligence.

"Here's what we know for certain, so far. Approximately twenty-seven hours ago, the Breen used an apparatus of Tzenkethi design to open a rift in the barrier between universes. This occurred just over the border between Breen and Federation space." An annotated star chart filled the wall monitor at the head of the table. Cole pointed at a red icon on the map. "We've pinpointed the source of the rift as an interstellar research post the Breen call Ikkuna Station. The rift was open only briefly, but long enough for them to move a *Reikin*-class fast-attack cruiser through it, into the alternate universe. This is the same kind of ship that attacked Earth during the Dominion War, and it's armed with the same energy-dampening weapons that wiped out our fleet at the Second Battle of Chin'toka. The vessel has been identified as the *Tajny*, and we have reason to think it's crewed by a company of Spetzkar—elite Breen military commandos."

A moment of silence gave those facts time to sink in. Then Cole switched off the wall screen, stood, and moved to the head of the table. "Available intel suggests the Breen are out to capture a wormhole-drive vessel from the alternate universe, but we have no idea which ship. Nor do we know where, when, or how they plan to stage that assault. What we do know is that we can't permit them to succeed."

Webb lifted his hand. "Are we planning to deploy into the alternate universe?"

"Yes."

"What kind of operational support can we expect over there?"

Cole frowned. "None. Once we cross the dimensional barrier, we'll be on our own. And as familiar as the alternate reality might look, I assure you, it will be foreign territory. Tread with care, people."

The next query came from Kitsom. "What's our tactical profile?"

"Trojan horse assault," Cole said. "We'll hit Ikkuna Station fast and hard. Primary objective: seize control of the station and use its rift generator to move our own ship into the alternate universe. Then we destroy the station behind us."

Sakonna arched one thin eyebrow. "Is this to be a one-way expedition, Mister Cole?"

"Perhaps. My superiors have decided that our return is not a priority. Keeping this technology from the Breen—and, by extension, the Typhon Pact—is our primary objective."

The Vulcan nodded. "Understood."

"You'll each be issued a sensor scrambler to mask your life signs, a comm interceptor for intelligence gathering, and a transporter beacon in case you need a fast exfiltration. As for weapons—" Cole paused at the sight of Bashir's raised hand. "Yes, Doctor?"

"If I might be permitted to inquire . . . have you shared this information about the Breen with Starfleet Intelligence or the Federation Security Agency?"

Cole let slip a cynical laugh before he re-composed himself. "Doctor . . . they're the *source* of our intelligence. Unfortunately, thanks to recent laws enacted by the Federation Council, and regulations put in place by Starfleet Command, both agencies are legally barred from conducting operations—clandestine or otherwise—in the alternate universe."

His revelation baffled Bashir. "Why?"

"A reaction to blowback from certain recent operations involving your former colleagues on Deep Space Nine. Whatever the rationale was for the legislation, it's black-letter law now. Which means that if the Breen's mission in the alternate universe is to be stopped, we're the only ones left who can do it." A smirk punctuated his point. "Any further questions, Doctor?" Bashir shook his head. No one else had anything to add. Cole nodded. "All right, then. Get ready, everyone. We'll be at Ikkuna Station in less than three hours—and we'll be hitting them hard, fast, and for effect. Dismissed."

Thirteen

The Alternate Universe

More than fifteen years had slipped away since Kersil Regon had last set foot on Bajor. The Cardassian spy had never harbored much affection for the Bajorans' culture. She found their art, music, and architecture uninspired, and except for *hasperat*, their cuisine was hopelessly bland.

The only fortunate circumstance of her present visit was that it had brought her to Hedrikspool Province, one of the hottest, most humid regions of the planet, the one that felt most like her beloved Cardassia. Located on Bajor's southern hemisphere, just below the equator, the province was home to the planet's largest wilderness preserve.

Standing in the center of that natural redoubt, surrounded by hundreds of hectares of lush rain forest in every direction, was the Elemspur Monastery—an ancient religious retreat that had become one of the Galactic Commonwealth's best-defended sites for high-level political conferences. High stone ramparts circled the monastery's interconnected buildings, whose defining elements included graceful arches, ornately sculpted façades, and high, elegant towers.

Regon could see little of the historical site from her vantage point more than half a kilometer away in the forest. This was as close as she and Kort had dared to approach, despite having taken the precautions of wearing camouflage and sensor-spoofing devices that would mask their life signs. He had told her to hunker down and wait while he circled the monastery's perimeter in the hope of scouting a less treacherous approach or an undefended entrance.

She checked her wrist chrono. Almost an hour had passed. The sun would be up soon.

Atop the high ramparts, several pairs of armed guards moved in patrol patterns. At numerous points along the barricades, sentries stood watch. A peek through her holographic scope had confirmed her suspicion. The troops manning the walls weren't Bajoran, nor did they hail from any of the slave races that now constituted the Galactic Commonwealth. These gray-skinned aliens had a fierce gleam in their eyes, and all of them carried energy rifles as well as axlike melee weapons. Their manner was that of professional soldiers. Born killers.

A low whistle in the darkness signaled her to expect Kort's approach. Half a minute later he emerged from the night, a silent shadow drifting to her side. "This is as close as we can get." He scowled at the alien soldiers guarding the monastery. "They're everywhere."

"There's more to security than manpower. What about gaps in the sensor screen?"

The Klingon shook his head. "Solid as a rock. I've never seen anything quite like it, which makes me think these new visitors are behind it."

It was dispiriting news, but Regon refused to give up hope. There had to be a way in. "I've heard rumors of underground passages between the monastery and the jungle. Maybe if we found one of the exit points, we could slip inside and pose as members of the civilian staff."

"A fool's errand." Kort pointed at far-off locations in the rain forest. "Scouring the jungle in a search pattern's out of the question. They have patrols outside the walls. I never saw them—to be honest, I never even *heard* them. But I smelled them. They were there." His surgically altered face tightened as he frowned at the soldiers on the ramparts. "If they're this thorough on the perimeter, I expect they'll be just as methodical defending the interior."

"But the Commonwealth's forces are manning the main gate, aren't they?"

A weary nod. "Yes, but they're not taking chances, either. The rebels learned much from living under our rule. They've set up a double checkpoint at the gate itself, and another inside. From what I saw, they're verifying everyone's credentials, no matter who they appear to be." He rubbed his smooth faux-Bajoran forehead. "It seems we let ourselves be butchered for nothing."

Regon drew a deep breath of the muggy predawn air. The night's breezes were rich with fragrances of rotting vegetation and sweet flowers, and the darkness was alive with the echoes of animal appetites, the sonorous buzzing of insects, and the plaintive musical cries of small birds. The rain forest was a lovely place, Regon decided. In some small way, she was relieved that she didn't have to mar its beauty with her and Kort's half-formed scheme to sow violence and chaos.

She pinched her nose's freshly cast ersatz ridges. "What do you suggest we do now?"

"We can't stay here." Kort gestured vaguely to either side of them. "If their patrols keep pushing into the forest, they'll find us sooner or later. I think it'd be best if we left before then."

"Then we'll head back to Jalanda."

Kort's eyes widened. He whispered through clenched teeth. "The capital? Are you mad?"

She extended her elbow and gave his arm a playful nudge. "Don't be such a grouch. It'll be like old times. Shadowing the junior attachés and the hungry young government staffers."

He grinned, amused by old memories. "Ah, yes. Waiting for them to drink themselves stupid and spill state secrets as they vie for mates and bragging rights . . . Could be fun."

"At the very least, it has to be better than sitting out here, waiting to get caught."

He considered that and nodded. "That much is true."

The Klingon in disguise skulked into the underbrush and beckoned her to follow. She stole after him, relying on slightly rusty decades-old training to avoid missteps that could betray their presence as they navigated through the overgrown foliage, back toward a seldom-used trail that would lead them north to their ground vehicle—and the road to Jalanda. As he turned back to speak, she cut him off with a simple declaration: "I'm driving."

A low growl rattled inside his broad chest. He kept walking as he muttered, "I hate you."

Regon smiled at the comfortable familiarity of the moment. *Just like old times, indeed.*

In all the years that Hanalarell sh'Pherron had commanded a jaunt ship for the Commonwealth, she had never been afforded the privilege of a direct audience with Saavik, the legendary director of Memory Omega who also, a century earlier, had been the last captain of the famed Terran warship *Enterprise*. It came as no surprise to sh'Pherron that her first audience with the famous Vulcan woman had manifested as an ass-chewing in front of her bridge crew.

Saavik's face loomed larger than life on the main viewscreen. *"Unacceptable, Captain. We verified an intrusion from the other universe. The ship responsible must be somewhere."*

It took all of sh'Pherron's hard-won discipline not to resort to sarcasm or profanity. "My crew confirmed the breach event, Director, but the intruder remains at large. My tactical chief and I think the culprit is using a cloaking device, of a model unknown to us."

"We have new cloak-penetrating protocols that might prove useful. My team at Omega Prime will upload them to your computer momentarily."

"It'll take some time to integrate the new protocols. Until then, we'll widen our search area." She considered keeping her next idea to herself, then chose to run with it. "We could execute the search far more quickly if we had another ship to share the workload."

The Vulcan lowered her chin and glowered at sh'Pherron. *"We have no ships to spare, Captain. If not for a confirmed breach, you would still be in spacedock at Erebus Station."*

"Understood. We'll look forward to receiving those new cloak-hunting protocols. *ShiKahr* out." A slashing motion of sh'Pherron's thumb across her throat cued Ensign Riaow to close the special quantum communications channel to Omega Prime.

Turak left the sensor console to stand beside sh'Pherron's command chair. "The new protocols are loading now, Captain. I can start a new sensor sweep of the area in two minutes."

"Good. Let me know the moment you get a lead on our prey."

"Of course." The Vulcan first officer lingered a moment before lowering his voice to ask a question. "Captain, are you upset about something?"

She answered him in a hushed voice. "Is it that obvious?"

"Yes, it is." Like most Vulcans, Turak had a knack for getting to the point.

"I'm annoyed that Saavik refused to send reinforcements for the hunt."

"I'm sure Director Saavik weighed all the relevant strategic and tactical considerations before arriving at her decision." Turak recoiled from sh'Pherron's sudden, poisonous stare.

She forced her stoic mask of command back into place. "Turak, to the best of your knowledge, how many times has a starship breached the universal barrier?"

He cocked an eyebrow as he searched his memory. "Only twice that I know of."

"Exactly. The first was a small ship, little more than a glorified shuttle. But this—if the initial report from Omega's right, it's *big*, Turak. A warship." Her stare narrowed and she felt her countenance take on a fierce edge as she gazed at the star-dusted sprawl of empty space on the main viewscreen. "And the fact that it's come cloaked tells me it's here looking for a fight."

He turned his gaze toward the starfield. "A logical inference."

"I hope I'm wrong, Turak. I really do. But in case I'm not, start running battle drills."

She kept her eyes on the viewscreen as Turak left to carry out her orders. Was it possible that the cloaked interloper was merely a research vessel? A peaceful explorer? She couldn't be certain it wasn't. After all, logically speaking, almost anything was *possible*. But was it likely?

Everything sh'Pherron knew of life told her not to count on it.

Fourteen

An aura of imminent violence enveloped Bashir as he and Sarina followed Cole out of the turbolift onto the command deck of their small starship. As soon as Bashir got a clear look at one of the companels, he recognized the alien symbols that filled its interface and intuited the origin of the vessel. "This is a Breen ship."

"Very good, Doctor." Cole directed Bashir and Sarina off to one side of the cramped bridge. "I'm glad you recognize it, because in a few moments, you and Miss Douglas will be playing the parts of its two most senior officers." He beckoned Webb and Kitsom from the shadows. The two men stepped forward carrying bundled beige-and-gray Breen military uniforms, which they handed to Sarina and Bashir. Sakonna approached from behind Cole and handed him his own disguise. She, Webb, and Kitsom were already dressed in borrowed Breen uniforms, except for the snout-shaped helmets, which Bashir glimpsed atop a storage crate tucked against the forward bulkhead. Cole stripped off his leather jacket and tossed it aside with a grin at Bashir and Sarina. "No time to be bashful. We need to hail our target in five minutes."

Bashir and Sarina mirrored each other's mild dismay for a moment before they doffed their Section 31 leather garb and donned the Breen uniforms, with help from Webb and Kitsom. As soon as their disguises were properly secured, their new colleagues spirited away their discarded articles of clothing and hid them from the communication system's visual sensors.

Cole gave their appropriated outfits a last check. "Perfect." He motioned Sarina toward one of the forward duty stations and ushered Bashir toward the center seat. "This ship is the *Królik*, a long-range Breen scout. It was captured less than three days ago, so it's unlikely the Breen know yet that it's been compromised. Doctor, you'll do most of the talking. After Ikkuna Station answers our hail, you'll identify yourself as Thot Kren and say your ship is in distress." He nodded at Webb and Kitsom. "We've crafted a false sensor profile that'll make us register as Breen and make our ship appear to be on the verge of losing life support and inertial dampening—crises that'll look potentially fatal for us but not a threat to them."

Bashir understood the nature of the ruse. "We request emergency docking for repairs, and they order us to shut down our engines. We comply with their orders and let them tow us inside the station with a tractor beam. And then—"

"Then we deploy into the docking bay and do what we do best." He handed Bashir a Breen-made data device similar to a Starfleet padd. "These are most of the command codes and challenge-and-response phrases we know the Breen have been using. Give it a look—we only have about ninety seconds before we get inside their sensor range."

Feigned jocularity added venom to Bashir's words. "Ninety whole seconds? Glad you gave me time to prepare. I'd hate to have to cram for something as important as this."

"Sarcasm gains us nothing, Doctor." Cole snapped his fingers at the others. "Helmets!"

Sakonna, Webb, and Kitsom pulled their own snout masks into place, and then they rushed the last three over to Cole, Bashir, and Sarina. Bashir put down the padd just long enough to force his head inside the claustrophobically snug helmet. It locked into place upon contact with the neck of his uniform, and its holographic heads-up display snapped on, giving him a remarkably clear view of his surroundings. Except for the HUD data superimposed over his simulated panorama, it felt surprisingly natural.

Just like the one I wore on the mission to Salavat. The bloody covert mission from years earlier still haunted him. His efforts to pull the Andorian species back from the brink of extinction had salved much of his lingering guilt over the innocent lives he had callously taken during the sabotage of the Breen shipyard in the Alrakis system, but as Ikkuna Station loomed large on the *Królik*'s main viewscreen, he feared he was about to repeat the sins of his past.

Cole slipped away to a starboard console. "Engage sensor camouflage."

Webb keyed in the command. "Engaged."

"All right, Doctor. It's your show now. Take us in."

Dread rushed through Bashir like an ice-water transfusion. He settled into the command chair and fixed his eyes upon the spindle-shaped Breen deep-space station. "Slow to half impulse, then cut engines. We'll need to drift in for them to buy the ruse."

"Slowing to half impulse," Sarina confirmed as she entered commands into the helm. "Engines cut. We're drifting into their sensor range in three . . . two . . . one. In range."

Now the fun begins.

Bashir stole a final look at the padd and tried to memorize as many of the challenge-and-response codes as he could in the scant moments he would have before—

"They're hailing us," Sakonna said.

"Vocoders on," Cole said. "Stay quiet and look sharp."

Bashir activated his helmet's vocoder, a device that translated speech—but only after masking its original nature and rendering it into garbled machine noise. It was just one of many oppressive technologies the Breen had devised to enforce their perverse sense of equality. Confident his true nature would now be hidden from the Breen on the station, he took a breath and prepared for a potentially awkward conversation. "Put them on-screen."

The viewscreen's image of the station was replaced by one of a Breen's masked head. He—she? it?—addressed Bashir in the harsh mechanized voice common to the Breen culture. *"This is a restricted area. Identify yourself."*

"Thot Kren, commanding the scout ship *Królik.* We have experienced critical failures of our inertial dampeners and life-support system, and require emergency assistance."

The head on the screen looked away, and Bashir surmised the individual was conferring with a superior—one who Bashir expected would take over the conversation at any moment. Instead, the underling manning the comm channel replied, *"Verify, six zark one."*

It was one of the first three codes listed on Bashir's padd. "Authorize, *zart* nine four."

Seconds passed while the Breen on the station checked Bashir's response.

"Confirmed. Continue on your present course. As soon as your vessel is in range, we'll tow you in. Repair teams will meet you in the docking bay."

"Acknowledged. *Królik* out."

Sakonna closed the channel, and the viewscreen reverted to the slowly growing image of Ikkuna Station. Bashir noted the sly turn of Sarina's head to look back at him, as if she were as surprised by the efficacy of their ruse as he was. He turned toward Cole. "Well, that was easy."

"Only because good people died to bring us the intel that made it possible." Cole stood, and the other Section 31 veterans did likewise. Bashir and Sarina were the last ones on their feet. The senior agent led them all toward the turbolift. "Step one of this mission went by the numbers. Let's hope the rest of the op goes as smoothly."

The implications of Cole's remark troubled Bashir. "And if it doesn't?"

"Then I hope you like blood, Doctor. Because if we botch this, there'll be a lot of it."

Bashir tightened his grip on his Breen-made disruptor rifle. Ahead of him, a sliver of brightness expanded as the ventral ramp of the *Królik* parted from the bulkhead and lowered to reveal the main docking bay of Ikkuna Station.

Kitsom's foot twitched. He was eager to spring into action. Too eager, Bashir feared.

It seemed Cole had noticed the younger agent champing at the bit. "Not yet. Stay cool." As the ramp continued to drop toward the deck of the docking bay, it became possible to see the Breen personnel waiting outside the ship. Cole charged his disruptor. "Set for heavy stun."

"I count nine hostiles," Sakonna said.

Cole flipped a switch on his helmet. "Sensors show seventeen Breen in the docking bay. The rest are behind us. Sakonna, Kitsom, take point, then cover the rear. Douglas, Bashir, watch our flanks. Webb, get us through the blast doors and into the base as fast as possible."

Webb powered up his CRM-114, a Breen-made handheld cannon typically used against vehicles and fortified installations. "Ask and ye shall receive."

"Watch your backs," Cole said, "and good luck." The ramp touched the deck with a dull scrape and a bright metallic *clang*. "Move out."

Angry shrieks of disruptor fire filled the air. Bashir didn't know who'd shot first—it might have been Sakonna, but it could just as easily have been Kitsom or Cole—but within seconds of Cole's order to attack, Bashir and Sarina were in the thick of the assault, laying down suppressing fire as they charged down the scout ship's ramp. They reached the deck and split up, Bashir to the right and Sarina to the left, to get out of the way of Webb's handheld cannon.

The Breen in the docking bay stood frozen as the barrage of disruptor blasts erupted from the hold of the *Królik*. Most of the technicians and engineers fell or were launched backward as the fusillade slammed into them. All those who stood between the Section 31 team and the sealed blast doors that led to the station's interior were downed within moments.

Bashir turned, crouched, and snapped off a flurry of shots at another group of Breen. He felled two in quick succession, then had to dive for cover behind one of the *Królik*'s landing struts, to dodge an incoming salvo from a Breen trooper in a guard post on an upper deck overlooking the docking bay. Before Bashir could recover his bearings to retaliate, Sakonna drew out the trooper with harassing fire, and Kitsom finished him with a precision head shot.

Then came the thunder.

Webb fired the CRM-114. A bone-rattling boom shook the docking bay and left Bashir feeling as if his innards had been quaked into pulp by sheer sonic force. Bright almost to the point of being blinding, a crimson flash leaped from the portable artillery piece and obliterated the blast doors at the far end of the docking bay. A storm of smoldering metal debris rode the rebounding shock wave and pelted the strike team and their ship. Bashir shielded his face with his arm until the shrapnel settled.

Cole barked, "Everyone up! We need to move!"

There was no time to protest or ask questions. Bashir sprang to his feet and followed Cole and the others toward the vast smoking breach. As they moved through the ragged gap wrought by the CRM-114, Bashir saw that the Section 31 agents had arranged themselves in a defensive formation around him and Sarina. Before he could remark on it, Cole turned, grasped Bashir's shoulder, and pointed him at a nearby wall console. "Know how to use that thing?"

"I remember the basics."

"Get on it. We need to scramble their internal sensors and find a route to the control room for the dimensional gate."

Sarina joined Bashir at the wall console. Together they keyed in commands, parsing the bizarre alien symbols and syntax with ease thanks to their photographic memories of the Breen idioms they had learned during the Salavat mission. Whenever one of them strayed off the mark, the other was there to catch it and correct the error. Within seconds they broke through the station's security lockouts, disabled its internal sensor grid, and called up a diagram of the station.

"Everything's in lockdown because we blasted through the bulkhead," Sarina said to Cole, pointing out details on the interactive map. "All the turbolifts are frozen, and security's mobilizing against us. We can expect to have some serious company in about sixty seconds."

"We'll be gone by then. Where's the control room?"

She highlighted it with a tap of her fingertip. "Up here. Operations level."

Cole pointed at the core. "We'll take the road less traveled. The station's guts are automated—lots of open space, no air, zero gravity. Douglas, find us a way in there." Alarms blared, and the station's interior lighting turned bloodred. Cole noted the new circumstances with a sanguine nod. "And not to put any pressure on you, but sooner would be better."

Sarina switched off the wall monitor and beckoned everyone to follow her. "This way."

Bashir fell in behind her, and the rest of the team scrambled back into their protective box formation around the couple. He appreciated the extra protection, but as they raced to the nearest core access hatch, he found himself suspicious of the team's desire to safeguard him and Sarina. *They could've done most of this without us. Everything we learned during the Salavat mission was recorded. So why go to all this trouble to bring us here? What are they really driving at?*

His questions would have to wait. The team charged into a terminal passage, and Sarina pointed at the pressure hatch on the far wall. "Through there."

Cole waved Kitsom forward. "Open it." The fair-haired young agent hurried to the hatch, unlocked it, and pulled it open. On the other side was an empty airlock.

The passageways behind the team resounded with the rumble of running footsteps and the angry buzz of mechanized voices barking orders. Time and options were both running out.

Cole waved the team past him. "It won't take 'em long to figure out where we went." He followed them inside the airlock and pulled the hatch shut behind him. "So get that next door open and move your asses before the Breen shoot them all off."

"Cover!"

Bashir huddled, head down, behind the corner with the rest of the team as Webb targeted the control room's reinforced door with the outrageous might of the CRM-114. The team's ascent to the operations level had been swift and uninterrupted, and now their access to the heart of the station promised to be just as quick.

"Fire in the hole!" A red pulse and a thundering boom disintegrated the entrance to the secret laboratory. Webb dodged toward the opposite corner, half a second ahead of the rebounding shock wave and its chaos of sparks and shredded, half-molten metal.

Bashir adjusted the filters of his helmet's holovisor to pierce the smoke, just as Cole windmilled his arm and marshaled the team into action. "Go!"

Kitsom and Sakonna sprinted down the smoke-filled passageway, firing suppressing shots through the jagged opening where the control room's door had been. Cole and Webb fell in behind Bashir and Sarina, who charged with their disruptors leveled ahead of themselves, prepared to face any counterattack head-on.

Energy pulses ripped through the gap, forcing the Section 31 agents to duck to either side and press themselves against the walls. A wild shot grazed the shoulder of Bashir's uniform with a sharp sizzle, followed by a puff of acrid smoke. He swatted the scar until it stopped smoldering, then shouted across the barrage to Cole, "We're pinned down!"

"Relax. We're just regrouping." The leader fired a quick series of shots at the lab's defenders, then hollered to the rest of his team, "Deploy spiders!"

Webb, Sakonna, and Kitsom slung their weapons. Each of them detached a pair of palm-sized, thin octagonal canisters from their uniforms' utility belts and tossed them to the floor. All six canisters sprouted eight legs on impact, then skittered with unnerving speed under the enemy's defensive barrage and scrambled into the control room.

Next came high-pitched whines and shrieks. Blue-white flashes filled the control room, which suddenly looked to Bashir like nothing less than a killing jar. The drones had the advantages of surprise, velocity, and superior accuracy. In a matter of seconds, all sounds of resistance from inside the lab ceased. Kitsom touched the side of his helmet, then he looked back at the rest of the team. "Clear."

Cole strode toward the control room. "Move up, two by two, covering formation."

Kitsom and Sakonna were the first ones inside. They split up to cover the Breen personnel who were still conscious. Bashir entered to see all of the control room's armed guards incapacitated, bodies sprawled on the deck in agonized poses—but still breathing.

Standing in the middle of the laboratory, surrounded by the six spider drones, were two unarmed persons. One wore a Breen military uniform bearing a *thot*'s rank insignia. The other was a resplendent Tzenkethi woman. Her silvery skin, deep-copper hair, and elegant facial symmetry were striking amid the aggressive drabness of the Breen.

Cole stepped past Bashir and Sarina to confront the enemy duo. "Thot Tran. Doctor Choska. It's a pleasure to make your acquaintances after all this time."

Choska's voice was as sweet as a lullaby. "And you would be . . . ?"

"Unimpressed by your charms." Cole aimed his disruptor at Choska's head.

Bashir blocked Cole as Tran stepped in front of Choska. "What are you doing?"

The agent's aim was steady, even with Bashir as its target. "Step aside, Doctor."

"I didn't sign on for this."

From the sides of the room came the low whine of charging disruptors. Kitsom and Sakonna took aim at Choska. Sarina leveled her weapon against Cole, who breathed a sigh that the vocoder parsed as crackling static. "Time is short, Doctor, and we only need one of them."

Tran raised his empty hands. "Do what you want to me. Don't hurt Doctor Choska."

In unison, Cole, Bashir, and Choska muttered with the same note of incredulity, "*What?*"

"I will cooperate," Tran said. "No tricks. All I ask is that you not harm her."

The Tzenkethi snapped at Tran, "What're you doing?"

"Saving your life. So be quiet." The Breen looked back at Cole. "I am in command here. Just tell me what you want."

Cole shook his head. "Sorry, Tran, but your dossiers make it clear she's the brains of this operation. I can't let her live just so she can rebuild all of this someplace else. I hope you both understand—this isn't personal."

Bashir seized the barrel of Cole's disruptor and forced it toward the ceiling. "You don't need to do this. He'll give us what we want."

"What we want is to stop the Typhon Pact from sending missions to the alternate universe. And the most reliable means we have of ensuring that outcome is to make sure these two *both* end up dead. But in the name of compromise, I'll settle for killing the smarter one."

"If they die, you die, I die—*everybody* dies."

To Bashir's dismay, Cole seemed to consider his offer. Unable to peer beneath the man's snout mask, Bashir had no way of knowing whether he had just struck a blow for diplomacy or had set in motion a bloodbath that would start with his own execution.

The tense standoff was interrupted by Webb, who noted with dry professionalism, "We have about sixty seconds before the security forces get here."

Cole lowered his weapon. "All right, Doctor. Have it your way." He leaned to look past Bashir at Tran. "You have one minute to power up your rift generator and program it to open us a passage to the alternate universe."

"Understood." Tran moved to a nearby master console.

Choska followed and leaned over his shoulder while he worked. "Are you mad?"

"Just do as I say, Choska. Initiate the stabilizer field."

Kitsom and Webb moved to covered positions from which they could defend the entrance. Cole stepped close enough to Tran and Choska to monitor their work. Sakonna kept her distance and stayed where she could cover both Bashir and Sarina.

Bashir watched Choska and Tran work as he asked Cole, "What's next?"

"Since you insist on letting them live, we'll need to change our exit strategy. Once our new friends activate the rift generator, we'll escort them to the nearest escape pod and put them in it. But someone has to stay here to trigger the self-destruct and sabotage the command systems to prevent it from being aborted." He frowned at Bashir. "Which job would you prefer?"

Sarina touched Bashir's arm. "I'll make sure the scientists get out unharmed."

He nodded. "All right. I'll stay here to trigger the self-destruct."

"So be it." Cole returned his attention to the enemy scientists. "How much longer?"

Tran entered a few last commands. "The generator is activating now."

A holographic projection along the wall opposite the entrance showed a sudden rent in the fabric of interstellar space. A radiant wound had appeared, as if slashed by a blade of titanic size. Choska made a few final adjustments to her console's settings, and the brilliant incision in the skin of the universe began to widen. Its edges grew ragged with wild energies that left its contours tattered and aglow with eerie fires of unknown origin.

"It's open," Tran said. "It should remain stable for about seven minutes, or until one ship passes through."

Cole offered the Breen a jaunty salute. "Well done, Tran. And my compliments to you, as well, Doctor Choska." He gestured for them to move toward the entrance. "Now if you'd be so kind as to vacate the premises?"

Choska glared at Cole even as Tran gently ushered her out at his side.

"Webb, Kitsom, see them to an escape pod, then decoy the incoming security force. No matter what, after ninety seconds, use your recall beacons to get back to the ship and prep for launch."

The two agents led Tran and Choska into the passageway outside the control room. Sarina paused at the doorway to look back at Bashir. All he could offer her was a single nod of encouragement. She parroted the gesture, then vanished into the smoky haze of the corridor to safeguard the fates of the two strangers for whom Bashir had just risked his life.

Cole pointed Sakonna toward the entrance, and she took over Kitsom's previous position so she could act as a sentry. Then Cole directed Bashir toward the master console where Tran had stood. "Work quickly, Doctor. Time's a factor."

"I never would have guessed." Most of the command systems resembled those Bashir had encountered during his mission to Salavat a few years earlier. It took him only a few seconds to isolate the command protocols and call up the interface for Ikkuna Station's self-destruct system. "I don't suppose you have command codes for—"

"Identify yourself as Thot Kren and use emergency command override five one *swit zmierz* nine nine three red."

Bashir activated the self-destruct. The main computer requested his authorization, and he repeated the identity and authorization code as Cole had recited them. Then the computer's mechanical voice prompted him, *"Set countdown duration for self-destruct."*

Cole instructed him, "Set two minutes, silent countdown."

Instead, Bashir told the computer, "Six minutes. Sound evacuation warning."

"Acknowledged."

A high-pitched alarm keened and echoed through the station's empty spaces. The computer's voice announced over the public-address system, *"Self-destruct sequence engaged. All personnel evacuate. You have six minutes to reach minimum safe distance."*

Cole punched a nearby console. Then he pulled off his helmet to shout at Bashir. "What the hell are you doing? I gave you an order!"

"True. But I never agreed to take orders from you—or to condemn innocent people to die." He turned his back on Cole and accessed the station's emergency systems. "Computer: Lock onto all registered station personnel inside the command center and beam them directly to the nearest unoccupied escape pods."

"Energizing." Seconds later, coruscating swirls of light cocooned the unconscious Breen troopers lying on the deck around Bashir, Cole, and Sakonna. Within moments, they all had vanished, shepherded to safety. *"Transports complete."*

"Computer: Launch those pods."

"Pods away."

Bashir took off his own helmet and stared back at Cole. *"Now* we can go."

"Not so fast. If you'd set the countdown I'd requested, we could leave. But for some asinine reason you insisted on giving the Breen six minutes—"

"They need time to evacuate a station of this size and crew complement."

"Perhaps. But by giving them time to evacuate, you also gave them time to *respond*. They'll try to retake this command center and override the self-destruct. So thanks to you, we need to stay here and make sure that doesn't happen." He put his helmet back on and charged his disruptor. "Take cover. You're gonna need it."

Bashir pulled his own helmet back on. He crouched between Cole and Sakonna, behind a long bank of consoles whose back faced the wide-open entrance. He checked the settings on his disruptor. "Say what you will, Cole. I know I did the right thing."

"No, Doctor, you did the *moral* thing." He peeked over the top of the console as the sounds of boots crunching over dust and debris filled the passageway outside. "Let's hope your renowned compassion doesn't get us all killed."

Like everything else made by the Breen, the escape pod was sturdy, functional, and soul-crushingly ugly. As a coffin it would have suited Thot Tran just fine, but it was a vessel most unworthy to ferry or contain Choska Ves Fel-AA's ineffable beauty.

Tran had no time to dote upon Choska—not now, with so much at stake. Using tools he always kept hidden in the folds and pockets of his uniform, he detached the faceplate of the escape pod's emergency communications system. He reached deep into the close-packed hardware that dwelled inside the pod's narrow, efficiently designed bulkheads.

Choska's enchanting voice filled his ears. "What are you trying to do?"

"I need to connect the comm system's main transceiver to the reserve power cells."

"To what purpose?"

"So we can generate a subspace signal powerful enough to pass through the rift and get a warning to the *Tajny*." His fingers found the power cables and adroitly wrestled them free. When he went to connect them to the transceiver, however, he grumbled bitter curses.

"Now what?"

"I can't feel the recessed auxiliary power port through my gloves."

She shouldered him aside. "You Breen and your costumes. Let me do it." Twisting like a slow flame, she snaked her limber arm inside the bulkhead and found the transceiver. After a few moments, a soft click from inside the machinery signaled her success. She extricated her limb and invited Tran back to the console. "All yours."

"Thank you." He powered up the comm system and opened an encrypted channel on the super-low subspace frequency that had been optimized for cross-dimensional transmissions and reserved for the *Tajny*'s use for the duration of its mission to the alternate universe. "Thot Tran to *Tajny*. This is a Priority One alert. Please respond."

He feared that the pod lacked sufficient power to send the message, or that the rift might be too unstable to let the signal pass through intact. But after several seconds, Thot Trom replied. "*This is* Tajny. *Go ahead.*"

"Ikkuna Station has been compromised. Its destruction is imminent, and a hostile vessel is about to pursue you and close the rift. Adjust your mission profile for return strategy *usta*."

"*Understood.* Tajny *out.*"

The channel closed abruptly, and the pod's comm system reverted to its normal standby mode. Tran reset the system to send distress signals on all Tzenkethi military frequencies. Then he breathed a heavy sigh and slumped against one side of the hexagonal pod, opposite Choska.

Outside the view ports, the endless night wheeled past, the scattered stars transformed into blurs by the slow but erratic tumbling of the pod.

Inside the cramped emergency vehicle, an awkward silence festered between Tran and Choska. The Tzenkethi woman studied him with eyes as cold as they were lovely. She regarded him the same way she scrutinized experiments that deviated too far from her predictions.

Tran had no idea what to say to her, so he felt great relief when at last she spoke. "What were you thinking, Tran?"

"When?"

"Back on the station. When you told the intruders, 'Do what you want to me. Don't hurt Doctor Choska.' What was *that* all about?"

Her question left him flummoxed. Then he realized the truth: *I have nothing left to lose.*

He had warned the *Tajny* and given its Spetzkar a fighting chance to defend themselves and find a new route home, but after surrendering Ikkuna Station to the intruders, his life would be forfeit if he ever returned to face his superiors in the Confederacy. His only hope of survival now lay in having the courage to do what he had wanted to do from the start.

He took off his helmet. Choska stared, wide-eyed, at the proud lines of his strong jaw, at his skin the color of rich, wet loam ready for planting, and into his chartreuse eyes. He peeled off his gloves and cast them aside. Then he reveled in the mild shock that came from touching her flesh as he kneeled and took her hand in his. The truth would be spoken, come what may.

"Dear, sweet Choska . . . my real name is Herlok Seltran, scion of the Clan Lokaar, born in the frozen north of Pacluro Prime, and I have something I need to tell you:

"I love you—*and I want to defect.*"

Leading the Breen astray inside the station had proved easier than Sarina had expected. Nearly half the force responding to the attack on the control room had detoured to pursue her, Webb, and Kitsom. Rather than engage the Breen directly, the trio of Section 31 agents had led them on a breakneck sprint through the station's upper levels—a chase that terminated by design in a dead end. As soon as they turned the last corner, Webb's order came through on their private comm channel via their Breen helmets: "Recall beacons!"

Still running, Sarina activated the automated signaling device on her uniform's forearm. With one stride she was in the corridor, racing toward a solid gray wall. Her next step carried her off the transporter platform inside the *Królik*. Kitsom and Webb bounded off the platform and sped past her, pulling off their helmets as they dashed out the door. "C'mon," Kitsom said. "We need to get to the rift!" She followed the two men on their mad dash back to the command deck, tossing aside her own helmet as they took their posts.

Kitsom dropped his helmet on the deck by the helm as he sat down and started tapping in commands. "Ventral hatch shut! Impulse engines online!"

Webb set his helmet atop the tactical station as he worked. "Disruptors charged! Firing!"

The ship's main disruptor bank fired with a furious shriek. Sarina winced at the flash of light on the whited-out main viewer. The glare faded to reveal the absence of the outer docking bay doors—because Webb had just vaporized them. He called to Kitsom, "Clear!"

Sarina felt the deck lurch ever so slightly as Kitsom engaged the impulse drive. The inertial dampeners lagged by a few thousandths of a second, apparently confused by the *Królik*'s sudden departure from the station's artificial gravity into zero-*g* deep space. "Coming about on course for the rift," Kitsom said.

"Hold at thirty thousand kilometers from the station," Webb said. "Warp drive to standby." He looked at Sarina. "Scan the rift. Make sure it's stable before we try to cross it."

"On it." Sarina pivoted toward the sensor console and made a comprehensive sensor sweep of the interdimensional rip. "Energy levels fluctuating. Quantum signature from the other side matches the known frequency for the alternate universe."

A quick, steady percussion turned her head. She tracked the sound to Kitsom, who anxiously tapped his index finger against the side of the helm console. The dark-haired agent stared at the split image on the main viewscreen. On one side was the fiery chaos of the rift; on the other was the panicked flurry of escape pods rocketing away from Ikkuna Station.

Kitsom's frown thinned and the creases in his brow deepened. "Where the hell are they? They should have beamed back by now."

With a quick jab at the tactical panel, Webb opened a comm channel. "*Królik* to Cole. What's your status and ETA?"

Static accompanied the whine of weapons fire over the channel. Cole's voice pitched with stress. "*Still helping the good doctor hold the control room!*"

Concern darkened Webb's expression. "Do you require assistance?"

"*Negative! Are you in position?*"

"Affirmative."

"*Stay there.*" The screeching of disruptor blasts became deafening. "*Hang on.*"

The channel closed with a click. Webb and Kitsom traded grim looks. Kitsom shook his head. "What the hell are they doing? It was supposed to be two minutes and out!"

"Facts on the ground," Webb said. "Gotta deal with what is, not what you planned."

Kitsom pointed at the flurry of departing escape pods. "And what the hell is that? Why did we give them so much time to escape? It has to be that moron Bashir's—"

"Enough!" Webb's sharp rebuke silenced Kitsom. Their reciprocal angry glares persisted for a fraction of a second longer than Sarina might have expected, before Webb broke the moment with a new order. "Plot the fastest course through the rift and get ready to go. I get the feeling we'll be cutting this one closer than usual."

Both men continued with their tasks as if nothing odd had transpired between them, but Sarina was sure she had witnessed an accidental slip, a clue that something serious was amiss. And whatever it was, it had to do with Julian.

An alert buzzed on Webb's console. He silenced it with a sweep of his hand. "They're back." He opened an internal comm channel. "Command to transporter room."

Cole shouted over the comm, *"We're all here! Go!"*

Webb pointed at the rift. "Punch it!"

The impulse engines thrummed, sending thrilling vibrations through the deck. The *Królik* leaped into motion, and the image of the rift swelled until its ragged edges slipped past the boundaries of the viewscreen's oblong frame.

Emergency alerts flooded the sensor screens in front of Sarina. "The station's exploding! Aft shields, now!"

Webb grimaced. "No shields inside the rift! We'll have to outrun it!"

Kitsom pointed at the horrifying image on the screen. "The rift's collapsing!"

Sarina pointed out the obvious. "If the station's gone, so's the rift generator!"

No one had to tell Kitsom to push the engines into overdrive. He released the safety lockouts on the impulse coils and accelerated the stolen Breen scout vessel through the rift.

The leading edge of a subspace shock wave made the *Królik* tremble as the aft hatch slid open and Cole, Sakonna, and Bashir scrambled onto the command deck. Sarina grabbed Bashir's arm and pulled him to her as she warned the others, "Brace for impact!"

It struck with a roar like a volcanic eruption. Darkness dropped; the viewscreen and the consoles all went black, and the musical droning of the impulse engines fell silent.

Violent invisible forces—momentum, deceleration, wild shifts in direction—hurled Sarina through the dark. She stretched out her arms in front of her head and face and tried to prevent her body from tensing with anticipation. *Stay loose, stay limber. Be ready to—*

Her back slammed against a bulkhead or a console, and something hard took a bite out of the back of her head. Purple spots swam in her vision as she was launched again into the dark, tumbling and flailing blindly toward her next collision.

She bounced off something, then off of someone, before the cacophony ceased. The artificial gravity resumed and slammed her back onto the deck.

Dull greenish emergency lighting snapped on at regular intervals where the bulkheads met the overhead. Seconds later, most of the command deck's consoles flickered back to life. The viewscreen displayed a grainy image cut by diagonal hashes of interference, showing the last remnants of the rift as it stitched itself closed and vanished from existence.

Cole pulled himself to his feet with a groan and walked with a stiff gait to the center chair. "Mister Kitsom, get a fix on our position. Everyone else, damage reports. Now."

Kitsom recalibrated the helm, then checked the navcomp readout. "We've made it to the alternate univese. Our position is the same as it was in our universe, on the edge of Breen space."

A slow nod from Cole. "Good. We'll start the hunt from here." He raised his voice. "Where are my damage reports?"

Webb spoke first. "Shields and weapons are good to go, but the cloak is fried."

"Can it be fixed?"

"Not a chance. It's a total loss."

Cole sighed and pointed at Sakonna. "Engines?"

The Vulcan coaxed an update from her engineering panel. "Minor damage to the port warp nacelle. We can have it fixed within the hour."

Sarina completed her own check and turned toward Cole. "All other internal systems check out. And the passive-detection system traced the subspace message Thot Tran sent through the rift after we ejected his pod. Which means we have an approximate position for the *Tajny*."

"Good work, everyone. Douglas, go below with Sakonna and get that warp nacelle fixed. Webb, load the cloak-penetrating sensor protocols the *Enterprise* crew developed last year when they tracked the Breen to Mangala." He lifted his arm and dramatically pointed at the stars. "Mister Kitsom, lay in a pursuit course, best possible speed." He smiled. "The hunt is on."

Fifteen

"**C**onfirmed breach!" Ensign Riaow looked up from her tactical panel and beckoned the *ShiKahr*'s captain with a wave of her white-tufted paw. "Same coordinates as the first event! Sensors indicate a vessel came through from the other universe!"

"All sensors on those coordinates now." Sh'Pherron left the center chair to review the data on Riaow's console. With a gingerly touch of her fingertip behind her ear, she activated her subcutaneous transceiver. "Commander Turak to the bridge, on the double." She sidled up to Riaow. "Show me what you've got. All of it."

Riaow reconfigured her panel into a grid consisting of half a dozen correlated sensor reports. She touched her paw to the top left corner. "The event was brief, no more than a few minutes, but the energy levels were even higher than the last one. There was also a major subspace shock wave before it closed, which suggests something big exploded on the other side."

"Okay. Did we get a clear reading on the ship?"

The Caitian called up a tactical scan from the center row of the grid. "Hull configuration suggests Breen design, but its energy signature is one we haven't seen before, not on any Breen ship. It might be something new, or it might have been modified by someone else."

"Or maybe the Breen make their ships differently in the other universe." Eager to move along, sh'Pherron pointed at the full-sector target-tracking scans. "Where's it going?"

"Bearing one-nine-nine mark twenty-six." Riaow pulled up a subspace signal waveform. "The same general heading as a two-way subspace transmission we picked up between the rift and an unknown source in this universe, somewhere in this subsector."

The highlighted subsector of the chart was interstellar deep space—no star systems, rogue planets, space stations, or even listening posts. Riaow's observation seemed to confirm what sh'Pherron had suspected all along. "A cloaked ship."

"Most likely, sir, yes." Another warning flashed on the console. Riaow subdued it with a swat of her paw. "The new arrival just jumped to warp nine point seven."

Thinking out loud, sh'Pherron pondered the evidence in front of her. "So, the first ship to come through the breach evades us by traveling cloaked. Then someone risks revealing the hidden ship's position by sending it a subspace signal, to which it responds. Now another ship arrives and follows that heading at high warp." The *shen* aimed a sidelong glance at Riaow. "What would you deduce from all this?"

"It would seem careless to risk sending a signal to a cloaked ship, unless something posed a threat to it." A sideways nod at the console. "Such as someone coming after it."

It seemed to sh'Pherron like a plausible reading of the facts. Still, she had to consider less favorable interpretations. "What if the first vessel is merely clearing the way for the second? Or the second is traveling uncloaked to serve as a decoy for the first?"

"Both are possible." Riaow shrugged. "Either way, we need to pursue the new target."

"Because?"

"It's what we have. If it's a decoy, capturing its crew could yield clues to the first ship's intentions. If it's in league with the first intruder, catching it will put us closer to both. And if it's tracking the other ship, then it might be of use—by flush-ing out our quarry for us."

The tactical officer's arguments rang true to sh'Pherron. "Well said. Carry on."

The starboard aft turbolift doors opened, and Turak emerged and moved to sh'Pherron's side. "Situation, sir?"

"We have a new interloper, one whose identity and objec-tives are unknown. Review the sensor data with Riaow, then design a pursuit-and-attack plan with Zareth."

The Vulcan man nodded. "When do you want to begin the assault?"

"I'm not sure yet that I do. I just want a plan ready to go."

Her answer put a confused look on Turak's face. "I do not understand."

"We don't know yet whether we're dealing with friend or foe. Until we do, track the ship from maximum sensor range. Observe and report any changes in its heading or behavior to me."

"Understood, Captain." Turak cocked an eyebrow. "And if they prove to be a foe?"

Sh'Pherron hoped that scenario wouldn't come to pass. She turned a hard and unforgiving stare toward her first officer. "Then we'll make sure they don't live to regret their mistake."

Thot Trom hunched over the star chart displayed on the com-mand deck's aft situation table. New details popped into view every few moments as data from the *Tajny*'s sensors refreshed in real time. Watching the tactical reality unfold this way helped Trom see patterns of activity more clearly, which in turn aided him in developing responses.

It was, in some respects, a lot like improvising a dance to a tune one had never heard before: feeling the tempo and learning to expect when the changes would likely come. And though Trom was not one to boast, in his youth he had been quite the dancer.

A turbolift arrived. Crin stepped through its parting doors and turned on his heel to join Trom at the situation table. "Has something changed?"

"Everything." Trom pointed at the tactical map. "Contingency *usta*'s been enacted."

The first officer stared at the tabletop star chart. "*Usta* hasn't been tested yet."

"Then we'll be breaking new ground." Trom tapped the hexagon of an adjacent subsector on the chart. "Ikkuna Station's gone, and whoever fragged it is coming after us."

Crin leaned closer to the tabletop. "A scout ship? That's the best they could do?"

"Don't get overconfident. It's one of ours, but its energy profile has changed. Which suggests that someone captured it and modified it somehow." Trom touched both hands to the interactive display and widened the scope of the star chart by setting his fingertips at opposite corners and pulling them together, toward the center. "Fortunately, it's traveling without its cloak, so we have time to lie low while we rethink our exit strategy." He tapped on the B'hava'el system. "This is our real problem."

"Bajor?" Crin looked up. "What's our interest in them?"

"In the Bajorans? Nothing. But their wormhole is our only remaining path home." Trom called up a classified report on the tabletop and rotated it for Crin to peruse. "According to secret Starfleet reports, there have been several crossings between our universe and this one over the past ten years—all of them utilizing the wormhole to one degree or another." He highlighted a topological wire frame of the Bajoran wormhole's interior. "That artificial structure is more than just a passageway between distant points in the Alpha and Gamma Quadrants—it's potentially a gateway to a nearly unlimited number of parallel universes."

Crin set his hands on the table's edges and leaned forward, mirroring Trom. "Is the large number of Commonwealth ships lingering around the Bajor sector any reason for alarm?"

"At the very least, it's cause for caution." Trom selected the hexagon containing the Bajor system. "I'm more concerned about the unpredictable nature of the nonlinear-time entities who inhabit the wormhole. During the Dominion's war against the Federation and its allies, the wormhole entities wiped out a fleet of Jem'Hadar reinforcements."

A slow grim nod from Crin. "So they might not be amenable to granting us passage."

"A distinct possibility."

Crin magnified the subsectors directly adjacent to the wormhole. "There's another wrinkle to consider. If we succeed in using the wormhole to return to our own universe, we'll emerge on the doorstep of Starfleet's new Deep Space Nine starbase. Even if we arrive cloaked, they'll see the wormhole when it opens, and they'll start scanning for us. They'd be certain to intercept us."

"I admit it's a less than ideal plan. But for now, it's all we have. Put Solt and his engineers on it. See if they can cook up a better alternative."

Rem lifted his visor from the tactical console. "Sir? We've picked up a new signal. There's another ship following us."

"I'm aware of that, Rem."

"No, sir—not the scout ship. Another vessel. Much larger." He checked his panel to confirm his facts before he continued. "I think it's the wormhole ship we saw before."

New sensor data appeared on the situation table as its display refreshed. Trom and Crin studied the icons representing their two pursuers. The first officer traced one gloved finger along the path of the hijacked scout ship. "They're heading straight toward us." He looked up at Trom. "Almost as if they have some means of seeing through the cloaking device."

Trom nodded. "They very well might. Such advantages tend to be short-lived." He reached out and tapped the icon representing the wormhole ship. "If the scout's following our trail, then the wormhole ship is probably shadowing the scout. Which means we can use the scout to lead our prey into a trap—and rid ourselves of two pests at once."

Crin reduced the volume on his vocoder. "That might not be wise, sir. What if the scout and the wormhole ship unite against us?"

"Unlikely." Trom's thoughts were a whirlwind of possibilities. "The wormhole ship is following the scout at long range. If they were in league together, they'd move as a pair— or else split up to cut us off. No, our hunters have become the hunted and might not even know it." He stalked away from the situation table and returned to the listing center seat. "Helm, bring us about. Set an intercept course for the scout ship pursuing us. Rem, charge all weapons and tell Solt we're going to need all systems operational within the hour. It's time for a showdown."

Sixteen

Sarina's voice was soft and her breath was warm in Bashir's ear. "What happened over there?"

He looked up from the sensor display and cast a furtive glance around the command deck to make sure the Section 31 agents weren't paying particular attention to their conversation. "Nothing. Just a short holding action."

"That's not how Kitsom saw it." She turned a wary look toward the crew-cut agent. "He got pretty bent out of shape about the delay. And he blamed you."

Bashir shrugged off the news. "He was right. Cole wanted a two-minute countdown. I set it for six, so the station's crew could reach the escape pods."

"Risky move." Her anxious eyes flitted toward Cole. "How'd he take it?"

"About as well as one would expect."

"So? Was it worth the risk?"

"Most of the station's crew survived. Their casualties were minimal and limited to armed combatants, and we accomplished all our mission objectives. So, yes—I think it was worth it."

She wore a skeptical frown. "I'd bet Cole and the others disagree."

He disarmed her warning with a smile. "And it's my pleasure to disappoint them."

Before Sarina could chide him any further, a fast-moving anomaly sent up chirps of alarm from the sensor console. Bashir turned to analyze the readings, with Sarina looking over his shoulder. More dire alerts sounded from the tactical console. Bashir raised his voice over the sudden din of feedback tones. "Neutrino surge! Dead ahead, moving on an intercept course, closing at warp nine point eight!"

Webb's eyes widened as he read the report on the tactical panel. "It's the *Tajny*! She's coming right at us!"

Cole snapped out orders. "Shields up! Evasive pattern romeo four! Charge weapons!"

Kitsom pointed at the viewscreen. "They're uncloaking!"

The Breen battle cruiser rippled into view, a ghost taking shape in the darkness. Then its main disruptor banks fired, and the image on the viewscreen flared. Half a second later, the bridge was filled with the ear-splitting boom of overpowering energy blasts pummeling the *Królik*'s shields. Something above Bashir's head let out a fearsome bang. He and Sarina dodged clear of a shower of white-hot phosphors that rained down from a ruptured plasma conduit.

"Forward shields collapsing," Webb shouted over the clamor of the attack.

Despite Cole's level tone, Bashir heard the stress in the man's voice as he issued new orders. "Transfer shield power to the aft and dorsal generators. Helm, come about, hard starboard! Get me a clean shot at their warp coil!"

Adrenaline put a tremor in Webb's report: "They're behind us!"

Another brutal impact rocked the *Królik*. The force of it sent Bashir tumbling forward. He slammed against a secondary duty console, then lost his footing as another thunderous blast sent him and the rest of the crew flying toward starboard. For a moment he was airborne, and then he landed on top of an auxiliary console, which cracked beneath him.

The lights went out. Bashir blinked, and a hazy, out-of-focus view of the command deck returned. He realized it wasn't the lights that had gone out—it had been him, stunned into a semiconscious state for who knew how many seconds.

Sarina pulled him off the shattered console and helped him onto his feet. "Get up! We have to abandon—"

"*Be advised,*" rasped a mechanical voice over the ship's internal comm network, "*this is Thot Trom, commanding the Breen expeditionary force aboard the cruiser* Tajny. *Surrender without condition or delay, or you will be destroyed. You have twenty seconds to reply.*"

On the viewscreen, the fearsome bulk of the *Tajny* orbited the smaller *Królik* like a massive carrion bird making a slow circle above its mortally wounded prey. Cole maintained his poker face while watching the cruiser. Around him, Sakonna, Kitsom, and Webb dusted themselves off but betrayed no sign of fear.

Quite the opposite, Bashir realized. *Before the attack, they all acted as if they were under hideous stress. Now their ship is crippled and they're about to be taken prisoner, and none of them shows a hint of concern. What are they up to?*

A burst of blue light swirled into existence behind the *Królik*. Bashir recognized its telltale event horizon, a cerulean storm of churning dust and high-energy particles: it was a wormhole. But its limited scope and near-perfect symmetry betrayed its origin: it was artificial, the product of a jaunt ship. The vessel that had created the instant tunnel through space hurtled out of it and cruised into an attack posture against the *Tajny*.

Cole shot a look at Webb. "On speakers. I want to hear what they say to each other."

The agent patched in an intercept of the ship-to-ship communications between the jaunt ship and the *Tajny*. "*Attention, unidentified Breen vessel. This is Captain sh'Pherron, commanding the free starship* ShiKahr. *Power down your weapons and drop your shields.*"

Kitsom reclined his chair, crossed his arms, and grinned at Webb. "Bet you a hundred credits the Breen don't even respond before they open fire."

"No bet," Webb said.

Sarina wrangled a sensor report from the stuttering hash of her console. "The *Tajny* is coming about to face the *ShiKahr*. Wait, I'm detecting a power buildup—"

The *Tajny* unleashed a massive pulse of energy at the *ShiKahr*. The brilliant white sphere slammed into the jaunt ship. A crackling cocoon of wild, sapphire-hued lightning enveloped the vessel from its needle-shaped primary hull to its ring-shaped secondary fuselage. The creeping tendrils of blue energy snaked inside the ship, whose running lights dimmed and went dark.

Bashir recognized the weapon that had crippled the *ShiKahr*. He had been aboard the first *Defiant* when it was laid low by the Breen's dreaded energy-dampening cannon. Although ships in his universe had since been hardened to repel that attack, the jaunt ships apparently had not.

As the same mechanized voice that had given its ultimatum to the agents on the *Królik* addressed the jaunt ship's crew over an open channel, Bashir realized that he and the rest of Cole's team had all just been played for fools.

"Crew of the ShiKahr. *This is Thot Trom, commanding the Breen expeditionary force on the cruiser* Tajny. *Surrender and prepare to be boarded."*

In every direction sh'Pherron turned, she found bad news. "Riaow?"

The Caitian tapped at her console, whose surface danced with wild blue fingers of electricity. "Weapons and shields offline! Tactical grid's fried!"

Zareth swiveled his *glenget*—a kneeling chair custom-made to suit his peculiar Chelon physiology with its inflexible back carapace—and faced the captain. "Helm's frozen!"

Turak stepped back from the master systems display, which had become a flickering mosaic of chaotic pixels. "All computer systems are off-line."

"Which means we can't initiate command lockouts or a manual override." Desperate for good news, sh'Pherron tried to open an internal comm channel to main engineering, but the interface beside her command chair transformed into a garbled mess and went dark. "Uzaveh's fire! What hit us?" She tapped the subdural communicator behind her ear and was relieved to hear the dulcet tone of the transceiver standing by to transmit. "Everyone, switch to personal communicators. Until we get the computer back, all comms need to be direct, from person to person. Riaow, tell security to repel boarders. Turak, let Mott know we need primary power and the main computer restored, as soon as possible. Zareth, contact the deck officers for casualty and damage reports, see if they—"

"Captain," Turak cut in. "Boarders reported in main engineering and auxiliary control."

"Have all personnel in those sections repel boarders by any means necessary, and—" Her train of thought was derailed by a singsong wash of noise and a flurry of light in the center of the bridge. "Hit the deck!" She turned her chair and raced to duck behind it.

A fury of white light was followed by a tooth-rattling detonation. By the time sh'Pherron realized what had happened, she was lying flat on her back, half blind, half deaf, and stunned.

Standing above her and the rest of her dazed bridge crew were a dozen Breen soldiers armed with disruptor rifles, stun batons, and flash grenades. The neon green glow of their visors cut through the smoky gloom of their attack's aftermath.

Acting on instinct, sh'Pherron tried to draw her phaser, only to have one of the Breen step on her wrist and pin it to the deck.

The hulking masked intruder loomed over her. A harsh scratch of mechanical noise spat from a speaker in the snout of his mask. A secondary speaker mounted beneath the snout translated the sounds for her. "I am Thot Trom. Do you command this ship?"

"Yes."

"Order your crew to stand down and surrender."

Trom waited several seconds for sh'Pherron to react, but she made no move to comply. Staring at the monstrous contours of his helmet, she felt her antennae twitch with revulsion.

Trom increased the pressure on sh'Pherron's wrist, which cracked loudly beneath his weight. She dropped her weapon. "Give the order, Captain. Tell your crew to stand down."

"No."

The Breen aimed his rifle and snapped off one shot. Its crimson blast struck Zareth, who let out a roar of pain as he vanished in a fast-spreading blaze of red fire that left nothing behind but a handful of dust and the echoes of his death cry. Then Trom leveled his weapon at Turak. "Tell your crew to stand down and surrender this ship, or I will execute your bridge officers, one by one. After they are gone, I will have my men execute the rest of your crew the same way. And I will make *you* witness every one of their deaths."

Handing over the ship went against all of sh'Pherron's training. Worse, it offended her on a personal level; losing her ship so decidedly, and so swiftly, was a smirch upon her virtue as an Andorian. But her pride was not worth sacrificing the hundreds of lives under her command. She slowly raised her empty hand and touched the transceiver behind her ear.

"Captain sh'Pherron to all *ShiKahr* personnel. Attention, all decks. This is the captain. Stand down. This is a direct order. Lay down your weapons and surrender." She glared up at the masked villain whose boot pressed on her wrist and whose rifle remained trained on her first officer. "Thot Trom is now in command of this vessel. That is all. Sh'Pherron out." Another light tap on her subcutaneous transceiver closed the channel. She looked up at Trom, her eyes and her heart full of hate. "The ship is yours."

"I know it is. Thank you, Captain." He removed his boot from her wrist, kicked away her weapon, and barked orders in his machine-noise voice. There was no translation this time, but none was required; the actions that followed were self-explanatory.

The Breen soldiers hoisted sh'Pherron and her stunned officers from the deck, herded them into a turbolift, and marched them belowdecks, to the brig.

Time was short and Thot Trom was impatient as he entered the *ShiKahr*'s transporter room. "Energize," he said as soon as he'd stepped through the doorway. One of his technicians, Chot Kine, initiated the transport sequence.

Trom faced the transporter platform. Half a dozen heavily armed Spetzkar troopers stood between him and the low dais. Six figures materialized on the energizer pads. As the prismatic whorl of light resolved into solid forms, Trom saw that his newest prisoners were wearing Breen military uniforms—but their faces were distinctly those of Federation-aligned species: four human males, a human female, and a Vulcan female.

As the annular confinement beam deactivated, freeing them from their in-transport paralysis, the Spetzkar troopers raised their weapons. To the prisoners' credit, none of them made even the slightest attempt to reach for his or her own disruptor pistol, which were plucked from their belt holsters by two of the Spetzkar.

"Which of you is in command?"

As Trom expected, the eldest human male, a trim figure with close-cut dark hair and green eyes, stepped to the front of the group. "I am."

"Name?"

"Cole."

"How did you come to possess a Breen military vessel?"

The human shrugged. "I never thought to ask."

"How did you learn of our mission?"

"What mission?"

Behind his helmet, Trom smiled at the human's insouciance. "Feigned ignorance? Is that all you have to offer? You disappoint me." He turned toward Thar Khol, the chief of the security detachment. "Take them to the nearest empty cargo bay. Have Doctor Nev meet us there with an interrogation kit." As his men seized the prisoners and forced them toward the door, Trom permitted himself a rare moment of gloating. "You want to play? Then let the games begin."

Seventeen

Bashir saw little of the jaunt ship during his forced march from the transporter room to the cargo bay—nothing but corridors either deserted or littered with the bodies of those slain by the Breen. The few details he noticed suggested the *ShiKahr* was a clean and orderly vessel, a bit tight on interior space but no less accommodating than many of Starfleet's smaller ships.

The small cargo bay to which he and the rest of the Section 31 team had been led was also nearly immaculate, and it exhibited an efficient use of space. If he had one criticism of the storage bay, it was that it felt uncomfortably cold, but he attributed that to the fact that he and the others had been compelled by their captors to remove their stolen Breen uniforms, which had left all of them barefoot and attired in only their undergarments.

He also blamed his crushing headache on the Breen, because they were the ones who had strung up him and the others by their bound ankles and dangled them upside down with their fingertips just shy of scraping the deck. As if hanging inverted hadn't been enough of an indignity, the Spetzkar guarding them until their commander's arrival insisted on circling the group and jabbing them with stun batons at random intervals.

Muffled grunts and stifled shouts of pain answered every crackling thrust of the batons. Bashir dreaded his next turn on the receiving end of the Breen's sadism. Just when he thought he might be spared another jolt, a stab of white heat in his ribs made his mind go blank.

Consciousness returned with a shudder. He had no idea how long he had been out. At first he thought it might have been only a few seconds. Then he assessed the size of the puddle of drool that had spilled from his mouth and gathered beneath his head, and he realized he must have been hanging stunned and limp for at least a minute, if not longer.

He turned his head toward Sarina, who hung like a rag doll beside him, and he mumbled under his breath, "If this is the Breen's idea of a suspended sentence, I can't say I approve."

His rewards for the bad joke were a wince from Sarina and a gut-punch from a Breen that left him gasping like a landed fish. The quip had been an admittedly lame attempt to bolster his broken morale, but more than once he had found comfort in gallows humor during times such as this.

The cargo bay's broad oval door dilated and vanished inside the bulkhead. A trio of Breen entered. Bashir recognized the insignia of the one walking in front of the others—it was the commander, Thot Trom. He surmised the others were two of Trom's senior officers.

Analyzing their gaits and body language from an upside-down vantage made it more difficult for Bashir to guess the species of the individuals beneath the Breen uniforms. Even so, he was fairly certain the commander was a Silgov, a humanoid species whose members could mingle easily among the peoples of the Federation. The other two were harder to gauge. The lightness of one's step led Bashir to think he might be an Amoniri, a low-density species whose need for cold had made refrigeration units standard issue on Breen uniforms; the other one was likely a Fenrisal, a lupine-featured race for whom the Breen masks had acquired snouts.

The Spetzkar officers approached the prisoners and spread out into a single rank before them. Trom looked at one of the Breen who had been guarding the group. Harsh noise spat from Trom's vocoder like sonic confetti ejected from a blender. Despite Bashir's experience with the Breen language, the device's near-perfect scrambling of vocabulary and syntax left him no chance of decoding the conversation transpiring right in front of his face.

After a brief exchange with his men, Trom activated his vocoder's translator circuit. "Who is ready to answer my questions?" His request was met by silence. "Your stoicism is laudable but futile. Most of you are unknown to us." He looked at Bashir. "But not *all* of you."

One of the other Spetzkar handed Trom the Breen version of a padd. He took a short look at it, then proceeded as if from memory. "Doctor Julian Subatoi Bashir. Human, genetically enhanced. Former chief medical officer, Starbase Deep Space Nine. Dishonorably discharged from Starfleet after a court-martial in absentia. I'll spare you a recounting of the formal charges."

"Too kind."

Trom pivoted toward his next subject of interest. "Sarina Douglas. Human, genetically enhanced. Former field operative, Starfleet Intelligence. Former deputy director of security, Starbase Deep Space Nine."

"*Senior* deputy," Sarina corrected.

He stole a brief look at his padd. "According to Breen Intelligence Directorate files, you and Doctor Bashir share more than a domicile. You also acted together on a covert mission to the Salavat shipyard, in the Alrakis system, three and a half years ago." He leaned down, as if to touch his helmet's snout to her face. "Your crimes on Salavat, including the murders you committed during your escape from interrogation, have not been forgotten, Miss Douglas. The Breen Confederacy considers you a fugitive from state justice."

"Oh, sure. You *say* you remember me. But did you call? Did you write?"

The Spetzkar commander straightened and took half a step back, putting him just out of Sarina's reach—not that she had showed any sign of making a move to attack. "Your former status as a Starfleet officer, as well as Doctor Bashir's, intrigues me. If you both have left Starfleet, whom do you now serve? Your dossier indicates that you belong to the Federation's civilian espionage and counterintelligence service, the Federation Security Agency." He regarded the rest of the team. "But we have no records of your associates."

"My associates? I don't know them. They were just hitching a ride."

Trom kneeled in front of Sarina and seized her by her throat. "I see your irreverence for what it is, Miss Douglas. Cease and desist, or I will kill one of these people. Understood?" Sarina nodded, so Trom let go of her and stood again. "Let's continue. Are these associates of yours non-official agents of the FSA?"

This time, Sarina said nothing. She closed her eyes and drew a long slow breath—no doubt to calm herself in preparation for what she knew was coming next. Trom nodded at one of the men who had guarded the group. "Doctor Nev? If you please."

Nev thrust his stun baton into the small of Sarina's back. Her screams were piercing and shrill, and they cut Bashir to his soul. All he could do was wince and shut his eyes. *I can't give in to save her. That's the Breen's plan—and it's the last thing she'd want me to do.*

After minutes that felt like forever, Sarina's monstrous howls came to a halt, and the Breen doctor—though Bashir doubted anyone capable of such horrors deserved to bear the title—stepped away to let the Spetzkar commander inspect his handiwork.

"She's done for now." Trom looked at the others. "Torturing the Vulcan would be pointless." He waved dismissively at Cole, Kitsom, and Webb. "They'd enjoy it." Then he looked at Bashir. "And our superiors have a bounty on this one. Him, we take home as is." The commander turned and walked away, uttering a string of untranslated vocoder gibberish.

Before Bashir had time to wonder what Trom had said, the synthetic ropes holding the team went slack, and the six prisoners crashed hard, heads first, onto the deck. Gloved hands seized Bashir by his bound ankles and dragged him across the deck. On either side of him, the rest of the team was hauled with the same lack of dignity, towed like garbage out of the cargo bay and through the frigid corridors, until they arrived, finally, at the brig, which was packed to overflowing with the *ShiKahr*'s officers and crew.

The low humming of a force field ceased just long enough for the Breen to hurl Bashir and his comrades into a cell. The six of them landed together in a heap. Then the force field snapped back on, filling the cramped space with its incessant angry buzzing.

As the Breen troops walked away, Bashir saw Sarina's left eye flutter half open.

"Sarina? Are you all right?"

"Shh. It's okay, Julian." She gave him a weak smile. "I have a plan."

Her smile faded as she passed out in his arms. He sighed. "I feel better already."

A sharp hiss roused Bashir from his all-too-brief nap. "Psst. Hey you." Bashir blinked slowly as he got his bearings. He was still in the brig, slumped against the bulkhead beside the force field. The hissing and the voice were coming from somewhere close by, to his right. He turned his head. Across the corner from his cell, behind the force field of another holding area, a young rust-furred Tellarite pointed at him. "Yeah, you. 'Bout time you woke up."

Bashir rubbed his eyes and surveyed his own cell. Sarina lay beside him, her head cradled on his thigh. Kitsom, Webb, and Sakonna slept on the deck. Cole had claimed the small space's only bunk, where he had stretched out with his back to the rest of the brig.

The Tellarite became more insistent. "Hey." He waited until Bashir looked back at him before he continued. "Don't I know you?"

Whispering so as not to wake his cell mates, Bashir said, "I doubt it."

"Your face is familiar. I know I've seen you before." He grimaced, as if the effort of thinking was too great a strain for him to bear. "I'm Chief Tunk. What's your name?"

"Unimportant," Bashir said.

He pointed past Bashir with his three-fingered hand. "Who are they?"

"Even less important."

The chief's snout twitched as if he smelled something rotten. "If you were nobodies, you wouldn't be locked in here with us. You're not part of our crew—I know everybody on this boat. So if you aren't with us, and you aren't with the Breen, what are you?"

"Stuck in the middle."

Tunk sounded annoyed. "You're full of snappy answers, eh?"

"If I said my friends and I were here to help you, would you believe me?"

The Tellarite shrugged. "I might want some proof."

"Sorry." Bashir gestured at his scant undergarments. "What you see is what you get."

Prisoners in other cells shuffled and shimmied closer to their force fields to join the hushed conversation. Most of them had no direct line of sight to Bashir, but he heard them moving: the scrapes of their feet on the deck, the soft rustling of fabric as they shifted position. Only a pair of faces, in the next cell down from Tunk's, had a view of Bashir. A Bajoran woman and a Bolian man peered through the shadows at him. Bashir tried to inch away, to take cover deeper inside his cell, but he hesitated to wake Sarina or disturb the others, which left him trapped and visible. He looked back out at the *ShiKahr*'s officers in time to see the Bajoran woman's eyes widen with surprise. "By the Prophets! Is that—it *can't* be him. He's *dead*."

Bashir turned his face away, but he knew it was too late; the damage had been done. He had recalled reading of his alternate-universe alter ego in one of Captain Sisko's after-action reports, but until now he hadn't considered the possibility that he might be mistaken for the man—or the risk that his counterpart might be dead, instantly making his own presence suspect. In his imagination, a whoop and cry were about to go up, branding him an intruder.

Instead he heard the Bolian shush his shipmate. "Quiet, Raya. Keep this to yourself. You, too, Tunk. Not a word, not to anyone. That's an order."

Mumbled acknowledgments of "Yes, sir" came back from Raya and Tunk. Bashir turned back and looked across the dim confines of the brig. The Bolian man met his stare, smiled, pressed his index finger to his lips, and nodded once. His message was clear: *Your secret is safe.*

He had no idea why it mattered, but all the same he was

grateful for the crew's discretion. He gave a small nod of thanks, then turned as he heard his cell mates stir. Cole rolled over and sat up. Sakonna, Webb, and Kitsom sat up and roused themselves quickly but quietly.

Their synchronicity baffled Bashir. Did they all have implanted alarms? Or had the junior agents been conditioned to adapt to their superiors' schedules? He decided it didn't matter how they had awoken together, at least not for the moment. He twitched his thigh beneath Sarina's head and jostled her gently from her light slumber. She squinted, then blinked as she sat up. "I see none of us are dead yet," she said under her breath. "So far, so good."

"The night is young." Bashir got up and stamped his feet to get his blood circulating. The other agents stood and stretched their limbs. In such close quarters, Bashir found the sudden profusion of movement awkward and intrusive of his personal space. He stopped his exercise and put his back to the wall. "Any plan to get us out of here, Mister Cole?"

The senior agent bent side to side, like a willow tree caught between competing winds. "Not at the moment, Doctor. Unless you have a plan you'd like to share."

Bashir ignored the verbal jab. "We're at a distinct disadvantage."

Kitsom cracked his knuckles. "Nice of you to notice."

"I'm serious. We've lost our uniforms, our equipment. Everything we had was on the *Królik*, and now it's in the hands of the Breen."

Sarina rested her hand on Bashir's shoulder. "Maybe we should relax, Julian."

"Relax? Are you serious?"

Cole shot a weary look at Bashir. "Patience, Doctor. Sometimes, if you wait quietly, opportunity knocks. But you need to be still in order to hear when it comes to your door."

"Patience? Opportunity? Forgive me, Mister Cole. I was under the impression that you and your 'organization' made a practice of planning for all contingencies. I find it hard to believe you didn't see this scenario coming from light-years away."

"Who says we didn't?" Cole folded his hands behind his back and stepped to within a millimeter of the invisible force field. He looked out at the imprisoned officers of the *ShiKahr*, and then he turned to face his own team. "Trust me, friends: This is far from over."

Eighteen

By some standards, half a day was not a long time; under the present circumstances, however, Trom found its duration interminable. He stepped out of the turbolift onto the bridge of the *ShiKahr*, hoping to put an end to the spell of waiting that was driving him to distraction.

He walked toward the center seat. His second-in-command relinquished the chair as Trom approached. "The bridge is yours, sir."

"I've had my fill of this universe, Crin. Tell me some good news."

Crin waved over the senior tactical officer as he began his report. "Main power restored. All overloaded relays have been replaced or bypassed. Command and control systems are back online. Communications are back up."

One detail was conspicuous by its omission. "What about the wormhole drive?"

Karn, the tactical officer, stepped in to answer Trom. "The jaunt drive, as this ship's crew calls it, sustained minor damage. Engineer Solt says repairs are complete. Pilot Yoab is making himself familiar with this vessel's helm controls and the navigation software for the jaunt drive. Rem is assisting him with the calculations for a jump to the B'hava'el system."

"Good work." Trom directed his next question at Crin. "Status of the *Tajny*?"

"We've taken it in tow with a tractor beam. Factoring in its additional mass and its effect on wormhole topology is part of what's complicating Rem's calculation of the jump."

That was less than ideal news, but Trom had expected it might be the case. "If bringing it with us becomes untenable, we'll have to set its self-destruct and continue without it."

"Rem is sure he can make the jump work. But just in case, I've put a skeleton crew on the *Tajny*. If the jump goes wrong, we'll cut them loose and abort."

It was a prudent plan, one that maximized the company's options. "Well done. But make sure everyone knows our priority is to safeguard *this* ship. It has to be delivered intact to our research teams. If that means sacrificing the *Tajny*, then so be it."

"Understood, sir."

"What about the scout ship the Federation agents were using?"

"It's in the main docking bay. It appears to have suffered heavy damage."

The first officer's choice of words stoked Trom's curiosity. "Appears to?"

"Our priority was to fix *this* ship, sir. I told Solt not to waste his men or his time on the scout. When we get home, we can release it to fleet operations, and let it be *their* problem."

"All right. How long until—"

Crin turned his head away and looked down; it was a habit of his when he received audio transmissions through his helmet. After a few seconds, he straightened and faced Trom. "Jaunt drive online, wormhole generator fully charged."

Trom pivoted into the command chair. It felt very different from the seats on a Breen starship. It wrapped around his upper body and offered a generous cushion beneath him. *Let's hope the lab rats back home think to copy these seats along with the jaunt drive.* He gripped the armrests and lifted his chin. "Yoab! Status!"

The pilot looked up from the helm and rotated his chair to answer Trom. "Calculations complete, sir. I was double-checking them to make sure I didn't miss any variables."

"And? Did you?"

"I don't think so, sir." Left to hang on his own noncommittal answer, Yoab corrected himself a few seconds later. "No, sir, I didn't. Course plotted and ready."

"Crin, sound general quarters. All hands to battle stations. Karn, advise the *Tajny* we're about to get under way. Yoab, how close will your jump take us to the Bajoran wormhole?"

Yoab checked his navigational chart. "Approximately nine point two light-minutes."

"Can you put us any closer?"

"Not without ripping us to shreds inside the Denorios Belt."

Trom beckoned Karn. "What's on long-range sensors?"

"Heavy activity in the B'hava'el system, sir."

"Military or civilian?"

Karn bowed his head by the slightest degree. "At this range, our sensor readings are inconclusive. We're picking up several energy signatures that could be from matter-antimatter warp drives, but we can't ascertain any details beyond that."

The commander nodded to mask his dismay. "So we'll be jumping in blind. That presents a tactical hurdle. Recommendations?"

"It might be prudent to avoid confrontation, sir. We have the advantage of being in a military vessel. If the majority of traffic in the system is civilian, it's unlikely anyone will try to challenge us. In which case, we emerge from the jump and set course for the wormhole. At warp two, we can reach it in less than ninety seconds."

"Relay those orders to Yoab and brief the crew on the *Tajny*. We go in one minute."

"Yes, sir."

Trom settled into the command chair and drew deep breaths to calm himself as the moment of action arrived. The seconds passed slowly, dragged down by the weight of adrenaline and anticipation. Then Karn signaled Crin that all was ready. The first officer looked at Trom, who nodded his assent, and Crin gave the order: "Activate jaunt drive."

"Engaging jaunt drive." Yoab keyed in the jump command.

An indigo mandala of supercharged gases swirled into being on the main viewscreen, directly ahead of the *ShiKahr*. The cloud expanded to epic proportions in a matter of seconds, and then its center dilated to reveal the yawning throat of a wormhole, a shortcut through space-time. The interior of this artificial tunnel through the stars rolled like the sides of a kaleidoscope. Bursts of energy flared and danced along its ever-shifting curves.

"Increase power to the tractor beam," Trom said. "Keep the *Tajny* as close to us as possible. Karn, charge the shield generators in case we need them. Yoab . . . take us in."

"Yes, sir. Proceeding into the wormhole at one-half impulse."

The maw of the wormhole filled the viewscreen as the *ShiKahr* accelerated inside it. Trom wasn't sure what to expect of a trip through a synthetic wormhole, but he was surprised at how smooth the journey proved to be. No turbulence, no eerie sonic feedback. Just a hypnotic array of blue radiance that soon yielded to a point of light, which expanded within moments into a vista of black space dusted with bright stars.

All at once the *ShiKahr* was free of the wormhole, shot out into normal space-time with hardly any sense of disruption. Trom was glad no one could see his grin through his helmet. *I could get used to this.* "Yoab, report."

"Right on target, sir. We've arrived in the B'hava'el system. Setting course for the wormhole, warp two."

"Engage when ready," Trom said. "The sooner we—"

"We're being hailed," Crin said. "On multiple frequencies."

Karn's console came alive with shrill alarms and flashing icons. "There's a fleet of Jem'Hadar battleships in formation near the wormhole. Another Jem'Hadar battleship orbiting Bajor." He paused as he saw the next detail. "As well as another jaunt ship."

Crin turned from the communications panel. "It's the jaunt ship that's hailing us."

"On speakers."

A rich tenor voice wafted down from the overhead. *"—why you've abandoned your assigned patrol sector. Repeat, this is Captain Jean-Luc Picard, commanding the free starship* Enterprise. *Captain sh'Pherron, please respond. Why has your ship—"*

A wave of Trom's hand cued Crin to mute the channel. "More than we bargained for." He looked at Crin and Karn, then at Yoab. "To the wormhole, warp three."

"Aye, sir." Yoab triggered the warp drive, and the stars on the screen distorted into streaks as the *ShiKahr* raced toward its most viable route home. "Twenty seconds out."

More alerts shrilled from the tactical console. "The Jem'Hadar fleet's moving to block the wormhole," Karn reported. "We should beat them there. Raising shields and—"

All the consoles went dark. The whine of the warp engines dwindled to a pathetic groan as the ship slowed and plunged back into normal space-time. Yoab struggled with the helm console, then slammed his gloved fists on its unresponsive interface. "We're adrift!"

"Main power's down," Crin said. "Tractor beam's off."

Karn delivered more bad news: "Shields and weapons are off-line."

Trom accessed his helmet's comm circuit and opened a channel to his chief engineer. "Solt! What's going on down there?"

"The warp reactor and jaunt coil are both off-line."

"I know that, damn you! *Why* are they off-line?"

"If I had to guess, sir, I'd blame either a computer virus or a command lockout."

"No one said our prey would make this easy." Trom had only seconds to choose what to do next. He made his decision as he saw the image of a wormhole forming on the main viewscreen—followed by the swift arrival of the *ShiKahr's* sister ship, the *Enterprise*.

That same deep voice wafted from the speakers again, unbidden this time: *"Attention, crew of the* ShiKahr. *This is the* Enterprise. *Stand down and prepare to be boarded."*

Trom sprang from his chair. "*Tajny*, this is Thot Trom. Beam all our people off this ship, right now. Do not engage the Jem'Hadar, and be ready to raise the cloak as soon as I'm aboard."

"Acknowledged," came the reply from the *Tajny*.

The commander switched to his internal helmet channel. "All personnel, this is Thot Trom. Stand by for beam-out. Thar Khol, do you copy?"

"Affirmative, sir. Go ahead."

"Can you secure the Federation agents for transport?"

"Negative. Boarders have already arrived. We're cut off from the brig."

"Then leave them behind. Stand by for emergency transport." Trom reverted to the ship-to-ship comm channel. "*Tajny*, this is Trom. Energize."

Trom cursed his luck as the transporter beam took hold

of him. *Now this'll have to get bloody.* The tingling sensation of dematerialization put his moment of grim reflection on hold.

After a momentary wash of green light and white noise, he was back aboard the *Tajny.* He hurried off the oversized transporter platform; it was one of several that the Spetzkar had developed for the rapid deployment and recovery of large numbers of commandos. By the time he'd reactivated his helmet comm, he was out the door and halfway down the corridor to the turbolift. "Command, this is Trom. Is everyone back aboard?"

The watch officer replied, *"Yes, sir."*

"Cloak and go evasive, sublight only, pattern *pioro.*"

"Cloak engaged. Going evasive."

"I'm on my way up. Keep us clear of the Jem'Hadar until I get there. Trom out."

By some standards, Trom knew his mission might be deemed a failure at this point. He had lost the element of surprise, been forced to surrender the ship he'd captured, and given up custody of six enemy agents who might be able to expose his objectives to his targets.

But he was still drawing breath, still had a ship, and still commanded more than a hundred of the best-trained special operations soldiers in this universe or any other.

It hadn't been a good day, that much was true.

But it wasn't over yet.

The corridors of the *ShiKahr* were eerily deserted and quiet. Invisible in her Memory Omega–designed full-body stealth suit, Commander K'Ehleyr did her best not to break the silence as she skulked from one section of the ship to the next. She supported her phaser with both hands as she advanced. The weapon's coating of optical camouflage particles kept it cloaked as long it remained in contact with the chameleon fibers of her stealth suit. Her aim was steady; her thumb hovered above the firing stud, ready to act at the first sign of hostile action.

Despite her advantage, she exercised caution as she neared intersections and corners. If the ship was under hostile control, there was no telling where traps might have been set. She let her suit's built-in sensors sweep the passageway ahead of her, to expose unseen potential threats. The scan turned up nothing out of the ordinary.

A few sections ahead, at the next intersection, she saw the shimmering silhouette of another stealth-suited boarder. Her mask's holographic HUD identified it as Lieutenant Dorina Arellano, one of the *Enterprise*'s senior security officers.

Arellano signaled all clear. K'Ehleyr returned the signal and directed Arellano to meet her at the entrance to the brig. Then she looked back and beckoned the rest of her camouflaged strike team to move up and follow her. Arellano's cloaked team followed close behind her.

Other teams had already secured the *ShiKahr*'s bridge, engineering section, auxiliary control center, and armory. The brig and sickbay were among the last areas to be searched. As K'Ehleyr met Arellano at the entrance to the brig, an update flashed on her HUD, superimposed over the bottom of her field of vision: SICKBAY SECURED.

Then this is our last hope. She entered a command override code into the control panel beside the door, which slid open. With quick gestures, she ordered Arellano to enter and flank right. The lithe human woman slipped through the open doorway, her phaser steady at eye level. K'Ehleyr followed, one stride behind Arellano's left shoulder.

In cells on either side of them, locked behind force fields, were the officers and crew of the *ShiKahr*. As far as K'Ehleyr

could see, a few of them sported bloodied faces or scorches
from disruptors set on heavy stun, but none of them appeared to have been seriously harmed. At the end of the entry
passage, Arellano led her team right, and K'Ehleyr took her
squad left.

More cells were packed with junior officers from all the
departments of the ship—but there was no sign of their captors. The passage curved aft and terminated at a dead end.
In the next-to-last cell were the ship's senior officers. Still
expecting a trap, K'Ehleyr ran a final sensor sweep of the area
but found no evidence of sabotage or booby traps.

She deactivated her stealth suit and peeled off the close-
fitting full-head mask. The rest of her team followed her lead,
and they all shimmered back into view, like mirages turning
solid. At once, the imprisoned officers of the *ShiKahr* leaped
to their feet, faces bright at the prospect of rescue—all except
their captain, who sat alone in the corner of the cell, eyes
downcast.

K'Ehleyr entered her command override code into the
control panel on the bulkhead outside the cell and deactivated all the brig force fields. She looked at her squad's
chief petty officer, a shaved-headed human man with a
close-trimmed goatee. "Foster, see if any of them need to be
beamed to sickbay." With a tap behind her ear, she activated
her transceiver. "K'Ehleyr to *Enterprise*."

Picard answered without delay. *"Go ahead, Number One."*

"The *ShiKahr*'s officers are alive and secure in the brig.
Waiting on a final head count, but it looks like they're all
here."

From the back of the cell, Captain sh'Pherron muttered,
"Not all of them."

A pall fell between K'Ehleyr and sh'Pherron. Then the
Vulcan first officer, Turak, stepped forward and said in a low

voice, "We lost Ensign Zareth. Our senior flight controller."

K'Ehleyr acknowledged the news with a slow nod. "Correction, *Enterprise*. We have one confirmed fatality among the *ShiKahr*'s senior staff, Ensign Zareth."

"Acknowledged. Be advised Commander Barclay will be beaming over with an engineering team to assist in repairs and check for any deep-level sabotage."

"I'll give their tool pushers a heads-up, sir. I'd suggest we also sweep all compartments and run a level-five diagnostic on—" Six strangers drifted out of the last cell on the block. Overcoming her surprise, she snapped her fingers once, and Foster appeared at her shoulder, his phaser rifle leveled at the motley half-naked and clearly brutalized group of four human men, a Vulcan woman, and a human woman.

Seeing the weapon pointed at them, the strangers came to a stop but remained quiet.

K'Ehleyr looked back at Turak. "Who are they?"

The Vulcan eyed the disheveled sextet with clear suspicion. "If my chief engineer and senior science officer are correct, these are visitors from the other universe."

"Hostile?"

"Unknown. But, like us, they were prisoners of the Breen."

It was a point in the newcomers' favor, but not enough to persuade K'Ehleyr to lower her defenses. Not yet, anyway. "The enemy of my enemy is not necessarily my friend, Turak. *Enterprise*, are you still receiving me?"

"Affirmative," Picard said. *"Go ahead."*

"I have six persons of unknown affiliation in custody. I need to have them beamed to the *Enterprise*, and I want a full security detail standing by to meet them and escort them to guest quarters for a full debriefing."

"Understood. Stand by for transport."

The half Klingon couldn't resist a smirk at the strangers' state of hapless undress. "One more thing, sir. Let the quartermaster know our guests are in need of some new clothes."

They were as nondescript a group as Picard had seen in some time, and yet looking their leader in the eye was profoundly unnerving. The six "compulsory guests"—he resisted thinking of them as prisoners when, so far as he knew, they had committed no offenses meriting the curtailment of their liberty—had been quiet, deferential, and cooperative. They sat on one side of the long oval dining table, opposite him, K'Ehleyr, and Troi.

So why did the stare of their leader, Cole, fill Picard with a sense of dread?

He tried to avoid direct eye contact with him as the interview continued. "You say you became aware of a Breen plot to enter this universe and hijack one of our ships. When did your organization first learn of this scheme?"

Cole was relaxed and his body language conveyed openness. "I don't know for certain. I know we monitor Breen military research as a matter of routine. But the briefings I received indicated the Breen began working on their dimension-breaching wormhole technology about ten months ago, shortly after they discovered the wreck of one of your ships on an uninhabited planet inside Federation space. Until they actually broke through the dimensional barrier, we weren't sure this was their objective. But once they started testing their rift generator, we put the facts together. At that point, we organized a mission to intercept them and stop them."

"I see." Picard glanced down. Troi sat to his right, with her right arm on the table and her left hand on her lap where Picard could see it. She had crossed her index and middle fingers—a signal that she sensed malicious deception from

Cole. Taking the empath's warning into account, Picard pressed on. "It appears, however, that your efforts were unsuccessful."

A humble shrug. "What can I say? We were outgunned."

Cole made a point of looking directly into Picard's eyes. It was a blatant power play, one that made Picard uncomfortable. Picard shifted his gaze to look past Cole, over his shoulder.

Outside the transparent aluminum view ports of the spacious guest suite—one of only a few such luxurious accommodations aboard the jaunt ship—the stars seemed almost static; if one paid close attention, however, their movement became noticeable.

The *Enterprise* was traveling at full impulse back to Bajor. Using a wormhole jump within the system to intercept the rogue jaunt ship *ShiKahr* had been a matter of necessity. Now that the intruders had escaped in their cloaked vessel and the *ShiKahr* was back under the control of its intended officers and crew, safer protocols were once more in effect.

Unable to ignore his interview subject for more than a few seconds without seeming rude or disengaged, Picard forced himself to resume the debriefing. "Our government has been under the impression that your Starfleet had actively discouraged further operations in this universe."

"That's my understanding, as well."

An artful evasion. "Then how do you account for your team's presence, Mister Cole?"

"Technically, we aren't acting on behalf of your Starfleet."

Picard hunched forward, his interest growing. "Then you're attached to a civilian body?"

"In a manner of speaking." The man's cold, disarming smile sent a chill through Picard. "I'm afraid it's all rather complicated."

K'Ehleyr leaned in, mimicking Picard's pose as she glared at Cole. "Simplify it."

"Our organization takes independent action to protect the people, culture, and institutions of the United Federation of Planets. We are self-directed and self-policing."

In his imagination, Picard substituted *Cardassia* for *the United Federation of Planets*, and he realized he had heard this mission statement before; it once had defined the now-defunct Obsidian Order. "In other words, you're the ones who watch the watchers. The secret police."

"It's nothing so dramatic, I assure you."

The fingers of Troi's left hand clenched into a fist. Malicious deception had degenerated into thinly veiled malevolence; she was warning Picard to tread with care. He decided it might be a good time to ease off the throttle. He put on his most ingratiating smile. "Well, whatever your charter might be, it seems we should be thankful for your efforts, even if they weren't as effective as you might have hoped. Thanks to you and your team, we now understand what the Breen are after, which gives us a far greater chance of ensuring they don't acquire it."

"Unfortunately, the Spetzkar escaped with their ship, which means the threat still exists, Captain. My team and I can't return to our universe until we verify that it's been neutralized."

"I appreciate your situation, Mister Cole. However, I'm sure you can understand why my superiors would rather not have your team operating without oversight in our jurisdiction. We are prepared to take any and all steps required to locate the Breen and eliminate the risk they pose, and we welcome your advice—but that must be the limit of your team's involvement."

Cole responded with a demure smile and a polite nod—both tagged as fake by Troi's signals under the table. "Of course, Captain. If we could have completed our mission without anyone knowing of our presence, that would have been ideal, but that's no longer possible. We'll do whatever we can to help your people prevent the Breen from finishing their mission."

"Thank you." Picard stood, which gave everyone else permission to do the same. "Commanders K'Ehleyr and Troi will arrange individual quarters for the duration of—"

The door behind Picard opened. He turned to confront the source of the unannounced interruption. Striding into the suite was Weyoun, the Dominion senior diplomatic counselor. "Captain Picard! The Founder requires an immediate report on the incident at the wormhole. Why did one of your vessels try to violate the terms of our agreement? What was the other ship it had in tow? And why did it flee and cloak when challenged?"

Picard stepped forward and intercepted the Vorta with outstretched, open hands. "Mister Weyoun, I assure you, we are investigating the incident—which, as your own fleet commander will attest, we resolved."

"Eris confirmed that your ship intercepted the *ShiKahr*. But that does not explain why you permitted the second ship to escape, or why the *ShiKahr* tried to enter the wormhole and gain access to Dominion territory!"

"The *ShiKahr* had been hijacked by a company of Spetzkar," K'Ehleyr cut in. "Elite Breen commandos, more than a hundred of them. The second ship was theirs. After the *ShiKahr* failed to provide proper recognition codes when we hailed her, we remotely disabled the *ShiKahr*'s command systems. We then boarded the *ShiKahr*, and the Breen abandoned ship by beaming back to their own vessel."

Weyoun pointed at Picard. "Which you then permitted to escape!"

"An error, I admit," Picard said. "At the time, it appeared to have been captured by a vessel that was under potentially hostile control. Our focus was on securing our sister ship. When the Breen vessel broke away and cloaked, we were unable to lock a new tractor beam onto it in time to prevent its escape. For that, Mister Weyoun, I take full responsibility, and I apologize."

"Your apology is welcome, Captain, but it fails to address the continuing . . ." Weyoun's voice trailed off as his gaze landed on something behind Picard. Then the Vorta's eyes went wide with fury. He stepped past Picard and pointed at one of Cole's men. "You!" The cluster of bodies between Weyoun and his subject parted, until the human with the ash-and-charcoal hair and beard stood alone, facing his accuser with a bewildered expression. The room went quiet, and Weyoun's next words spilled forth in a cry of hatred: "You killed a Founder!"

Frozen in place by Weyoun's manic charge of murder, Bashir lost precious seconds struggling to understand what was happening. His mouth dropped open, but no words came out.

Weyoun filled the stunned silence with a tirade. "Fifteen years and eight months ago, this man killed the Founder known as Odo. He shot him down like an animal."

Picard stepped between Bashir and the Vorta. "How can you know that?"

"Did you think we came through the wormhole without investigating what lay on the other side? We sent several agents ahead of our fleet. One of them learned the fate of Odo, with whom we'd lost contact decades earlier." He circled around Picard to keep his eyes on Bashir. "He tracked down a backup of Terok Nor's security records in an archive on Bajor. Those records show the slaying of Odo in perfect detail."

Old memories rushed back to Bashir, recollections of a time and a place he had long preferred to forget. Near the end of his second year of service on the original Deep Space 9, a navigational accident inside the Bajoran wormhole had thrown him and Major Kira Nerys into this alternate universe, which had been visited a century earlier by four officers from Captain Kirk's famed *Enterprise*. Once here, Bashir and Kira had been taken prisoner by her counterpart, the villainous Intendant Kira. Hastily struck bargains and alliances, coupled with a bit of luck, had made possible their escape aboard the runabout *Rio Grande*—but in the process of freeing himself from enslavement in the ore refinery, Bashir had been forced to defend himself from Overseer Odo. Not realizing the disruptor he had stolen from a Bajoran guard had been set to kill, he had fired a lethal shot at the Changeling— one that blew Odo, literally, to pieces.

Now Bashir was confronted by a representative of an interstellar power that would never forgive such a killing, and he realized he had yet to account for the life he had taken.

Weyoun pivoted toward Picard. "Our investigation also revealed that Odo's killer was an interloper from another universe. Because we assumed we would never have a chance to face him, we decided to hold the powers of the Alpha Quadrant blameless for this heinous crime. But now, providence brings us this gift: an opportunity for justice, at last!"

Troubled looks passed among the *Enterprise* officers. Picard faced Weyoun. "What, precisely, do you mean by that?"

"Captain Picard, on behalf of the Dominion, I demand the immediate and unconditional extradition of Doctor Julian Bashir, so that he can stand trial for the murder of Odo!"

Nineteen

It galled Thot Trom that he and his men had been forced to slink away from a fight. From a tactical standpoint, retreat had been the best option. He had withdrawn his troops with only a few fatalities. Now they were safe aboard the *Tajny*, which drifted, cloaked and radio silent, within the Denorios Belt, well hidden from the probing sensors of the jaunt ship *Enterprise* and its Dominion allies. When a new opportunity to attack presented itself, Trom knew he would have at least nearly the full strength of his Spetzkar company at his command.

Regardless, he was angry. And he wanted answers.

He entered the *Tajny*'s briefing room with long strides and no patience. "We had our prize, and then it was taken from us. Someone explain to me why." He looked down the plotting table ringed with his senior officers, then pointed at his second-in-command. "Crin, you start."

"After-action review of our sensor logs suggests there were undetected comm signals passing between the *Enterprise* and the *ShiKahr*."

"What type of signals?"

"Ultralow frequency, encrypted subspace radio pulses." Crin tapped on the interactive surface of the oblong plotting table and called up an annotated sensor report on its central holographic display for everyone to look at as he continued. "It's a system similar to the one Ikkuna Station used to warn us about the Federation team on the *Królik*."

Trom spent a few seconds reviewing the projected data.

"Backdoor command codes. We missed some kind of challenge-and-response, so they used this to take remote control of the *ShiKahr* and locked us out." He looked at Solt. "How do we prevent that next time?"

The chief engineer traced a few lines in a schematic on the table's display. "To receive that type of signal requires a special antenna. We can disable it next time."

"I presume you'll know where to find it."

"It would be part of the main comm array. Once we find its input node on the transceiver router, we can trace that back to the antenna, and to any backups it has."

"Good." The next commando in Trom's sights was his computer specialist and second officer. "Rem, is it possible there might be some other frequency the Commonwealth crews could use to hijack a jaunt ship from us?"

Rem shook his head. "No. Their computer cores are shielded against outside signals, and we'd be able to monitor the other comm channels. Now that we know about this security exploit, we won't let them use it again. We'll be ready for them next time."

That was an answer Trom could accept, so he shifted his attention to someone new. "Karn, how did their boarding teams reacquire control of the *ShiKahr* so quickly? You assured me we had all the key areas of the ship secured."

The tactical specialist shifted his weight, a telltale sign that he was nervous. "We aren't entirely sure, sir. I've reviewed some of the recordings from our teams' helmet comms, and as far as I can tell, they followed procedure. At the first sign of hostile transporter signals, they engaged the shroud circuits on their armor and assumed ambush positions."

"And yet most of those men are dead, Karn."

An anxious nod. "Yes, sir. A few of them reported picking

up trace signals of other shrouded personnel shortly before
being engaged by the enemy. My current hypothesis is that
the Commonwealth starship crews also possess personal
stealth technology—perhaps even one superior to our own.
They also seem to possess superiority in their small-arms
technology."

Karn's bad news drove Trom to pace while he considered
his response. "If we can't rely on a technological advantage,
then we'll need to exert tactical superiority the next time we
board one of those ships. Work up a battle plan that neutral-
izes the enemy crew as quickly as possible."

"What about prisoners?" Karn held up his padd. "You
said we had orders to bring back prisoners familiar with the
operation of the jaunt ship."

"Countermanded. The lab rats will have to reverse-
engineer it on their own."

An obedient nod. "Understood, sir."

Trom tapped the tabletop to summon a control interface.
He relayed images of the two jaunt ships over Bajor, plus a
slew of sensor data, to the central display. "As if we don't have
enough hurdles to clear on this mission, we've just uncovered
a new one. Energy readings from the two jaunt ships indicate
they're both upgrading their deflector harmonics and shield
geometry to negate the effect of our energy dampener. It was
a nice trick the first time we used it, but these people learn
and adapt much faster than the Federation did during the
Dominion War. So not only have we lost the element of surprise, we've also lost our most effective weapon." He looked
around the table at his command team. "Suggestions?"

A deathly silence followed. No one said it, but Trom
imagined them all thinking the same thing: *Abort this disas-
ter of a mission and go home.*

"While you're all thinking that over, consider this, as well:

the Jem'Hadar battle fleet is dead set on denying us passage through the Bajoran wormhole. In other words, not only has our mission just gone from insanely difficult to damned near impossible, but even if we somehow pull it off, we currently have no way home. So I need you all to collaborate on two new tactical plans: one for how to breach a jaunt ship's defenses and then secure it against counterattack, and one for drawing the Jem'Hadar out of position and clearing us a path to the wormhole." He checked the ever-advancing chrono in the corner of the plotting table's display area. "And I need both plans as soon as possible." He switched off the plotting table and stepped back. "We reconvene in eight hours." Groans of discontent were muffled by helmets with momentarily muted vocoders. Trom felt the slump in his officers' morale. He did his best to project confidence. "I know starting from zero isn't easy, and it's not what we were counting on. But I, for one, don't plan on going home empty-handed—and neither should you. Dismissed."

Twenty

Two security guards—one Andorian, one Kaferian, both male—escorted Bashir through the corridors of the jaunt ship *Enterprise*. They had collected him at the temporary quarters he shared with Sarina, now that they had been separated from the rest of the Section 31 team, and they had walked on either side of him, leading him through turns at several key intersections and what had felt like the longest, most awkward turbolift ride of his life.

They stopped at a closed door. The insectoid Kaferian pressed one clawed manus against the visitor signal. While awaiting a response from the compartment beyond the portal, Bashir noted the nameplate mounted above the door's control panel: PICARD, CAPT. J.

The captain's deep voice answered over the door's comm, *"Come."*

The door slid open. The Kaferian entered, and the Andorian motioned Bashir inside. He followed the Kaferian while the Andorian stayed a few steps behind him.

In rapid fashion, Bashir took in the details of the captain's quarters. Muted illumination was augmented by reflected light from Bajor's surface through the sloped view ports along one side of the main compartment. The furnishings were simple but looked comfortable and clean: a table with four chairs, a sofa, a desk with a holo-projector mounted on its surface. Wall-mounted shelves were lined with old books and a few pieces of antique-looking bric-a-brac. A few small objets d'art sat alone on certain shelves or were mounted on

the bulkheads. Through an open doorway, he saw a neatly ordered bedroom; beyond that, a private lavatory and refresher
nook.

Picard stood next to the main room's replicator, whose
mellisonant *whoosh* of creation was just finishing. The captain picked up a small cup and saucer and walked toward
Bashir. He nodded at the two guards. "That will be all. Please
wait outside."

The security officers exited without question or even a
word of acknowledgment. Picard waited until the door closed
before he spoke again.

"Can I offer you something, Doctor? Tea, perhaps?"

A polite wave of rejection. "No, thank you, sir." Even
though Bashir was no longer in Starfleet, old habits proved
hard to overcome. Such as calling a superior officer *sir*.

The captain set his tea on the dining table, pulled back a
chair, and, with a gesture, invited Bashir to join him. They sat
across a corner from each other.

The older man took a slow, careful sip of his hot beverage.
"It seems we have a delicate situation on our hands."

"I wasn't aware 'delicate' was a synonym for 'explosive' or
'potentially disastrous.'"

Picard cracked a half smile. "I've also been surprised to
learn how versatile that word can be when used in a diplomatic setting." He took another sip of his tea. "Are you familiar with the abilities of Betazoids?"

"I am."

"My chief of security is half Betazoid."

Bashir risked a deductive leap. "An empath?"

"Precisely. She assures me that Mister Weyoun is quite
sincere in his belief that you are a fugitive from Dominion
justice and that this isn't merely some ploy for advantage at
the negotiation table. However, I'm not prepared to hand

over a free sentient being to a foreign power about whose legal system I know very little, merely on the accusation of one man."

"I'm glad to hear that, Captain."

Picard's expression turned grave. "However, I am obliged to investigate."

A slow nod. "I understand."

"As we speak, Mister Weyoun is asking his superior, the Founder, to lodge formal charges against you and to petition the government of the Galactic Commonwealth for your extradition. Before that happens, I would like to hear your side of the story."

Bashir shook his head. "There's not much I can add to what he's already told you, except that I acted in self-defense. I was being held as a slave on Terok Nor. When the alarm sounded, people were running in every direction. It was total chaos. I saw a chance to steal a disruptor from a guard's holster, so I did. Overseer Odo—the Changeling—saw me. He drew his weapon and aimed at me. I aimed back at him, and I fired first. Then . . ." The memory was so grotesque and disturbing to Bashir that it took him a few seconds to articulate it. "He exploded."

"Exploded?"

"The weapon was set to kill, but I didn't know that before I fired. If I had, I would have changed it to a stun setting. Anyway . . . where most humanoids would have vaporized, Odo's body just *erupted*. It was one of the most horrible things I've ever seen. But there was no time then to dwell on it, so I ran. I kept running until I found Kira so we could get off the—"

"Intendant Kira?"

"No, Major Kira. The one from my universe. We came through together, by accident."

"I see. Go on."

"Well, that's all there is."

Picard frowned. "So, Weyoun calls it murder. You call it self-defense."

"It *was* self-defense."

The captain shook his head. He stood, picked up the teacup and saucer, and carried them back to the replicator. He touched a button on the control panel, and the machine dematerialized the cup and saucer in a whirlwind of glowing particles and a rush of pleasant high-pitched sound. "Cases such as this have unpredictable outcomes, Doctor. Your fate is likely to rest not with the evidence but in the sympathies of your judges."

Bashir stood, paced a few steps away from Picard, then turned back. "Weyoun said the Dominion's agents had acquired copies of Terok Nor's security files from an archive on Bajor. If those files are as accurate as he claims, they'll prove my innocence."

"Perhaps." Picard's mien turned more glum by the moment. "Such files can be tampered with. But even if they depict events as you claim, we have no idea how Dominion law works. Its people revere the Founders as if they were deities. They might not consider self-preservation to be an affirmative defense when it comes to the death of one of their own."

Those were sensible points, Bashir realized. The prospect of being held accountable for murder in spite of the facts gave him a new reason to be wary of his every word and deed in this *universum incognitum.* "What do you suggest I do?"

"I would humbly recommend you apply to the Commonwealth for asylum."

"Excuse me?"

Picard held up his open hands, as if to forestall an argument. "I can't promise you'd be spared charges or a trial, but you might stand a better chance of a fair hearing in our courts than in theirs. The Commonwealth is a civilization of laws, Doctor, but it's also one of compassion."

"Do you really think the Dominion would let me go that easily?"

"I'm no solicitor, but Terok Nor was a Bajoran possession at the time of your alleged offense. Now that Bajor is a member of the Commonwealth, events that transpired here in the past but are brought to light only now would fall within our jurisdiction. Likewise, any jury that might be called to hear your case would be one with no love for the Alliance—or for slavery."

"I appreciate your offer, Captain, but I have to ask: How would a grant of amnesty affect your ongoing negotiations with the Dominion?"

Picard waved off the query. "That's not your concern."

"I can't just accept that. I'm not sure I'd want my fate to be the reason a vital treaty discussion fails."

This time, the captain looked away and permitted himself a low, cynical snort of derision. "This has been an extremely complicated negotiation, Doctor. There are *hundreds* of reasons it might fail." He calmed himself with a deep breath, then he turned back toward Bashir. "I should also make clear that I can't promise the Commonwealth will grant your request—or, if they do, that they'll shield you forever. If the Dominion can show that it has sufficient cause to bring a criminal case against you, and that their system of justice meets our standards of evidence and reasonable doubt, then the Commonwealth Assembly might vote to authorize your extradition."

"I have to say that sounds more than fair."

"I agree. But unless you ask for our help, you'll have no

legal standing here—and we'll have no right to refuse the extradition request, which could arrive at any moment."

"All right, then." Bashir adopted his most formal tone of voice. "Captain Picard, I request asylum aboard your vessel, and within the Galactic Commonwealth."

Picard stepped forward and shook Bashir's hand. "Request granted, Doctor."

No sooner had Picard emerged from the turbolift onto the bridge of the *Enterprise* than he saw K'Ehleyr and Troi converge to intercept him at his command chair. He preempted their questions and protests with a raised hand, a stern look, and two words: "Ready room."

The two women accepted his request with dour looks. They walked ahead of him toward his private sanctum, which was located just off the forward starboard quarter of the bridge. Its portal slid open. K'Ehleyr and Troi stepped inside and parted to let Picard pass between them on his way to his desk. As he sat down, they moved closer, and the door shut behind them. K'Ehleyr's trademark veneer of calm was shattered by a sudden flaring of her temper. "Is it true you granted that doctor asylum? Without consulting us?"

He met her criticism with an arched eyebrow. "As the commanding officer of this ship, I am afforded a certain measure of latitude—particularly in matters of life and death."

The lanky first officer reined in her emotions before she replied. "Yes, sir. I understand that. But offering the doctor protection could jeopardize our talks with the Dominion."

"I'm well aware of what's at stake, Number One. But I won't let political expediency deprive this man of his right to due process. He is entitled to face his accusers and mount a defense, and I plan to ensure he has that opportunity."

Troi waded with caution into the conversation. "Still, it

might have been prudent to vet this man before inviting him to take refuge aboard the *Enterprise.*"

Picard considered Troi's post facto advice. She had been his companion for many years before they had signed on to help lead the Terran Rebellion to victory; they had saved each other's lives many times, and he loved her as if she were his own daughter. Consequently, her disapproval cut him more keenly than K'Ehleyr's had. "You've interviewed him. Do you think he represents a threat to this ship, or to the Commonwealth?"

"I'm not sure. He seems to speak truthfully about the incident with the Changeling on Terok Nor, but I sense he's hiding greater secrets."

K'Ehleyr snickered under her breath. "Who isn't?"

"Be that as it may," Troi added, "I'm less concerned about him than about his friends."

Intrigued, Picard leaned forward to signal she had his attention. "Explain."

Troi struggled to put her concerns into words. "I can't describe it. Except for their leader, they exhibit no direct feelings of hostility, and I've yet to feel as if I've caught any of them in a lie. But they exude deception. They have a hidden agenda, and I think it involves us as much as it does the Breen."

Her vague warning drew a sarcastic glare from K'Ehleyr. "Really? You think a team of covert intelligence operatives has a hidden agenda?"

"Mock me if you like, but I know they're not being honest with us."

Picard intervened to stifle what promised to be a pointless debate. "Deanna, assume that the agents from the other universe *are* misleading us. What do you suggest we do?"

"Hold them in the brig until we know what they want."

Picard knew better than to ignore Troi's keen empathic

senses, especially when they pertained to people whose motives were less than clear—but the anarchic era of the rebellion was in the past. Frontier justice was no longer the code they lived by. They were sworn to obey and to uphold the law of the Commonwealth. "We can't detain them without reason, Deanna. Merely being from the other universe is not a crime. Legally, they've done nothing wrong."

"That we know of," Troi grumbled.

"Precisely. That we know of. The law requires evidence of wrongdoing to charge someone with a crime, or to deprive him or her of liberty. And at the moment, we have none."

K'Ehleyr tilted her head at a rakish angle and cracked a wan smile. "Which isn't to say we have *nothing* of interest. I had Kadohata run background checks on our guests, to see if we knew anything about their counterparts in this universe. I sent you the results. Have a look."

Picard activated his holographic terminal to the ship's computer. It automatically scanned his retina and genetic profile to confirm his identity, then presented his command interface. He opened the message K'Ehleyr had routed to him. Several dossiers appeared in new holographic extensions of the interface, which wrapped around him in a shallow curve. At a glance, he recognized all the faces attached to the files: Cole, Bashir, Douglas, Webb, Kitsom, and Sakonna. Then he noticed the one thing all their records had in common. "They're all dead."

"Yes, they are." The lanky half Klingon pointed at the various files; the holographic screens appeared translucent on her side despite being nearly opaque on Picard's. "Sakonna and Douglas both died at the Battle of Empok Nor—the same battle where the Alliance captured General Bashir. Webb and Kitsom were freedom fighters who were killed while trying to liberate Betazed. And Cole was one of hundreds the rebellion lost when Terok Nor was destroyed."

Knowing that his guests all were alternate-universe echoes of people who had died in this one sent a subtle chill down Picard's spine. It was as if they were hosting ghosts. Then the rational portion of his mind rebelled against superstition. "Could this be coincidence?"

"Maybe," K'Ehleyr said. "But I have to say, Mister Cole and his group don't strike me as the sort of people who leave anything to chance."

Picard closed the dossiers and deactivated the holographic screens. "You think they knew before they came here that their counterparts in this universe were dead."

Troi seemed convinced. "It would be a sensible precaution for a covert-ops team. If they know ahead of time that no one in their team has a double here, they reduce the risk of their group being infiltrated by a look-alike who can fool a biometric scan."

"I'll admit, it's an interesting notion, but it's hardly proof of hostile intent."

Discouraged looks passed between Troi and K'Ehleyr. The first officer crossed her arms. "How do you wish to proceed, sir? Should we cut them loose?"

"I said we can't hold them, Number One. I didn't say give them the keys to the ship."

Her mood took a turn for the mischievous as she sensed Picard's true intentions. "Sir?"

"Their vessel is docked aboard the *ShiKahr*, correct?" Off the first officer's nod, Picard continued. "The report I saw from Mister Barclay and his engineering team suggests Cole's ship is in dire need of repairs. It seems to me we could assist with those repairs—and offer to host Mister Cole and his team here on the *Enterprise* until the work is complete."

Troi's frown became a sly smile as she caught on. "And if

we happen to glean a few secrets about the latest Breen star-ship designs—"

"Or the newest Romulan cloaking technology," K'Ehleyr interjected.

"Or whatever else Mister Cole and his team have seen fit to bring with them to our universe," Picard said. "I think we'd have to call that a serendipitous reward for our generosity."

K'Ehleyr looked amused. "I'll have Barclay assemble re-pair teams right away."

Troi feigned concern. "It would be a shame to fix Mister Cole's ship only to find out the Breen had booby-trapped it. Maybe I should lead a security team to sweep its interior."

Picard dispatched his two most trusted officers with one shared order: "Make it so."

Twenty-one

The solarium was a riot of living color. Flowers in full bloom dotted the vines wrapped around the trellis over the entryway. Planting boxes erupted with new blossoms, and the trees were heavy with ripening fruit. Outside its force field–reinforced walls of transparent aluminum, the grounds of the Elemspur Monastery were lush and vibrant with as many shades of green as there were in Bajor's pristine seas. Every breath Saavik took was perfumed with floral scents and the rich fragrance of dark soil that was freshly turned and ready for planting.

The only sour note in the enclosed garden came from the unyielding visage of the Founder. She and her counselor, Weyoun, sat opposite Saavik and Chairman Eddington. Looming behind the two Dominion dignitaries was the Jem'Hadar known as Taran'atar.

Looking back at the Honored Elder from behind Saavik and Eddington was their chosen bodyguard, Nyyl Saygur, a Brikar with a body like a large hill and a voice like a rockslide in a thunderstorm. Although Saygur had extremely high density for a humanoid, he wore a gravity compensator on a belt around his waist; with its assistance, the hulking Brikar could move with shocking speed and grace without sacrificing any of his fearsome native strength. Whether he had the nerve to prevail in his staring contest against Taran'atar, only time would tell.

The Founder broke the uncomfortable silence that had prevailed since the solarium's doors had been closed to guarantee the meeting's privacy. "I was profoundly dismayed to learn of the actions taken by the captain of the *Enterprise*."

As the Commonwealth's elected representative in the room, Eddington was responsible for answering the Dominion's head of state. "Could you be more specific?"

"There is no need to be so coy, Mister Chairman. We both know what we're discussing."

Eddington struck a deferential note. "I don't assume to know the minds of others."

His deflection only sharpened the edge of the Founder's manner. "Your starship commander granted legal and political asylum to Doctor Julian Bashir of the parallel universe. He did this knowing full well that we are seeking Bashir's immediate extradition."

"Captain Picard's log shows that Doctor Bashir made a formal petition for asylum," Eddington said. "The captain was well within his authority to grant that request."

The Changeling's slow burn of anger intensified. "By what right do *any* of your people claim authority over this matter?"

"Bajor is a charter member of the Galactic Commonwealth. As such, it falls—"

"At the time of Odo's murder, it was a protectorate of the Klingon-Cardassian Alliance. Because that political entity no longer exists, any retroactive claim to jurisdiction over Terok Nor is voided. Further, because Terok Nor was destroyed while still technically a possession of the Alliance, neither Bajor nor your Commonwealth has any right to assert authority in this matter."

Saavik saw from the reddening of Eddington's complexion and the throbbing of the veins in his temples that the chairman was losing his patience with the Founder, but she was reluctant to interrupt him without cause. He leaned forward as his voice began to grow in volume. "We can sit and argue over jurisdiction as long as you like, Madam Founder. But the fact is, we have jurisdiction on Bajor, and our laws give us retroactive jurisdiction, whether you like it or not. No matter how weak you might think our claim to authority, I guarantee: yours is weaker."

"Do you think us unfamiliar with your laws, Mister Chairman? Our finest Karemma and Vorta barristers studied your civil and criminal codes in preparation for this visit. I think you will find that because Doctor Bashir—a citizen of a foreign state—killed a Dominion citizen while under the jurisdiction of a political entity that no longer exists, the formerly secondary jurisdiction of the Dominion now obtains primary status, and by virtue of precedence trumps any retroactive authority your government might now choose to assert, regardless of Bajor's accession to such. In other words, custody of Doctor Bashir rightly belongs to the Dominion."

"Prior to his request for asylum, that might have been a correct interpretation of our laws. But the fact is, asylum was requested and granted. Until you satisfy our terms for extradition, he'll be under our protection."

The Changeling's body language resembled that of a coiled serpent tensing to strike. "How can we negotiate for extradition when we have no treaty in place?"

"Perhaps this would be a good time to resume our talks, then."

"Of all the impudent—"

"Madam Founder," Saavik interrupted. "Might I offer a suggestion?"

The Changeling delegated her reply to Weyoun with a dismissive glance. The Vorta leaned forward with his hands folded together in a pose of mock obeisance. "Forgive us. We remain unclear on what role you play in this discussion."

"The same as yours," Saavik said. "Senior counselor."

Weyoun bowed his head like a corrected pupil. "I see. Carry on."

"Perhaps both our concerns could be addressed by trying Doctor Bashir in a Commonwealth court. An impartial jury—"

"Impartial!" the Founder snorted.

Saavik remained aloof from the room's rancor. "I assure you, Madam Founder, our people would have no reason to favor him or disfavor him. He is a stranger, not only to our worlds but also to our universe."

"But he is a solid, just like the rest of you."

"It might surprise you to learn that 'solids' feel no sense of communal identity such as your people suggest. If the Dominion can present compelling enough evidence to persuade a jury of Doctor Bashir's guilt, he would be sentenced accordingly."

Distrust infused Weyoun's reply. "Meaning what, exactly?"

"If he is convicted of murder, he would face lifetime imprisonment."

The Vorta shook his head and waved one hand. "Unacceptable. The penalty for murdering a Founder is death."

"Corporal and capital punishment are banned in the Galactic Commonwealth."

Weyoun raged, "But his crime wasn't committed against one of *your* people, it was committed against one of *ours*! And not just any person, a *Founder*."

Saavik was confused. "I fail to see why such a distinction would be legally relevant."

The Vorta gestured emphatically as he struggled to explain himself. "How would you feel if someone your people considered sacred was murdered in the Gamma Quadrant by a stateless actor from another universe? Then, when agents of your Commonwealth finally identified the culprit in custody aboard a Jem'Hadar ship, the Dominion refused to let the criminal face your justice. Would you be so calm, then? Would you demur and let others dictate terms to you?"

The elderly Vulcan woman refused to be baited or browbeaten. "First, Mister Weyoun, the Commonwealth does not venerate any individual, class of persons, or species above any other. It considers all sapient life sacred. So much so, in fact, that the state has been denied the power to end the lives of individuals under its authority. Murder is murder, regardless of whether it is committed by an individual, a group of persons, or the state. Second, I would be more than satisfied to see such a person face criminal charges in a Dominion court of law, so long as the proceedings were public, impartial, and conducted according to strict rules of evidence, and the sentence imposed was humane and proportional to the offense."

"In other words, you lack the will to mete out real justice and fear to let others exact the retribution that you cannot. Your moral cowardice sickens me."

"Weyoun!" the Founder snapped. "Enough." She sighed. "It seems, Mister Chairman, that we remain at an impasse. A most regrettable outcome." She stood, and Weyoun did the same. The Founder turned to leave, but she paused to look back at Eddington and Saavik as the duo rose from their seats. "You and your Commonwealth have ventured down a perilous road. You are about to learn that defying the Dominion comes with dire consequences."

The foreign dignitaries made a swift exit from the solarium. Eddington and Saavik watched them leave, and then he turned to her, his face drawn with dismay. "Now what?"

"We prepare for the worst. Because I predict that's exactly what's coming."

On the edge of the Denorios Belt, the Bajoran wormhole exploded into view, a blue flower unfolding in the endless night of space. As the throat of the wormhole dilated, a glorious fountain of light spilled from it, a white jet of pure energy coursing from the azure storm of ionized gas that ringed the wormhole's maw. It was one of the most beautiful of all the galaxy's wonders, and it captivated Jean-Luc Picard every time he saw it.

Standing on the bridge of the *Enterprise*, he marveled at the furious majesty of the wormhole depicted on the viewscreen, even though he suspected the moment was about to take an unwelcome turn. Then the pillars of light streaming from the wormhole darkened with the silhouettes of dozens of enormous warships. Ominous shadows coursed in formation and made wide swooping turns to clear the way for the steady stream of ships that followed them.

Troi monitored the new arrivals from the tactical console. "Seventy-five Jem'Hadar vessels, ranging in size from attack cruisers to battleships, have joined the Jem'Hadar fleet holding station four hundred thousand kilometers from the wormhole."

K'Ehleyr leaned toward Picard from her chair on his right. "They sure know how to make an entrance, don't they?"

"I can't deny it's an impressive display of power. But we can't afford to be goaded into a mistake, Number One. It's possible this is all just for show, an empty bit of saber rattling."

On the viewscreen, the wormhole contracted and twisted in upon itself with alarming speed. It vanished with a final flash of light, leaving only a star-flecked expanse of darkness. The Jem'Hadar fleet was lost in the yawning gulf of the cosmos—until the image on the viewscreen was magnified to reveal the fearsome Dominion warships in crisp detail. Within seconds, Picard noticed signs of shifting parallax in his view of the fleet from the Gamma Quadrant, and he deduced what was happening before Troi reported it.

"The Jem'Hadar fleet is moving," Troi said. "It's on a direct heading for Bajor—and us."

Picard knew the crisis at hand might have repercussions far beyond the fate of his ship and crew. This was no time to act rashly, or to make decisions in a vacuum. "Lieutenant Commander Troi, hail Chairman Eddington on Bajor. Make it clear this is an emergency."

"Aye, sir." Troi keyed in the command. After a few seconds she said, "Channel open."

"Mister Chairman," Picard said. "We have a rather tense situation developing in orbit."

Eddington sounded as unflappably calm as always. *"Let me guess, Captain. A sizable force of Jem'Hadar reinforcements has come through the wormhole?"*

"Precisely, sir." Picard checked the tactical details with a look at the command screen next to his chair. "The combined Dominion fleet is en route to Bajor. ETA, five minutes."

"Captain, I want the Enterprise *and the* ShiKahr *to maintain their positions in orbit. Do not fire unless you are first fired upon. Is that clear?"*

"Yes, Mister Chairman."

"Good. Carry on. Eddington out."

A palpable air of anxiety took root on the bridge as the channel closed. Picard took the shift in the collective mood as his cue to stand and address his officers. "Friends, this is a test of not just our resolve but also of our restraint. Our leaders and our people are depending on us to stop this situation from escalating into armed conflict. The Jem'Hadar fleet will try to provoke us by approaching Bajor. Its commanders will try to intimidate us with their superior numbers. But the purpose of our mission, the reason we are here, is to safeguard these negotiations. If we attempt to meet this force in kind, we risk destroying any chance of a diplomatic solution to—"

His call to arms was cut short by a staccato series of brilliant flashes on the viewscreen. In less than ten seconds, two dozen of the *Enterprise*'s sister ships jaunted into the system, each through its own self-generated artificial wormhole. The Commonwealth reinforcements arrived already in near-perfect formation, between Bajor and the approaching Dominion forces. A few seconds later the Dominion fleet slowed and came to an abrupt halt.

Alerts chimed on Troi's console. "We're picking up audio communications between the Jem'Hadar fleet commander and Captain Siddiqui on the *Syrinx*."

Despite his well-founded dread at what he might hear, Picard gave in to his curiosity. "On speakers, Commander. From the beginning."

The Dominion commander's voice was feminine, articulate, and as cold as vengeance. *"Attention, Commonwealth vessels. This is Eris. I have orders from the Founder to bring our fleet into orbit of Bajor. Cease and desist obstructing our approach."*

"Eris, this is Captain Shiraz Siddiqui of the free starship Syrinx. *Any attempt to bring your fleet into orbit of Bajor is a violation of the protocols for this treaty summit. You and your fleet are ordered to withdraw at once to your assigned coordinates adjacent to the wormhole."*

Eris replied, *"Our fleet will enter orbit, Captain, with or without your permission."*

"If your fleet attempts orbit without *my permission, it'll do so in the form of burning scrap. Stand down and return to your assigned coordinates,* immediately."

K'Ehleyr looked up at Picard with world-weary eyes. "You were saying something about 'a diplomatic solution,' Captain?"

He frowned at the high-powered standoff taking shape

high above Bajor. *I came to help broker a new peace, and instead I find myself with a front-row seat to a new war.* He sat down and distilled his fears and regrets into one eloquent word, spoken under his breath.

"*Merde.*"

Kort poked at the lukewarm lump of rolled dough and brined vegetables that lay on his plate, and then he shot a disgusted look at the other patrons enjoying late-night dinners at the open-air café in the heart of Bajor's capital. "How can anyone stand to eat like this?"

Regon, his dining companion and fellow traveler in Bajoran guise, looked up from her own lunch. "Are you referring to the cuisine or the setting?"

"Either. Both. Pick one."

She took a bite of her own *hasperat* and mumbled as she chewed, "Tastes good to me."

The surgically altered Klingon sulked behind his weak Bajoran nasal ridges. "Of course you'd say that. You're Cardassian. Your kind always has been partial to Bajoran cattle feed."

She glowered at him. "Say it a little louder. I don't think the state security agents in the next restaurant heard you."

Before he could retort, the waiter arrived with Kort's second course. "*Arnisios* steak," the young Bajoran man said as he set down the platter. "The cook prepared it just the way you asked, but he wants me to warn you that eating undercooked food can be dangerous, and—"

"Thank you." Kort waved off the youth. "I'm fine. Go."

The waiter backed away, warily at first, and then he turned and hurried to the far end of the café, as if he couldn't wait to get as far from his peculiar raw-meat-eating patron as possible.

Kort's wet chomps and smacks of mastication were almost too much for Regon to bear without wincing. She felt her façade of politesse crumble while she watched him stuff his maw with huge forkfuls of purple-blue meat that had barely been kissed by the grill's flames.

"The concept of being undercover and in disguise means nothing to you, does it?"

He gulped down a massive bite of half-gnawed raw flesh. "I need to eat. Not my fault these heathens can't serve a meal without burning it to a crisp."

"Luckily for us, you're not the most interesting thing in the café today." Regon draped one arm over the back of her chair as she turned to watch the news report on a nearby public holoscreen. A fair-haired female Trill's talking head prattled between cutaways to fuzzy images of the two fleets of starships that were, at that moment, faced off in orbit above Bajor.

"The standoff began today at just after fifteen twenty hours, Capital Time," the Trill newscaster said, her manner earnest and authoritative. *"Communications between the two fleets have been encrypted, so we're unable to report precisely what has been said by their respective commanders. Furthermore, a spokesperson for the Assembly has so far declined to comment on what appears to be a significant turn for the worse in the Commonwealth's negotiations with the Gamma Quadrant power known so far only as the Dominion."*

Kort forced down an oversized mouthful, then blocked a belch with the side of his fist. "This is a bomb waiting for a spark. A shame neither of our governments has the will to act."

"I wish we had some idea what instigated this," Regon said. "Then we could target the sore spot. Aggravate it. Exacerbate it. Make it bleed, and then stand back and enjoy the show."

"Dream on." Kort washed down his quickly devoured raw

steak with a mouthful of *wotyr*, a clear and extremely potent hard spirit distilled from rare tubers grown only in the Jokala Mountains of Bajor. He sleeved a sheen of blood and liquor from his lips. "You know these Commonwealth types. All talk. They'll yammer on until the Dominion loses the will to fight."

Regon stole another look at the Dominion fleet in the news vid. "I'm not so sure. The Terrans and their ilk might have underestimated their enemy this time."

A dubious shrug. "Maybe. But I'll bet my finest *bat'leth* the Commonwealth won't fire the first shot. And unless this Dominion is stronger than it looks, I doubt it wants to go toe-to-toe with those jaunt ships. Which means this little standoff probably won't amount to much."

"Not without a push."

"From who? Regent Duras? Legate Damar? Don't make me laugh."

A dastardly notion put a taut smile on Regon's face. "We need to think beyond our own borders. Our peoples don't want to get in the middle of this. And neither the Dominion nor the Commonwealth wants to see this situation turn bloody. So we need to seek help from someone who stands to gain by turning this standoff into a shooting war."

She sat back and enjoyed the befuddled look on Kort's stupid-looking fake Bajoran face while he struggled to catch up to her runaway train of thought. Then a sharp gleam illuminated his eyes. He grinned as he leaned forward and lowered his voice. "The Taurus Pact."

"Exactly. The Gorn are too far away to be of much use, but the Breen and the Tholians are right on Bajor's doorstep. Both would love a chance to bloody the Commonwealth's nose."

"They won't work for free," Kort said, thinking out loud. "Neither will the Tzenkethi."

"Revenge is what drives the Tholians. They're still angry about the crimes of the Terran Empire. They've said many times they'll gladly take out their grudge on the Commonwealth."

"True, the bugs are single-minded to a fault. But the Breen are opportunists. They won't get involved unless we can show them what they stand to gain." Something amused him. "Of course, what they *think* they'll get and what they receive don't need to be the same thing."

"For example?"

"If we let them infer they might acquire control over the Bajoran wormhole—and with it a monopoly over traffic between the Alpha and Gamma Quadrants—that might be enough to enlist the aid of a Breen attack squadron. Maybe even two."

Regon understood Kort's endgame. "Then the dust settles, and a joint armada of Klingon and Cardassian forces secures Bajor—for the good of its people."

"And ensuring the safety of Bajor would require securing the wormhole."

"Naturally. That only stands to reason." She toasted her colleague with her last sip of spring wine. As she set down the glass, her enthusiasm for their new scheme was dimmed by a sudden flash of recollection. "There's just one problem."

"That being?"

"The Pact's consular chief on Bajor."

Concentration wrinkled Kort's brow. "Why? Who is it these days?"

With great reluctance, she told him the consul's name.

Kort downed the rest of his *wotyr* in one swallow. "On second thought, kill me now."

Twenty-two

House arrest aboard the Commonwealth starship *Enterprise* was far from what Bashir considered a hardship. The accommodations were spare but comfortable, and they came with a view that faced aft, toward the jaunt ship's ring-shaped secondary hull and its sleek warp nacelles. As limited as its replicator's menu was, the food it produced was enjoyable. There was even a fair selection of freely available entertainment media, including books, vids, and music—a privilege Starfleet had denied him during his brief incarceration several months earlier, after he was arrested for stealing classified information in order to save the Andorian people from slow extinction. If not for the locked door with guards standing outside, Bashir would have felt more like a guest than a prisoner.

But the door was locked, and he was alone. It felt like solitary confinement again.

His enhanced hearing detected the cessation of a low hum from the door's magnetically secured dead bolts, which retracted with a soft click most people would not have noticed. The door to the corridor slid open, and Sarina rushed in. Behind her, Bashir saw the female Deltan security officer who had been assigned to shadow Sarina from one secure space to another—a precaution extended to all members of the Section 31 team. The bald woman halted shy of the door's threshold. The door closed as Sarina hurried to Bashir, who stood by the view ports.

She threw her arms around him. "Are you all right?"

"I'm fine." He tightened his embrace for a moment, then relaxed. She backed away, and they let each other go. "Where have you been?"

"They've been debriefing us all, one by one."

"What lies are Cole and the others spinning now that they're in custody?"

Sarina seemed bewildered. "They've been telling Picard's people the same thing they told us: that we're tracking the Breen and trying to prevent the theft of a jaunt ship."

"Which is a fairly good indicator they've been lying to us since the start."

"How do you figure?"

"If Thirty-one tells you something in secret, then openly tells the same thing to someone else, then you're part of a misinformation campaign. Halting the theft of a jaunt ship *might* be part of their op, or it might just be the cover story. Either way, I'm now sure it's anything but the real reason we're here." He took a breath and looked out at the stars, then at Bajor. "Do I even want to know what's happening out there?"

"Probably not."

"Tell me anyway."

Sarina joined him in gazing out into deep space. "To put it mildly, the Dominion was *irked* when it found out Picard had granted you asylum."

That boded ill. "How irked?"

"They brought another fleet of reinforcements through the wormhole and made a run at Bajor. Then the Common-wealth sent in a couple dozen jaunt ships, and now we're smack in the middle of a standoff that's just waiting to go wrong."

He nodded. "So, better than we expected."

"Much better. I figured the Jem'Hadar would've glassed Bajor by now."

"Be grateful for small mercies. Any leads on the Spetzkar?"

"No, but it's not like anyone's all that keen to keep us in the loop. Most of them treat us like we're in the way, even when we're offering to help."

He cracked a sly smile. "Almost as if we're outsiders."

"Well played." She stretched her arm across his back and rested her head against his shoulder. "What are we supposed to do if you get extradited?"

"I don't know. Get me a good lawyer?"

She looked up, a flash of anger in her eyes. "We can't just let the Dominion take you. I won't see you tried in some Gamma Quadrant kangaroo court."

He took her by her shoulders. "If it comes to that, we might not have any choice. Thirty-one has its tricks and its gadgets, but one team of agents can't take on the entire Dominion." He pulled her close and adopted a more soothing manner. "But no one's voted to hand me over yet. If the Assembly grants my request for asylum, I won't be going anywhere."

"That's almost as bad. What are you supposed to do then? Spend the rest of your life looking over your shoulder for a Dominion extraction team?" She turned away and anxiously pushed her fingers through her flaxen hair. "Hell—what if you get asylum, and the Dominion responds by leveling Bajor and the rest of the quadrant?"

The soft chime of the door signal spared Bashir the indignity of admitting he had no answers to her questions. Sarina faced the stars. He turned toward the door. "Come."

Cole walked in, leaving behind his security shadow, a male Triexian. The three-legged, three-armed alien moved on down the corridor as the door closed between him and Cole, who folded his hands behind his back and adopted an at-ease posture. He seemed oddly calm for a man at the potential flashpoint of a war. "How are you holding up, Doctor?"

"I've had better days."

"I know what you must be thinking."

"I doubt that."

"I just want to assure you that no matter how the rest of this op pans out, we won't leave you behind. And we damned sure won't let you be extradited to the Dominion."

Despite his contempt for Cole, Bashir resisted the urge to stoop to naked sarcasm and mockery. "Does this mean we'll be getting back in that ship of yours and heading home?"

The question drew a grimace of frustration from Cole. "Not right away, no. Even if we wanted to leave now, our ship is stuck aboard the *ShiKahr*. 'Under repair,' Picard says. Every time I ask how long until it'll be spaceworthy, they tell me 'a few more hours.'" He shook his head. "It's like dealing with a Pakled mechanic at a Ferengi used-spaceship lot."

Bashir parsed Cole's statement in his head, gnawing on a detail that troubled him. "What did you mean when you said, 'Even if we wanted to leave now'? Why do we want to stay?"

"Because we have no choice. Our mission's not done yet."

"But the Commonwealth has been warned. They're on the hunt for the Breen."

Cole scolded Bashir with a waggle of his index finger. "Never trust someone else to do your work for you. We came here to terminate the Spetzkar's mission with prejudice, and we'll stay here until we know they've been permanently neutralized."

"And how do you propose we do that without access to our ship or our equipment?"

"One thing at a time, Doctor." The older man smiled, turned, and walked toward the door. "One thing at a time."

Saavik stood alone in the transporter room of the Dominion command ship, facing a trio of Jem'Hadar soldiers. Each of the hulking creatures was armed with a battle rifle. The two on either end also carried *kar'takin*, short pole-arms with massive cutting blades that ended in long stabbing points. None of them spoke, blinked, or so much as twitched. In that place and moment, it was as if they had been born for no other purpose than to stand watch against her, one elderly Vulcan woman, lest she take an unauthorized step off the transporter dais onto the hallowed ground of their drab, hyperutilitarian starship. Their eyes bored into her with cold malice.

The door behind them opened, and their commander returned. Taran'atar's deep voice was freighted with authority. "Let her pass." His subordinates moved aside as Saavik stepped down to the deck. He regarded her with the same savage intensity as his men. "Follow me."

He led her through the command ship's narrow passageways and ladder wells. They passed only a handful of other Jem'Hadar as they traversed the ship, and each time the others tucked themselves into nooks or niches to make way for Taran'atar and Saavik.

It took a few minutes for them to descend three decks and reach one of the sections in the heart of the vessel. They stopped outside a door that bore no markings. He pressed his palm to a sensor panel. It shone with bright blue light. He removed his hand. "She is here."

The panel turned from blue to a warm shade of amber, and the door slid open. Taran'atar entered first, and Saavik followed him. The compartment was empty. No furniture, no creature comforts, no decoration or signs of habitation. Two rows of narrow, translucent white panels on the overhead filled the room with low, diffuse light. There were no other doors inside the room. For a moment, Saavik wondered if she had been led into a trap.

One of the bulkheads started to melt. The gray metal surface deformed and slid into a puddle on the deck. In seconds, the gray goo transformed into an amorphous blob of luminous golden liquid, transmuted itself into a humanoid shape, and finally solidified into the smooth-featured, gray-robed form of the Founder. The Changeling met Saavik's emotionless gaze with a cryptic, almost beatific smile. "You are a most *persistent* visitor." She looked at Taran'atar. "Wait outside."

The Jem'Hadar First opened the door, stepped out, and closed it after himself.

Saavik faced the Founder. "Thank you for seeing me."

The Founder folded her hands together. "Perhaps I should thank you for coming in person. I suspect it's you I should have been dealing with all along."

"My presence is a violation of protocol. Chairman Eddington is the elected head of state."

"But he doesn't represent the true power of the Commonwealth, does he?" She sized up Saavik with a keen, penetrating stare. "That's your role, isn't it? It's why you're here now."

It was vital, Saavik knew, not to let the Changeling sidetrack her. "I am here to urge you to accept some measure of compromise, so that we can resume our treaty negotiations."

"I've made my position clear. No half measures. No compromises. We want Bashir."

"This is a complex matter, Madam Founder. Intractable demands and thinly veiled threats of military reprisal—"

"Our threats are not the least bit veiled."

So much for an appeal to reason. "I would like to show you something. A recording I made several years ago, for the benefit of the Commonwealth's more belligerent neighbors."

"As you like."

Moving with caution and transparency of action, Saavik

took a small holographic projection disk from a pocket inside her tunic. She kneeled, set the disk on the deck, and activated it with a single touch. A three-dimensional image of a lifeless, rocky planet appeared, suspended in the empty space between her and the Founder. A female voice filled the room.

"This is the planet Rhenvara Five, a Class-G world in an unpopulated star system that lies just beyond the Terran Neutral Zone, inside sovereign Terran space. It has no natural resources worth exploiting, and its lack of indigenous life-forms is well documented."

The Founder remained stoic as a fiery streak manifested from thin air and arced slowly past her from behind, on a direct path toward the holographic planet. *"This is the Genesis Device, a technology we mastered nearly a century ago."*

The projectile made impact and detonated. A shock wave expanded from the blast point, spread at hypersonic velocity, and engulfed the entire surface of the planet in crimson fire.

"Genesis is capable of transforming lifeless worlds like Rhenvara Five into lush, Class-M worlds capable of supporting humanoid life—not over the course of years or even months, but in a matter of hours. Know this: if a Genesis Device is deployed on a world where life-forms already exist, it will destroy such life in favor of its new matrix. And remember that our mastery of wormhole propulsion means we can deploy these devices at any time against any world in the galaxy." The image of the burning world faded away.

Saavik searched the Founder's face for a reaction, only to find the Changeling's mask utterly devoid of expression. "Do you understand my meaning, Madam Founder?"

"Indeed." The Founder's mood turned pensive. "It was a most chilling demonstration. Such a weapon, if delivered with the speed and precision demonstrated by your jaunt ships, could obliterate every world in the Dominion so swiftly that by the time we knew we were under attack, the war would be over."

"I should also add that the Genesis Device represents the *beginning* of our arsenal, not its end. We've been developing far more devastating technologies for over a century." She squatted, picked up the miniature projector, and pocketed it as she stood. "With that in mind, are you now ready to discuss a compromise regarding Doctor Bashir's extradition?"

"No."

Saavik did a double take. "Excuse me?"

"There will be no compromise."

"You would continue to push us toward war, even knowing we can destroy you?"

The Founder's countenance was serene. "Principles betrayed are worthless. A civilization that lacks the courage of its convictions, even in the face of certain annihilation and oblivion, does not deserve to live." In the space of a breath, her blank visage turned doleful. "We had hoped that your Commonwealth would share our commitment to the rule of law."

"The Commonwealth is a civilization of laws, Madam Founder. But it is also much greater than that. The law needs to be more than an arbitrary and inflexible code. It represents a blueprint for the social contract between a government and its people—and the spirit of that contract is just as important as its letter."

"Perhaps. But without respect for the law's letter, its spirit has no agency in the world." She touched a panel on the bulkhead and opened the door. As soon as the portal slid aside, Taran'atar entered and looked at the Founder, who gave him new orders. "Take Director Saavik back to the transporter room and see that she is returned safely to her point of origin on Bajor."

"Yes, Founder."

Saavik paused at the doorway and looked back. "Is your wrath toward Doctor Bashir worth risking the survival of your civilization?"

"Is exempting him from responsibility for his actions worth committing genocide?"

Both questions were left unanswered as Saavik made her exit, troubled as much by the implications of the Founder's moral calculus as she was by her own.

Twenty-three

"I thought our circumstances couldn't get any worse. Once again, I am proved in error." Thot Trom and his command team had reconvened ahead of schedule to assess the rapidly changing tactical scenario that confronted them. "How many is that now?"

First Officer Crin manipulated the holographic image above the briefing room's plotting table to magnify the details of the two opposing fleets. "Over a hundred Jem'Hadar warships and twenty-four Commonwealth jaunt ships."

Rem added, "All sitting in front of the wormhole at high alert. A perfect blockade."

"What's impressive," Karn added, "is that the jaunt ships are outnumbered nearly five to one, but they repelled the Jem'Hadar advance on Bajor and pushed it all the way back here." The tactical officer triggered a time-compressed playback of the Dominion ships' retreat and regrouping. "I don't think I've ever seen a Jem'Hadar attack group react that way to anything."

"All of which underscores why we were sent here to capture one of those ships." Trom reset the hologram to show the fleets' current deployments. "However, thanks to this standoff, our plan to lure the Dominion ships away from the wormhole has gone from outrageously difficult to practically impossible." He looked around the table. "Any new ideas?"

The first to speak was Rem. "What if we modify a torpedo for passive deployment? We could release it inert while we stay cloaked. Then we maneuver clear. After a preset delay, the torpedo activates and locks on to the nearest ship in the blockade."

"To what end?"

"Sir?"

"What would that accomplish?"

Rem nodded at the projection. "We fire the first shot. They fire the rest and blow each other to bits. When they're done, we cruise through the wormhole at our leisure."

"An interesting theory, Rem. But what if the Dominion emerges victorious? Our job is to capture a jaunt ship, not scoop up the fractured debris of one. Who else has a plan?"

Solt lifted his snout. "I have some ideas, but I'm not sure how feasible they are."

"As long as they don't involve goading the Jem'Hadar into blowing up our target, you can speak freely."

The chief engineer took control of the projection above the table. Detailed schematics of two complex machines appeared and rotated slowly in opposite directions, side by side. "The first challenge we need to address is how to get aboard a jaunt ship. We don't want to risk a direct attack, and without the energy dampener, we have no way of disabling their shields—which means we can't use transporters for the boarding phase of the assault." He pointed at the schematic closer to him. "I dug up some old plans for a dimensional shifter and—"

Trom interrupted, "A what?"

"A folded-space transport system. Some variants were called inverters."

"Stop," Rem said. "I've read about these things. They damage organic tissue."

Doctor Nev cut in, "Only gradually, over the course of several exposures to the inverter's energy field. A single use will cause some tissue damage, but nothing that can't be managed."

"More important," Solt continued, "folded-space transport can bypass shields, force fields, and any other surprises those jaunt ships have locked inside them. We can even use it without dropping the cloak—which means we can stage a true sneak attack."

Trom was satisfied that the benefits outweighed the risks. "All right. Can you build one?"

"Maybe. My team is replicating the component parts. Unfortunately, the schematics we have all rely on mutually exclusive systems for directing the transport coordinates, and because they were all stolen from other powers' research facilities, we have the specs for the hardware but not the software. Still, I think there's a good chance we can reverse-engineer it."

"How good a chance?"

"Exponentially better than our odds of surviving a direct attack on a jaunt ship."

"Carry on, then." Trom pointed at the second holographic schematic hovering above the plotting table. "What is this?"

"The second part of my plan," Solt said. "Getting onto a jaunt ship is one thing. Getting it home is another. At this point, I think we need to accept that trying to slip past the blockade to the Bajoran wormhole isn't going to work." He deactivated the image of the dimensional shifter and enlarged the remaining design to fill the empty space. "This is a miniaturized version of the rift generator Thot Tran built on Ikkuna Station."

It was Trom's duty to ask, "Where did you get that?"

"I took the liberty of accessing his lab's computers and downloading his research before we deployed. It occurred to me that we might find ourselves in a predicament such as this, and I thought it best to take appropriate precautions."

"When we get home, Solt, I'm putting you in for a commendation and a bump in pay grade." With a wave of his hand, he added, "Continue."

"From what I've seen of the jaunt ship's wormhole propulsion system, I think it might be possible to modify it with some of the components from the Ikkuna rift generator. Balancing the flow of energy in a jury-rigged system will be dangerous—but if we're successful, we'll be able to use a jaunt ship's own propulsion system to breach the dimensional barrier to go home."

Trom's imagination reeled at the possibilities raised by such a leap in technology. Not only would he and his team be able to deliver their superiors' most sought after prize, they would be improving it in the process—and extending the reach of the Breen Confederacy farther than anyone had ever dared to dream possible. "How long do you need?"

Solt shrugged. "Not sure. We can probably turn our transport platforms into dimensional shifters in about a day. As for upgrading the jaunt ships' wormhole drives, we can make the parts in about twenty hours. But I can't be sure how long it'll take to integrate them once we're aboard a ship. Might be a matter of minutes, might take all day."

"We won't have that much time after we're aboard. Do whatever you can to minimize the refit time. We won't be able to buy you more than an hour, at best."

"Noted."

"Crin, task anyone with a Level Five or higher tech rating to assist Solt's team on the dimensional shifters. Rem, take point on that project, get it done. Solt, I want you and your best engineers working on the wormhole drive modifications." Trom straightened and switched off the holographic projector. "Men, this might be our last shot. Make it count."

There was so much to do, so many places to be, so many egos to appease. The Commonwealth was teetering upon the precipice of war over a matter of principle and the life of one man. All Saavik wanted was to find some way to craft a compromise, but she found herself snared between the immovable fanaticism of the Dominion and the fragile idealism of the fledgling interstellar power she and her colleagues in Memory Omega had midwifed.

Now, instead of addressing the myriad issues already at hand, she found herself answering the summons of a stranger.

Two guards, a male Tellarite and a female Trill, stood watch outside a suite of guest quarters on the *Enterprise*. Although Saavik wore no uniform, both security officers recognized her; neither challenged her as she approached. She asked them in her most polite manner, "Unlock the door, please." The Trill pressed her hand to the biometric sensor beside the door, which sighed open. "Thank you," Saavik said as she walked inside.

Cole was alone, seated in an armchair upholstered with gray microfiber. The dark-haired human set down the padd from which he had been reading and stood. "Director Saavik. Thank you for coming. I hadn't expected you so soon."

Saavik stepped away from the door's proximity sensor, allowing the portal to close. She regarded him with cool reserve. "What do you want, Mister Cole?"

"A chance to talk." He beckoned her toward the sofa perpendicular to his chair. "Please."

She kept her eyes focused on his. "My time is limited."

"Of course. But still, have a seat. We needn't be so formal."

As if to set an example, he relaxed back into the armchair and crossed one leg over the other. His change of situation suddenly made Saavik's pose seem needlessly confrontational. She crossed the small room to the sofa and sat down. "What do you need to discuss?"

"The guards on my door, for starters. I know that Doctor

Bashir needs to be kept under watch until his legal status is resolved, but I was led to understand the rest of my team and I were here as guests—not as prisoners."

"An unfortunate consequence of our confrontation with the Dominion armada. Under normal conditions, you and your people could have been granted limited access to non-classified areas of the ship. But with the fleet on combat alert, all privileges are rescinded."

"Ah." Cole stroked his stubbled chin. "It's good to see you're taking the Dominion threat seriously. They're far more dangerous than you might realize."

"Is that so?"

A grave nod underscored the import of his words. "In my universe, the Dominion were a threat second only to the Borg. My people waged a war against them that cost millions of lives. Entire worlds were laid waste. To be frank, they nearly beat us. The only reason the Federation finally came out on top was a few lucky breaks right near the end."

She studied his face for microexpressions that might betray an attempt at mendacity or evasion. "That sounds like an exaggeration, Mister Cole. Surely, luck can't have been the only thing that decided the war's outcome."

A grimace and dubious tilt of his head. "Not the only thing, no. But an important one."

He was a gifted liar, Saavik decided, one practiced in the art of deception. It was almost as if he believed his own prevarications. "Why tell me this?"

"Because it looks to me like you're on the verge of war with the Dominion."

"And you think my people need your advice?"

A faux-humble shrug. "I doubt it could hurt. The organization I work for amassed a significant amount of actionable intel against the Dominion in our universe. I know not everything is exactly the same on this side as it is back home, but I'd be willing to bet our intel could give you options you might not have considered. Alternatives to glassing all their planets with your stacks of Genesis torpedoes."

How did he know about— She halted her speculation. Cole was a covert intelligence agent. It was possible—even probable—that the entity he served had some means of monitoring events in this universe and of intercepting messages, such as Omega's warning to the Alliance.

"Let us presume, Mister Cole, that the information you offer is of value to my people. Why would it be in your interest to share it?"

"For the same reason it was in our interest to cross the dimensional barrier to stop the Breen commandos from capturing one of your ships." He sat forward, folded his hands together, and rested his arms on his thighs. "It's in the best interest of the Federation to know that it has a stable and nonhostile power calling the shots on this side of the barrier. We don't want someone like the Breen or the Dominion getting hold of the kind of technology you people possess."

Saavik's suspicion manifested in the form of an elegantly raised gray eyebrow. "In that case, Mister Cole, one might wonder how your organization feels about the fact that my people possess this technology. Is it even possible for you and your masters to trust someone else?"

"We trust everyone. We just like to verify that our trust isn't being abused."

"Sensible."

"We like to think so."

She admired his restraint. It was obvious that he had omitted a crucial detail from the conversation, but he appeared content to wait for her to broach the topic.

"Let's cut to the heart of the matter, shall we? What do

you want in exchange for this allegedly valuable information about the Dominion?"

"My team and I would like to be moved out of your impending war zone, to safer ground."

"Such as?"

"Such as wherever it is that you go when you're not brokering peace treaties."

He wants access to Memory Omega. To the headquarters, Omega Prime.

She shook her head. "There are numerous neutral worlds where—"

"We'd still be vulnerable in a place like that. Especially since Captain Picard and his friends on the *ShiKahr* don't seem to be in any hurry to give us back our ship. But even if we were back on the *Królik*, we'd be at a distinct disadvantage in this universe."

"What disadvantage?"

He gestured at his confining quarters. "We'd still be pilgrims in a strange cosmos. What's the preferred euphemism? 'Stateless actors'? As long as we remain out in the open, we're people without citizenship. No matter where we go in this universe, we're legally nonpeople."

"I assure you, that is not the case within the Commonwealth. We welcome those dispossessed from other states. All who seek refuge here are protected under the law."

Cole frowned. "I'd like to trust you, but for the sake of my team, I can't take that chance. What if I sweeten the deal? My organization has all kinds of intel on the Breen, not to mention detailed files on the Delta Quadrant. If you'd be willing to bring me and my team to safe ground, we'd share all of it."

"Tempting. But I think you and your team are better situated here on the *Enterprise.*"

"Is that the last word? Is there anybody I can talk with other than you?"

She stood. "If you like, I can ask my peers if they wish to consider your proposal."

He got up as well. "Please do." He offered her his hand. "Thank you for coming."

Reluctantly, she shook his hand, but only for a moment. Then she let go and stepped back. "I will let you know what the board decides. Good day, Mister Cole."

He watched her as she left the room. She had no doubt that he was, by training and by nature, contemplating all the means by which he might escape, as well as those by which he might take her life. Knowing this did not trouble her, for one simple reason.

She had already decided how Cole was going to die.

Precision and attention to detail were essential traits in effective Jem'Hadar soldiers. Taran'atar made certain to arrive in the strategy room of Battleship 774 several minutes before the appointed hour. As not just the First but also the most senior Honored Elder, he was obliged to serve as an exemplar for his men. He had summoned his four chief lieutenants to join him there at the top of the day's seventeenth hour, as measured by the ship's chronometer.

Half a minute before the top of the hour, the door to the strategy room slid open, and his men entered in descending order of rank: Second Ankan'igar, Third Keltan'iklan, Fourth Morgul'itan, and Fifth Golgan'adar. Aboard their own vessels, among their own regiments, they each held the title of First; here, however, aboard the Founder's command ship, in Taran'atar's presence, they reverted to subordinate ranks in deference to his venerable status.

Just after they had taken their places in a line before

Taran'atar, the chronometer changed over, marking the top of the hour.

The Honored Elder welcomed them with a nod. "Let's begin." He stepped to his left and used a freestanding control console to activate a display on the bulkhead in front of his men. The first image to appear was the likeness of the human Bashir. "The Vorta Weyoun and our revered Founder have demanded that the Commonwealth extradite this man, a human physician named Julian Bashir, to stand trial for the murder of the Founder Odo." He added a second image, one of another human, an older man with a bald head. "Captain Jean-Luc Picard of the *Enterprise* has granted the fugitive Bashir asylum aboard his vessel. Consequently, he and the Galactic Commonwealth have refused our leaders' requests for custody of Bashir."

Taran'atar noted his men's intense focus on the images of the two human men. These were the gazes of soldiers memorizing the faces of future targets. "Any questions so far?"

Second Ankan'igar pointed at Bashir. "Is he still aboard the *Enterprise*?"

"All available intelligence suggests he is. The reason we are here is to develop a viable strategy for boarding the *Enterprise*, taking custody of Bashir, and returning him alive and with minimal injury to this vessel so that he can be held accountable for his crime." Taran'atar switched the image to a schematic blueprint of the deck plans for a jaunt ship. "These are an approximation of the *Enterprise*'s interior, based on sensor analysis and limited firsthand observation by covert operatives."

"Question," said Fifth Golgan'adar. "How heavily guarded is their brig?"

"Its automated defenses are formidable," Taran'atar said. "But that is of no concern. We have intercepted communications that suggest the fugitive Bashir has been confined to guest quarters, along with the rest of his associates. That should facilitate his capture and repatriation."

Third Keltan'iklan nodded at the schematics. "These plans show several suites of guest quarters. How are we to find the correct one before the ship's security forces intercept us?"

"We will go aboard shrouded and remain so while we scout the vessel. As there do not appear to be other 'compulsory guests' on the *Enterprise* at this time, we need only determine which suite is under armed guard. That will be the one containing Bashir."

A turn of Fourth Morgul'itan's head telegraphed the next question. "How are we to board the vessel? Any approach by one of our ships will cause the *Enterprise* to raise its shields before we achieve transporter range."

"The mission profile calls for us to be smuggled aboard the *Enterprise* as passengers on a shuttle carrying the Founder. We will shroud ourselves and debark the shuttle after the Founder and her Vorta entourage have departed."

Doubt crept into Second Ankan'igar's tone. "Why would they not beam over?"

"We will express reservations regarding the safety of the transporter systems on the Commonwealth's vessels. Though we were willing to beam the Founder to the surface, we will refuse to entrust her life to a hand-off between our respective systems."

The explanation did not seem to sit well with Keltan'iklan. "If they don't believe us?"

"Then we will have no choice but to board the vessel and take Bashir by force."

All the subordinates responded with nods of affirmation. Morgul'itan studied the jaunt ship's plans with keen eyes. "If the Founder or one of her Vorta could disable the *Enterprise*'s primary shield generator for just a few seconds, we could beam over." He stepped forward and tapped a point on the schematic. "If we materialize here, we could split into two groups and investigate all the guest suites in under two minutes."

"Yes, good," Golgan'adar said. "But this plan's viability depends upon the response time of the *Enterprise*'s security forces." He looked at Taran'atar. "Do we have any intel on them?"

"Not as such. However, intercepted comms suggest they were able to retake their own commandeered vessel *ShiKahr* from hostile forces in under four minutes."

A low growl of respect from Ankan'igar. "They're not amateurs, then."

Taran'atar met his second's inquisitive look. "No, they are not."

Golgan'adar was unfazed by the news. "We should always assume we face opponents who are, at the very least, our equals. Given that presumption, how do we propose to exfiltrate the prisoner Bashir alive? Can we count on the *Enterprise*'s shields staying down long enough for us to transport out once we secure him?"

"Unlikely," Keltan'iklan said. "The jaunt ships seem to have multiple redundancies built into their key systems. We might knock down the shields long enough to get aboard but not long enough to complete the search and transport back out."

"There is another concern," Morgul'itan said. "The *ShiKahr* remains in orbit with the *Enterprise*. If the crew of the *Enterprise* deduces our objective, even if they cannot raise their own shields, they could call upon the *ShiKahr* to protect them with its defensive screens."

Ankan'igar bristled. "Then we mount simultaneous assaults on both ships!"

"How?" asked Golgan'adar. "Our initial attack upon the *Enterprise* depends upon a covert strike against its defensive systems from within. If we mount an open attack on the *ShiKahr* at the same time, the result will be a full-scale engagement between our fleets."

"That's a likely consequence if our mission succeeds," Ankan'igar said. He turned toward Taran'atar. "Is that the Founder's goal? To trigger a war with the Commonwealth?"

The second's query unleashed a flood of similar questions.

Keltan'iklan asked, "Are we expendable in the name of protecting Bashir?"

"What are the Founder's orders regarding collateral damage?" asked Morgul'itan.

It was Golgan'adar who asked the question that left Taran'atar dumbstruck. "When does the Founder want us to launch the mission?"

Their attention weighed upon Taran'atar. He had been born incapable of lying to his own men. The effectiveness of the Jem'Hadar as a martial entity depended upon unbreakable unit cohesion at all levels of the command hierarchy, from the most venerated Honored Elders to the lowliest of new hatchlings waiting their turn to draw their first blood and earn their names. He did not want to tell his soldiers the truth, but he knew they would discern it from his silence.

Keltan'iklan's countenance became grave. "Who ordered the planning of this mission?"

"No one," Taran'atar said.

Dark, paranoid glances passed among his men. Ankan'igar was the first brave enough to meet Taran'atar's stare. "You launched this operation on your own initiative?"

It was imperative that Taran'atar correct his soldiers' misunderstanding. "I have not *launched* this operation. No action has been initiated. I have anticipated one possible request the Founder or her agents might make of us, and I am ensuring that if such a request comes, we will be ready to carry it out without delay. That is all, and nothing more."

Slow nods of fearful caution. Once again, the others let Ankan'igar speak for them. "We understand, First."

"That will be all for now. Dismissed."

Taran'atar faced the jaunt ship schematic as his soldiers filed out of the room. They had accepted his explanation, just as they and all of their kind had long ago been genetically programmed to do. This was the way of things, the shape of their existence.

Hidden from their sight by the closing of the strategy room's door, Taran'atar surrendered to a bitter flush of shame and self-castigation.

What was I thinking? How could I have dared to think I might know the mind of a Founder well enough to anticipate one's desires? Never has a Jem'Hadar been so arrogant!

He could only hope that none of his men had discerned his error of judgment. Because if any of them reported this irregularity in his behavior to any of their Vorta, then this first mistake born of pride would likely be Taran'atar's last.

"Come in, sit down, and start talking. And do try to get to the point. I don't have all day."

As brusque as the Taurus Pact consul's invitation was, Kersil Regon accepted it with a gracious smile and a follow-me-inside glare at Kort, who plodded into the diplomat's office. The two spies in disguise settled into the comfortable armchairs that faced Zolim Fel Tun-A's desk. Regon smiled. "It's a pleasure to see you again, Zolim. It really has been too long."

The aging Tzenkethi squinted at his two guests. Though he once had been luminous like so many other members of his species' upper echelons, his glamour had faded with time's passage. His golden hair had dulled, and his majestic complexion, which once had sparkled in the right light, now betrayed an ashy texture. Even his eyes had darkened and given up their inner light. Just as withered now was his patience. "I'm sorry, but I don't recognize you."

"Nor should you. We've had quite a bit of work done recently, and Tellus Prime was such a long time ago." A diabolical smirk lifted one corner of her mouth. "How's your knee?"

She saw that her invocation of places and events from their shared past had jogged his memory. His mild annoyance became surprise, and then it gave way to barely contained rage. "Regon." He shifted his glare to her companion. "Which means this must be Kort."

"Yes, I must be." The surgically altered Klingon looked himself over, and then he shrugged, as if to say without words, *What is one to do?* "What do you think, old friend?"

"First, I was never your friend. Second, you've looked better."

Regon harrumphed. "We could say the same." She looked around at his barren office. "Never thought I'd see you give up intelligence work." Unable to help herself, she added with a cruel note, "I guess the Autarch finally put you out to pasture, eh?

Zolim's manner grew sharper by the moment. "Last I heard, you were the one left out in the cold. A shame your masters in the Obsidian Order lacked the foresight to provide you with a retirement plan." He snickered under his breath at Kort. "Or the compassion to keep you on the payroll long after you'd outlived your usefulness."

Kort tensed to spring from his chair. Regon slapped her

hand against his chest to keep the ill-tempered old coot in his seat. "You'd be dead before you got across the desk."

The Tzenkethi steepled his long fingers. "Heed her well. She just saved your life."

"Yours as well, *petaQ*." Kort eased back into his chair.

Regon put on her most businesslike demeanor. "As much fun as it's been catching up with you, Zolim, we're here for a reason."

"What a relief. I was starting to think I'd have to kill you for nothing."

She settled back into her own chair and crossed her legs. "I presume you're aware of what's going on in orbit?"

"The great showdown? I might have caught a few details on the news."

"Well," Regon said, "how long would it take the Taurus Pact to muster a few battle fleets on either side of this fast-brewing apocalypse?"

Zolim laughed. "Why would we do that? This isn't our problem."

Kort leaned forward. "We never said it was. In fact, we think you and your allies ought to be looking at this calamity in the making as an unparalleled opportunity."

The sales pitch garnered Zolim's suspicion—but also his interest. "How so?"

"Obviously," Regon said, "the Taurus Pact has nothing to gain from going head to head against either the Common-wealth or the Dominion. But if those two titans square off, there's a good chance they'll do each other a lot of damage, especially in the sectors adjacent to this one."

Picking up the rhetorical baton, Kort continued. "Not only would the Pact be well positioned to lay claim to stra-tegically valuable planets and star systems; if you had forces here when the fighting starts, you could lay claim to the Bajoran wormhole—and seize control of all shipping and passage between here and the Gamma Quadrant."

"In other words," Zolim said, "you want my people to do your people's dirty work."

Regon shook her head. "Not at all. If done correctly, no one ever needs to know the Taurus Pact lit the fuse on this war. The Commonwealth and the Dominion will each blame the other for firing the first shot. And while they're busy wiping each other off the map, the Pact—and, yes, the Klingon Empire and the Cardassian Union—can divvy up the Commonwealth's shipping lanes and vital resources." A rakish tilt of her head. "And if we happen to find, floating amid the wreckage of their fleets, some of that secret technology they've been using to keep the rest of us running scared for the last few years . . . so much the better."

Zolim reclined his chair and pondered their proposal. "Would I be correct if I presumed the two of you had a plan in mind for how to make this happen?"

Sly looks passed between Kort and Regon. She flashed a sinister smile. "You would."

The weathered old Tzenkethi spy turned diplomat got up and walked from his desk to a small low cupboard against the wall. He opened its two front-facing doors. He removed three glasses, which he set on top of the cupboard. Then he took out a squat decanter filled with pale liquid and poured two fingers of liquor into each glass.

He handed one glass to Regon and another to Kort; he set the third on his desk. The careworn ex-spy slumped back into his chair. His face brightened as he picked up his drink and lifted it as if to toast his visitors. "Now then, my *old friends* . . . tell me *everything*."

Twenty-four

M *y mind to your mind.*

Sakonna pressed her ear and her fingertips to the bulkhead. Its insulation would prevent most sound from carrying through to the quarters in which she and the rest of the team had been confined, but her psionic talents—which the organization had honed far beyond her native gifts—could penetrate the duranium and its embedded cabling and machinery with ease.

My thoughts to your thoughts.

She felt the presence of the sentient mind on the other side of the locked door. When a pair of security officers had escorted Cole from the suite a short while earlier, Sakonna had seen a dark-haired woman standing in the corridor beside the entrance. It had been only a brief glimpse, but to her trained eye she had looked human. Her eyes had been hazel, so she had ruled out the possibility that she might be a Betazoid; full-blooded members of that telepathic species had solid black irises. She also had lacked the distinctive hairless protrusion near the temples that identified Ullians, another telepathic threat. Also absent were epidermal spotting patterns, which meant there was almost no chance Sakonna would encounter the dual mind of a joined Trill.

Open your mind. Feel my thoughts becoming your thoughts.

One by one, the layers of the young human's psychological defenses melted away. Her mind was untrained. Each new wave of suggestions from Sakonna washed over the ramparts of her psyche like a neap tide overpowering a sand castle. Surge after surge wore down the weak battlements of her unconscious, until at last her will vanished, swallowed up by the Vulcan's.

Sakonna heard the woman's thoughts echo her own: *My mind to your mind.*

Her memory became an open book to Sakonna. Her name was Bonnie Burton. She was an ensign, a graduate of the first class of cadets formally trained for service in the Commonwealth military. Her pride at being part of the vanguard of a new era in galactic history was powerful to the point of being intoxicating. The colors of her thoughts were bright and hopeful. It was almost a shame to use her so cruelly, but Sakonna had her orders.

The Vulcan withheld her thoughts from Burton. Instead, she projected an irresistible suggestion into the human woman's beautiful mind. *Unlock the door to the guest suite.*

It was almost too easy. Burton turned toward the control panel on the bulkhead by the door. She entered a security override code that she knew by virtue of rote repetition. The door's magnetic locks released, and the portal slid open.

Remain still, Sakonna directed her psionic puppet. She pushed away from the wall, stepped through the door, and walked quickly to stand beside Burton, who remained locked in place, a statue of flesh and bone. The Vulcan touched her fingertips to key neural junctions on the side of Burton's face, initiating an even deeper telepathic link. *You will stay at your post. You have seen nothing out of the ordinary. You will not remember our link.*

Burton stood, rigid and unblinking. *I will stay at my post. I have seen nothing out of the ordinary.* After reciting the first two directives, her mind turned as blank as virgin parchment.

Sakonna withdrew her hand from Burton's face and

walked away at a brisk pace. She had to reach the nearest transporter room before any other member of the ship's crew saw her outside her quarters. Voices from a short distance ahead made her duck down a side passageway. She pressed her back to the bulkhead and held her breath as two of the ship's crew, a Bolian male and a feminine Andorian (Sakonna had never been able to discern that species' multiple genders), passed by without so much as a look in her direction.

As soon as the corridor was clear, Sakonna was moving. It was fortunate that whoever had designed the Commonwealth's jaunt ships had taken pains to post informative signage and deck diagrams at regular intervals in all the main passageways. Two minutes after escaping her confinement, Sakonna reached a transporter room. She extended her psionic senses through the bulkhead and determined to her satisfaction that the compartment was unoccupied.

She hurried inside and moved to the control panel. Its interface was highly intuitive, and most of its controls were similar enough to others she had used that she was able to power up the console with ease. The target coordinates posed a more serious challenge. She had to access the *Enterprise*'s sensor network and locate its sister ship, the *ShiKahr*.

To her relief it was orbiting Bajor in close proximity to the *Enterprise*, likely as a precaution after having recently been boarded. She focused the transporter's targeting sensors on the *ShiKahr*'s main docking bay, and then she fine-tuned its coordinates to the interior of the *Królik*, which remained under guard inside the *ShiKahr*. A quick review of the transporter's sensor data confirmed there were no personnel currently inside the *Królik*. Sakonna programmed her beam-in coordinates for the interior of the *Królik*'s main fuselage and decoupled the security circuits on the transporter panel, so that it would not alert the *Enterprise*'s bridge crew of an unauthorized transporter activation. As for the *ShiKahr*, she could only hope that its crew was too distracted by its ongoing repairs and security review to notice this brief visit of hers.

Sakonna activated the dematerialization sequence on a five-second delay and hurried onto the platform. She positioned herself beneath an energizer coil and stood still as the world around her blanched to pure white and filled with melodious noise . . .

. . . and resolved instantly into the dim gray interior of the *Králik*. As soon as the annular confinement beam released its hold on her, Sakonna raced forward and opened a hidden panel in the deck. Underneath was a second panel, this one equipped with a biometric sensor. She pressed her palm against it.

"Sakonna. Clearance, tango nine four red oscar seven blue echo."

The disembodied masculine voice of the ship's computer replied, *"Confirmed."*

A *thunk* and a subtle vibration in the deck indicated the panel was now unlocked. Sakonna lifted it open. Inside were four large bundles, each just over a meter long and forty centimeters in diameter. She pulled them from the secret storage space, closed the inner panel, and waited until she heard its locks reengage. Then she closed the outer panel.

She slung a pack over each shoulder, picked up the other two by their protruding handles, and hauled them to the *Králik's* transporter room. Its interfaces roused themselves from standby mode as she entered the compartment. She walked to the transporter platform, issuing orders to the computer as she went. "Lock on to viridium tracer signals in subjects Webb and Kitsom."

"Coordinates locked."

"Set for stealth transport and beam me to those coordinates." She took her place on the platform, beneath the foremost energizer coil, facing the control console. "Energize."

Next came the quickest of flashes. Sakonna barely felt the touch of the annular confinement beam because its embrace was so brief. In the space of a breath and a blink, she was back inside the guest suite on the *Enterprise*. Webb and Kitsom jogged toward her.

"That was fast," Kitsom said as he took hold of the bundle stenciled with his name.

Webb grabbed the bundle that had been marked for him. "Nice work."

"Thank you." Sakonna tossed them the other two bundles. "Retrieve the parts and assemble the machine before Cole returns. We don't have much time."

It all had happened so quickly. Not that the swiftness of Memory Omega's response to his offer had surprised Cole in the slightest. Based on what the organization knew about them, Cole's circumstances fit Omega's documented modus operandi.

One moment he had been relaxing in the guest suite he shared with Webb, Kitsom, and Sakonna on the jaunt ship *Enterprise*; the next he had been collected by a pair of armed guards, who now delivered him to Saavik in a nearby transporter room. "The board has agreed to meet with you and hear your proposal," Saavik said. Before he could mutter so much as a thank-you, she pulled him with her onto the transporter pad and snapped, "Energize."

They disappeared into a wash of white light and a mellifluous curtain of sound, then they materialized inside a long, high-ceilinged tunnel. As soon as they were free of the transporter's confinement beam, he sensed the perfect fluidity of real gravity exerting its hold upon him. Long ago he had learned to distinguish the subtle differences between artificial gravity and the natural pull of a planet's mass. Because Bajor was the only world within the range of most starships' transporters, he deduced he was somewhere on the planet's surface.

"Follow me, Mister Cole." Saavik led him a short distance down the tunnel to a set of double doors that parted as they approached. Beyond them lay an imposing silolike chamber. In its center was a short dais surrounded by high-tech terminals, all of them manned by personnel wearing white laboratory jackets. His hostess acknowledged one of them, a male Zakdorn. "Good morning, Doctor Ropaal. My guest and I are bound for Omega Prime."

"Very good, Director. Please step onto the platform."

Saavik led Cole up a short set of stairs onto the main dais. He looked around, uncertain what he was getting himself into. "What is this?"

"A subspace transporter. For security reasons, our destination's coordinates must remain a secret." She looked at Ropaal. "Energize."

The Zakdorn worked the controls of his panel with deft movements of his long digits. A crushing force seized Cole and knocked the air from his lungs. Before he could signal anyone for help, another pulse of light and sound erased his surroundings for a moment that felt strangely elongated. His senses returned, and he found himself and Saavik in a nearly identical chamber, surrounded by different scientists wearing similar long white jackets.

The Vulcan woman stepped off the dais and beckoned Cole. "Welcome to Omega Prime, Mister Cole." He followed her out of the subspace transport chamber.

Together they moved through what Cole imagined had been designed as a labyrinth of corridors. None of the junctions or compartments were marked in any way. He was sure that someone who lacked his ability to memorize routes and minuscule details would become disoriented within a matter of minutes inside this maze. *If they think these cheap tricks are enough to confuse me, they're in for quite a surprise.*

Saavik led him to a door, which opened ahead of her. They entered a long room. Its walls and floor were dark. At the far end of the room, opposite the entrance, a holographic display was projected in front of a blank wall. A long conference table dominated the room; its surface was polished obsidian. Gathered around it, seated in high-backed chairs, were several persons, all in civilian garb. Saavik took the empty seat at the head of the table, and she motioned for Cole to take the chair to her left. "Thank you all for coming on short notice."

Her thanks were met by nods of acquiescence. Cole sat down and did his best to project calm and confidence. Once he had settled, Saavik opened the meeting. "Everyone, this is Mister Cole. A visitor from the other universe." She furrowed her brow and asked him in a confidential tone, "Forgive me—do you have a first name?"

He couldn't help but crack a wan smile. "Just Cole will suffice, Director."

"As you prefer." She went around the table, starting from her right, making introductions. The first member of the board was a female Betazoid. "This is Dannis Palancir of Betazed." Next was a Bajoran man with a receding hairline and hostile eyes. "Ruxin Ejor of Bajor." At the end of the far side of the table was an Andorian *thaan* with a warrior's hard mien. "Fallanooran th'Sirris." At the foot of the table, opposite Saavik, sat a black-maned Tellarite. "Kol jav Megh." On Megh's right was a pie-faced Bolian man of middling years. "Mister Veen." One seat closer to Cole was a burly male human. "Yoshi Dehler."

The last person to be introduced was the professorial-looking Trill woman sitting next to Cole. "And this is Inglis Arkel."

"A pleasure to meet you all," Cole said. None of the board members tensed or flinched as he reached inside his tunic and removed an isolinear data chip from an inside pocket. *Okay, so we know they're not jumpy. Maybe they're overconfident.* He held up the data chip. "This contains several hundred gigaquads of classified intelligence my employers have gathered over the past decade regarding such powers as the Dominion, the Breen Confederacy, and the Tzenkethi Coalition. Although there are bound to be differences between them and their counterparts in this universe, I think that you'll find enough of value in these documents to—"

"How did he bring that here?" asked Palancir.

Saavik arched her brow at the Betazoid. "I warned you he was resourceful."

"Never mind how I got it here." Cole slid the chip across the table to Palancir. "I'm giving it to you. No questions asked. As a show of good faith."

His gift was received with incredulity. Ruxin snorted derisively. "Good faith?"

Palancir picked up the chip. "It does seem . . . unlikely."

"Everything we know about the Breen's mission to steal one of your jaunt ships is on that chip. Along with all the data we collected on their dimension-breaching technology, and intel on the new Romulan-made cloaking devices they're using."

Megh leaned forward to get a clear look at Cole. "Nothing of value is ever given freely. What are you hoping to obtain, Mister Cole?"

"Your trust. And your help. I was sent here with two missions. The first was to stop the Breen from acquiring your jaunt ship technology. The second was to open a direct line of communication between your organization and mine. Call

it a back channel between our universes. Our goal is to safeguard the Federation at all costs. And unless we're mistaken,
your mission is to do the same for the Commonwealth. We
both benefit by having each other's back."

The mood in the room turned cold and suspicious. Cole
had known this might be a hard sell, but until that moment he
hadn't realized just how much resistance he would face from
the puppetmasters who pulled the Commonwealth's strings.

It was th'Sirris who broke the silence. "Why should events
in your universe concern us?"

"They already do. The Breen are here, and they're a threat.
And they won't be the last."

The Andorian remained unconvinced. "And why should
the events of our universe be of any consequence to yours?"

"Because if you people can't keep your technology under
wraps, your carelessness might cost trillions of lives in my
universe—and destroy the Federation I've sworn to protect."

Grim looks were volleyed around the table until Saavik
abruptly halted the meeting. "We'll take your advice under
consideration, Mister Cole. But until we reach a decision, I
fear the time has come for me to escort you back to your confinement on the *Enterprise.*"

Silence and suspicion defined Cole's chaperoned return from
Omega Prime. From the moment Saavik had ended his meeting with her peers, she had not spoken to him except to dole
out curt directions: "This way." "Turn left." "Stay in front of me."
They had returned to Bajor via the subspace transporter and
then had beamed back up to the *Enterprise.* The old Vulcan
woman led him to his quarters and nodded at the female security officer guarding the door. With simple, quiet efficiency, the
human woman unlocked the door to the guest suite.

Saavik ushered Cole back inside his gilded cage. "I will

inform you when the board reaches a decision. Until then, make yourself comfortable."

"Too kind." He met her stare and extended his hand. She shook it, feigning politeness, but she was visibly uncomfortable with the tactile nature of the gesture. Cole stepped through the doorway, which Saavik closed and locked behind him as soon as he had cleared its threshold.

Sakonna, Webb, and Kitsom emerged from the private sleeping quarters situated off either side of the suite's main room. The men wore hopeful expressions.

Cole let slip the slightest glimmer of self-satisfaction.

With the merest lift of an eyebrow, the Vulcan woman prompted him to elaborate.

"It went well." He moved toward the middle of the main room, and the others met him there. Sakonna opened her clenched left hand to reveal a privacy module: the tiny device enveloped the four of them in a cone of silence augmented by spoofed sound waves. Anyone eavesdropping, either by ear or by device, would hear a sanitized version of their conversation, one devoted to the most mundane topics: dinner, sleep schedules, and a host of petty complaints about minor maladies and inconsequential inconveniences.

The four agents huddled. "Since you have that," Cole said, "I presume you made it safely back aboard the *Králik*."

"I did. All the gear we set aside is stowed in our private rooms."

"Did you meet any resistance?"

"None." Her eyes shifted toward the door. "The woman guarding our door is an open book to me now. We can make her do whatever we need of her."

Cole nodded. "Outstanding." He pried open the lids of his left eye and with his right index finger gingerly removed one of the high-tech contact lenses he had been wearing since before the team's capture by the Breen. He passed the first lens from his fingertip to Sakonna's, and then with gentle care he removed the second lens from his other eye and passed it to her in the same manner. "I got detailed scans of the entire route through their facility on the planet, and their headquarters facility. I'm pretty sure I also got a look at a few screens in the distance that had base schematics. Look those up and magnify them. They should help us locate the target."

Webb activated a tiny encrypted-signal receiver; it resembled a stylus with a data port on one end. "I'm downloading the data from your transceivers now. Signals look good."

The transceivers were tiny subdural implants, each half the size of a grain of rice. They were implanted behind Cole's ears and had circuits that made them register on most scanning devices as benign nodules of fatty tissue. In fact, they were extremely sophisticated devices; one recorded with perfect fidelity every sound Cole heard. It could store several months of audio data. The other scanned and recorded each new genetic profile it detected.

A red progress light crept across the receiver's side. When it turned green, Cole switched off the device. "Done."

"Pull up Saavik's voiceprint first, then get a transcript of her orders." He extended the back of his hand toward Kitsom. "Are Saavik's fingerprints legible?"

The serious-faced young man scanned Cole's hand with a miniaturized tricorder. "Yes."

"Webb, how long until Sakonna's prosthetics are ready?"

He thought it over. "Five hours. I need time to set up the fabricator and mask its energy signature from the ship's sensors. Once it's ready, we can program a voice patch and configure a sensor-spoofing transceiver that'll mask Sakonna's genetic profile with Saavik's."

Kitsom nodded. "As long as you got a straight look into

Saavik's eyes, we can copy her retinal patterns." He glanced at his tricorder's display. "And we have all the prints for Saavik's right hand. As long as no one asks Sakonna for a blood sample, she ought to be golden."

Cole nodded. "From what I've seen, they all defer to Saavik, regardless of rank."

Webb asked, "How 'bout snagging some of those Memory Omega stealth suits for us?"

"My new puppet will provide them," Sakonna said. "She knows the location of the ship's armory and has a high enough clearance code to gain access. When we're ready to deploy, I'll send her to retrieve three of their stealth suits. She'll hand them over when she unlocks our door. Then we can all walk out together and not have to fear being accosted by the ship's crew."

"Sounds like a plan," Cole said. "Let's get this new intel analyzed on the double. Every second we shave off this op gets us one second closer to going home."

Twenty-five

Drawn from his ready room by the whooping of the Red Alert siren, Captain Picard stepped onto the bridge of the *Enterprise* expecting to face a worst-case scenario. He was not disappointed.

K'Ehleyr met Picard in the middle of the bridge. "Long-range sensors have picked up three battle fleets converging on our position from separate vectors."

"Whose fleets, Number One?"

She nodded toward the main viewscreen. "Tholia's Third and Fourth fleets, bearing one-nine-seven. The Breen Confederacy's Seventh Fleet on bearing three-five-three. And the Tzenkethi Coalition's Gold Fleet, bearing one-five-five." The lanky half Klingon frowned. "All are en route at maximum warp. They all have the same ETA, five hours and nine minutes."

Picard frowned. "A coordinated assault." He tried to make sense of it. "Why is the Taurus Pact taking such an aggressive stance? We've done nothing to provoke them."

"Not directly," K'Ehleyr said. "Not recently, anyway."

Troi spoke up from behind them. "They're capitalizing on our standoff with the Dominion. Apparently, the Taurus Pact believes hostilities between us are imminent."

"They aren't the only ones," K'Ehleyr grumbled.

Ignoring his first officer's cynicism, Picard asked Troi, "To what end?"

"If I had to guess? I'd say they hope to land forces on

Bajor, and perhaps attempt to salvage the wreckage of our ships and the Jem'Hadar's for new technologies."

Confronted with such base motives, all Picard could do was scowl and clench his teeth. "Send an encrypted request for reinforcements."

K'Ehleyr recoiled in mild surprise. "Really? We already have nearly half the fleet here."

"I'm prepared to face a single hostile force that has a five-fold advantage in numbers," Picard said. "But we can't prevail against a four-front attack outnumbered twenty-five to one."

"Aren't you always telling me 'pessimism is a misuse of imagination'?"

"You must have me confused with someone else."

Troi interrupted, "We're being hailed by the Dominion command ship."

That can't be good. Picard turned and faced forward. "On-screen."

The image of the Dominion warship orbiting behind the *Enterprise* was replaced by the fearsome visage of Taran'atar. *"We have detected three battle groups converging on this star system."*

"As have we," Picard began, only to be cut off.

"They will not arrive in time to save your fleet."

"I doubt they have any intention of doing so," Picard said. "Those vessels belong to a political alliance known as the Taurus Pact. They are not our allies—nor are they yours."

Taran'atar narrowed his eyes, as if doing so would enable him to pierce some imagined veil of lies. He sounded almost insulted. *"The Jem'Hadar have no need of allies."*

Picard had no idea how to overcome the Jem'Hadar's innate distrust. "You're missing my point. The inbound attack groups have no wish to engage in battle. Their true aim is to push us closer to violence and then feast upon the scraps of whatever our two forces leave behind."

"*Then they act in vain. Because when our battle is done, we will leave no trace of you or your precious technology. You have one hour to hand over the fugitive Bashir. If you refuse, we will take him by force—and destroy you in the process.*"

The transmission ended, terminated from the Jem'Hadar's side. The image on the screen reverted to the threatening profile of the hulking Dominion battleship.

Already exhausted, Picard settled into his command chair with a heavy sigh.

So much for diplomacy.

The news was not unexpected, but it sank Bashir's spirits all the same. "An hour?"

"Less than that now," Picard said. He stood in front of Bashir and Sarina, who sat together on the sofa, their hands entwined. "We have just under forty-nine minutes until the Dominion makes this a contest of arms rather than one of ideas."

Bashir absorbed that with a slow nod. "And the Taurus Pact?"

"Poised to make the most of our diplomatic failure. If this goes as badly as I fear, we could lose more than half the Commonwealth's fleet—as well as Bajor."

The notion of seeing another Bajor fall beneath the jackboot of an alien occupation made Bashir sick. "This has gotten out of hand."

"I quite agree," Picard said. "It feels as if the vultures are circling." He had the demeanor of a man defeated. "This was to be a peace summit. A negotiation for trade and exploration." He looked away, out a view port, at the stars. "All lost because neither side wants to compromise its principles.

Theirs are too old, too entrenched. Ours are too new, too fragile."

Sarina turned her pleading gaze toward the captain. "What if we found a way back to our universe? If we go away, the problem goes away, right?"

Picard shook his head. "It's not so simple. At this point, there is almost no way you can return to your universe without our help. In which case, I, my crew, and the Commonwealth as a whole would be complicit in aiding your flight from the Dominion. Your disappearance now would provide just as much of a pretext for war as the crisis we already have."

"He's right," Bashir said to Sarina. "Running away won't solve this. If anything, it'll make it worse." He looked at Picard. "I think there's only one solution to this problem."

"I can't ask you to do that, Doctor."

"No one has to ask. I should never have put you, or your crew, or your people in this predicament at all. I caused this. It's my duty to resolve it."

Sarina grabbed him by the front of his shirt. "Julian! You *can't* be serious."

Bashir let go of Sarina's hand. "I can't let two civilizations go to war when I have the power to prevent it. I won't let billions die just to preserve the chance that I might be spared." He stood and shook Picard's hand. "Thank you, Captain, for everything you and your crew have done. I'm in your debt. But effective immediately, I formally withdraw my request for asylum, and I ask that you convey the following message to the Founder." He swallowed hard and mustered his courage to say what needed to be said.

"Please tell her . . . I surrender."

Twenty-six

The waiting was the worst part. Bashir knew it would take time for his message to wend its way through the appropriate channels, but as the minutes dragged past he was living in slow time.

One immediate consequence of his surrender was that he had been separated from Sarina, escorted out of the guest quarters by armed security personnel and locked in the *Enterprise*'s brig. Captain Picard had assured him the change was only a formality, a matter of protocol and not a judgment on the merits of the Dominion's accusations. Bashir wanted to believe him, but it was difficult to hang on to hope in the gray isolation of solitary confinement.

The door to his private section of the brig slid open. He expected to see a phalanx of armed Jem'Hadar, and perhaps a Vorta, come to haul him away to a sham tribunal.

A single person entered and stood on the other side of his cell's force field. Bashir stood and faced her. "Director Saavik, I presume?"

The old Vulcan confirmed his guess with a bow of her head. She eyed him like a biologist studying a lab specimen. "Captain Picard says you wish to surrender to the Dominion."

Bashir nodded. "That's right."

"A noble decision, Doctor, but an unnecessary one."

He was taken aback by her coldness. "I disagree. Countless lives are at stake."

"Including your own. You will be safer with our protection than without it."

"But at what cost? Never mind the price in lives. As a matter of principle—"

"You're acting illogically, Doctor." Her eyes followed him as he began to pace the short length of his cell. "As formidable as the Jem'Hadar fleet is, Memory Omega has the power to obliterate them—and the Dominion they serve. I won't deny that the Commonwealth will suffer casualties, but our losses will be negligible compared with the Dominion's. So why give yourself up to them when our strength supports your asylum?"

He stopped pacing and faced her. "Because this isn't about strength. Justice isn't decided by power. It isn't born through the force of arms. It comes from people of conscience taking responsibility for their own lives—and accepting the consequences of their actions." He saw in Saavik's empty stare that she didn't understand his point. "I don't care who prevails in your fight with the Dominion, or with the Taurus Pact. I don't care who suffers the most casualties. What I care about is the fact that *anyone* is being asked to suffer or die *because of me*."

Saavik pondered his argument in silence for a few seconds. "We could facilitate your return to your universe and tell the Dominion you escaped."

Bashir let slip a derisive huff. "You really think they'd believe that? I know I wouldn't. But even if you could persuade them that I'd eluded you, they might still hold you accountable. The same carnage would unfold, regardless of my absence." An unpleasant truth nagged at him. "I think we also need to consider that the Dominion might be in the right on this."

A confused look. "How so?"

"Weyoun and the Founder have a sound basis for legal jurisdiction."

"Then why did you request asylum?"

He found it hard to meet Saavik's stern gaze, so he looked at his feet instead. "Because I was afraid. I'm ashamed to admit it, but it's the truth." With effort, he looked her in the eye. "Captain Picard encouraged me to ask for asylum, and I reacted out of fear."

"Fear of what, precisely?"

"That I won't receive a fair trial at the hands of the Dominion. That I'll be standing accused in a culture that still employs the death penalty. That they might not consider my plea of self-preservation a legitimate defense."

She frowned. "Given the circumstances, those are reasonable concerns."

"Maybe. But they're not enough to justify letting millions, or possibly billions, of sentient beings die just so I can walk away." He sighed and shook his head. "I'd rather stand alone before a court of harsh justice than live with knowing I'd allowed so many to suffer and perish because I lacked the courage to account for my own actions."

Saavik nodded slowly. "Thank you for your honesty, Doctor. It seems to be an increasingly rare commodity in these dark times."

"You're wel—" His answer caught in his throat as he watched Saavik shimmer and liquefy. The craggy lines and weathered details of her face melted away, and her dark gray robes fused with her body, until she was a radiant form of golden fluid. It was a phenomenon Bashir had witnessed many times before: the transmogrification of a Changeling. When the transmutation was complete, he found himself facing the Founder.

She turned toward a small panel mounted on the bulkhead beside her. "Come in, please."

The door behind her opened. Captain Picard entered,

followed by the real Saavik, Weyoun, and Taran'atar. It gave Bashir a jolt of déjà vu to see the Jem'Hadar again after all these years and to realize this was not the being he had known on Deep Space 9 but an even older and more experienced creature, one tempered by a very different life in this universe.

The Founder looked at Saavik and Picard. "I am satisfied with the sincerity of Doctor Bashir's answers. Are you satisfied, as well?"

Picard and Saavik gave nods of concurrence. The captain regarded Bashir with a bittersweet countenance. "I have no doubt of Doctor Bashir's honorable intentions."

"Nor do I," Saavik added.

The Founder looked at Bashir. "Doctor, do you still wish to surrender to our custody?"

"I do."

Picard turned off the force field. Taran'atar handed Weyoun a pair of magnetic manacles. Bashir stepped forward and offered his outstretched hands. The Vorta clamped the manacles around Bashir's wrists. The metal rings closed with a low *clack*. They were cold against his flesh. "Doctor Bashir," Weyoun said, "I arrest you for the killing of the Founder known as Odo." He faced Taran'atar. "Escort Doctor Bashir back to our command ship."

Taran'atar seized Bashir by his shoulder. The Jem'Hadar's grip was tight enough that Bashir knew it would leave a bruise.

As Bashir was led out of the brig, Picard whispered to him in passing, "*Bon chance.*"

In the corridor, a trio of Jem'Hadar soldiers fell into step around Bashir, grim escorts for what he expected to be the last journey of his life. Following them to his fate, he felt his fear fall away, along with his hope. All that remained was the cold comfort of knowing he had done what he knew to be right. If this sacrifice was to be his last measure of devotion to the Hippocratic Oath, it was a burden he was proud to accept.

I've made my mistakes. Committed my sins of action and omission. But whatever else history might tell of me . . . at least now it can say I deserved to be called a doctor.

There was barely time for Bashir to glimpse the stark, empty passageway on the other side of the doorway as the Jem'Hadar soldiers pushed him into it. As soon as he had cleared its threshold, the door behind him snapped shut with a hiss and bang, plunging the narrow passage into darkness. The only light was a crimson glow cast upon the door at the far end. His instructions from Taran'atar had been simple and clear: "Walk to the far door and, when it opens, step through it to the other side."

His footsteps echoed in the pitch-black confines. He reached the far door and stood before it, wondering how long it would take to open. No one had told him what to expect on the other side. He didn't dare to imagine it for himself.

The door opened.

A narrow walkway stretched away in front of Bashir and led to a small disk-shaped platform suspended in a starless sea of black. The edges of the path were demarcated by pale yellow lines that shone with the soft glow of fluorescent chemicals. The Founder's voice resounded in the yawning emptiness that surrounded the widow's walk. "Enter, Julian Bashir."

He crossed the narrow bridge to the circular platform. When he turned to look back, he no longer saw the door through which he had entered—nor any sign of the walkway. He was alone on a tiny island of firmament in the void.

Again, the Founder's voice filled the formless darkness. "State your full name."

"Doctor Julian Subatoi Bashir."

"Do you know the crimes of which you stand accused before this tribunal?"

He had come willingly, but that didn't mean he had to make this easy for them. "Why don't you enlighten me?"

"You are accused of causing the wrongful death of the Founder known as Odo. Before we review the evidence, do you wish to confess to your crimes?"

"No, I do not."

"Very well. Weyoun, please present the prosecution's opening statement."

A dim light came to life somewhere high above Bashir, on his right. The Vorta sycophant Weyoun stood upon a small, low-walled balcony. He was lit from below, giving his features a sinister cast, and his voice was amplified to the point where its sonic force hurt Bashir's teeth.

"Fifteen years and twenty-two days ago—as measured in the standard calendar of the native culture of the accused—Doctor Julian Subatoi Bashir was a guest aboard the Klingon-Cardassian ore refinery Terok—"

"Guest? I was a prisoner!"

"Silence!" bellowed the Founder. "Continue with the charges, Weyoun."

The Vorta collected himself and picked up from midsentence. ". . . the Klingon-Cardassian ore refinery Terok Nor. During his sojourn on the station, he was employed—"

"Enslaved," Bashir muttered.

"—as an ore processor's assistant. During an emergency evacuation of the refinery level, Doctor Bashir stole a sidearm from one of the station's Bajoran security personnel and used it to maliciously slay the Founder Odo." He bowed his head. "With your permission, Founder, I shall now present evidence, in the form of firsthand witness testimony and an archived security recording of the killing."

"Proceed."

"My first witness is a fellow worker who was there during the evacuation." Weyoun looked up. Bashir followed the Vorta's eye line to a higher balcony that lit up to showcase a middle-aged Trill man. "Please state your full name, sir."

"Vallo Lorom."

"Mister Lorom, were you serving in the same section of the refinery as Doctor Bashir on the day and at the time the emergency evacuation occurred?"

The Trill looked around, his mien wary and fearful. "I was."

"Did you see the accused, Doctor Julian Bashir, there at that time?"

"I did."

"And did you witness his actions during the evacuation?"

A reluctant nod. His verbal answer was inaudible.

Weyoun snapped, "Please speak up, Mister Lorom. For the record."

Lorom seemed to resent being barked at. "Yes. I saw him during the evacuation."

"Did he arm himself at any point?"

"Yes. He took a disruptor from one of the guards."

That answer brightened Weyoun's mood. "Did you see Doctor Bashir use that disruptor during the evacuation?"

"Yes. He shot Odo."

"I'm sorry, could you repeat that please? A bit louder?"

The witness raised his voice and stared daggers at Weyoun. "He shot Odo."

"Thank you, Mister Lorom."

Weyoun's key light dimmed, and another brightened,

opposite him. Bashir's eyes adjusted to discern the fine grada-
tions of shadow that surrounded him. He began to see that
he was in a cylindrical chamber a few dozen meters in diameter and several dozen meters tall. When the light opposite
Weyoun achieved full brightness, Bashir saw a female Vorta
standing on a balcony. The Founder's voice announced, "Eris
shall stand in defense of the accused."

"Thank you, Founder." Eris looked up at the witness.
"Mister Lorom, how did you come to be employed on the
ore-processing level of Terok Nor?"

"I was arrested on suspicion of terrorist action against the
Klingon-Cardassian Alliance."

"Would you say your employment in the refinery was
voluntary or coerced?"

Lorom seethed. "I was led to work every morning at gun-
point, and taken back to my cell each night the same way. You
can call that coerced, if you like. I call it slavery."

Weyoun cut in, "Objection! Relevance?"

"All will be revealed in time," Eris said. "But I'm prepared
to move on." She looked back at the witness. "Mister Lorom.
You say that you saw Doctor Bashir kill Overseer Odo. When
the incident occurred, where were you, exactly?"

"He was in front of me on the way to the exit. An arm's
length away, if that far. If I hadn't ducked, he might have
shot *me*."

"So you were facing Doctor Bashir, and you had an unobstructed view of him?"

"That's right."

"And at the time Doctor Bashir fired the shot that killed
Odo, were you facing Odo?"

"No, he was behind me."

"Thank you, Mister Lorom." Eris looked up into the darkness. "Nothing further."

The light shining up at Lorom went dark, stealing him from sight. Eris's light dimmed, cloaking her in shadows as Weyoun's light returned to full strength.

Weyoun pivoted toward a lower balcony and a new witness, an athletic Bajoran man. Unlike the first witness, this one had a proud and wrathful quality to his bearing. More alarming to Bashir, he knew this man's counterpart in his own universe, but until now he hadn't realized this was one of the souls he had encountered during his previous visit to this universe.

The Vorta smiled at the witness. "Please state your name."

"Major Cenn Desca."

"Major Cenn, were you present when Overseer Odo was killed?"

"I was." Simple words, but Cenn had infused them with great anger.

"In your own words, please tell us what happened that day."

Cenn stole a hateful look at Bashir, then directed his answer to Weyoun. "I was a junior deputy with the Bajoran security force on Terok Nor. Odo was my supervisor. On the day he was killed, I was standing guard on the ore-processing level. I saw Odo talking with one of the workers"—he pointed at Bashir—"that man, Julian Bashir. Then there was an explosion and an alarm. Odo said it was a thorium leak. He ordered us to open the security doors and evacuate the level. I was helping workers toward the exit when someone hit me—first in the gut, then on the back, just below my neck. By the time I knew what had happened, Bashir had taken my sidearm from its holster. He moved toward the exit with the other prisoners. Just before he reached the exit, he stopped, aimed, and fired at Odo. That one shot destroyed Odo. He just . . . *exploded*. There was nothing any of us could do to help him."

Weyoun absorbed the testimony with a sympathetic expression. "Thank you, Major." He shot an insincere smile at Eris. "Your witness." His light faded as hers came up.

Eris squinted at Cenn. "Major, did you pursue Bashir as he moved toward the exit?"

"I tried, but he warned me off by waving my disruptor at me."

"So you kept your distance?"

He nodded. "Yes."

"Did you at any point turn your back on him?"

"While he was holding a deadly weapon? Of course not."

"So at the moment when Doctor Bashir aimed and fired his weapon, your back was to Overseer Odo—wasn't it?"

Cenn blinked as if he had been struck. He was slow to answer. "I . . . yes. It was."

"Nothing further," Eris said.

Her balcony light dimmed again, returning the illumination and focus to Weyoun. He folded his hands in front of him. "With your indulgence, Founder, I should like to enter into evidence a composite holographic re-creation of the death of Odo, compiled from numerous recordings made by Terok Nor's own security system and recovered from the Central Data Archive on Bajor. The master archivist herself has vouched for the accuracy of this record."

"You may proceed."

Suspended in the darkness before Bashir was a scene from his memory, resurrected in three dimensions and living color. He could almost smell the acrid tang of toxic fumes, feel the heat of the smelting furnaces and the smoke that had stung his eyes, and taste the bitter metallic dust that had coated every surface inside Terok Nor's grimy refinery level. Spectres in filthy rags slouched from one backbreaking bit of tedium to the next. The hiss of old hydraulics and the steady rumbling of heavy machinery filled his ears.

In the forefront of this shadowy tableau, Bashir's past came to life. He saw the image of his younger self, clean-shaven but smeared with filth, sitting hunched and facedown over an ore bin. Overseer Odo kicked the bone-weary, half-conscious younger Bashir in the back, a rude awakening. The Changeling's words were slow and heavy with contempt. "You're not accustomed to this workload, are you, *Doctor*? You have much to learn. It's a shame this is going to be your *last* night on the job."

A blast lit up the smoky darkness behind Odo, who tapped his combadge. "Engineering! We have a thorium leak down here!" He pointed toward the exits. "Release the security locks!"

Workers fled toward the exit, and Bashir's younger self seized the opportunity to retreat with them, making a run for cover and for freedom. He struck a few fast surprise blows to a Bajoran guard who blocked his path and plucked the disruptor from the man's hip holster. Weapon in hand, the bruised and beaten-down physician backpedaled toward the exit.

Odo pivoted and saw the doctor on the verge of escape. Wide-eyed, the Changeling aimed his already drawn sidearm at Bashir, who fired off a reflexive snap shot that struck Odo in the chest—and blasted him to pieces.

The playback froze, suspending Odo's explosively ejected viscera in midseparation.

Weyoun spread his arms, like an old-time preacher delivering a sermon. "Could it be any clearer, Founder? A cowardly sneak attack upon a guard, and a single lethal shot delivered so expertly that its victim never had the chance to respond."

Indignation creased Eris's fair brow. "Did we just watch the same security vid? Because if we did, Weyoun, I think you must have had your eyes closed. Reset to time reference thirty-four thirteen point two, please." The hologram reverted to an earlier moment in the recording. Eris crossed her arms. "Pay close attention, please. Resume playback."

Odo sneered at young Bashir. "It's a shame this is going to be your *last* night on the job."

"Freeze playback," Eris snapped. "Here we have a clear threat by Odo. There is nothing in the record to indicate that Bashir was being considered for release from custody. The most reasonable inference from Odo's statement is that he intended to kill Bashir imminently." She nodded at the hologram. "Reset to time reference thirty-four forty-seven point five."

Younger Bashir was crouched and backing toward the exit with his stolen disruptor in hand. On the other side of the refinery level, Odo pivoted and saw him—and aimed his own weapon at Bashir.

"Freeze," Eris said. "Note the relative positions of Odo, Doctor Bashir, Mister Lorom, and Deputy Cenn. Odo has aimed his weapon at Bashir but appears to have been momentarily blinded by smoke. Lorom and Cenn are both facing Bashir and have their backs to Odo. Neither can see that Odo has already trained his deadly armament upon Doctor Bashir. Note also that the doctor's weapon is not aimed at anyone in particular." She shot a meaningful look at Weyoun. "Odo was the first to act with deadly intention, after having threatened Bashir's life. I contend that Doctor Bashir acted justifiably, in self-defense."

No one spoke for a handful of seconds that felt to Bashir like a lifetime.

Then the Founder rendered her verdict.

"The evidence supports the defense's argument that Doctor Julian Subatoi Bashir acted in self-defense. Consequently, this court finds him not guilty of criminal culpability in the death of Odo. Doctor Bashir . . . you are free to go."

Twenty-seven

Even after hearing the verdict, Bashir found it difficult to believe. He had spent so long convincing himself that he would find no justice under the auspices of the Dominion that it struck him as nothing short of surreal now that he finally had.

The catwalk he had crossed to the circular platform reappeared, as did the door at its far end. He crossed the narrow bridge, and the door slid aside as he drew near. The cramped passageway on the other side now was brightly lit, and the door at the other end also was open. He emerged into a regular corridor inside the Dominion command ship and found Taran'atar waiting for him. The Jem'Hadar removed Bashir's manacles. "Follow me."

Bashir trailed him down the corridor to a nearby turbolift. As soon as they both were inside, the doors closed and the lift hurtled into motion, suggesting that their destination had been decided in advance. Half a minute later the doors opened, and Taran'atar led Bashir out of the lift, down another long corridor, and finally to a door that stood open. "In here."

He stepped past the Jem'Hadar and through the doorway to find an empty compartment. Standing in the center of the antiseptically bare space was the Founder. A faint smile gave a small measure of humanity to her unnaturally smooth face. She looked over Bashir's shoulder at the Jem'Hadar, her demeanor one of absolute calm. "Leave us."

Taran'atar withdrew. The door closed, leaving Bashir and

the Founder to speak in privacy. She folded her hands in front of her waist. "You seemed surprised to be acquitted. Did you doubt your own innocence?"

"Not at all. I doubted it would matter."

His criticism amused her. "You know nothing of us, but you hold us in low esteem."

"I've had a great many unpleasant dealings with your counterparts in my universe."

"Some would have said the same about your alter ego in this one. When we first investigated Odo's death, we mistakenly attributed your actions to this universe's Bashir. He was despicable, simple, and violent." She cocked her head and regarded Bashir with deep curiosity. "I've been pleased to learn just how little you and he have in common."

He held up a hand. "Wait. What evidence led you to investigate him?"

"The archived security recordings."

His mind reeled, and his temper flared. "You'd *seen* it before?"

"Naturally."

"So you knew all along that I'd acted in self-defense."

"That was our impression."

His hands curled into fists. "Then what was the point of all this? Why make me take part in this bloody sideshow attraction if you already knew the truth?"

"To my people, the law is not some mere code. It is a *way of life*. Order must be preserved. So we investigate and adjudicate *all* offenses, even when we think the verdict will be benign, and we follow our protocols without fear or favor. No one is above the law in the Dominion, not even a Founder. Because our laws are fair, and our enforcement uniform, we are able to keep the peace among all the worlds and peoples who live beneath our banner."

Bashir began to understand. To an outsider, the Dominion in the alternate universe might seem as severe in its customs and manners as the one he knew at home, but there was a crucial difference between the two entities. "Forgive me," he said. "I should have known better than to judge you based on your counterpart. Your similarities are outweighed by your differences."

"I presume the Dominion you knew lacked our reverence for the law."

He let slip a short, mirthless chortle. "That would be an understatement. They shared your commitment to order and discipline, but their means of preserving those qualities were often tyrannical and quite brutal. What led them into conflict with my people was the fact that what they desired more than anything was control—over their own people, and over others."

The Founder's smooth forehead betrayed a crease of concern, and the corners of her mouth turned downward in disapproval. "They sound like a culture driven by fear."

"Very much so. Their early interactions with 'solids' went badly. They were met with fear and distrust. So they retaliated in kind. And it defined them from that moment forward."

"How tragic," the Founder said. "My people were also met with suspicion when we first encountered solids. Some of them tried to kill us. But we never desired retribution or control. Our only interest—then and now—was justice, coupled with order and tempered with reason."

Bashir smiled. "Actually, that sounds a lot like the Odo I know back home."

"Is he still alive in your universe?"

"As far as I know. After the war against our Dominion, he returned to the Great Link to shape a new order based on peace and justice. As of last year, he was leading the Dominion."

"Tell me about him. What kind of a person is he?"

"He's the most fair-minded being I've ever met, and the most passionate defender of the law I've ever known. And he sees all sentient beings as equals." Hearing his own words made Bashir realize how much he had missed Odo during his prolonged absence. "He's a great man."

The Founder's mood took a wistful turn. "One almost has to wonder whether our universes might have traded Odos at some point."

"It wouldn't surprise me," Bashir said without irony. "Not one bit."

Twenty-eight

No matter how many times Sakonna put on another person's face, she never got used to seeing a stranger's reflection looking back at her.

She walked the corridors of the jaunt ship *Enterprise*. In nearly every section, an interactive companel dominated one bulkhead. Between the panels' ever-changing details, she caught fleeting glimpses of herself in their pristine black surfaces. Her disguise was impeccable. Her head and her hands were encased in full prosthetics, and Webb had programmed one of the ship's replicators to produce a perfect duplicate of the attire the real Saavik had worn that day. Fitted to her as a second skin, her stolen visage mirrored even her most subtle microexpressions.

A few *Enterprise* personnel passed her. Enlisted crew and noncoms avoided eye contact with her. The one officer who strolled by, a young male Tellarite with a honey-colored mane, managed nothing more than a low utterance of "Director" before quickening his pace to get away. To an introvert like Sakonna, it was a welcome state of affairs.

Once again, proof that rank has its privileges.

By design, there was no evidence of her three companions, but she had no doubt they were close behind her. Sakonna had found it easier than she had expected to telepathically compel security officer Burton to procure the stealth suits for her friends. Now, thanks to the human woman's unwitting assistance, Webb, Kitsom, and Cole had the advantage of being invisible while they followed Sakonna through the jaunt ship's passageways en route to the first stop on their perilous and improbable journey: the ship's subspace transporter.

Sakonna had found the restricted compartment while using one of the ship's companels to find the locations of the nearest five transporters, in case she or the others were forced to alter their route for any reason. Although Saavik had beamed down to the planet and used a subspace transporter on the surface for the trip to Omega Prime, finding the same technology aboard the jaunt ship had made it possible for Sakonna and her teammates to cut one step off their itinerary.

The subspace transporter compartment was slightly farther away than the nearest regular transporter room, but Cole had assured Sakonna and the others that it would be worth it to make the most of this shortcut. Now that Sakonna was approaching the door, she saw the logic in her superior's decision. Despite a minor increase in the risk of their absence being detected while they were still aboard the *Enterprise*, they now would be able to head straight to their target—and from there they could proceed home without delay.

Eager to stave off unwelcome inquiries, she put on a stern mien as the door opened ahead of her. She paused in the doorway to make sure her team had time to follow her through before the portal closed—its sensors would be unable to detect them while they were hidden in the full-body stealth suits, and she couldn't risk them being stranded on the other side.

While she stood in the doorway, the half dozen white-jacketed technicians who worked in the vast compartment looked up at her with alarm and deference. One of them, a spry sixtyish Trill woman with silver hair and beige spots on her pale skin, stepped away from the master console to greet her. "Director. We weren't expecting you."

A light tap on Sakonna's lower back told her that her team was ready to follow her inside. She stepped past the threshold and moved to her left, on a direct line toward the Trill woman. "I need to return to Omega Prime at once."

"Omega Prime?" The Trill traded worried looks with her colleagues. "That'll take a lot of power. The relay station on Bajor would be better suited to—"

"Time is a factor. I need to go now. Please set the coordinates." Without waiting for the Trill to demur, Sakonna played her part as the one in charge and climbed the short steps onto the central dais. She stood proudly while the techs in their white coats raced to set the coordinates and siphon the requisite power from the ship.

One of them, an orange-haired young human, whispered something to the Bajoran woman on his right; she, in turn, leaned and whispered to the Trill woman in charge. Eyes wide, the older woman looked up at the visitor she thought was Saavik. "Director . . . can you confirm your authorization code, please?"

Sakonna had known it might not be so easy to escape the ship by impersonating such a well-known individual. Regardless, she remained calm as she asked, "Are the coordinates set?"

"Yes, but we'd like to confirm your command code, please."

"Is there a problem?"

Furtive glances and worried frowns spread among the technicians. The Trill began to reach toward the corner of her master control console. Then she froze and her eyes opened wide.

Webb's voice issued as if from thin air. "Everyone, step away from your consoles." He deactivated the stealth function of his body suit and shimmered back into view—standing behind the Trill woman and holding a phaser to the back of her head. "Back away from your panels or she dies." The tech-nicians were slow to obey, so Webb shouted, "Now! Move it!" He put a hand on the older woman's shoulder. "You too. Let's back up, nice and slow."

As she was guided away from the console, the Trill woman shot a frightened look at Sakonna. "Director . . . don't move . . ."

Sakonna cocked her head at the Trill. "Why? Are you trying to warn me there are two persons standing on the dais with me?"

Kitsom and Cole switched off their stealth circuits and rippled back into the visible spectrum. Both men had their phasers drawn. Cole nodded at Webb. "Good work."

Cole fired and stunned two of the technicians. Kitsom snapped off three perfect shots and felled the rest of the Trill woman's team. Webb finished the job by knocking the Trill unconscious with a single stunning blast to her back.

"All right," Cole said. "So far, so good. Webb, are you sure you can operate that thing?"

"No problem. It's all set for you. Once it recharges, I'll set it to send me home. Are you sure you guys can get back on your own?"

Cole dismissed the question with a wave. "Child's play. See you at the debriefing." He and Kitsom reactivated their suits and disappeared like mirages swallowed by the fall of night. Then Cole said from his vantage unseen, "Energize."

Cole watched Webb initiate the subspace transport sequence. A crushing sensation took hold of him. His world turned to white energy and a bright ringing like tinnitus—and then he, Sakonna, and Kitsom materialized inside the much larger subspace transporter room of Omega Prime.

He recognized the faces looking up at Sakonna. They

were the same technicians who had been on duty when he had visited here hours earlier with Saavik. He saw by their various reactions of surprise that they had expected three persons to materialize on their dais, not just the one they now saw. Because nothing good would come of prolonging their confusion or letting them interrogate Sakonna, Cole made an executive decision to resolve the problem directly.

He fired his weapon while still in stealth mode. Kitsom did the same half a second later. Phaser pulses flashed in the dim light, and the screeching of the weapons filled the cavernous space with wild echoes. When the chaos ceased, the technicians all lay stunned on the floor.

"Let's go," Cole said.

Sakonna led them out of the subspace transporter facility and into the industrial-style environs of Omega Prime. Cole had to trust the Vulcan woman's memory to guide them to their target. Though Cole had not been able to gain direct access to the secure lab during his earlier visit, one of the command screens recorded by his ocular implant had revealed a handful of level plans for the Omega Prime facility—and one of those had been marked in a way that led him to believe the prize they sought was there.

While he and Kitsom focused on moving silently, Sakonna strode with pride. The slight upward tilt of her chin and the way she shifted her gaze while she walked were nearly perfect imitations of the real Saavik's mannerisms, despite the fact that Sakonna had seen the other Vulcan woman only a couple of times in brief passing. Her evocation of the Memory Omega leader was truly uncanny. Even as she passed other denizens of the hidden redoubt, people whom Cole expected knew the real Saavik quite well, no one so much as looked askance at her. There were no double takes or curious glances. Just polite nods and curt greetings.

They filed into a turbolift. Kitsom and Cole each tapped Sakonna's back to confirm they were inside. She instructed the computer without missing a beat, "Observation lab."

A low hum filled the circular lift pod. It hurtled with hardly any sensation of acceleration or deceleration, and in a matter of seconds it arrived at its destination. The doors parted, and Sakonna stepped into a security checkpoint area. The walls, floors, and ceiling all were solid plates of metal, fused at their corners. Opposite the turbolift was a locked blast door. The antechamber had no visible sensors or countermeasures, but Cole knew better than to think it was just an empty space. It was a kill box. One that Cole and his team had no choice but to enter. Whether any of them ever left it alive was now up to Sakonna.

Kitsom pressed the manual control to hold the lift pod's doors open while the Vulcan crossed the room, emulating every nuance of Saavik's gait. No doubt, hidden biometric scanners were verifying her retinal patterns, body mass distribution, and genetic profile. All that remained to be verified were Saavik's voiceprint and her command authorization code. The former, Sakonna had. The latter, unfortunately, had defied discovery by her and Cole.

Consequently, they had decided that a workaround was in order.

Sakonna flexed her hand back from her wrist, triggering the drop of a small spherical device that had been hidden up her sleeve. She caught it and closed her hand around it. Her thumb pressed a pad on its surface. Then she dropped the sphere ahead of her.

It rolled across the floor and struck the far door.

Cole shut his eyes a fraction of a second before the flash. The light faded, leaving perfect darkness. "Sakonna, light the flare."

A rustling of fabric told him Sakonna was retrieving the

emergency flare she had hidden inside her disguise. Next came a sharp crack as she activated it with a quick bend that broke its interior seals and mixed its binary chemicals into a fluorescent compound.

Pale chartreuse light filled the anteroom and spilled onto Kitsom and Cole. Their stealth suits had stopped working, leaving them visible. Kitsom asked Cole, "Did it work?"

"Let's go find out."

He and Kitsom edged out of the lift pod into the checkpoint. No alarms sounded. No antipersonnel systems activated. For once, a piece of technology from the organization's research-and-development group had functioned exactly as had been promised. The sphere was based upon the Breen's energy-dampening technology. Stripped of the need to penetrate the high-energy barrier of a starship's shields, the device could cripple most unshielded systems that relied on artificial power. The drawback, of course, was that it had rendered their stealth suits useless, along with their phasers.

Fortunately, chemical reactions were unaffected by the Breen energy dampener weapon. A binary explosive compound, concealed as flat strips inside Sakonna's disguise, was going to open the last set of doors barring Cole from the prize for which the organization had sent him across the dimensional barrier. He nodded at the Vulcan. "Set it up."

Sakonna extricated the strips of explosive from her costume. Kitsom helped her attach them to the door, and then he armed a primitive molecular fuse. He attached it to the demolition strips. He motioned Cole and Sakonna back toward the lift pod. "Fire in the hole!"

The trio scrambled back inside the pod and pushed themselves to the sides, away from the stuck-open doorway. Several seconds later an ear-splitting blast shook the room. Smoke and dust billowed into the lift pod.

Cole swatted it away as he peeked out. The doors had buckled into the next chamber, folded aside like the petals of a flower in bloom. "It's open. Let's move."

They crossed the anteroom and entered the small octagonal chamber beyond the demolished doors. There were no details, only shadows, until Sakonna edged forward and pushed past Cole with the flare held in front of her.

The room was empty.

Kitsom stumbled past Cole and pivoted full circle in the middle of the room. "What the hell? Where is it?"

Cole looked at Sakonna. "Are you sure this is the right place?"

Her voice had reverted to normal, now that the energy dampener had disabled her voiceprint synthesizer. "I'm sure this is the chamber we saw on the floor plans."

Before Cole could speculate further as to what had gone awry, he heard the voice of the real Saavik from overhead. "This is the right chamber, Mister Cole. It's exactly the one we'd intended you to find. I'm quite pleased you did not disappoint us."

Kitsom, Sakonna, and Cole looked up as a viridescent glow brightened above them. The octagonal chamber had a balcony level, like an operating theater. The emerald hue of chemical lights, coupled with their odd upward angle, turned sinister all the faces that looked down upon them. More than a dozen sharpshooters of various species were crouched along the perimeter, aiming rifles at Cole and his partners. He knew at a glance they were projectile weapons that would be unaffected by the energy dampener.

Gathered above the blasted-in doors was a group that consisted of Saavik, Sarina Douglas, Julian Bashir, and Webb—who had been restrained with his hands behind his back and was escorted by a fearsome-looking pair of masculine Andorian guards. Saavik said to her doppelgänger, "You can remove your disguise now, Miss Sakonna."

Sakonna tore the prosthetic mask from her head and threw it aside.

Flushed with anger and embarrassment, Cole cursed himself in silence. He had blundered into a trap. "This isn't the real observation lab, is it?"

"It's not even the real Omega Prime," Saavik said.

The jig was up, and Cole was in no mood for games. "I guess you'll want to know how *we* know about your quantum window technology."

Saavik remained cool and detached. "We already know. Your organization—which I believe some refer to as Section Thirty-one—intercepted one of our field agents who was on a reconnaissance mission to your universe. You tortured him until he revealed our existence and told you about our ability to spy on other universes."

"Actually, he told us you used it to steal technology from other universes. Like your precious jaunt drives, for instance. We just thought it was time you shared the wealth."

"Then you thought wrong." She addressed her troops: "Arrest them."

A dozen more guards entered the room from behind Cole and his team. In less than a minute, he and Kitsom were stripped of their stealth suits. Sakonna's costume was torn away, and all three of them were left in their undergarments and bare feet. The Memory Omega personnel finished their work by using high-tech tools to extract the transceivers from behind Cole's ears, and they confiscated every last bit of technology from Kitsom and Sakonna.

The security officer in charge looked up at Saavik. "They're ready."

"Take them away."

Another officer seized Cole by his arm, but he resisted being hauled off long enough to aim a murderous stare at Sarina Douglas. "You're traitors, you and your boyfriend. Don't think you'll get away with this. I promise, the organization will find out what you did here."

She returned his hatred with equal venom. "Probably. But not from you."

He glared at Bashir. "You picked the wrong side, Doctor. You're just too blind to see it."

The physician regarded Cole with cold contempt. "Good-bye, Cole."

Several pairs of strong hands overpowered Cole and his colleagues and hauled them away. He had no idea what fate Memory Omega had prepared for them, but if any of the reports he had read about the secret army created by the late Emperor Spock had been true, he was certain no one from his own universe would see him, Sakonna, Webb, or Kitsom ever again.

Twenty-nine

"**S**omething's *happening.*" Those two words over the comm from Crin made Thot Trom sprint from his quarters to the command deck of the *Tajny*. Trapped in the turbolift, he felt like a bomb on the verge of detonation. When the doors opened, he exploded through them, firing off an order to his first officer as he moved toward the center seat. "Crin, report!"

"The standoff is over." He tapped his console and magnified the image on the forward viewscreen. Jem'Hadar vessels were breaking formation, coming about, and navigating into the open blue maw of the Bajoran wormhole. "The Dominion fleet is heading back to the Gamma Quadrant, and the Commonwealth ships are jumping away."

It seemed too good to be true. Trom met the news with suspicion. "Jumping to where?"

"Unknown. But at least they're gone. Apart from the two in orbit, there are five jaunt ships left, and they're all powering up their wormhole drives."

Trom saw a moment of opportunity taking shape. "Karn, how long until the Dominion reinforcements are clear of the wormhole?"

The tactical officer checked his console. "At their current rate of progress, nine minutes. That includes the original Dominion fleet as well. They're all powering up for departure."

"Nine minutes. Very well. That's when we'll strike." Trom opened a channel to the engineering deck. "Command to engineering. Solt, have you made any headway on your calculations for breaching the dimensional barrier with one of the jaunt drives?"

"*Some. I'm having trouble locking down a few of the variables.*"

"What about the dimensional shifters? Are they ready?"

"*Working prototypes are operational on platforms one through four,*" Solt said. "*We'll have the rest ready in about twenty minutes.*"

"You've got eight. Put everyone you can on getting those folded-space transporters operational, because we need to attack the moment our path to the wormhole is open. Command out." He closed the intraship channel and resumed his conversation with Crin. "Pull everything out of the armory. Weapons, demolitions, shroud suits, all of it. I want all our people armed and ready to join the assault on the jaunt ship, including us and the rest of the command crew."

Crin hesitated before he replied. "All of us, sir? Who'll be left to crew the *Tajny*?"

"We're committing all our resources, Crin. This ship has served us well, but we'll need to sacrifice it if we're to have a chance at victory." He directed the first officer's attention toward the viewscreen. "All the intel we acquired was from the *ShiKahr*, so that's the ship we're going to take. But I can't let the *Enterprise* interfere the way it did last time. Once we've beamed aboard the *ShiKahr*, the *Tajny*'s role will be to cripple the *Enterprise* at all costs."

"What about the Dominion command ship?"

Trom smiled behind his helmet. "It's not their fight. They won't interfere."

"Are you sure about that?"

"I'm sure enough. Start distributing the armory surplus. And tell the engineers to take all the tools they can carry. We might need them once we're on the *ShiKahr*."

Crin nodded. Then he asked Trom, "What of the jaunt ship's crew? It took several minutes to subdue them last time—even before the *Enterprise*'s crew interfered."

"No prisoners." It was a ruthless policy, but Trom knew he had no choice. "Before we go aboard the *ShiKahr*, make sure that our people know we'll be shooting to kill."

Thirty

Each time Bashir thought he had known what was happening in this off-kilter twin reality of the one he knew, something had shattered his expectations. In the span of a single day he had been captured, liberated, accused, granted asylum, surrendered, put on trial, acquitted, and then invited to bear witness to the entrapment of those who had brought him here. Now, as a pair of human security officers escorted him and Sarina to a guest suite on the *Enterprise*, he almost dreaded to learn what awaited him on the other side of the door.

The portal slid open, and he and Sarina stepped through the doorway. Seated on a sofa in the suite's main room was Saavik, who stood to greet her two guests. "Welcome." With a slow sweep of her arm, she motioned them toward the sofa opposite hers. "Please. Sit down."

"Thank you." Bashir and Sarina crossed the room and settled onto the sofa.

As they relaxed, Saavik sat down across from them. "Can I offer you anything?"

Sarina made no effort to conceal her defensiveness. "How about the truth?"

"About what?" The Vulcan almost let slip a faint smirk. "The truth is like the multiverse. It contains endless possibilities, many of which depend entirely upon one's point of view."

"Let's start with why Julian and I are still here, and the rest of our team isn't." It was a very direct inquiry—perhaps more confrontational than what Bashir would have chosen, but he suspected Sarina's methods might prove better suited than his to getting results in this instance.

Saavik steepled her fingers. She kept her eyes locked on Sarina's, as if the two women were engaged in a silent battle of wills. "I think we all know that you and Doctor Bashir were part of their team in name only. They never told you their true objective, did they?"

This time, Bashir answered for both of them. "Not as such, no."

"Why do you think that was?"

He shrugged. "Their organization has a habit of compartmentalizing information."

"Yes, it does." Saavik shifted the tilt of her head from one side to the other as she studied him. "I find it curious that you would call it *their* organization. Not *the* organization. Not *ours*. But *theirs*." Her eyes narrowed. "You still see yourself as separate from Section Thirty-one."

She had phrased it as a declaration, but her inflection had made it sound like a question. Bashir nodded. "I always have." As Sarina held his hand, he added, "We both do."

"Then it should come as no surprise that they've seen you both the same way."

Bashir felt his body recoil from Saavik's revelation. "Excuse me?"

"They know all about you. That you're both really working for Starfleet Intelligence, trying to infiltrate them as a prelude to sabotaging them from within."

There was no point dissembling. It was obvious that Saavik knew too much to be deceived by any lie he might try to spin. Bashir exhaled the breath he belatedly realized he had been holding. "How did you know?"

"Quantum windows—the same technology Cole and his

friends came here to steal." She crossed her legs. "We began using it to collect intel from your universe after three of our agents vanished there on recon missions. In time, we learned that the group you call Section Thirty-one was responsible—and that its agents had become aware of us and our extra-dimensional surveillance capability. It was only a matter of time before they tried to steal it."

The more Bashir heard, the more he felt like a pawn in a game whose players he could barely perceive, much less understand. "If they didn't need me or Sarina to help them take the quantum window technology, why did they bring us here?"

"I think they hoped your presence would serve as a distraction, for us as well as for the Commonwealth and its military. Thirty-one has a number of agents operating in this universe, and one of them must have learned of our summit with the Dominion. When Thirty-one's leaders cross-referenced that fact against your service record, they would have been reminded of your slaying of Odo on Terok Nor—and immediately seen an opportunity to put you in jeopardy."

"While concocting a political and legal crisis that would command your full attention."

"Precisely." She lifted one eyebrow. "Had we not already been aware of their intentions, it might have been a very successful ruse. However, I think they also underestimated the ethics of the Dominion in this universe. They went to so much effort to ensure your presence would be detected that I believe they were certain you would be executed for Odo's death."

Bashir nodded. "Yes, I'd have to call that an ironic development." A troubling notion occurred to him. He looked up at Saavik. "What happened to Cole and the others?"

"They've been dealt with."

Sarina echoed Bashir's tone of alarm. "How, exactly?"

Saavik seemed reluctant to answer. Then she relented. "They were exiled."

Still not satisfied, Bashir asked, "To where?"

"Technically? To Bajor." Saavik seemed prepared to let her answer stand until Bashir and Sarina's reproachful glares compelled her to add a few details. "We used the subspace transporter to shift them across the dimensional barrier to a quantum reality whose frequency is known to only a few of our scientists. Cole and his accomplices will live out the rest of their lives in a universe that has everything it needs to sustain life but contains no other sapient beings—only plants, animals, and microorganisms." She sighed. "Technically, it is neither corporal nor capital punishment. But no one in our universe or yours will ever see them again."

What could Bashir say in reply? Thanking her seemed gauche, but condemning her felt ungrateful. From one perspective, she had done him and Sarina a favor; from another, she had put them in a difficult situation if and when they returned home: how would they explain the loss of Cole and the others to Sarina's handler? Ultimately, all he could say was, "I see."

Before anyone could render the moment more awkward than it had already become, they were interrupted by the whoop of the ship's alert sirens. A woman's rich and husky voice announced over the ship's internal comms, *"Yellow Alert. Senior staff, report to the bridge."*

Saavik stood. "Do the two of you still wish to help us neutralize the Breen threat?"

Bashir and Sarina exchanged excited glances. He looked up at Saavik. "Definitely."

"Then come with me."

*   *   *

Sometimes being first was a privilege; sometimes it was nothing less than a leap of faith. For Rem, being the leader of the first Spetzkar team to pass through the folded-space transporter for the strike mission against the *ShiKahr* was the latter.

He and two squads of his fellow commandos stood on the transporter platform, flanked by bulkheads that had been torn open for last-second modifications. Loose cables spilled like guts from the gaps in the walls, and the exposed machinery in the spaces beyond them radiated heat and hummed with wild energies.

At the control console, Solt completed his final system check. "Coordinates locked!"

"Charge rifles," Rem said. He and his men powered up their weapons to the maximum kill setting. "Activate chameleon circuits." He engaged his armor's shrouding system, a technology the Breen Special Research Division had developed after studying the natural abilities of Jem'Hadar it had secretly abducted during the Dominion's war against the Alpha Quadrant powers. In less than a second, Rem and his men vanished from sight—but to each other they appeared as frost-blue silhouettes, a useful safety feature designed to minimize friendly fire casualties during shrouded operations.

Solt keyed commands into the transporter console. "Starting dimensional shift . . . *now.*"

Traveling through space-time via the dimensional shifter wasn't like being moved by a transporter. There was no sense of being seized by the annular confinement beam, no gradual dissolution of one's surroundings, just a blinding white flash—

—and they were inside the jaunt ship's computer core. The towering space was a huge, hollow cylinder, inside which stood another cylindrical structure, the ship's main computer.

Pale blue light blazed inside its sophisticated matrix of linked databanks and faster-than-light processing cores.

Half a dozen of the ship's technicians halted their work and reacted in shock to the flashes of light that had erupted all around them. One of them, a male Bolian, asked, "Did anyone else just see that?"

A female Bajoran replied, "Maybe we should alert the bridge."

Rem aimed at her and fired. His red disruptor pulse incinerated her head. A fraction of a second later, the rest of his team unleashed perfectly targeted head shots that dropped the rest of the technicians.

Before the whine of their rifles had faded, the Spetzkar heard the shrieking of the ship's intruder alarms. Rem paid them no mind. All the warnings in the universe would make no difference now. "Kine, Yuay, disable the ship's internal sensors and comms. Treyd, shut down their intruder countermeasures. Rowk, take their command systems off-line."

He stood back and watched them work. They moved with the precision of surgeons and the detachment of butchers. In a matter of seconds, they had gutted the *ShiKahr's* main computer core and left the entire ship defenseless. Kine faced Rem. "Adjustments complete, sir."

The computer specialist activated his helmet's subspace transceiver. "Rem to *Tajny*."

"Go ahead," Trom said.

"The *ShiKahr's* computer is ours. Continue the attack."

Bursts of light filled the bridge of the *ShiKahr*. Captain sh'Pherron sprang from her command chair, ready to meet this new threat—but the light was gone almost as soon as it had appeared, and nothing on the bridge seemed to have changed. It took a fraction of a second for her to remember that the *Enterprise* teams that had liberated her ship the day before had reported encounters with shrouded enemy personnel. She turned to warn her first officer—

The first disruptor shot burned into her back. She fell face-first to the deck.

Lying on her belly with her head twisted to the left, sh'Pherron bore mute witness to the slaughter of her bridge crew. A furious barrage from the forward end of the compartment cut down everyone in its path. Turak collapsed, robbed of his face by a lethal headshot. Riaow was thrown against the aft consoles, her fur burning, a smoldering wound blasted deep into her chest. Though sh'Pherron couldn't turn her head, she heard the death cries of the Lagorian helmsman, Ensign Gunnd, and the human operations officer, Lieutenant Caswell.

The piercing shriek of energy weapons gave way to a deathly silence. A sparse and ragged pall of gray smoke lingered over the carnage. Humanoid shapes formed in the hazy aftermath, their outlines rippling like heat distortion for a moment before they became first translucent and then opaque. It was a squad of Breen soldiers in scaly black-and-silver armor, with gold bands atop their snout-shaped helmets, extending from front to back.

They moved among the dead, prodding the corpses with their booted feet. One of them nudged Riaow. The felled Caitian let slip a low, pathetic groan. The Breen trooper aimed his weapon and fired a coup de grâce. Then he fired again, ensuring the kill.

One of the commandos wore a helmet whose gold band was bordered by crimson stripes. He snapped orders at the others, in the machine-noise gibberish that spewed from their vocoders.

Sh'Pherron didn't need to speak the Breen's language to know what they were doing. She saw the updates on the master systems display. The Breen had armed the ship's intruder countermeasures—and turned them against the *ShiKahr*'s crew.

She wanted to curse at the troopers, to spit her last bit of bile at them. All she could do was splutter helplessly and cough indigo blood onto the deck.

The Breen commander took note of her dying spasms and turned away from his men. He walked over and loomed above her, his intentions hidden behind his helmet.

On some level, sh'Pherron hoped there might still be some measure of mercy, however small, lurking behind that grotesque mask.

He pointed his rifle at her face and fired.

With a searing white flash, the dimensional shifter moved Crin and his platoon through a wrinkle in space-time to their designated strike area.

Dozens of faces looked up and around, all of them bewildered by the mysterious light show that had heralded the Breen commandos' unseen arrival. Crin smiled. It was liberating not having to worry about taking prisoners. That meant anyone in the *ShiKahr*'s engineering section who wasn't limned by the pale glow of Spetzkar chameleon armor in shroud mode was fair game. And this was the most target-rich environment Crin had seen in years.

He activated the private channel that linked him to his strike team. "Weapons free."

A storm of fire tore through the *ShiKahr*'s engineering crew. High-power blasts ripped into multiple targets at once. It took only a few seconds for the wails of the panicked and the dying to drown out the screams of the Spetzkar's disruptors.

The platoon divided into squads as it moved aft, clearing each compartment and section along the way. Crin was disappointed by how few of the jaunt ship's personnel tried to run. So many of them cowered, as if they might be spared. But when did the universe ever show mercy to cowards? He gunned down the ship's multispecies menagerie of fools while cursing them for robbing his victory of its sport.

By the time he reached the ladderway to the lower decks, the other platoon leaders were there, each on a different level, some looking up, others down. Crin switched over to the command channel. "Engineering deck officers, report."

One by one, they all replied, *"Clear."*

Quick and ruthless—just as Thot Trom had wanted.

"Have your grunts police up the bodies and beam them into space. Solt, do you copy?"

"Go ahead," the chief engineer replied.

Crin checked his chrono as he double-timed back the way he had come. "Power up the jaunt drive. We have less than ninety seconds before the *Tajny* starts its attack run."

Reports flooded in on all the encrypted channels used by the Spetzkar. The key areas of the *ShiKahr* were secure, and the jaunt ship's own intruder countermeasures had eliminated those members of its crew stationed in its less consequential sections.

We've been lucky so far, Trom reminded himself. *But luck doesn't last.*

"Yoab, have you unlocked the helm controls?"

"Almost." The pilot checked his console. "Wait—sir, the jaunt drive is locked out."

"Don't worry," Trom said. "If this works, we won't need it."

The doors to the aft starboard turbolift opened. Rem

and Crin stepped onto the bridge. The first officer headed toward Trom, and Rem passed Karn at the tactical console on his way to the ship's operations panel. Crin took his place at Trom's side. "The ship is secure, sir."

"Well done. The *Tajny* starts her run in twenty seconds. Stand by to receive the *Enterprise*'s request for assistance. Tell them what they want to hear."

"Yes, sir." Crin moved away to the communications console.

"Karn, stand by to raise shields. Yoab, plot a course for the wormhole at warp four, then hold for my order. Everyone else, get rid of these bodies before they start to stink."

As the corpses littering the deck were hauled away and stowed in the commander's ready room, Trom kept his attention on the viewscreen. His plan was moments away from its next crucial step. He was about to learn whether he had underestimated the tactical capabilities of the jaunt ships. If he had, then he and his men were going to suffer badly for his mistake.

But if he had guessed right, they would soon be welcomed home as heroes.

"Continue tracking that ship," Picard snapped. "It's come out of hiding for a reason. I want to know why—and I want it found." He turned at the swish of a turbolift door opening. Director Saavik strode onto his bridge, followed by Bashir and Douglas, the two interlopers from the other universe whom Saavik hadn't condemned to extradimensional exile.

He turned away to conceal his annoyance. His ship was potentially mere seconds away from a combat situation. The last thing he needed now was a distraction.

Saavik stood beside him in the middle of the bridge. "What do we know, Captain?"

"The Breen are back." He stared at the starscape on the viewscreen. "And they're close."

K'Ehleyr moved to stand on the other side of Picard from Saavik. "We picked up a sudden local increase in tetryon particles. Then we noticed it was moving at full impulse."

The Vulcan mirrored Picard's concern. "Is it continuing its evasive maneuvers?"

"No. It's getting closer." Picard's already grim mood darkened. "It's looking for the right angle from which to launch an attack." He decided on a course of action. "I'm not waiting for them to make the first move. Commander Troi, raise shields and arm all weapons."

"Aye, sir." Troi primed the *Enterprise*'s tactical systems with a single tap on her console.

"Number One, apprise the *ShiKahr* and the Dominion command ship of the situation, and recommend they raise shields as well."

K'Ehleyr delegated the order with a nod to a Tellarite officer. She turned back toward Picard and lowered her voice. "Should we prep another boarding party?"

"That would be prudent. Make it so."

She stepped away to relay his orders discreetly to Troi, leaving him in the unsettling company of Saavik. "Director, it might be safer if you and your guests returned to—"

The keening whoop of the Red Alert siren cut him off.

Troi pointed at the viewscreen. "They're uncloaking!"

Picard saw the menacing bulk of the Breen cruiser bearing down on the *Enterprise*. Its nose was lowered a few degrees, a classic attack profile. "Target that—"

Emerald beams from the Breen ship slashed through the darkness and filled the viewscreen. Bone-jarring impacts rocked the *Enterprise*. A momentary overload of the inertial dampeners and a hiccup in the power supply to the artificial gravity generators combined to send Picard, Saavik, and her two guests tumbling to starboard.

"They're firing all they've got," Troi shouted over the painfully loud clamor of disruptor blasts hammering the *Enterprise*'s shields.

K'Ehleyr snapped, "Fire back!"

Troi triggered a retaliatory strike. Orange streaks of phaser energy lashed out and pummeled the oncoming Breen ship, and a volley of four quantum torpedoes slammed into it head-on. The first two collapsed its shields. The second two ripped through the cruiser's hull and eviscerated long swaths of its infrastructure before erupting from the ship's underside.

It was a brutal and decisive blow, one that Picard was sure would put an end to the Breen's mad assault. "Target their engines as they break away. Shoot to disable."

He waited to see the Breen ship veer off so that Troi could take out their impulse coil and warp nacelles. Once the ship was immobilized, he would—

What are they doing?

Troi's eyes widened. "They're not breaking off, Captain."

K'Ehleyr was the first to see the obvious. "They're on a collision course!" She sprang to Troi's side at the tactical console. "Lock all phasers! Fire!"

Vermilion beams scissored through the Breen cruiser. It charged ahead, into the cruel barrage, accelerating all the way. Then it dived and rolled, burning like a Catherine wheel.

Picard threw himself into his command chair as he shouted, "Evasive maneuvers!"

It was too late. The fiery wreck of the Breen ship rammed into the *Enterprise*'s shields.

The viewscreen filled with gray static for half a second, and then it went dark, along with all the other bridge consoles and the overhead lights.

A deafening crash left Picard clutching his chair's arm-rests white-knuckle tight and gritting his teeth against a sonic assault that threatened to shake them loose from his jaw.

When the cacophony subsided, Picard felt as if he had been pummeled by a prizefighter. He looked around, half in shock, as dim emergency lights faded up. His first priority was to make sure his officers were alive. They all were at least in the vicinity of their posts, and neither Saavik nor her guests appeared to have been injured. He twisted and looked over his shoulder toward K'Ehleyr. "Number One. Damage and casualty reports."

"Internal comms are down. Switching to backup channels."

He turned a hopeful look at Troi. "The Breen cruiser?"

"Destroyed." She struggled with her flickering console. "But we're not much better."

The overhead lights slowly climbed back to full brightness. Several of the major duty stations' consoles ceased stuttering and reset their interfaces. The main viewscreen hashed with interference for a second, and then its image resolved to show a vista of fiery destruction. The *Enterprise* was enveloped in a cloud of smoldering debris from the Breen cruiser.

K'Ehleyr sat in her chair, beside Picard's. She turned her command screen so they both could see it. "Multiple injuries, no fatalities. Medical teams are responding."

"And the ship?"

"Heavy damage to the shields. Overloads all through the tactical grid. Subspace comms are down. Hull breaches on Decks Eleven through Sixteen. And the jaunt drive is off-line."

It was a far from ideal outcome, but his ship and his crew were still here, albeit a touch worse for wear. *At least we've fared better than our attackers.* "Commander Troi, hail the *ShiKahr* on short-range comms. Tell Captain sh'Pherron we need her to return yesterday's favor. Any engineering and medical personnel they can spare, as well as spare parts and—"

"Captain," Troi interrupted. "The *ShiKahr* is breaking orbit."

He stared at her. "What?"

"They've changed course—toward the wormhole."

She changed the viewscreen's vantage to obtain a clearer angle of the *ShiKahr*—which promptly streaked away in a spectral blur of light as the ship jumped to warp speed.

K'Ehleyr spoke in a horrified whisper. "The cruiser must have been a decoy. I don't know how they did it, but the Breen are back on the *ShiKahr*. And they're *getting away.*"

Picard stood. "Like hell they are. Helm, set a pursuit course, best possible speed."

Lieutenant Tolaris delivered bad news with dry detachment. "The ship is limited to full impulse until Mister Barclay gets main power back online."

Picard lifted his voice. "Bridge to engineering."

Barclay sounded out of breath. *"Go ahead, sir."*

"How long to restore main power?"

"At least ten minutes."

Picard looked at Troi. "How long until the *ShiKahr* reaches the wormhole?"

The security chief grimaced. "Four minutes. Unless they jaunt to it."

Saavik put herself in Picard's eye line. "They can't. The *ShiKahr*'s jaunt drive is still locked down. But without warp power, we can't reach them in time. Which means we need to ask for help from the only ship that can."

He knew what Saavik was suggesting. It was a conversation he did not want to have.

"*Merde.*"

*   *   *

It was not Taran'atar's habit to offer unsolicited opinions on the affairs of his superiors, so he swallowed his contempt for the softness and ineptitude of the Commonwealth jaunt ship's crew. Their captain's face filled the forward holoframe as he petitioned the Founder. *"Madam Founder, I would not ask this of you if there were any other way."*

The Founder's face was inscrutable. "We have no wish to involve ourselves in your affairs. The hijacking of your vessel is not our concern."

"I disagree," Picard replied. *"The ShiKahr is heading toward the wormhole, which will take it to the Gamma Quadrant. If the Breen escape with that ship and learn how to build a jaunt drive, they'll be able to use it against your people and ours. The entire galaxy will be in peril."*

"Why would that risk be any graver than allowing your Commonwealth to retain its monopoly on wormhole propulsion?"

Her question seemed to exasperate Picard. *"I can guarantee you, the Breen Confederacy will not wield this power with the same restraint we've shown. We've had this power for eight years now. If we had wanted to abuse it, we could have. But we didn't. So I'm asking you to accept our pledge of good faith— and return the favor. While there's still time."*

After a moment of consideration, the Founder turned toward Eris. "Can this vessel reach the wormhole ahead of the *ShiKahr*?"

"Barely," the female Vorta said. "And only if we go now, at maximum warp."

"Lay in the course and execute immediately." The Founder faced Picard's larger-than-life visage on the screen. "We will do our best to waylay your stolen vessel, Captain. But if its hijackers turn its weapons against us, we will defend ourselves."

"Understood. We'd rather see it destroyed than stolen."

The transmission ended, and the Founder looked at Taran'atar. "Prepare for battle."

Warp-streaked stars retracted to cold points of light as the *ShiKahr* dropped back to full impulse. Thot Trom leaned forward in the command chair. "Time to the wormhole?"

"Thirty seconds," Yoab said from the helm.

Good fortune was a rare commodity in wartime, and Trom meant to make the most of it. His team's backup plan for returning to their own universe involved using a known and proven method for triggering a dimensional jump inside the Bajoran wormhole. Though it was commendable of Solt to have theorized a means of making the same jump using the jaunt ship's artificially generated wormholes, Trom was grateful not to have to put that notion to the test.

Ahead of the *ShiKahr*, the wormhole unfolded as if from nothing, a midnight-blue flower blossoming in the cold night of space. Light poured majestically from its dilated mouth, and a faint tremor of gravimetric distortion shook the jaunt ship as it approached its destination.

"Take us in, Yoab. Crin, alert all decks to brace for turbulence. Rem, stand by to—"

A coruscating burst of light washed out the details on the viewscreen. When the blinding glare abated, the Dominion command ship filled the screen. It was a gunmetal leviathan that completely obstructed the *ShiKahr*'s flight path to the wormhole.

Karn looked up from tactical. "Their shields are up, all weapons have been armed. They're locking onto us and"—he paused to silence a new alert tone—"they're hailing us."

"Put them on-screen."

A Jem'Hadar's terrifying visage glowered back at Trom. *"Attention, Commander,* ShiKahr. *I am First Taran'atar. Drop your shields and surrender your vessel."*

Trom stood and stepped forward. "Let us pass, First. Our battle is not with you."

"*You are mistaken. Yield in ten seconds or be destroyed.*"

So much for the Dominion staying out of this.

Trom signaled Crin with a subtle gesture to mute the channel. "Karn, target the known vulnerabilities of the command ship."

"I've already tried," Karn replied. "Their ship isn't the same as the ones in our universe. I can't find the same weak spots. It might not have any."

Rem swiveled away from the sensor console. "The *Enterprise* is inbound at warp eight."

Karn shook his head. "Even if I find a chink in the Jem'Hadar's armor, we can't fight them and another jaunt ship at the same time."

Their ten seconds of grace from the Jem'Hadar were about to expire. Trom let go of his delusions of good fortune and chose to face the bitter truth. "Close the channel. Helm, full evasive. Get us away from the command ship and take us back to maximum warp."

With one hand, Yoab accelerated the *ShiKahr* into a rolling, diving turn beneath the Jem'Hadar battleship; with the other, he started plotting warp-speed coordinates. "Heading?"

Trom returned to his command chair. "Anywhere but here." He glanced at a star chart on the monitor beside his seat. "Head for Klingon space—maybe they won't follow us."

"Laying in the course and jumping to warp . . . *now.*"

On the viewscreen, the starfield stretched into blurred streaks.

Crin moved to Trom's side. "The Jem'Hadar are still at the wormhole, but the *Enterprise* is right behind us. If they call in reinforcements before we get the jaunt drive online—"

"I know. Get down to engineering. Tell Solt he has to break the lockout right now. Then he has to rig the drive to get us home. Otherwise, this entire mission's been for nothing."

Impatience was a fault to which Picard rarely succumbed, but watching the stolen jaunt ship hurtle away by an ever-growing margin had him at wit's end. "Helm! Time to intercept?"

"Intercept?" Looking back, Tolaris protested, "Sir, we can barely keep pace."

Picard shot a look at K'Ehleyr, who knew what his pointed glare was asking. "Barclay's doing all he can. He says he can get us up to warp eight point eight in a few minutes."

"Not good enough, damn it! Not good enough! They could be gone by then!" Picard got up and stalked over to Troi's console. "Are we close enough to use quantum torpedoes?"

She shared his disappointment and frustration. "They're just out of range."

He breathed an angry sigh and paced along the aft duty stations. As he passed Saavik and her guests, Bashir spoke up. "Captain? Your ship has subspace transporters. Perhaps you could beam a strike team aboard the *ShiKahr*."

It was so preposterous an idea that it made Picard angry. "Are you mad? Subspace beaming between two points moving at different warp factors?"

The *Enterprise*'s senior science officer, Lieutenant Kell Perim, joined in the mocking of Bashir. "We might as well just cremate you and eject your ashes from the shuttlebay." The Trill turned back to her console as she added, "We'd use less energy and get the same result."

Picard looked over Perim's shoulder. "Any luck restoring subspace comms?"

"Almost there, sir. Just a few more minutes."

"Tell me the moment they're back online."

He left her to her work and returned to his chair. He couldn't catch his foes, attack them, or summon reinforcements. All he could do was watch the *ShiKahr* slowly widen the gap between itself and the *Enterprise*. He promised himself the Breen would pay for this—and that he would be the one to collect the debt.

Thirty-one

If there was any rhyme or reason to the design of the jaunt drive, it eluded Solt. The Spetzkar engineer stood surrounded by the mind-boggling amalgam of technologies that had been united to create the Commonwealth's marvel of propulsion. Some of its components looked as if they were of Romulan design; others evinced classically Cardassian aesthetics. A few discrete elements showed evidence of Tzenkethi origin. More than a dozen were so bizarre that Solt had no idea where they had come from, or how they had been compelled to work in concert.

This engine is the work of a madman.

Ominous rumblings underscored a jolt of impact that rocked the *ShiKahr*. Solt grabbed hold of a load-bearing strut and braced himself.

A few of his engineers were slower to react and ended up in a tangled pile on the deck at his feet. One of them did a double take as another blast shook the jaunt ship and made its hull ring with violent percussion. "What was that?"

"We're being torpedoed," Solt told his men. "Get up, all of you. We need to find a way to override the lockout and bring this drive online."

He opened an access panel and was dismayed by the high-tech puzzle it contained. There had to be a logic to it. It was all geared toward a single shared function—the generation and maintenance of a stable artificial wormhole. He knew that a team of dedicated engineers could reverse-engineer this perplexing jumble of hybridized parts. All it would take was time.

More blasts hammered the jaunt ship's shields.

Time, Solt fumed. *The one thing we're fast running out of.* "Does anybody see anything? Talk to me!"

Lar, a mechanic's mate, waved his free hand. "Over here!"

Solt pushed past the other engineers between them. "Report."

"I think this might be the core command relay." Lar reached in and laid his gloved hand on a dodecahedronal module. The head-sized device had one unobstructed facet, which served as its interface panel. The other nineteen facets were festooned with cables and hard connections. At a glance, Solt saw the unit was linked into nearly every other part of the jaunt drive.

"Good work, Lar. Step clear." He reached in to activate the interface. Another salvo of enemy fire quaked the ship and knocked Solt off balance. Lar and another engineer caught him and set him back on his feet. He promised himself he would thank them later; for now they had more pressing concerns. A few quick taps activated the node's command interface. All its options were dimmed, and a red overlay contained flashing alphanumeric symbols in some alien language. Half a second later, the translator circuit in his helmet's holovisor parsed the warning: COMMAND OVERRIDE— LOCKDOWN IN EFFECT.

The junior engineers pressed closer, crowding Solt. Lar peeked over his shoulder and asked, "Can you break the lockout?"

"With finesse? Not a chance."

Solt pulled loose a power cable from an adjacent non-critical system. Using his free hand, he drew his knife and pried open the interface facet of the command node. Nothing inside the unit looked familiar, so he made an educated guess as to which component was its main bus capacitor. Then he jabbed the exposed end of the power cable against it.

Sparks blasted upward, and a burst of light shorted out the holovisor in his mask for a split second. Then his holovisor reset—and so did the interface screen of the command node.

The message made Solt smile: SYSTEM REBOOT IN PROG-RESS.

"We're in business. Set up the mods, just like we practiced! And be quick about it!" His technicians and mechanics scrambled away, rushing in all directions to modify key subsystems of the jaunt drive. The chief engineer activated his helmet comm. "Solt to Trom."

"Go ahead."

"Lockout defeated. We're modifying the drive now."

"How long to breach the dimensional barrier?"

It was time to deliver the bad news. "Not sure. Still working on the equations."

"Work faster. Our shields won't last much longer, and if the Enterprise *calls in reinforcements, we're as good as dead."*

"Understood. Solt out."

He closed the channel, tuned out the roar of ever louder torpedo blasts, and struggled to program the jaunt drive to create an artificial wormhole with interdimensional topology.

I guess this would be a bad time to tell Trom I only got an average rating in subspatial calculus. His hands trembled as he worked. *Yeah, I'll save that story for the medal ceremony.*

There was little for Bashir to do on the bridge of the *Enterprise* but stand with Sarina and Saavik near the aft port-side turbolift and try to stay out of the crew's way.

of the bridge officers were hunched over their con-
'Ehleyr moved from one to the next, offering sug-
ollecting updates as she went. At the end of her
ned to Picard's side. "This is our best possible

Her news vexed him. "We just need another tenth of a warp factor."

"We can fix only so much of the warp drive while we're using it." She threw an anxious look at the image of the fleeing *ShiKahr* on the viewscreen. "The good news is, they're working with most of the same restrictions we are."

The captain looked at Troi, clearly hoping for better news. "Any luck accessing their command override system?"

"None. We can't establish contact. They've disabled their ULF subspace antenna." She tapped a launch trigger on her console and fired another round of torpedoes at the *ShiKahr*. The five-missile salvo sped away in brilliant golden streaks; seconds later, they flashed against the other jaunt ship's shields. "Our torpedoes are having only minimal effect."

"Continue firing. Their shields won't last forever."

"Neither will our supply of torpedoes," K'Ehleyr said. "And if we use them up on these long-range pokes at the *ShiKahr*'s aft shields, we could end up in real trouble if they turn around and decide to start shooting back."

It was sound advice, but Picard received it with a dark glare. "Very well. Cease fire."

Bashir leaned toward Sarina and whispered, "Should we tell them now?"

"I don't think they're in the mood to hear it."

"I'm not sure we can wait."

Sarina held Bashir's hand, perhaps to lift her own spirits as much as to buoy his. "Okay."

Together, they stepped forward. Then they halted in midstep as Lieutenant Perim sprang from her post and crowed to her shipmates, "All comms are back up!"

In an instant, Picard's bad mood evaporated. "Send a quantum signal to fleet command! Tell them the *ShiKahr*'s been hijacked and request assistance from all available vessels." He stepped toward the viewscreen with clenched fists. "Let's keep them busy till help arrives. Arm another volley of torpedoes and fire!"

"Torpedoes away," Troi confirmed as she tapped the launch trigger.

K'Ehleyr noted that Bashir and Sarina had moved toward the center of the bridge. "Do you two want to contribute something?"

A nod from Sarina encouraged Bashir to speak for both of them. "We need to warn you not to underestimate the Breen. These aren't the usual privateers or mercenaries that operate outside their borders. The *ShiKahr*'s been taken by Spetzkar—elite commandos."

"We're aware of that," K'Ehleyr said. "What's your point?"

"They're more than capable of breaking the lockout on the jaunt drive. And if they do, we think there's a real risk they might use it to take that ship back to our universe."

His admonition was met with grave concern by Picard. "Is that even possible?"

"It's happened before," Sarina said. "That's why the Breen came here, remember? One of your jaunt ships crashed in our universe a couple of years ago. The Breen found the wreckage in Federation space and tried to salvage it. That failed, so they've come here to steal one directly."

The discussion drew Perim away from her station. "Hang on. You think the Breen might try to break through the dimensional barrier with a jaunt drive?" Nods of confirmation turned her slack-jawed surprise to wide-eyed horror. She turned toward K'Ehleyr and Picard. "Sirs, we can't let that happen!"

Picard adopted a calming manner. "We know the risks if they succeed."

"Never mind if they *succeed*," Perim said. "I'm worried

about what happens if they *fail*. They could unravel space-time as we know it—not just here, but across the galaxy. They might even cause a chain reaction that can unravel reality as we know it in this universe *and* theirs."

K'Ehleyr shifted her sidelong stare from Perim to Picard. "I won't pretend I understand what most of that means, but I have to say, sir—it sounds pretty bad."

"I'm forced to agree." Picard took a deep breath and looked at Bashir and Sarina. "But I still think we should wait for the rest of the fleet."

Bashir shook his head. "That might be too late, even the way your ships move. If the Breen are modifying that engine, we need to stop them *now*."

Picard's temper frayed. "And how do you propose we do that, Doctor?"

Sarina stepped between them. "With all respect to you and your science officer, you're wrong about the limitations of the subspace transporter. It is possible to compensate for the effects of differential warp velocities. I've seen the equations. I can give them to you."

Everyone turned to face Saavik, who had come forward to join the debate. "What you propose is extremely danger-ous, even if your calculations are correct. Anyone sent in this manner would run a high risk of dying in transit. Why should we risk it?"

"We're not asking you to," Bashir said. "Send the two of us."

Dubious looks passed among the *Enterprise* officers. Before any of them could object, Sarina interjected, "These Spetzkar came from our universe, and we were sent here to stop them. This mission is our responsibility, so the risk should be ours alone."

Saavik betrayed neither hope nor skepticism. "What would you need from us?"

"Two stealth suits," Bashir said. "Weapons. A briefing on the jaunt ship's weak spots."

"And an exit strategy," Sarina added. "Just in case we live through this."

The old Vulcan looked at Picard. "The decision is yours, Captain."

"Number One, have Mister Barclay meet Doctor Bashir and Miss Douglas with their equipment in Transporter Room Three. Make sure he's ready to brief them on their targets." He turned toward Bashir and Sarina, and a small, grudging smile broke through his dour mood. "Let's hope you don't come to regret this sudden bout of heroism."

Thirty-two

Time was the enemy now. Trom knew it. He felt it in his bones. His pilot Yoab was pushing the *ShiKahr* to its ultimate limit, coaxing every last bit of speed he could from the vessel. Down in the bowels of the ship, Solt was rebuilding the jaunt drive—the very prize they had come for—into the one thing that could take them home. All they needed was time—

—but a brutal concussion of torpedo blasts made it clear the enemy had no intention of giving it to them. Trom hung on to the command chair. Consoles stuttered, and bodies fell through the strobing light in surreal slow motion.

Crin stumbled across the pitching deck as another salvo hit the *ShiKahr*. He fell across his own chair, to the right of Trom's. "Long-range sensors are reading new signals, sir."

"Klingon?"

"Jaunt ships. Dozens of them. They're jumping in all around us."

Trom kept his curses to himself. "The *Enterprise* restored its comms sooner than we expected." He used the command interface beside his chair to open a channel to engineering. "Solt! We're being surrounded. Are your modifications ready?"

"Almost. We'll be ready to cross the dimensional barrier in ten minutes."

"Keep me posted. Every second counts. Command out." He closed the channel and looked at Crin. "We're almost home. Divert just enough power from the aft shields to fire four rounds of torpedoes from the aft launcher. Let's see if the *Enterprise* likes a bloody nose."

"Yes, sir." Crin slipped away to relay the order to Karn.

Trom looked forward to seeing his harassers swallow a bit of their own medicine, but behind his brave talk, he knew he had nothing but bluster. His ship was only minutes away from being trapped by a vastly superior force. Unless Solt proved to be a genius without equal in the field of starship propulsion, Trom and his men were on the verge of annihilation.

Victory was within his grasp, but already he felt it slipping like water through his fingers.

Suffocating force, scintillating light, and a wash of white sound all surrendered their hold on Bashir, who blinked to find himself free of the subspace transporter beam and standing beside Sarina, inside a remote compartment on the lowest engineering deck of the *ShiKahr*. They both had been rendered effectively invisible by their borrowed Memory Omega stealth suits, but to each other they appeared as ghostly green figures, a feature of the software built into the holovisors of their full-head masks.

Sarina drew her phaser. Because it was coated with stealth materials that reacted to the ones in her gloves, the weapon was also invisible. "Which way?"

"Forward to the main junction." Bashir drew his own phaser and pointed down the passageway. "You cover the left, I'll take the right."

Together they skulked forward. It amazed Bashir how perfectly quiet his and Sarina's footfalls were, even in the close confines of the narrow corridor. Part of the credit was due to their genetically enhanced dexterity, which made them light on their feet when they needed to be, but he knew the stealth suits were doing most of the work. The soles of their shoes were padded with layers of material that absorbed sound waves and let them move like ghosts.

The first intersection was on Sarina's side. She signaled Bashir that she would aim high. He gestured back that he would duck in low behind her. He darted behind her as they reached the corner. They turned together, and he crouched as he pivoted on his leading foot.

All was clear. Bashir moved ahead, taking point. Sarina fell in behind him as they hugged the right wall of the corridor until the next intersection. This time, he cued her with hand signals that he would aim high. She acknowledged with a nod and ducked low, close to his back.

They turned as one. A dozen meters down the maintenance passage, a pair of Breen commandos were busy rearranging the internal components of some part of the ship's engines.

In the holographic heads-up display provided by his mask, Bashir noted the red targeting crosshairs that indicated precisely where his phaser shot would fall. A second set of yellow crosshairs informed him that Sarina was targeting the other Spetzkar trooper. He steadied his aim. Softly exhaled a deep breath. And fired.

His single phaser pulse struck one of the Breen in his head. A fraction of a second later, Sarina's head shot took down his partner.

There was no time to check the bodies. He and Sarina were shooting to kill now, and time was short. They advanced, trading places again to let her take point to the octagonal main intersection. She hugged the left wall, and Bashir stayed close to the opposite bulkhead. They padded into the open junction. Four sides of the octagon were open and led away at ninety-degree angles—one main passageway running forward to aft and another that crossed the deck from port to starboard. On the other four sides of the octagon were turbolifts.

"This is where we split up," Bashir said. "Activating transceiver now." He tapped the tiny device tucked into his left ear. Sarina did the same, switching on her own concealed transceiver. Speaking in a whisper, Bashir said, "Do you copy me?"

Her hushed voice was intimately close thanks to the implanted device. "Loud and clear."

"All right. Promise me you'll stick to the plan. We hit our targets and get out."

"I promise. It's not as if we have time to do anything else, anyway."

She sounded calm and professional, but he knew what would happen if she let her emotions take over. All he could do was hope she stayed in control this time. He walked to his turbolift, and she walked to hers. They pressed their respective call buttons, and both sets of lift doors opened to reveal waiting pods. He stepped into one, and she entered the other.

Looking diagonally across the intersection at her, he gave her a small salute with his phaser. "I'll see you when I see you."

She returned the valediction with the same forced aplomb. "See you when I see you."

The doors of their turbolifts closed, and Bashir hoped their farewells would amount to more than just wishful thinking.

When the doors of Sarina's turbolift slid apart on Deck Four, she had her back against the side of the lift pod, to the right of the door. As she had expected, a Breen commando who had been posted to guard the deck from intruders leaned inside the pod to investigate.

She snaked her invisible right arm behind his back and over his shoulder. Then she seized his chin with her right hand and braced her left hand against his back as she twisted with all her enhanced strength. The commando's neck broke with a wet crack. His body went limp in her grasp, and she struggled to lower him to the floor of the pod without making any noise. Then she pulled him the rest of the way inside, stepped over his corpse, and slipped out into the corridor.

Her hand was on the grip of her phaser, ready to draw if it turned out the dead trooper had a partner waiting in the passageway, but there was no one there. Ever cautious, she treaded lightly and kept her back to the wall as she snuck toward the entrance to the *ShiKahr*'s computer core. Every few steps, she threw a quick look back, to make sure her six was clear.

Avoid unnecessary confrontation. That had been Saavik's advice to Sarina and Bashir before they had beamed over. There were more than a hundred Breen on this ship—far too many for Bashir and Sarina to face alone in combat, no matter what advantages they had received from their genetic augmentations or Memory Omega's high-tech equipment. Evasion and diversion would be her and Bashir's best hope of finishing this mission and living to tell about it.

Two sections shy of the computer core, a Spetzkar marched down the center of the corridor. He carried his rifle tucked against his left side, the barrel angled downward, his finger hovering beside the trigger rather than in front of it. He moved with a strong and even stride, and his gaze swiveled slowly while he walked, taking in everything around him. He glowed frost-blue in Sarina's visor, which suggested he was concealed by his armor's shrouding circuits.

Sarina sidestepped, pivoted, and put her back to one wall—all without making a sound. She held her breath and remained motionless as the commando stalked past her.

He stopped.

She stared at him, her breath still caught in her chest. *What's he doing?*

The Breen kneeled down and ran his gloved fingertips over the deck where Sarina had just walked. He looked away, down the path from which she had come.

What if their masks see infrared? What if he can see my heat signature?

He turned back and looked directly at her.

If he saw Sarina's invisible blade before she thrust it into his throat, he didn't have time to stop her. She plunged the stealth-coated knife of Tholian obsidian deep through the flexible neck guard of the Spetzkar's armor, and then she twisted the blade and forced it up into his skull. His gurgling death rattles were muffled by his mask.

Can't just leave him here. Sarina looked over her shoulder. A bulkhead tag identified the compartment behind her as unassigned quarters. *Good enough.* She unlocked the door, which parted with a soft hiss. As quietly as she was able, she dragged the dead Breen inside, dumped him to the left of the entrance, and cleaned his blood off her blade by wiping it on the legs of his uniform. She sheathed the knife, then paused to verify the corridor was still empty. Satisfied, she locked the compartment behind her on her way out, to prevent an accidental discovery of the dead trooper.

Fast, light steps carried her to the entrance to the ship's primary computer core. A pair of Breen stood guard just inside the doorway, which someone had apparently locked open. Sarina squatted low and crab-walked along the wall of the corridor opposite the entrance, using her lower vantage to see more of the towering open space on the other side of the doorway.

Five Breen technical specialists were moving around the

computer core, tampering with various systems as they went. The two guards paid the techs no mind and talked to each other, as if they were bored with their assignment.

If it's excitement they want, I'm happy to give it to them.

It was all going to be about timing.

From a small utility pocket on the belt of her stealth suit, she took a miniaturized smoke bomb. The device was as small as a marble, and according to Saavik it was designed to arm when it was thrown and to detonate a few seconds after its initial impact on any surface.

Sarina edged up next to the doorway to the computer core and lobbed the smoke charge down the corridor. It struck one bulkhead, then rolled away, around a curve in the passageway.

At the first click of contact, one Breen asked the other, "Did you hear that?"

The two guards charged down the corridor. One of them pointed in the direction that Sarina had thrown the smoke marble. "It sounds like it's coming from—"

A low boom echoed in the tight space of the corridor. Green smoke billowed from the detonation and created an impenetrable wall. The Breen in charge moved to the far wall and kneeled down while barking orders: "Cover me! Switch to UV, it'll cut through the haze."

His subordinate dropped to one knee on the other side of the corridor—right in front of Sarina. She silently retrieved another Memory Omega implement from her suit's utility belt: a stealth-coated monofilament wire with a fist-sized grip at either end. Or, as it was more commonly known in the jargon of espionage tradecraft, a garrote.

With a single pull she released an arm's length of slack on the monofilament. Then she crept forward, looped it over the junior Breen guard's head, lowered it in front of his neck, and violently yanked the two ends together.

She neither felt nor heard the monomolecular wire slice through the Breen's armor and flesh. All she knew was that his head, once solidly connected to his neck, was now falling to the deck, trailed by a spray of fuchsia blood.

In the split second it took the Breen's severed head to fall and strike the deck, Sarina let go of one side of the garrote and drew her phaser. The other guard turned at the unexpected thud of a helmeted head clattering against the deck plates—just in time to see the phaser beam that punched a scorching hole through his own visor.

No time to lose now. The sound of the phaser shot would have the techs inside the core on alert. She couldn't risk them warning the rest of their company of her presence. She pivoted and marched through the doorway, her eyes keen to every movement.

She froze: none of the technicians were anywhere in sight.

They took cover. Smarter than they look.

There was nothing to gain by letting them set the rules of engagement or summon reinforcements, so Sarina moved deeper inside the five-level compartment. Circular platforms, all with waffle-grate deck plates, ringed the twenty-meter-tall main core, creating a vertiginous sense of open space above and below. Sarina took soft steps and utilized the sparse cover afforded by the control panels that were set at regular intervals around the center level.

She stopped at the nearest companel and logged into the core using an administrator's override code that Saavik had shown her while she had been suiting up on the *Enterprise.* The panel's interface changed from lockout crimson to full-access green.

Time to muzzle the techs. She ramped up the Cochrane distortion coil inside the core far beyond its rated maximum.

The CDC's principal purpose was to enable the core to execute computations in a holographic matrix at many multiples of the speed of light. Faster-than-light processing was an essential element in most starship computers—but it had limits. If one generated too powerful a Cochrane distortion field inside the computer core, any number of onboard systems would suffer as a result—chief among them, communications.

That ought to do the trick.

Her next task was to swap out one of the panel's isolinear chips. To her chagrin, there was no quick way to do so without attracting the commandos' attention and giving away her position. If she wanted the freedom to finish her sabotage, she would have to deal with them.

She locked the console back down. Then she stalked forward to the staircase, scanning above and below for any sign of her quarry. Just before she reached the stairs, she saw them. The five Breen had split up. Two had climbed up two levels and were lying prone, their rifles aimed downward. Two were backed up against the walls on the level beneath her, with their rifles aimed upward. The last one was crouched on the steps, one level above her, his head on a swivel, looking for a target.

She respected their expertise. They were ideally placed to defend one another and concentrate their response to any assault. She couldn't attack any one of them without betraying her position to the others. Her only advantages lay in the facts that her stealth camouflage was superior to theirs and that she had cut off their communications with one another as well as with the rest of their company.

All I need to do is figure out how to neutralize all five of them at the same time. She rolled her eyes at her predicament. *I hope Julian's having better luck than I am right now.*

* * *

Wild shots and screaming ricochets tore out of the open hatchway and kept Bashir pinned to the bulkhead, hoping that the next shot didn't bounce back and cut him in half. He winced at another near miss. *I hope Sarina's having better luck than I am right now.*

A prompt blinked in his holographic heads-up display: ENGAGE ASSISTED TARGETING? He wasn't sure what that included, but he reasoned that any advantage was better than none in his situation. He focused on the prompt and blinked twice to assent to the suggestion, which then changed to read ASSISTED TARGETING ENGAGED.

An inset frame was superimposed over his field of vision. At first he was confused by it. The targeting function seemed to have done nothing more than magnify an area of the floor in front of him. He shifted his weight and saw that the inset frame moved oddly. It took him a moment to understand that his mask's holovisor was giving him his phaser's point of view.

He kept his back to the wall and eased his weapon around the corner into the open doorway. A view of the upward-curving meter-wide walkway inside the ship's ring-shaped jaunt drive filled his HUD's inset frame. As soon as the software detected a potential target, it painted the Breen trooper with a blinking three-point yellow cursor. Bashir adjusted his aim until the cursor turned green and stopped flashing, then he pulled the trigger.

A perfect head shot sent the trooper reeling. His comrade fired back a wild flurry of energy pulses that screamed past Bashir and filled the corridor around him with bouncing sparks and acrid smoke. He put an end to the mad barrage with another precise shot that punched straight through the Breen's chest and dropped him dead beside his partner.

The echoes of battle faded. Bashir's enhanced hearing

detected the scuffling of movement from a few sections away. He focused his attention and heard at least three people. *No, four.* They were trying to sneak up on him, but the Breen's armor had been made for invisibility and resilience, not for stealth. Regardless, that was a fight for which he had neither the time nor the advantage. He moved inside the jaunt drive's ring structure and hurried past the two dead Breen, eager to reach his assigned target quickly.

Gravity inside the ring pulled one outward, away from the main hull of the ship. Moving along the curved walkway reminded Bashir of early space stations, which had relied on rotating ring structures to simulate gravity. It also felt like orbiting a planet, always chasing the curve of the close horizon, and knowing it would forever remain just out of reach.

His pulse raced as quickly as his thoughts. He had to keep track of his pursuers, whom he heard enter the ring far behind him; he noted the markings on the access panels on his left and stayed alert for any sign of hostile contact that might suddenly appear in front of him. Then his eyes fixed upon the panel he had been told to find. He keyed in the command override code that engineer Barclay had shown him in passing on the *Enterprise*, and as the panel unlocked and sprang open, he was thankful once again for his nearly flawless memory.

The clatter of booted feet closed in on him from both directions. He pushed back against his fear and made himself see nothing but the delicate array of components in front of him. This, Barclay had told him, was the key to the entire jaunt drive: the chroniton integrator. It was a system that enabled a jaunt ship to collect sensor data from several seconds into the future—an almost prescient technology that was essential to hyperaccelerated faster-than-light propulsion, as well as to the generation and targeting of stable artificial wormholes.

He entered the override code into the chroniton integrator's main interface and unlocked its configuration panel. *Don't destroy it*, the *Enterprise*'s chief engineer had warned him. *Just . . . tweak it a little bit.* Following that sage advice, Bashir nudged a couple of the device's perfectly attuned calibrations a mere few billionths of a percent off kilter. Then he closed the configuration screen and shut the access panel, which locked automatically.

Now all I need to do is get out of here alive.

In front of him and behind him, the feet of two ghostly pairs of shrouded Breen crept into view. They had him boxed in. Even if they never saw him because of his stealth suit, within moments at least one of them was certain to collide with him on the narrow walkway.

Bashir drew his phaser. Moving with slow care, he lay down on his back and stretched his arms behind his head. He drew a deep breath, then softly exhaled to steady his aim. In the pause between heartbeats, he pressed the firing stud.

A single full-power blast struck one of the Breen behind him in the groin. The Spetzkar he'd hit doubled over and fell to the deck—and the other three opened fire, all of them aiming high as they shot blind around the bend. Crazy ricochets careened down the narrow passage and caromed off the insulated bulkhead panels. Stray shots grazed Bashir's arms and legs, but most of them slammed into the other Breen, who presented the broadest targets.

Two seconds after it had started, the crossfire ended.

Searing pain underscored Bashir's every movement. His stealth suit flickered for a second, and then it stuttered out, leaving him visible and exposed. *So much for the advantage.*

He struggled to his feet and tapped the transceiver behind his ear. "Sarina, do you copy?" No response came. "Sarina, what's your status?" Again, his message went unanswered.

She could be in trouble. He pushed that thought away. Of course she was in danger. They both were. The dilemma he faced was what to do next. His assignment was done. The mission plan called for him to fall back to the exfiltration point—but his heart rebelled at the notion of leaving Sarina behind. If she was cut off, she might need his help.

He looked down at his damaged stealth suit. *How much help can I be like this?* He considered stealing a suit of armor from one of the dead Breen, but then he imagined himself being gunned down by Sarina in a case of mistaken identity, and he ruled it out.

On legs that alternated between jolts of pain and feeling half numb with shock, Bashir limped back to the hatchway through which he'd entered the jaunt drive's ring. His limbs were stiff and burning with fresh pain as he climbed back out into the corridor.

The smart choice, he knew, would be to head aft, back to their beam-in site, which had also been set as their extraction point. Instead, he hobbled forward, toward the turbolifts.

He was going to leave this ship with Sarina at his side . . . or not at all.

It wasn't a perfect plan, but Sarina didn't have time for perfection.

She stood at the same console she had used to ramp up the core's Cochrane distortion. It was just outside any of the commandos' sight lines. As long as she didn't attract their notice by making too much noise, they were unlikely to abandon their concealed positions. At least, that was Sarina's hope. She needed them to stay still for just a few more seconds—just until the site-to-site transport sequence engaged.

The mellifluous drone of the transporter beam filled the core compartment, and on the other side of the core, above and below her position on the middle level, a golden radiance flared and then abated in tandem with the wash of white noise.

Accessing a transporter remotely had been easy. Targeting the Breen inside the core compartment through the Cochrane distortion had been hard. Making the transporter start the dematerialization sequence had entailed overriding several safety warnings.

Sarina had taken the liberty of dispersing the Breen commandos' scrambled patterns into space. Compared to the gruesome agonies that would have awaited them on the other side of a rematerialization sequence, it had seemed to her like the merciful choice.

Time to move now. She pried open the maintenance panel on the underside of the companel. The main bus was arranged exactly as Barclay had shown her in his hurried briefing minutes earlier. Following his instructions, she found the master control chip inside the panel, pulled it out, and substituted the isolinear chip Saavik had given her.

As soon as it snapped into place, the companel's display became a frantic hash of activity happening at the speed of faster-than-light nanoprocessors. Saavik had been deliberately vague about what the substituted chip would do. "It will safeguard our secrets and make the *ShiKahr*'s jaunt drive unreliable," was all the explanation she had offered, and all that Sarina had needed.

Satisfied her work was done, she darted to the open doorway and checked the corridor. *So far, so good.* Choosing speed over caution, she sprinted back the way she had come.

A squall of mechanical noise, like grinding gears and static, spat from the ship's overhead speakers and echoed through the corridors. The universal translator circuit inside Sarina's stealth suit parsed the Breen's vocoder gibberish: "At-

tention, all decks. This is Thot Trom. Prepare for dimensional breach in ninety seconds. Command out."

Sarina reached the turbolift and pressed the call signal. She stepped against the bulkhead beside the lift's doors, in case the pod that arrived turned out to be occupied. Phaser in hand, she tensed when she heard the faint thrumming of the magnetically propelled lift pod's arrival. The doors parted with a low hiss. All was still.

She pivoted to enter the lift—and found herself looking into the muzzle of a phaser. She raised her own weapon in a flash, as the one pointed at her jerked away. She deactivated her stealth suit. "Julian! What the hell?"

"You didn't answer." He stepped back to let her inside the lift. "I thought—"

"That you might get yourself killed? Your suit's not even working!"

He sighed. "Level Twenty-five, Section Ten. Priority transit." The doors closed, and the pod began its swift descent into the bowels of the ship. He frowned. "You're welcome."

No one had asked for an update on the *ShiKahr*'s worsening tactical status, but Crin blurted one out before Trom could silence him. "Fifteen jaunt ships inbound. Ninety seconds to intercept."

"Steady." Trom did his best to project certainty from the command chair. His posture was straight, and his movements were minimal. The crew had their orders; there was nothing to be gained by filling the air with chatter. He had to trust that if he just let them work—

Solt's voice filtered down from the overhead speakers. *"Solt to command. Equations complete. Ready to breach the dimensional barrier."*

"Well done. Lock in your formula and stand by." Now it

was time to act. "Helm. Power up the jaunt drive and patch in Solt's new subspatial geometry."

"Yes, sir." Yoab keyed in the commands, then paused to look back at Trom. "Sir, I need to remind you that we'll have to drop out of warp to use the jaunt drive."

The pilot's report lifted Karn's focus from the tactical console. "Sir, the *Enterprise* is right behind us. If we drop to impulse, we'll be vulnerable."

"No choice, Karn. Arm all weapons and route all backup power to the aft shields. It's up to you to keep the *Enterprise* at bay until we've made it back to our universe."

Karn accepted the burden without further complaint. "Understood."

Yoab finished his preparations at the helm. "Jaunt parameters updated. Ready, sir."

Trom stood. "Attention all decks. This is Thot Trom. Prepare for dimensional breach in ninety seconds. Command out." He stepped forward. "Helm. Take us out of warp."

"Dropping to impulse . . . now." Yoab disengaged the warp drive, and the streaks of starlight on the main viewscreen retreated to cold points.

"Evasive maneuvers," Trom said. "Tactical, stand by to harass the *Enterprise* with preemptive fire."

"Here they come," the tactical officer said. "Firing." Soft feedback tones from his console heralded slashes of phaser light and the blazing streaks of torpedoes across the viewscreen. The *ShiKahr*'s opening salvo was swiftly answered by the thunder of the *Enterprise*'s counterattack.

Trom raised his voice above the rumblings of battle. "Command to Solt."

"Go ahead, sir."

"Power up the jaunt drive. It's time to go home."

* * *

Bashir and Sarina sprang from the turbolift. Together they sprinted aft, abandoning stealth or caution in favor of speed. Every surface of the ship resonated with the rising hum of the jaunt drive, which was on a fast buildup to activation, and the deck rocked with the devil's drumbeat of weapons fire punishing the *ShiKahr's* shields.

By necessity, their beam-in location was also their exfiltration site. Because the *Enterprise* crew couldn't scan through the *ShiKahr's* shields to establish a transporter lock, they had to rely on being able to target their dematerialization sequence on a very limited area inside the ship. That meant the departure point had to be set in advance, and leaving from the same point at which they had arrived would entail the fewest new calculations.

They were three-quarters of the way down the corridor to the exfiltration point when a disruptor shot screamed past Bashir's head from behind.

He ducked by reflex, then spun about-face and threw himself against the bulkhead, narrowly evading another flurry of shots down the middle of the passageway. In the fraction of a second it took him to turn about, Sarina reactivated her stealth suit.

Through his suit's holovisor, he saw her hit the deck and roll onto her back. Bashir filled the corridor behind him and Sarina with a wild barrage of phaser fire, and then he crouched to make himself as small a target as possible.

The pair of Breen commandos who had spotted them poked their rifles back around the corners and returned Bashir's mad attack with one of their own. One shot drilled through Bashir's gut and launched him backward. Another tore into his thigh as he fell.

A perfect shot by Sarina struck one of the commandos' rifles. The weapon exploded in the trooper's hands, and the blast obliterated him and his comrade.

Sarina kneeled above Bashir and deactivated her stealth suit. "Are you all right?"

He couldn't answer; white-hot pain filled his body. All he could do was grit his teeth, focus on breathing, and try to hold back the primal scream that was building in his chest. She surveyed his wounds. "Can you walk?" He shook his head.

Trom's voice echoed down the passageway. "*Stand by for dimensional breach.*"

Sarina holstered her weapon, grabbed Bashir by his arm, and helped him sit up. Despite her slight frame and fragile appearance, she possessed tremendous strength. She got beneath him and draped his weight across her shoulders. Then she lifted him from the deck and stumbled aft in trembling steps, plodding toward their designated exfiltration point.

Bashir winced as the jaunt drive's rising whine became deafening. The *ShiKahr's* doomed jump was imminent. He shut his eyes. *We're not going to make it.*

"I know what you're thinking," Sarina said through clenched teeth. "And shut up, because we're getting off this boat"—she collapsed onto her knees, plucked the recall beacon from her utility belt, and pressed its transmission switch—"right now."

Seconds passed, and they were still sitting in the passageway.

Sarina looked with dismay at the recall beacon, then at Bashir. "Or not."

Shouted reports overlapped strident alarms on the bridge of the *Enterprise* as it traded one salvo of phaser and torpedo fire after another with the *ShiKahr*. In all the commotion, there was one fact that Picard needed above all others, and his first officer used the power of her voice to get it from Troi. "Can you confirm the signal or not?"

"There's too much interference from the *ShiKahr*'s jaunt drive!" Troi fought with the interface on her console. "I'm boosting the gain on the receiver."

"Quickly, Commander," Picard said, putting rare pressure on his security chief. "If they've triggered their recall beacon—"

She shot a pointed stare at him. "I'm *working* on it."

Tolaris's voice snapped Picard's attention forward. "Their jaunt drive is spinning up!" On the main viewscreen, an eerie nimbus of energy formed around the *ShiKahr*. In seconds, the azure halo became a rippling shell of distorted space-time that enveloped the fleeing jaunt ship.

"Signal confirmed!" Troi's hands flew across her panel. "Trying to target the subspace transporter." Her excitement became frustration and then dismay. "Still too much interference from the *ShiKahr*'s jaunt drive!"

K'Ehleyr opened a channel from the console beside her chair. "Bridge to engineering!"

"Go ahead," Barclay replied.

"Reg, we can't lock the subspace transporter for beamout. Can you filter out the interference from the *ShiKahr*?"

"Already on it. Hang on!"

Precious moments slipped away, and it felt to Picard as if time accelerated while he watched a wormhole unlike any he'd ever seen form in front of the *ShiKahr*. Instead of the soothing blue swirl he had come to expect, this one was the color of blood, and flashes of crimson light spilled from its seemingly bottomless maw. Whereas all the other artificial wormholes he had ever seen had evoked for him images of doorways to some mythical higher plane, this one looked like a pit to some fiery underworld—and the *ShiKahr* was racing into it.

Picard turned toward K'Ehleyr, his heart full of hope and dread. "Number One?"

She deflected his seeking gaze with a questioning look at Troi.

Troi kept her eyes and hands on her console, as if she were fighting to conjure a miracle.

On the viewscreen, the *ShiKahr* hurtled into the dark vortex, which contracted shut behind it. A blinding flash erupted as the wormhole closed.

Warnings shrilled on Tolaris's console. The Vulcan yelled, "Brace for impact!"

Hellish thunder engulfed the *Enterprise*. A hard lurch sent Picard sprawling across the deck. He collided with K'Ehleyr, who was also rolling to port—and then they and the rest of the bridge crew were thrown upward as something overwhelmed the ship's artificial gravity and its inertial dampeners. Picard's balding pate slammed against one of the overhead lights. Then the ship righted itself, and everyone plunged back to the deck.

Picard felt the sting of the fresh cut on the top of his head, and a warm trickle of blood traced an erratic streak down his forehead. He shook off the dizziness of the blow and made himself stand up. Beside him, K'Ehleyr slowly regained her balance. He reached out and took her arm to steady her until she nodded that she was all right, and then he looked at Troi.

She hunched over her stuttering console and poked at its controls. Then she looked up at Picard and read his question in his eyes. A smile lit up her face. "Mister Barclay confirms Douglas and Bashir are safely aboard—and they're reporting 'mission accomplished.'"

Finally, some good news. "Tell Mister Barclay I said, 'Well done.'" He added with a rakish smile, "Then tell him I want full damage reports and repair estimates in two hours."

"Aye, sir."

K'Ehleyr sidled over to Picard and dropped her voice to a confidential hush. "Barclay had to keep his tweaks to the *ShiKahr*'s jaunt drive subtle so the Breen wouldn't detect the changes. Are we sure we did enough to prevent it from getting through?"

Picard thought of the spinning vortex of fire that had swallowed the *ShiKahr*. "All I know for certain, Number One, is that I'm glad I'm not aboard *that* ship right now."

Flames lapped at Trom's arms as he ducked for cover from the bridge's cascade of exploding consoles. Sparks fell like rain from ruptured plasma conduits overhead. If not for the air filters in his mask and the haze-penetrating filters of his visor, he had no doubt he would be blind and choking on hot, bitter smoke. Staggering across the yawing deck, he stumbled over Crin's dead body and fell hard against the back of Yoab's chair. "What happened?"

"No idea, sir!" The pilot entered one futile set of commands after another into the helm. His vocoder was unable to conceal the panic in his voice as he shouted above the banshee wails of the ship's engines. "The wormhole's completely unstable!"

An explosion knocked Trom sideways with a bowel-shaking shock wave. He picked himself up off the deck and climbed the operations console to get himself back to upright. "I'll try to patch reserve power into the—"

"It's gone," Yoab interrupted. "We're on batteries, and they're bleeding power fast."

Trom fought to make the operations panel obey him. All he needed was one small break in his favor: another ounce of power, a working subspace comm circuit, a shield generator that hadn't overloaded. But it was no use. The wormhole had reduced the *ShiKahr* to a wounded, defenseless husk that was mute and robbed of power.

We were so close, Trom lamented. *We had it all—*

The twisting fires of the wormhole vanished with a searing flash and a crushing thunderclap. The macabre shrieks of the jaunt drive went silent. Trom looked at the main viewscreen. Through the jittery hash of interference, he saw the comforting normalcy of deep space peppered with stars—and then the broad, shallow curve of a cinnamon-hued planet looming large directly ahead of them.

"Report," he snapped, prompting Yoab out of his stupor and back into action.

The pilot checked his console. "Engines are still off-line. No warp, no impulse, nothing."

A review of the operations panel yielded nothing but more bad news, which Trom kept to himself. His stolen ship, his prize beyond measure, was crippled, powerless, burning on multiple decks, and venting plasma as it dived without shields or communications toward the reddish-brown orb whose gravity had taken hold of it.

Had they at least made it home? He looked at Yoab. "Where are we?"

"Somewhere inside Federation space," Yoab said. "Alpha Quadrant, I—" He froze.

Trom got up and loomed over Yoab's shoulder. "What's wrong?"

"The chronometer," Yoab said.

The commander looked at it, and his blood ran cold. "That can't be right."

"I computed the date by comparing star positions against the closest Federation temporal beacon." He looked at Trom. "The ship's time matched our suits' chronometers before we left."

No. Trom backed away from the console. It wasn't possible. The date had been the same in both universes when Trom and his team had traveled through the rift at Ikkuna Station. But if the new chrono readings were correct, then something had gone terribly wrong. Going by the Federation's standard calendar, they had begun their journey in January 2386.

Now the *ShiKahr*'s chronometer registered the date as 3 August 2383.

Why does that date sound so familiar?

He stared with growing horror at the ruddy landscape toward which the *ShiKahr* fell. "Yoab . . . what planet is that?"

It took Yoab a moment to coax the data from his console. "Tirana Three."

Trom staggered back to the operations console and collapsed into the chair, the weight of his defeat too great to bear while standing. He remembered his first briefing for this mission, and the report about the strange extradimensional starship that the Special Research Division had sacrificed so much to recover, only to fail in disgrace. Then he recalled the name of the planet on which their botched salvage had taken place.

Tirana III.

The mission had come full circle. Trom's hard-won treasure was doomed to become the bait that would lure his countrymen to wrack and ruin. The SRD's failure was now complete and guaranteed by the immutable laws of temporal causality.

I am become the agent of my people's destruction. I am history's fool.

Regardless, protocol had to be preserved.

Trom drew his disruptor and shot Yoab in the head. The pilot's corpse slumped over and fell to the deck.

Alone at last, Trom took off his own helmet and cast it aside. Wreathed in fire, he cackled like a madman until the ship struck the surface, shattering its hull and expelling him and the remains of his men with the last of its air onto the barren world that fate had made their grave.

Thirty-three

Cold wind stung Regon's face, which was still raw from its second cosmetic surgery in as many weeks. She was glad to be herself again, but the lingering pain was an unwelcome side effect of the procedure. *To think—some people bear this for the sake of vanity.*

Kort stood at her side, his own Klingon visage restored to its former weathered glory. Together they gazed out across the rippled waters of the lake at the sun-splashed wreckage of Stratos. He buried his hands in his pockets and grunted. "Back where we started."

"It was always a long shot. We knew that going in."

He kicked a loose rock down the hillside toward the shore. "Of course we did." He squinted against a frigid gust. "But I hate to walk away having accomplished nothing."

"I wouldn't say we achieved *nothing*." She favored him with a crooked smile. "Word is, Zolim's been recalled to Tzenketh. It seems the Autarch wants him to explain why he advised the Taurus Pact to send three fleets on a fool's errand to Bajor."

The news elicited a low rumbling laugh from Kort. "Serves the lazy old *petaQ* right." He shot an approving look at Regon. "Maybe we made a difference, after all. Like old times."

"Like old times." She offered him her hand. "Die with honor, Kort."

"I plan to." He shook her hand. "But not today."

They parted ways neither allies nor enemies; they weren't

intimate enough to be friends, but their aims had always been too closely aligned for them to be rivals.

We're just two ghosts on the same road to an uncertain future, Regon decided.

She didn't know if their paths would ever cross again. Secretly, she hoped they would. But if this moment turned out to be their last farewell, she could live with that, as well.

If her years of service to the Obsidian Order had taught her nothing else, it was that there were always far more terrible ways for things to end.

Never one for the niceties of diplomacy, Taran'atar remained alert but uninterested as the Founder concluded her treaty signing with the human leader of the Galactic Commonwealth. There were hundreds of persons in attendance, not counting the rather large contingent of Jem'Hadar that he had insisted be present throughout the Elemspur Monastery for security purposes. The civilians in the former monastery's great hall all were riveted by the words and actions at the table on the ground floor, while the Jem'Hadar and their assorted counterparts from the Commonwealth's military observed the crowd, ever vigilant for danger.

Chairman Eddington inscribed his signature at the end of a ponderous document that, for reasons Taran'atar failed to appreciate, had been printed on a long, continuous roll of durable paper. Then the human rotated the document toward the Founder, who sat waiting with her own stylus. She favored Eddington with a faint, polite smile, and then she, too, signed the document. As soon as she lifted her pen, she handed it to Weyoun; Eddington handed his pen to Saavik. The treaty was rolled up and whisked away by a tall, regal-looking Andorian of a feminine gender. The audience filled the hall with sustained applause.

The Founder stood, and so did Eddington. They shook hands and exchanged a few brief words, but they spoke too softly for Taran'atar to hear what was said.

Ankan'igar stepped to attention beside him. "You have news from Eris."

Taran'atar retrieved his holographic eyepiece from his belt and fixed it into place on his head. It registered his retinal scan and then retrieved the message from his Vorta commander. Her update was brief, and its details were welcome. He turned off the eyepiece and put it away.

The roar of applause tapered off. Eddington and the Founder said good-bye and went their separate ways, each retreating into the company of his or her entourage. Taran'atar timed his stride to slip in between the Founder and Weyoun as they passed him. "Eris reports that the Taurus Pact fleets that have lingered just outside this system since the Breen's attack on the *Enterprise* have set new courses—back to their points of origin."

His news drew an enigmatic smile from the Founder. "No doubt a decision they made the moment they heard we'd signed a nonaggression pact with the Commonwealth."

Weyoun added, with a droll touch, "There would appear to be a correlation between the timing of the two events. On the other hand, perhaps they merely had a change of heart."

"A most charitable assessment of the situation." The Founder touched Weyoun's arm. "Would you excuse us a moment? I need to speak in private with Taran'atar."

"Of course." Half bowed, Weyoun withdrew in backward steps.

The rest of the Dominion entourage melted away as the Founder led Taran'atar down a deserted hallway of the old religious retreat. Ensconced in stony shadows, she stopped and turned to confront him. "Do you know why I want to speak to you, First?"

"No."

"You wouldn't care to guess?"

It was an odd question. The more he thought about it, the more it felt to him like an accusation. "It would not be my place."

Her face registered benign disappointment. "I am aware of your recent moments of initiative, Taran'atar—your willingness to anticipate my desires and prepare accordingly."

Shame overwhelmed his thoughts. "Forgive me, Founder. I was wrong to presume I could know your mind. I sought only to serve." He bowed his head. "I will have Second Ankan'igar take my life as punishment for my hubris."

"You will do no such thing." Her rebuke stunned him. "Look at me, Taran'atar." She waited until he raised his head and met her stare. "I have long been curious to know what a being of your unique experience and potential might be capable of, in different circumstances."

"I do not understand."

She studied him with an almost compassionate air. "Not only were you born without a natural dependency on the white, you have lived longer than any other Jem'Hadar in history. No other member of your kind has your experience, your discipline, your unique constitution. Now the Great Link wants to know whether you have the ability to learn and adapt to a life other than the one for which you were bred. That is why you will be remaining here in the Alpha Quadrant when our ship returns home."

"Will the Commonwealth permit my regiment to remain on their soil?"

The Founder shook her head. "Not your regiment, Taran'atar. Only you. I have decided that you'll stay on as part of Ambassador Weyoun's entourage."

He thought he understood now. "As a bodyguard."

"Not as such, no. I want you to learn about the peoples of the Alpha Quadrant—in particular, those who have banded together to form the Commonwealth. In short, the role I have in mind for you would be more that of a . . . cultural observer."

It was difficult for him to conceal his revulsion at the prospect. Purely out of reflex, his posture stiffened, and he lifted his chin. "I was designed and born to be a soldier. I earn my life through service and battle. Without those duties, I will have no purpose."

The Founder smiled. "Your purpose will be to learn to live as a free being."

The very notion paralyzed him. "I have no idea how to live such a life."

She answered as she walked away. "That's all right, First. I'm sure you'll figure it out."

Despite a lifetime of being spoiled by the miracles of Federation medicine, Bashir had to admit a profound respect for the sickbay facilities of the Commonwealth's jaunt ships. It had been less than three days since he had been narrowly plucked off the *ShiKahr* by the *Enterprise*'s subspace transporter. He had returned from the mission suffering from multiple disruptor wounds. His injuries had been excruciating as well as life-threatening. Had they been attended to in a Starfleet sickbay, he might have expected to feel lingering phantom pains for up to a week after his treatment. Instead, he had been restored to peak physical condition within a few days.

Maybe I should have taken notes.

Doctor Tropp, the *Enterprise*'s grouchy Denobulan chief medical officer, wasn't keen on small talk, however, so all of Bashir's attempts to wheedle some insights into how the man had achieved such exemplary outcomes had been rebuffed with grunts and grumbles. He switched off the display above Bashir's biobed and pointed at the door. "You're done. Get out."

By the time Bashir replied, "Thank you, Doctor," he found himself talking to Tropp's back.

So much for professional courtesy.

The main sickbay doors opened. Captain Picard entered, followed by Saavik and Sarina. The captain beamed at Bashir. "I trust you're feeling better, Doctor?"

"Quite. Thank you, Captain." He added with a nod to Saavik, "Director."

The Vulcan tilted her head toward the door. "Come. We can talk on our way." Without waiting for him to agree, she turned and made her exit. Picard and Sarina followed her.

Bashir trailed them into the corridor. "Where are we going?"

"The subspace transporter room," Picard said. "From there, the two of you will be heading home."

In contrast to the deserted passageways Bashir and Sarina had seen on the *ShiKahr*, the corridors of the *Enterprise* bustled with activity. Its multispecies crew looked very much like those Bashir had come to know when he served in Starfleet. Being surrounded by such diversity working in harmony filled him with a nostalgic yearning for the career he had sacrificed in the service of his conscience and the name of duty.

He quickened his step to walk beside Picard. "Remarkable ship you have here."

"Yes, it is." A shadow of remorse passed over his stately features. "As was the *ShiKahr*. A pity she had to be destroyed— but better that than to see her fall into the wrong hands."

Double doors parted ahead of Saavik, who ushered them into the subspace transporter room. "We owe you both a debt of gratitude. You risked your lives to prevent the Breen from finishing their mission. Thanks to you, we were spared the risk of sacrificing many ships and lives to stop them."

"Just cleaning up our own mess," Sarina replied. She paused at the steps to the transporter platform, then turned to face Saavik. "But y'know, this might not be the last time a problem from one of our universes bleeds into the other. If you'd like, I could suggest to my superiors at Starfleet Intelligence that they set up an intel-sharing program with you."

Saavik shook her head. "That won't be necessary, Miss Douglas. We've been sharing information and coordinating our activities with Starfleet Intelligence for a few years now. That's how we came to know of Mister Cole and his organization."

"I see."

"Do you? Because I don't think either of you appreciates the danger they pose to you. Their resources are not unlimited, but they are formidable, at least on the level of clandestine operations. Until now, you've underestimated them."

"A mistake we won't repeat," Bashir said, "thanks to you. Now that we know they're aware of our plans, we can adjust our strategy accordingly."

"For your sake, I hope that's true." Saavik reached into a pocket of her robe and took out two small cylindrical devices. She handed one each to Bashir and Sarina. "These are quantum transceivers. If you choose to continue your mission to destroy Section Thirty-one from within, you're going to need them. They work by sharing signals between quantum-entangled subatomic particles. Their transmissions cannot be intercepted or blocked." She pointed at their controls. "Use the white buttons to contact each other from across any distance—even across the barrier between universes. Use the red buttons to contact me, if you need help from Memory Omega."

Bashir and Sarina pocketed the transceivers. "Thank you," Bashir said. "For everything."

Saavik accepted their gratitude with a subtle bow of her head, and then she stepped over to the master control console. She keyed in a few commands, and the cavernous compartment trembled with the low vibrations of tremendous energies. "I'm going to beam you to a top secret subspace transport platform in your own universe, one located on the surface of Bajor."

"Wait," Bashir said. "There's a subspace transporter on *our* Bajor?"

Captain Picard smiled. "As she said, we've been busy—and so have your comrades."

Saavik asked Sarina, "I trust you can devise an explanation that will satisfy your Section Thirty-one handler?"

"I'll think of something." She took Bashir's hand and led him up the steps to the subspace transporter platform. Looking back, she patted the transceiver in her pocket. "And just so you know—these things go both ways. If you ever need us, feel free to call."

Saavik arched one eyebrow. "We just might do that, Miss Douglas." She tapped a pad on her console. "Energizing."

Now that Bashir knew what subspace transporting felt like, he knew to exhale rather than hold his breath before the coils charged to full power. When the oppressive grip of the annular confinement beam took hold of him, the pressure felt slightly more bearable on his empty lungs.

A beautiful curtain of light fell between him and the subspace transporter room inside the jaunt ship *Enterprise*—

—and then the radiance dimmed, the sound faded, and the pressure melted away. As form and color returned to the world around him, Bashir saw that he was in a subspace transporter chamber very similar to the one he had left, but with two major differences.

The first was the two banners suspended on the far wall, facing the platform: the official flags of the Third Republic of Bajor and the United Federation of Planets.

The second was the stunned-looking Bajoran behind the console that faced the platform. He wore a Starfleet uniform with lieutenant's pips. Gaping at Bashir and Sarina, he stammered and tripped over half-formed words. "I, uh, you—but—this—"

"We know exactly how you feel," Bashir said.

As he and Sarina stepped off the platform, the Bajoran found his voice. "Hang on! Who are you? Where did you come from?"

Sarina answered as she and Bashir walked out the door.

"Trust me, Lieutenant. You don't want to know."

Thirty-four

Sarina and Julian materialized in front of their villa on Andor. She felt as fatigued as she had ever been. The couple's unexpected arrival at a top secret Starfleet Intelligence facility on Bajor several days earlier had stirred up considerable attention, and containing the news had proved to be a difficult and delicate task. Only after SI had provided them with new, ironclad identities and nondescript clothing had they been cleared to book passage home on a civilian transport.

Eight days and three ship transfers later, they had beamed down from Andor's orbital transit hub, each of them carrying only a half-filled shoulder bag, and been delivered to within meters of their own front door. Julian plodded toward the house. "It's good to be home."

She trudged after him, up the slight incline. "Dibs on the bath."

The front door unlocked as it sensed their approach. Julian opened it, took two steps inside the foyer, and stopped.

Noting his rigid posture and tense demeanor, Sarina halted in the doorway. "What's—"

She saw what it was—or, to be more precise, *who*. Seated in an armchair in the living room, facing the foyer, was L'Haan, her Section 31 handler. The Vulcan woman sat with her legs crossed and her fingers steepled in front of her chest. "Welcome home."

Sarina tossed her shoulder bag into the corner by the door and stepped forward, between Julian and L'Haan. "We've had a long trip. Can this wait?"

"Of course. My apologies. Please, take a few hours to unpack and shower while I sit and wait for the courtesy of your attention. After all, it's not as if *my* time has any value."

Vulcans might not have invented passive-aggressive sarcasm, Sarina mused, *but they've clearly raised it to an art form.* She looked back at Julian and nodded. He frowned at Sarina, set down his bag, and shut the front door. They walked together to the sofa opposite L'Haan and sat down. Sarina met her handler's cold stare in kind. "Let's get this over with."

"I'm here for your after-action report." L'Haan reached inside her black leather tunic and took out a small device. She pressed a button on its side. A red light on its top indicated that it was recording. She set it on the coffee table between them. "Where is the rest of your team?"

"Lost in action." Sarina chose her words carefully. Telling the truth, even while withholding vital details, would help her avoid the facial microexpressions that betrayed lies. "We were forced to complete our assignment on our own, without their help."

"How were they lost in action? Please be specific."

"We were following the Breen cruiser when it came about and attacked us. They crippled our ship. Julian and I were left adrift in space until the Breen beamed us to the jaunt ship they'd captured during the battle. After that, we were their prisoners."

L'Haan narrowed her eyes. Did she know Sarina was lying? Her hands parted, and she set them on the armrests of her chair. "Did you see the other members of your team die?"

"No," Julian answered. "We were in a different part of the ship."

Not bad. Until that moment, Sarina hadn't realized what a splendid liar Julian could be.

Now that he had drawn L'Haan's attention, she directed

her next query at him. "Tell me about the end of your mission. How did you stop the Spetzkar from stealing the jaunt ship?"

"I made my way to the lowest level of the engineering section. Sarina went to the ship's computer core. She sabotaged their comms and the software for their jaunt navigation. I tampered with the chroniton integrator, which made the jaunt drive's artificial wormholes unstable. Then we—"

"I thought you said you were prisoners of the Breen."

"We were," Sarina cut in. "Some of the Commonwealth officers helped free us from the *ShiKahr*'s brig. They also told us what systems to hit to prevent the Breen from escaping with their vessel."

Julian nodded. "We couldn't have done it without their help."

The Vulcan looked down her nose at the duo. "Continue, Doctor."

"After we sabotaged the ship, we escaped before the Breen activated the jaunt drive. By the time they found out what we'd done, we'd been picked up by a Commonwealth starship."

Sarina leaned forward and hoped to shift the conversation's direction. "The Breen ship didn't make it through, did it?"

"Not as far as we've been able to tell. Our latest intel from the Breen capital is that Domo Pran has scuttled the wormhole research program—due in no small part to the fact that its chief scientist, Thot Tran, defected to the Tzenkethi Coalition."

L'Haan's news reminded Sarina of Tran's chivalrous defense of his female Tzenkethi research partner, Doctor Choska. A mirthful smirk slipped through her mask of disinterest. "Good for him."

"Pardon me?"

"Nothing. Just a small salute to the power of love."

The Vulcan wrinkled her brow in disapproval. "Nature's most overrated aberration." In a breath, she expunged all vestiges of emotion from her face. "Are there any other relevant details I need to know regarding your mission?"

Sarina shook her head. "No, that's it. I'll have a more detailed written report ready for you tomorrow."

"Very well." L'Haan got up, and Sarina and Julian stood to see her out. "I'll be in touch, Agent Douglas." She dipped her chin at Julian. "Doctor."

They followed her to the front door. The Vulcan let herself out, and she pulled the door closed behind her.

Julian stepped past Sarina and cracked open the door to peek outside. Then he closed it and turned a baffled look at Sarina. "She's gone."

"And not a moment too soon." She took his hand and tilted her head toward their bedroom suite. "C'mon. I hear a shower calling our names."

He scooped her up in his arms and carried her with a grin toward the bedroom. "You need to get your hearing checked, my dear. Because *that* siren call is coming from the bed."

Thirty-five

Tangled together beneath the sheets, Bashir and Sarina lay facing each other. Her skin was warm against his, and the air between them was rich with the scents of their coupling.

Tucked under Bashir's pillows was a surveillance-blocking device developed by Starfleet Intelligence to shield them from Section 31's seemingly omnipresent eavesdropping. He activated the scrambler to keep their whispers private. Then he stroked a lock of Sarina's blond hair from her forehead and tucked it gently behind her ear. "Do you think she believed us?"

"No idea." She pressed her forehead against his. "But I don't think it matters. If they're on to us, they'll think we killed Cole and the others, even if we show them proof we didn't."

He sighed. "You may be right."

"So? What now? If our cover's blown, we should walk away from this."

"It's too late for that." He felt the truth like a weight on his chest. "We're in too deep. We've seen too much, and they know it. Thirty-one can't let us walk away. If we try to scrap the mission, they'll have no choice but to kill us."

Disbelief put an edge on her voice. "It's too dangerous. They know our true objective. How are we supposed to finish our mission if they've already seen us coming?"

"It's a double bluff," Bashir said. "They know *why* we're working for them—but they don't know we've been warned our cover's blown. But if we run—"

"—they'll know," Sarina said, seeing his point, "and they'll kill us. But if we go forward, we'll be able to see the traps they set for us. We'll be expecting them."

"Exactly."

There was fear behind her words. "But what's our *plan*, Julian?"

It was a question he had dreaded answering. He knew what had to be done, though he still had no idea how to do it. But the only way to set the future in motion was to say the words.

"We no longer have time to go slowly. We have to jump ahead to the endgame as soon as we can."

She looked into his eyes, perhaps in search of some reassurance that he wasn't out of his mind. "Meaning what?"

"We have to turn the organization's agents against one another. We need to make Section Thirty-one destroy itself from within."

Sarina shook her head. "No, that's insane. It's *too soon.* We don't have the time or the resources. It takes years to pull off an op like that."

"It doesn't matter anymore." He hugged her close and whispered into her ear. "Because it's the only move we have left."

Enlarged holographic images of the other senior coordinators' heads surrounded L'Haan inside the audience chamber. They were being transmitted over secure subspace channels so that they all could remain in seclusion as much as possible—a precaution made necessary by the increased attention the organization had received from Starfleet Intelligence in recent years.

Every whisker in Vasily Zeitsev's snowy beard looked as thick as rope, and the wrinkles in his old and weathered face had been rendered as if they were tiny canyons in a sun-bleached desert. He asked in his heavy Russian accent, *"Do we believe them?"*

L'Haan considered his question. "I see no reason we should."

"*Then why not put an end to this charade?*"

"Because we can't be certain of what happened to Cole," L'Haan said.

"*And because Douglas and Bashir might still be useful,*" said Caliq Azura. The Betazoid woman's black irises were overpowered by her broad streaks of lavender eye shadow. Despite her youth, there was a shrewdness in her gaze. She had a knack for exposing others' secrets—and for making everyone she met see her as whatever they hoped she might be. "*It never hurts to have willing pawns.*"

Her argument failed to sway Kestellenar th'Teshinaal, the organization's eternal pessimist. "*Pawns that turn against their own hardly seem worth keeping.*"

Zeitsev scowled at the Andorian's remark. "*We were never their own, Tesh.*"

"*All the more reason to be rid of them,*" said Jhun Kulkarno. The Zakdorn was a veteran of the organization, one whose decades of service were exceeded only by those of Zeitsev and L'Haan. "*We know they want to act against us. How many chances should we give them to destroy everything we've fought and bled for? When do we say* enough *and cut them loose?*"

"*When I say so,*" replied the only disguised voice in the conversation, the one that belonged to an ominous but conspicuously undefined silhouette—that of their mutual superior, the one they all knew only as Control. "*Then, and no sooner.*"

Julian Bashir and Sarina Douglas will return in

SECTION 31: CONTROL

Acknowledgments

Kara, my wife: Thank you for waiting until I finished writing this novel before starting our new diet. And thank you for persuading me to go on a diet. And for not smothering me when I snore.

My esteemed editors, publisher, and licensor: I offer you my gratitude for letting me continue to play with the coolest toys in one of science fiction's all-time greatest sandboxes.

To former *Star Trek: Deep Space Nine* writer-producers Ira Steven Behr, Bradley Thompson, and David Weddle: Thank you, gentlemen, for incepting Section 31. Without shadow, light has no definition, and your creative contributions to the *Star Trek* universe have made it a richer and far more fascinating milieu, one that my imagination loves to call home.

Lucienne, my agent: Yes, I will get to work writing a new original novel now. Thanks for being patient. I'll do my best to make my next original manuscript not suck.

Bourbon and vodka: You complete me. At the very least, you make it possible for me to complete my manuscripts. Don't ever change, you crazy kids.

Last, I extend my gratitude to you, gentle readers, for continuing to support my flights of fancy, my acts of linguistic mendacity, my crimes of literary deception. Without you, there would be no reason for me to continue spinning tales in this fictional setting that I've loved all my life. So, because your support has made it possible for me to go on contributing to a shared universe whose core message is one of hope for the future, I say to you all: Thank you.

Until next time, *adieu*!

About the Author

David Mack is too weird to live and too rare to die.
Find out more at his official website:
www.davidmack.pro
Or follow him on Twitter:
@DavidAlanMack

Prophetical-Priestly Ministry

The Biblical Mandate
for the 21st-Century Pastor

Prophetical-Priestly Ministry

The Biblical Mandate
for the 21st-Century Pastor

Darius L. Salter

Evangel Publishing House

Nappanee, Indiana 46550

Toll-Free Order Line: (800) 253-9315
Internet Website: www.evangelpublishing.com

Unless otherwise noted, biblical quotations are from the New American Standard Bible®, copyright © 1960, 1962, 1963, 1968, 1971, 1972, 1973, 1975, 1977, 1995 by The Lockman Foundation. Used by permission.

Edited by Helen Johns
Cover Design by Bateman Design

Publisher's Cataloging-in-Publication Data

Salter, Darius, 1947-
  Prophetical-priestly ministry : the Biblical mandate for the 21st-century pastor / Darius L. Salter. — 1st ed.
  p. cm.
  Includes bibliographical references and index.
  LCCN 2001099440
  ISBN 1-928915-25-6

  1. Pastoral theology. I. Title.

BV4011.S35 2002   253
                    QBI02-200085

Printed in the United States of America
  04 05 06 / 10 9 8 7 6 5 4 3 2

On September 16, 2001, churches across the
United States of America were packed with people,
many of whom attend church spasmodically or not at all.
We can speculate about the motivations for attending church
on the Sunday after the terrorist attacks of September 11,
and our conjectures may be true to some extent.
No doubt, many came to participate in the collective
prayer mentality that suddenly seized the American people.
I suspect all who attended on that Sunday desired to hear
words which would somehow make sense
of the most disastrous day experienced on American soil.

Many pastors groped for the appropriate words.
The words did not come easily, but they came.
Parishioners heard words of hope, courage, faith, love, and
reassurance.

This book is offered in gratitude to over one-half million pastors
who took the risk to enter into the aching disillusionment
of millions of Americans. This timeless task will endure
until the return of our Lord Jesus Christ,
when all things will be made right.

Table of Contents

Introduction

Information rains down on us today. This proliferation of information and communication—intensified by cable TV and cyberspace—serves to construct countless personal versions of reality. As a result, William Donnelly designates this as the "Confetti Generation."

> Nurtured in an autonomous generation, the confetti citizen consumer will be inundated by experience and ungrounded in any cultural discipline for arriving at any reality but the self. We will witness an aggravated version of today when all ideas are equal, when all religions, lifestyles, and perceptions are equally valid, equally indifferent, and equally undifferentiated in every way until given value by the choice of a specific individual.[1]

This explains why so many independent, nondenominational churches are not in the business of broadcasting the gospel, but *narrowcasting* it. Narrowcasting is aimed at target groups with addictions, emotional needs, upwardly mobile lifestyles, and particular music or entertainment tastes. Instead of the seeker encountering God through the revelation of His holiness, God is supposed to encounter the consumer at the point of need, not to mention taste. In fact, independent megachurches offer some of the same qualities as cyberspace: remoteness, nonparticipation, immediacy, privacy, anonymity, autonomism, and voyeurism.

Both the Christian faith and American society are more fragmented today than ever before. Thus, the first task of pastoral ministry is offering the *non*-optional option: the faith delivered to the saints. Present-day pastors to cyberspace residents are facing a more difficult task than any of their predecessors.

---

[1]William Donnelly, *The Confetti Generation: How the New Communications Technology Is Fragmenting America* (New York: Holt, 1986), 182.

Myriad conflicting currents have displaced meaning with mass information. In reference to the nineteenth century's explosion of newspapers and periodicals, Alvin Gouldner writes, "This sheer increase of information intensified the problem of information processing and above all of clarifying the meaning of the information. Acquiring meaning, not information, [became] increasingly problematic."[2] The problem is even more acute in America during the twenty-first century.

The present infatuation with media personalities is undermining any serious attempt to pursue truth and meaning, whether political or religious. We have become people who are more interested in the slick and sensational than in any kind of sane sorting through of issues that would align us with Scripture and the mind of Christ.

The only hope for the church is to recover a consensus of faith from the cauldron of conflicting religious claims being stirred by our self-fulfillment society. The Christian clergy must place themselves within the pastoral succession, aligning with the content and spirit of what the apostles believed and taught—proclaiming meaningful *words* of faith and sound doctrine.

Indeed, it is time to begin at the house of God, which no longer echoes with the trumpet's certain and clear tones of truth. The church must place priority on the authoritative affirmation of the truth of Christ and the claims of that truth on everyday life. The evangelical church needs prophet-priests who speak for God, in God, and for God. Their model is found in Christ, who spoke with power and said, "All authority has been given to me in heaven and on earth…and lo, I am with you always, even to the end of the age" (Matt. 28:18b, 20b).

The mastery of words is a lifelong pursuit of ministry. The words themselves may vary with different generations, but their task is the same. Ministers' concerns today are the

---

[2]Alvin Ward Gouldner, *The Dialectic of Ideology and Technology: The Origins, Grammar, and Future of Ideology* (New York: Seabury Press, 1976), 93.

same as those carried by Jeremiah and Christ. *Theology* (literally, "a word about God") and the words that express theology are the currency of ministers of any era, the currency that gives meaning to life. Prophetic-priestly words convey a theocentric comprehension of life as represented by Jesus Christ and illuminated by the Holy Spirit. The minister's words must not be compromised or diluted by marginal pursuits. The bewildering call of multitudinous pastoral options means that a minister must focus on biblical rootedness and clarity of communication, more than ever. To this task, the prophet-priest in pastoral ministry gives constant attention.

Above all, pastors today must learn a language that is adequate to meet the needs of people. The words of this language create godly emotions, desires, plans, and actions. They carve meaning out of life's nothingness, light out of darkness, encouragement out of despair, and belief out of unbelief. Words represent ideas. Ideas inspire action. Without effective words, a minister will see no action or, at best, the action will be meaningless.

How do we acquire this prophetic-priestly language? We must begin at the very same place the apostles began: We must give ourselves to prayer and the reading of Scripture. Out of a rich storehouse of biblical words, the church can begin to reform society and help people in their quest for meaning.

Is there a language—a word paradigm—that transcends culture and time? Is there a particular kind of communication that enables a minister to do ministry God's way and carry out God's intentions? This book argues that there is a model of communication that is biblically informed, theologically driven, and culturally astute. We call this model the prophetical-priestly paradigm for doing ministry.

Darius L. Salter
Nazarene Theological Seminary
Kansas City, Missouri

CHAPTER 1

The Changing Paradigm of Ministry

In 1955, a new family moved into a certain Midwestern town. A hard-earned five hundred dollars purchased the four acres that would serve as their home site. But there were no jobs in the small town. The husband's monthly pension from Navy retirement was insufficient to feed this family of two adults and three small children. The credit rendered by the local grocer and the Sears catalogue quickly became an insurmountable debt.

Before marrying at the age of thirty, this man had spent his life drinking, gambling, fighting, and carousing. His war experience produced a serious case of bleeding stomach ulcers. The man was unemployable.

His wife had been raised in a single-parent home that was nominally Christian. Her parents had divorced before her birth. She was filled with anger, bitterness, and self-pity.

This small family was religiously and spiritually rootless. In today's terminology, they were a textbook example of a dysfunctional family.

Probably not more than one family moved into this small community each year, and no more than one family moved out. Not much that happened there remained a secret. So when this new family tumbled into town, it was in full view of everyone. Yet no pastor of the community's established churches ever called on them.

Then, within the providence of God, one pastor threw the family a lifeline. This pastor was a flaw in the town's social fabric. He was not a seminary graduate and he lacked spit-and-polish, but he knew he had a mission. He had come to the community with a wholehearted devotion and a single-minded intention. He was determined to fulfil the pastoral office in loving, prayerful concern, proclaiming the gospel with passion and conviction, and reaching out to people through visitation with unswerving fervency.

He invited the new family to church. They heard the gospel enunciated loudly and clearly. The preacher covered the basics of the Christian faith in his preaching: justification, sanctification, heaven, hell, assurance, sin, righteousness, and forgiveness, all with appropriate application. He gave a definite invitation, bathed in prayer, for his listeners to step into the benefits of Christ's atonement.

The prayer was not without hands and feet. The pastor and his congregation visited the home of the new family, placing a circle of concern around them. In today's terms, the visitation seemed oddly deficient because the church offered this family no social or legal advocacy. They provided no tangible assistance in the way of food, clothes, or medicine. The family received no church, state, or community assistance. All the family ever got from the people of this little church were words—convicting, hopeful, eternal, redemptive words.

In his visits, the pastor talked in effervescent tones of Christ and salvation. He made no carefully scripted presentation of the gospel. Instead, his conversation flowed with a natural theological current: Time is short; life is fragile; death is sure; eternity is long; heaven will be worth it all. His words sprang from a way of life, a way that offered affirmation, encouragement, and potential for change. The verbal exchange consisted of what Walter Bruggemann refers to as "gospel modes of discourse."[1]

What did salvation mean for this family? The wife was converted to Christ and found harmony with her existence. The husband found the Christ of physical and emotional healing. He was now able to work and provide for his family. Each of the children made commitments to Christ that would be played out in their education, vocations, marriages, children, and adult decisions. This family found direction, purpose, and security. They attained the freedom to love and embrace one another because they had been loved and embraced.

Indeed, words were life-changing for them. The pastor and church members extended their life-altering invitation as prophets and priests. God called them and empowered them to engage in that endeavor.

The twenty-first century has now arrived and things have changed in that little town. After reaching a population of 40,000 in 1995, the town even changed its name. Many people in the town commute to a nearby metropolis to work, taking pride in the fact that they don't have to live in the big city. A grandson of the 1955 couple, his wife of five years, and their two children have just moved into the bustling little town. They are college graduates, having attended their denomination's flagship school. He is employed in a local electronics firm and she teaches fourth grade in a public school. Both of their children are enrolled in a church preschool program.

Outwardly, things seem to be going well for this young couple. They live in a new subdivision and drive late-model

[1]Walter Bruggemann, *Biblical Perspectives on Evangelism* (Nashville: Abingdon, 1993), 45.

cars. Actually, they are "running on empty." The mother is plagued with guilt every time she drops the children off for daycare, because her teaching job is taking more time than she ever imagined. She often finds herself wide awake at 4:00 A.M., worrying about the pressures of the day. The father's computer programming job also demands long workdays, so their marriage is subject to a good deal of tension. They owe fifty thousand dollars in student loans and their debt seems increasingly staggering. The young father escapes to the golf course, but does not find that nearly as satisfying as when he played with his college buddies.

This couple know they are not where they need to be spiritually. They rarely talk about their relationship with God. Within their current schedule, a personal devotional life seems out of the question. They tried attending the church of their grandparents, but the worship service was dull. The facility had not been updated for decades and the whole place seemed lifeless. Even though the pastor made a follow-up visit and tried to persuade them that this was the church where they would be most satisfied, they were not convinced.

They tried several other churches. The pastors of most of those churches had attended church-growth seminars, so they fully understood the felt needs of the young couple. In fact, many of the twenty-five churches of this town would be able to meet the couple's needs in terms of child rearing, marriage enrichment, money management, and all other kinds of educational programs. Many of these congregations had tailored their programs to the young couple's schedule and tastes that the newcomers would not have to change their lifestyle to get involved. The couple's gnawing spiritual hunger was partially assuaged with the affirming sermons and upbeat worship services and they found enough reassuring sentiment to get them through another week.

In a sense, the needs of this young couple are much different from those of their grandparents. They live life at an entirely different pace. In the last fifty years, transportation, entertainment, communication, education, recreation, and even religion have gone through a metamorphosis. Religion is no longer a way of life; it is an option to be fitted into other options. So many options are vying for the young couple's attention that life is bewildering.

From another perspective, however, the needs of the young couple are exactly the same as their grandparents'. They need to hear the same eternal truths—truths borne by prophetic-priestly words that will confront, convict, and connect them to the Redeemer. These words will need to possess sufficient accuracy to guide the young couple to repentance, justification, and sanctification. The words must also represent a biblical ethic that enables the young couple to address their lifestyle and assess their value system before it is eternally too late. They need a pastor who can relate to their current way of life, someone who knows how to communicate the truth to them. They need a pastor who can speak in a contemporary idiom. In short, they need a pastor who is a prophet-priest.

The New Environment

Actually, the plight of this young couple is more desperate than that of their grandparents for two reasons. First, they are hedged about by so many possessions and activities that their essential needs, if not completely neglected, are at least subverted. They measure up to their ancestors culturally, but they are dwarfs spiritually. And since they cannot differentiate between the beguiling voice of their culture and the voice of biblical priorities, they find themselves in a puzzling malaise.

Second, their situation is more desperate because the people who would render them pastoral care have adopted a new paradigm of ministry. This paradigm promises the young couple spiritual welfare while keeping their present materialistic lifestyle intact. In other words, they are told it is possible to become a full-fledged member of most of the churches in their town while still being enslaved to the priorities of the secular community. They get the message that the kingdom of God has not come to earth; it has been adapted to earth. Thus, it is much more difficult for this twenty-first-century couple to become liberated by Christ's kingdom, a kingdom that transcends the normative assumptions about happiness and blessedness.

The pastor who ministered to this young man's grandparents fit more readily into the prophetic-priestly role than do the present-day pastors of this town. He spent a good deal of time reading the Word of God and praying on his knees. The language of Scripture became his language. The concerns of Scripture became his concerns. In both his lifestyle and speech, he expressed an urgency that is alien to today's ministers. Today, soul concerns are camouflaged by more temporal pursuits. Bringing people into the presence of God has been replaced by teaching them coping techniques. Despite all this, the young couple can and may pick up many good things by attending the churches in their new hometown. The local pastors may even enable them to make sufficient adjustments to call themselves Christian.

A Technological Approach To Ministry

Times change. People, cultures, social theories, world views, and professions change. Christian ministry changes, too. Its evolution has been more subtle than what we have seen in professions that depend more upon technological innovation. But there have been distinct changes in ministry, clearly characterized by the changes in its word paradigms. Seventeeth-century ministry was characterized by a theological word, eighteenth-century ministry by a revivalistic word, nineteenth-century ministry by a methodological word, and the twentieth century by a therapeutic word. Ministers believe each change was an advancement on the past, bringing about a deeper understanding of both individuals and society than their ministerial predecessors possessed.

Today, we have a new paradigm, a technological approach to ministry. Pastoral success is thought to depend on having the best "system." A ministry system can be taught via a seminary and replicated in a chart. What persons need is the driving motif of today's church. However, their needs are seldom defined by the historical church, but by contemporary society.

This partially explains the current rise of the megachurch and the demise of the small church. We ministers are convinced that only the ministry system most attuned to society's rapidly rising expectations will survive. So the new system's leaders are creative geniuses who grow large churches, hold seminars, and sell books to the rest of us. We have accepted the proposition that a word about managing and marketing the ministry system is as important, if not more so, than a word about God.

But every minister has a part in shaping the word paradigm of twenty-first-century ministry. Our society's understanding of the gospel will depend on each pastor's understanding of words, and how those words interpret and communicate the unchanging Word to a changing world. This calls for a fresh application of pastoral language, enabled by the Holy Spirit, to attend to the living Christ who is forever relevant to the world.

CHAPTER 2

The Impact of Words about God

In his illuminating history, *Lincoln at Gettysburg,* Gary Wills dismantles the myth of Abraham Lincoln's hastily scribbling a few words for off-the-cuff remarks at the Gettysburg cemetery. In all likelihood, Wills says, the speech was honed over a period of several days, being fine-tuned even on the morning of the cemetery dedication. Lincoln was obsessed with finding the right word, and the right word to follow that word. He would have agreed with Mark Twain that the difference between a right word and the nearly right word is the difference between lightning and the lightning bug.[1]

Lincoln's speech on the "new birth of freedom" was conceived in 272 words. The words acted. Lincoln's words of peace instilled peace in the crowd. His words of hope inspired

---

[1]Gary Wills, *Lincoln at Gettysburg: The Words That Remade America* (New York: Simon and Schuster, 1992), 163.

hope. His words of unity bound the grieving nation together. Later, in his second inaugural address, Lincoln's words about "malice towards none, charity for all" would both console and forgive. The distinction between words and deeds is often artificial. Words *are* deeds.

Lincoln's words evoked a comprehension of the past and a vision for the future. His simple words were amplified by his humanness and his magnanimous spirit. Lincoln's spirit comprehended the spirit of the moment. He combined common language with uncommon grace and power, to enable others to understand the world as it is and as it can be.

The kind of speech delivered by Lincoln is what J.L. Austin calls "performative utterance."[2] The ability of words to work change in the lives of its hearers stands on the twin pillars of authority and appropriateness.

Is it possible that today's pastor could rediscover the revolutionary precision of speech exemplified by Abraham Lincoln? And why has this precision been lost? More important, could pastors recover the kind of congregational authority necessary for a prophetical-priestly role? This God-anointed role would manifest itself in preaching, worship, counseling, visitation, and the various types of crisis intervention that are common to the ministerial task. People of the congregation would have a renewed sense of confidence because the pastor is able to utter a right word in due season.

Part of the reason for mundane pulpit speech stems from the confusion concerning the word *extemporaneous,* literally meaning "from the moment." The two following definitions demonstrate that *extemporaneous* has highly diverse meanings:

> (1) composed, performed, or uttered offhand, without previous study or preparation; unpremeditated, as an extemporaneous address. (2) in speech classes, etc., spoken with

---

[2]J.L. Austin, *How To Do Things With Words* (Cambridge, Mass.: Howard University Press, 1978).

preparation, but not written out or memorized, distinguished from impromptu.[3]

Unfortunately, most evangelical American ministers have adopted the first definition rather than the second when they think of "extemporaneous preaching." *Extemporaneous* is assumed to mean spontaneous—i.e., without preparation. Yet no effective American preacher ever has adhered to this premise. For those who divorce the life of the mind from the life of the spirit, pulpit speech becomes benign and shallow. They do not realize that the anointing of the Spirit is best found in a constancy of devotion, rather than in an occasional impulse.

Christian people can endure and prevail in Christ, supported by faithful pastoral words. Failure to provide this support is a betrayal of the ministry's most basic call. Of course, just as pillars vary in thickness, design, and strategic placement, so do the different aspects of a pastor's ministry. The effectiveness of a pillar's construction is often difficult to assess; we hope we don't have to wait until a building falls down before we evaluate its construction. Likewise, careful attention should be given to the construction of a pastor's supportive ministry. In this book, we call the process *becoming a prophet-priest*. Prophet-priests draw other persons to the ultimate pillar, Jesus Christ.

"You should hear his words. You have never heard anything like his words," a lady said to her friends. She spoke of a pastor who was about to preach at her husband's funeral. In faith, she had bestowed on a trusted spiritual director life's ultimate privilege, the final word. The final word opens the door to life's mysteries, paradoxes, and inherent contradictions. We must have a deft touch in opening the door to peer beyond death. Every ear and eye are open and every individual is poised to experience the other side. Imprecision through lack of spiritual preparation, careless thought, or the inability to seize the significance of the moment, is a sin.

---

[3]*Webster's New Twentieth Century Dictionary Unabridged* (New York: Simon and Schuster, 1983), 648.

Those who hear a funeral sermon deserve that in which the prophet-priest should excel—words fitting for the moment. The hearers wait expectantly, but not always confidently, for Spirit-anointed and Christ-centered words.

All of life is a crisis. The prophet-priest has the deep realization that daily human existence carries the potential for conflict. Words can be used for both conflict prevention and conflict resolution. Pastors who fail to face life as it is by applying biblical truth are as bland as a computerized sales pitch on the telephone. They fail to change people's lives because they are both impersonal and irrelevant. By contrast, a prophet-priest can enter a crisis with differentiating, penetrating, revealing, unmasking, and inspiring speech. This calls for a marshaling of all of the minister's resources. It requires all of the prophet-priest's character, knowledge, and skill to meet the demand of the moment.

Even when a minister says nothing, it is not out of a lack of knowledge. A faithful minister's silence will not come out of ignorance, but from a thoroughly honed sensibility that there is not an appropriate word to speak on this occasion. But eventually, like Job's friends, we will be called upon to speak, for better or worse.

Prophetical-priestly words call for an emotional and spiritual investment that is draining. Facing falsehood with truth, tearing down evasive facades, calling for decision, and rebuilding character is tough work. For that reason, throughout the history of the church, prophet-priests have needed times of retreat. The confronting, interacting, uplifting, and resurrecting nature of the minister's job requires incredible stamina. The requisite resources are not found in the human storehouse. The prophet-priest must be wary of spiritual depletion. For that reason, we read of Christ, "The news about him was spreading even farther, and great multitudes were gathering to hear him and be healed of their sicknesses. But he himself would often slip away to the wilderness and pray" (Luke 5:15-16).

Words that do not issue from such times of spiritual retreat will become chit-chat, prattle, and idle talk. Unfortunately, much of professional ministry majors in these kinds of words. In contrast, prophetical-priestly words are intentional. They intend to create Christian heroes and heroines, who rise above self-service. They intend to create visions of the kingdom of God on earth. Most important, they intend to create action that will bring the kingdom of God to earth. All of this is idealistic, but prophet-priests will not stop short of the ideal. They are never satisfied. They know that life could be better for someone. Thus, there is the wild hope that they can plant a word that will be replicated *ad infinitum* in the lives of Christian disciples until Christ returns.

Neil Postman equates "word meaning" with "world making." The church continually competes for the dominant world view. The gods of economic utility and technology always seek to displace the radical monotheism of the Hebrew and Christian Scriptures. The only way by which we can effectively describe the one true God is via our shared narrative. Telling the Christian story has never been more critical. Postman writes, "Our genius lies in our capacity to make meaning through the creation of narratives that give point to our labors, exalt our history, elucidate the present and give direction to our future."[4]

The pastor is responsible for the perceptions of his or her people. Lack of a clear Christian perception of the world leads to an amalgamation with the prevalent world view of the secular culture. This world view is deadly. We can escape only by being summoned to God's transcendent ideals. Unless leaders of the Christian community sound a certain trumpet from the mountaintop, the people's allegiance to God surely will be compromised.

When we accept the call to ministry, we accept the duty to get the Christian narrative correct. Relating the definitive

[4]Neil Postman, *The End of Education: Redefining the Value of School* (New York: Alfred A. Knopf, 1996), 7.

narrative—i.e., the drama of Christ's redemptive work—to the totality of life is the prophet-priest's primary task. This work is as deliberate as the worship of Job, who rose up early in the morning and offered burnt offerings according to the number of his children. "'Perhaps my sons have sinned and cursed God in their hearts.' Thus Job did continually" (Job 1:5b). Spoken words which bear prophetical-priestly application will be no less premeditated. They begin with the Christ perspective. They end by asking, "What is the Christian implication of the words which accompanied my latest task or encounter?" All ministerial tasks bear this kind of accountability.

A minister accepts the fact that her or his words are more than words, and never spoken for words' sake alone. The Jewish author Elie Wiesel, in reflecting on his life's work, commented:

> For me, literature must have ethical dimension. The aim of literature...is to disturb. I disturb the reader because I dare to put questions to God, the source of all faith. I disturb the miscreant because, despite my doubts and questions, I refuse to break with the religious and mystical universe that has shaped my own. Most of all, I disturb those who are comfortably settled within a system—be it political, psychological, or theological. If I have learned anything in my life, it is to distrust in intellectual comfort.[5]

All of life tends toward comfort. The comfort that a minister fears, or ought to fear, is the comfort of ministry itself. For that reason, few of us persist in ministry's most intrinsic task. Myriad pastoral duties offer escape from the toil of soul-care. Likewise, the prophet-priests of biblical history were often lured away from their assignment. Their task was simple—to address the spiritual condition of their people.

Right words are expensive and should be carefully chosen. The writer of Proverbs says:

[5]Elie Wiesel, *Memoirs: All Rivers Run to the Sea* (New York: Alfred A. Knopf, 1995), 336-37.

Like apples of gold in settings of silver
Is a word spoken in right circumstances.
Like an earring of gold and an ornament of fine gold
Is a wise reprover to a listening ear (Prov. 25:11-12).

The writer goes on to express apt analogies for faithful words, refreshing words, soft words, false words, inviting words, and controlled words. Words affect people's lives. Words determine people's actions.

So godly words are means of grace. John Wesley defined the means of grace as "outward signs, words, or actions, ordained of God, and appointed for this end, to be the ordinary channels whereby he might convey to men, preventing, justifying or sanctifying grace."[6] These ordinary channels have been constant through the history of the church. Pastoral ministry consists of spoken and acted words, offered in the name of Christ.

Eighteen years ago, a woman came to my church office for counseling. She attended my congregation, along with her three children. She wanted me to rubber-stamp what she had already decided to do—divorce her husband. Her argument was persuasive: He had been maritally unfaithful; he no longer showed any romantic interest in her; he paid little attention to the children; and he misused the family's finances. To add insult to injury, he had a Corvette sitting in the garage which the family could ill afford.

Like thousands of other pastors, I found myself standing between the biblical text and the human text. After hearing the sordid details of the human text, I wanted to blurt out, "Go ahead and divorce the no-good bum. He's not worth your time."

But my first obligation was to the biblical text. "Marriage is to be held in honor," Scripture says (Heb. 13:4). "For I hate divorce," God declares (Mal. 2:16). The dissonance be-

[6]John Wesley, *The Works of John Wesley*, Third Ed. (Kansas City, Mo.: Beacon Hill Press, 1978), 5:187.

tween God's Word and the immediate crisis was clear, but we lacked a simple solution. So I stalled for time. I said, "Sue,[7] let's give it three weeks. Covenant with me to pray, and let's expect God to work a miracle." Why I designated three weeks, I did not know.

Three weeks later, almost to the day, the couple's oldest son was found to have an aneurysm (a ballooned blood vessel) in his brain. He was a walking time bomb. The first time I met Bob was at his son's hospital bed. The boy's critical condition awakened Bob from his hedonistic coma. On the night before his son was to be taken to a distant hospital specializing in the surgery he needed, I visited the family at their home and prayed with them.

Though I did not know it, Bob made a covenant with God that night. He promised that if God would heal his son, he would begin attending church. The surgery was successful and Bob kept his promise to God. Each Sunday thereafter, Bob was in church. He and I regularly had lunch together and talked about what really matters in life. Bob eventually gave his life to Christ and became a leading member in that church. God not only restored the health of his son, but redeemed Bob's marriage and revitalized his relationship to his family.

I recently had an opportunity to visit that congregation again. After I preached, Bob and Sue met me in the foyer. Bob wept uncontrollably, hardly able to speak. Sue repeatedly said, "He's a changed man."

The right words—words far beyond my wisdom—had served as tools of redemption eighteen years earlier. The Holy Spirit had rendered the Scriptures effective in ways that only He foresaw.

Every parishioner deserves a pastor who speaks the language of the Kingdom rather than mimicking the ideas of a confused society. Translating both the written text and the human text is critical to the work of the prophet-priest. God's Word must be applied to the human heart.

---

[7]The names of this couple have been changed to safeguard their privacy.

All of us who claim to be Christian ministers must keep in mind what Jesus told His disciples: "The words that I have spoken to you are spirit and are life" (John 6:63b). Christ's words are truly the difference between life and death.

Paul's First Epistle to Timothy describes the core identity of a pastor. The one gift most necessary for an "overseer," a leader of the people of God, is the ability to teach—to use prophetic words (3:2). "The elders who rule well are to be considered worthy of double honor, especially those who work hard at preaching and teaching" (5:17). This epistle frequently alludes to the task of teaching and reminds young Timothy that it is essential for the welfare of the church (1:3, 5; 4:11, 13, 16; 6:2, 17). The following exhortation is as applicable to pastors in our own day as in any other:

> Preach the word; be ready in season and out of season; reprove, rebuke, exhort, with great patience and instruction. For the time will come when they will not endure sound doctrine; but wanting to have their ears tickled, they will accumulate for themselves teachers in accordance to their own desires, and will turn away their ears from the truth, and will turn aside to myths (2 Tim. 4:2-4).

Even those who were physically closest to Christ were unable to comprehend adequately the "fullness of the Godhead" in Christ, much less express it in words. God had revealed himself via the living Word, "the creative principle of the cosmic order."[8] That incarnate Word represented everything God had ever been or ever will be. Ministers have been striving ever since to find proper words to describe and communicate that Word. This is the challenge and the art of the prophet-priest.

Who was Christ and how did words figure in His ministry? Christ on earth was the embodiment of all God's attributres. Christ carefully selected a series of disclosures

---

[8]Mark Taylor, *Erring: A Postmodern Theology* (Chicago: University of Chicago Press, 1984), 46.

and discourses to reveal His identity. For the multitude, He chose signs and wonders. For those closest to Him, He chose words. In the absence of this explanatory speech, Christ would have been a complete mystery. Christ entered the lives of His followers by speaking of himself: "I am the way, the truth, and the life; no one comes to the Father but through Me" (John 14:6).

In Christ, the world discovered that there is a purpose and direction in history. He demonstrated that the Word of God defies fate and chaos. Christ could usher in the Kingdom and redeem history by becoming a part of history. "I am the Alpha and the Omega, the first and the last, the beginning and the end" (Rev. 22:13). The essence of history is rational discourse. In the absence of rational discourse, there can be no self-discovery. Only through properly aligned words can a person discover that she or he is not an accident. Thus, we can say that history is not only theocentric, but logocentric.

The New Testament narrative is not simply made of words, it is largely *about* words—the words of angels, prophets, Mary, Zachariah, Anna, John the Baptist, and ultimately, the Christ. The point is well made that the New Testament centers on the redemptive deed—the death and resurrection of Christ. But that deed would have little or no meaning without the perspective offered by words. The Messiah's coming was preceded and followed by prophetic words. The angels are the harbingers:

> Glory to God in the highest,
> And on earth peace among men
> with whom he is pleased (Luke 2:14).

Christ announced the purpose of His own coming: "Thus it is written, that the Christ would suffer and rise again from the dead the third day, and that repentance for forgiveness of sins would be proclaimed in His name to all the nations, beginning from Jeruslaem" (Luke 24:46-47).

John the Baptist's ministry consisted of words, so much so that he was often called the "voice." A single message has never been more timely, succinct, and critical than the one which he preached: "Behold the Lamb of God who takes away the sin of the world!" (John 1:29b). John's words instructed Roman soldiers, prepared hopeless peasants, and rebuked King Herod. He was put to death because his words had been unhedging and unequivocal. He left no monument, healed no disease, and performed no miracle. (At least none is recorded.) Yet Christ said of him, "Truly I say to you, among those born of women there has not arisen anyone greater than John the Baptist!" (Matt. 11:11a).

By contrast, Jesus came performing all sorts of supernatural acts. In fact, he used the miracles to validate his ministry to John when the "voice" wondered whether he had made the correct identification of the Messiah. Jesus' supernatural acts were primarily intended to get people's attention, to prepare them to listen to His words: "The blind receive their sight and the lame walk, the lepers are cleansed and the deaf hear, the dead are raised up, and the poor have the gospel preached to them" (Matt. 11:5). Rarely, if ever, did Jesus perform one of these acts without declaratory words. He often prefaced a healing with a command: "Go; it shall be done for you as you have believed" (Matt. 8:13). "Get up, pick up your bed and go home" (Matt. 9:6). "Little girl, I say to you, get up!" (Mark 5:41b).

Jesus often connected a miracle with a spoken promise: "It shall be done to you according to your faith" (Matt:9:29b). "Your brother shall rise again....Did I not say to you that if you believe, you will see the glory of God?" (John 11:23, 40). The signs were sometimes concompassed by prayer and blessing. Consider for example Jesus' feeding of the multitude: "Ordering the people to sit down on the grass, He took the five loaves and the two fish, and looking up toward heaven, He blessed the food, and breaking the loaves He gave them to the disciples, and the disciples gave them to the crowds" (Matt.

14:19). On all of these occasions, He could have said nothing. But had He said nothing, the meaning would have been lost.

Doing and speaking were uniquely combined in Christ's act of blessing. He blessed the bread and blessed the children. The greek word for "bless," a combination of *eu* ("well; good") and *logeo* ("speak"), literally means "to speak well of." It was the appraisal that God gave of the created order in the beginning. Christ gave the same appraisal while on earth, an appraisal that continues to refute Gnosticism, Manicheanism, and other false dualisms between spirit and matter. Sovereign grace continues to validate all existence, placing it under the possibility of redemption. Christ's blessing is the ultimate word of hope.

Jesus' healing ministry seemed rather to go in reverse. By the end of his earthly sojourn, His healing miracles had virtually ceased. The last eight chapters of Matthew, the last six of Mark, the last six of Luke, and the last nine of John contain no healing miracles of Christ, except for repairing the damage Peter did to Malchus' ear. What we have instead in these chapters are the two essential things that Jesus came to bring: His atoning death for the sin of the world and His words.

A primary task of the church during its first five hundred years was to accurately define who Christ is. No movement in the history of the world has given more attention to the precision of language than did the church during that time.

The seven Ecumenical Councils of the church were the most important events to take place following its birth at Pentecost. The most critical of the councils was held at Nicea in A.D. 325. Three hundred assembled bishops, after weeks of discussion and debate, concluded that the historical Christ is the eternal *Logos*. They stated that the eternal Christ is of one being with the Father and is of one substance with the Father (*homoousios*). Thus, Christ is not less than the Father, but co-eternal, co-equal, and co-substantial with Him. Church historian Philip Schaff observed, "In the development of doctrine, the Nicene and post-Nicene age is second in productiveness and importance only to those of the apostles and of the Reformation. It is the classical period for the objective fundamental dogmas, which constitute the ecumenical or old Catholic confession of faith."[9]

The champion of Nicene orthodoxy was a young unofficial recording secretary named Athanasius, who was not given a seat or voice in the proceedings. He was to become Bishop of Alexandria in 328, three years after the Nicene Council. Athanasius captured the genius of orthodox Trinitarian doctrine with one clear, precise word, *homoousious* ("of one essence"). He would continue to defend his understanding of the deity of Christ until his death in 373, although he was banished from his home and bishopric five times by various emperors who did not agree with him. The Council of Constantinople in 381 confirmed the decision of Nicea and Athanasius' subsequent theological defense.

Athanasius crystallized the uniqueness of Christianity, the essential biblical doctrine that God became man. God is not an aloof deity. The Son is not less than the Father. We are partakers of the divine nature because we live in Christ. Indeed, Christ is the proper object of our worship because he is the perfect, absolute revelation of God. Christ is the only person physically to represent God accurately and infallibly. This representation is the *telos* ("goal") toward which the Christian moves, especially the pastor, though perfection is never achieved. Athanasius' unflagging zeal should remind us that Christ's representation of God will be preserved for the church only by a mentality that stands in service of faith, enabled by grace. The unity of Christianity was made possible by the well-chosen words of the Nicene Creed. Gerhard Kroedel calls it a "communication by the Church to its members on how to speak the gospel."[10]

---

[9]Philip Schaff, *History of the Christian Church* (Grand Rapids, Mich.: Eerdmans, 1949-50), 3:6.

[10]Quoted in Emilianos Timiadi, *The Nicene Creed, Our Common Faith* (Philadelphia: Fortress Press, 1983), 7.

The Nicene Creed also reminds us that theology is best formulated in consultation with other Christians. The present-day church is not called to formulate any new doctrine. There are fresh ways of expressing the gospel in modern idioms, relevant applications, and more accessible languages; yet even this is tricky business. The quest demands prayerful dialogue in the same spirit as the apostolic Jerusalem Council, who said, "It seemed good to the Holy Spirit and to us..." (Acts 15:28).

Chapter 3

The American Tradition
Of Pastoral Ministry

The Protestant Reformation was built upon a single foundation, *sola scriptura* ("Scripture alone"). From the authority of Scripture came the doctrine of justification by faith. For both Luther and Calvin, the highest act of worship was the proclamation of Scripture. David Buttrick writes, "In Calvin's mind the preacher was to be a voice for God, and therefore, of necessity, preachers were to be brainy theologians, exegetes, and teachers—not to mention God obsessed!"[1] In fact, preaching was so central to pastoral care and worship that Luther referred to the church building as a "mouth house." Luther wrote, "Christ will be of no benefit to you and you will not be able to avail yourself of him unless God translates him into words whereby you can hear and

---

[1]David Buttrick, *A Captive Voice: The Liberation of Preaching* (Louisville, Ky.: Westminster John Knox Press, 1994), 47.

know him....He must be brought to you, prepared for you, and translated into words for you by means of the inner and external Word."[2] *work of mouth*

The primary concern of Puritans was Restorationism, a desire to restore the church to the primitive teachings of Christ. Thus, the symbolism that had accumulated through centuries was abandoned. The Puritan preachers defined words as the heart of their vocation. Words exalted the character of God, described the majesty of Jesus, invited the sinner to conversion and the believer to a life of holiness. Puritan preaching was biblical, systematic, passionate, personal, credible, and convincing. According to J.I. Packer, the first task of Puritan ministry was preaching. The Puritan pastor devoted major time to the preparation of sermons that would be the chief means of grace and the climatic liturgical act of the church. The Puritan divine John Owen wrote, "The first and principal duty of a pastor is to feed the flock by diligent preaching of the Word....The feeding is the essence of the office of a pastor."[3]

The incessant preaching of the Puritans was driven by the deep conviction that the proclaimed word was the chief means of grace. Words were active because the Word was pure act. David Hall argues that the New England seventeenth-century pastor believed the central attribute of God was action. "This conception of his nature passed from Calvin through the brotherhood to all the preachers in New England."[4] For the Puritans, the purpose of all pastoral ministry, especially preaching, was an encounter with an active, present God.

The identity of the pastor in American history has been defined primarily by the call to preach. The pastor is more

[2]Buttrick, 39.
[3]J.I. Packer, *A Quest for Godliness: The Puritan Vision of the Christian Life* (Wheaton, Ill.: Crossway Books, 1990), 283.
[4]David D. Hall, *The Faithful Shepherd* (Chapel Hill, N.C.: University of North Carolina Press, 1972), 59.

often referred to as "preacher" than by any other label. Of course, this narrowly defined paradigm of ministry was often constructed out of ignorance. The less educated a pastor, the less he or she was acquainted with a full conception of pastoral ministry. A case in point would have been the Methodist pastors of the nineteenth century. Because many of them were untrained and often unordained, it was left to the presiding elder to come around quarterly to chair the business meeting of the church, administer the sacraments, and implement a bit of conflict management. The pastor preached, provided consolation in personal crisis, and did a fairly regular round of parish visitation.

But other elements also defined early American pastoral ministry primarily as preaching. Jesus had come preaching and teaching. Even a casual reading of the New Testament reveals that the essential medium for spreading the Kingdom was the spoken word. Synonyms for the word *tell* appear in the New Testament an astounding twenty-four hundred times. The pattern was set by Christ and the early disciples. When Christ was no longer present physically, the apostolic commission could be realized through absorption and application of the biblical Word. American preachers well understood that they, as well as the original Twelve, were beneficiaries of Christ's high priestly prayer: "Now they have come to know that everything you have given me is from you; for the words which you gave me I have given to them" (John 17:7-8a).

A New Breed Of Puritans

The Protestant preachers who came to America were freshly minted by European Puritanism. The centrality of preaching had been restored to the church. The revival of personal piety and corporate worship had grown out of the dogmatic affirmations of *sola scriptura* and *sola fides* ("faith alone"). The Puritans brought with them a fierce commitment to protect these critical reference points through preaching, teaching, and creedal affirmation. They did not come to America for the sake of religious freedom. They came to ensure that their tenacious hold on biblical religion would not be lost. They could be ensured only as the Word was proclaimed. They well understood what Geoffrey Wainwright calls the "dynamic component which is written into the New Testament canon." That is to say, the New Testament is canonical in terms of both its substance and its methodology. "The New Testament writings show us in exemplary manner that the gospel is always to be preached into particular circumstances where it will meet with a particular response according to these circumstances."[5]

Something else characterized America's earliest preachers. There were no "givens" of American church life. Except for the few Anglicans, Presbyterians, and Congregationalists who came from Europe to established churches, the American church was carved out of the wilderness. If a preacher didn't have a church, he started one. The success of a local church or its parent denomination was determined by the evangelistic effectiveness of its preachers. The most effective denominations made sure that their preachers, at great sacrifice, stayed within hearing distance of as many people as possible. In describing the mass movements of Christianity across the American landscape, Nathan O. Hatch writes:

> Each was led by young men of relentless energy who went about movement-building as self-conscious outsiders. They shared an ethic of unrelenting toil, a passion for expansion, a hostility to orthodox belief and style, a zeal for religious reconstruction, and a systematic plan to realize their ideals. However diverse their theologies and church organizations, they all offered common people, especially the poor, compelling visions of individual self-respect and collective self-confidence. Like the populist movement at the end of the nineteenth century, these

---

[5] Geoffrey Wainwright, *Doxology: The Praise of God in Worship, Doctrine, and Life* (New York: Oxford University Press, 1984), 168.

movements took shape around magnetic leaders who were highly skilled in communication and group mobilization.[6]

America's Resident Bishop

In the two hundred years of America's existence before the Civil War, no one so effectively pronounced the prophetical-priestly word as did Francis Asbury. Notwithstanding his enormous religious shadow, Jonathan Edwards appeared to many of his parishioners as erudite, isolated, and aloof. George Whitefield was almost void of organizational skills or an encompassing ecclesiology. In contrast, Francis Asbury placed evangelism within the context of connectedness, intimacy, and nurture. He combined a hierarchical understanding of church government with a love for the common person, to the extent that Methodism grew seven times as fast as the United States population during the first ten years of the nineteenth century. Asbury was autocratic in church government while exhibiting a highly democratic style of ministry.

Asbury's means for claiming and taming the frontier country was the anointed preaching of the Word. He believed the Word of God was "one grand dispensary of soul diseases, in every case of spiritual malady."[6] He preached 16,500 times—at a paper mill, under a jail wall, in a prison, at an executioner's stand, at a poor house, in a tavern, from the door of a public house, in a courthouse, in a barn, in the woods, from a camp-meeting stand, in a borrowed church, and at Yale University. He addressed and comprehended spiritual death and moral laxity by the proclamation of the "pure Word of God."

Asbury knew that the "pure Word of God" could be proclaimed only in the active presence of God. Zeal, passion, and subsequent fruit were realized by the gracious effusion of the Holy Spirit. Sinners were melted, stricken, convicted,

[6]Nathan O. Hatch, *The Democratization of American Christianity* (New Haven, Ct.: Yale University Press, 1989), 4-5.

and captivated by the thunderous lightning of the spoken word. Asbury exhorted his preachers to preach as if "they had seen heaven and its celestial inhabitants and had hovered over the bottomless pit and beheld the tortures and the groans of the damned."[7] This was not an exhortation to feign a technique, but a genuine urgency ignited by Asbury's primal concern to bring an individual and collective Pentecost. "What is preaching—without turning to God? It is daily unction that we want, that the Word may be like a hammer and 'fire' from our mouths to break hearts and to kindle life and fire."[8]

For Francis Asbury, Pentecostal proclamation was far more comprehensive than public discourse. Asbury quickly embraced the camp-meeting methodology, which had been started by the Presbyterians. On the other hand, he understood the private, personal nature of spiritual formation. America's resident bishop quite possibly visited more homes than any other individual in post-Revolutionary War America. His most frequent overnight accommodations during his forty-year, 270,000-mile odyssey were in private homes. The facilities were often primitive: lack of clean water, a dirty floor, three to a bed, and filth that could have been shoveled from the floor with a spade. The following is a remarkable account of Asbury's life with his parishioners on the frontier:

> I too have my sufferings, perhaps particular to myself: pain, and temptation; the one of the body, and the other of the spirit; no room to retire to—that in which you sit common to all, crowded with women and children, the fire occupied by cooking, much and long-loved solitude not to be found, unless you choose to run out into the rain, in the woods: six months of the year I have had, for thirty-two years, occasionally, to submit to what will never be agreeable to me; but the people, it

---

[7]Francis Asbury, *The Journal and Letters of Francis Asbury*, Elmer T. Clark, ed. (Nashville: Abingdon, 1958), 1:403.

[8]Asbury, 2:783.

must be confessed, are amongst the kindest souls in the world. But kindness will not make a crowded log cabin, twelve feet by ten, agreeable: without are cold and rain; and within, six adults, and as many children, one of which is all motion; the dogs, too, must sometimes be admitted. On *Saturday*, at Felix Earnest's, I found that amongst my other trials, I had taken the itch; and, considering the filthy houses and filthy beds I have met with, in coming from Kentucky Conference, it is perhaps strange that I have not caught it twenty times: I do not see that there is any security against it, but by sleeping in a brimstone shirt:—poor bishop! But we must bear it for the elect's sake.[9]

For the elect's sake, Asbury ceaselessly uttered the Word through Scripture reading, prayer, exhortation, teaching, and family worship. Every overnight stay would involve spiritual examination of the residents and subsequent catechism. There would be no idle words. "My mind was powerfully struck with a sense of the great duty of preaching in all companies, of always speaking boldly and freely for God as if in the pulpit."[10] This included calling "the family into the room and addressing this pointedly one by one concerning their souls."[11] The following statement shows how Asbury combined the prophetic utterance and the priestly conservation which was at the heart of Methodism's effectiveness:

> I spent part of the week visiting from house to house. I feel happy in speaking to all I find, whether parents, children, or servants. I see no other way; the common means will not do. Baxter, Wesley, and our Form of Discipline say, "Go into every house." I would go farther and say, "Go into every kitchen and shop, address all, aged and young on the salvation of their souls."[12]

---

[9]Asbury, 1:316.
[10]Asbury, 2:411.
[11]Asbury, 1:708.
[12]Asbury, 2:51.

The Rise of the Seminary

Of the 116 colleges founded in America before the Civil War, 113 were founded by religious movements, many of them for the express purpose of educating clergy. As preparation of ministers advanced to higher levels of attainment, schools fully devoted to professional ministry were envisioned. The first major theological seminary was founded at Andover, Massachusetts, in 1808 as a reaction against heterodoxy at Harvard.

Seminaries are so called because they dis*seminate* words about Christ. They are founded on the supposition that persons can rightly speak of God and his revelation in Jesus Christ. Seminaries are places of discourse, where people believe that discourse is critical to individual and corporate spiritual growth. This discourse begins with the Apostle Peter's own affirmative question, "Lord, to whom shall we go? You have the words of eternal life" (John 6:68). These words are "trustworthy and true."

Theological discourse assumes that the same meanings of the words spoken by Christ are available to us through careful biblical scholarship and dependence upon the Holy Spirit. Thus, theological discourse calls for the utmost diligence and dependence. We have received the oracles of God, the greatest gift that can be given a people. Yet we live between having received and fully comprehending the Word. Theological discourse attempts to more completely comprehend the Word, while at the same time seeking to be comprehended. The former takes place as one "rightly divides the word of truth." The latter takes place as the Word is inscribed on the human heart by the Holy Spirit. Thus, seminaries ought to be communities of both knowledge and formation. "Be transformed by the renewing of your mind, so that you may prove what the will of God is, that which is good and acceptable and perfect" (Rom. 12:2b). They are communities not so much given to mastering the Word as to being mastered by the Word. Only those who have had the

Word implanted within them will be zealous to plant the Word in the lives of others.

Seminaries are founded on the conviction that the world needs redemptive words. They give themselves to the task of discovering the most accurate and relevant words possible to represent the God who has spoken and who still speaks today. This is the same sacred trust that was given to the early apostles. "But we will devote ourselves to prayer and to the ministry of the word" (Acts 6:4). In the very beginning of the church, the Twelve nearly got sidetracked with kitchen chores, conflict resolution, and the administration of social services. They had sufficient insight to keep their job description clear and simple: "prayer and the ministry of the word." This is the highest and most critical endeavor that can be entrusted to a person in ministry.

Seminaries (or other dialogical communities) are a necessity for this enterprise. However, in terms of being able to interpret the biblical text, seminary students may be less able to engage the Scriptures than they were a century ago. A modern emphasis on technology, management, and marketing have eroded the students' ability to do serious Bible study. Our seminary students today are far less likely than previous generations to have taken undergraduate courses in logic, rhetoric, speech, and literature. Today's evangelical pastors are far less apt to be acquainted with the biblical language than their seventeenth-century counterparts.[13]

We have moved from word analyzing to word processing. Ironically, word processors have rendered us less able to handle words capably. My own observation is that students are becoming more off-the-cuff in their methods of organizing and synthesizing ideas. The trend leads to David Wells' sad indictment: "We now have less biblical fidelity, less interest in truth, less seriousness, less depth, and less capacity

---

[13]My own seminary, which is a very conservative institution academically, does not require any of the biblical languages for a Master of Divinity degree.

to speak the Word of God to our own generation in a way that offers an alternative to what it already thinks."[14]

Yet Christian seminaries and other Christian communities devoted to theological discourse are the church's last hope. They are the last forums where rational discourse is taken seriously, and they should be. They are founded on the two essential truths of life: (1) There is a God who has disclosed himself in an historical person; and (2) The physical disclosure of the eternal *Logos* makes his ongoing disclosure through words possible. My finite word has value and meaning as I apply it to the service of the Infinite Word. There can be an ultimate orientation for human discourse because the *Logos* entered into a dialogue with the world. That dialogue is the grounding and standard for all other meaningful conversation. That dialogue is recorded in a Book, which is the written revelation of that Person. Christian communities study, contemplate, and discuss the written Word because it describes Someone worthy of serious, undivided reflection. Our reflection upon the Word furnishes the self and the surrounding world with value and purposeful guidance.

Christ, Paul, Athanasius, Luther, Calvin, and Asbury devoted themselves to the ministry of precise, Spirit-anointed words. For them, no hour was too late, no distance too far, no home too humble, no institution too intimidating, no sacrifice too daunting to deliver the most precious commodity known to humankind—words of life.

---

[14]David F. Wells, *No Place for Truth, or Whatever Happened to Evangelical Theology?* (Grand Rapids, Mich.: Eerdmans, 1993), 12.

Chapter 4

The Most Important Communications Medium

Jesus is back from the dead. It is the day of the Resurrection, Christ's first day back on earth. How would you have spent that day if you were He?

I think I might have appeared in Pilate's bedroom and said, "It wasn't just a dream!" Or possibly I would have paid a visit to the Sanhedrin, asking, "Do you boys want to talk a little theology?" Certainly, I would have enjoyed a confrontation with the high priest with the question, "Have you repaired that veil into the Holy of Holies yet?"

Only one event, and that recorded by only one Gospel writer, recounts what Jesus did during the daylight hours of that first Easter Sunday. The event was a walk from Jerusalem to Emmaus. The seven-mile stretch of rocky, winding road would have taken three or four hours to traverse. Granted, Jesus may not have traveled the entire distance. But

note what He did during the trip. Jesus joined the conversation of two disciples on the road, who rehearsed the events
of the prior several days. In response, Jesus "explained to them
the things concerning himself in all the Scriptures" (Luke
24:27). This discourse must have taken at least an hour, possibly more.as darkness fell, Christ reclined at table with His
fellow travelers, breaking and blessing bread with them.

Let's be clear: Christ spent the better part of the most
critical day in Christian history trudging over a dirty, winding road with two persons of whom we have never heard,
going to a town whose location has been lost to antiquity,
and dining there in the most meager of circumstances. But
was this not the way Jesus had spent most of His earthly ministry, itinerating and dining with the marginalized people of
society, all the while blessing their common lot of life? The
day of the Resurrection did not mean an escape from everyday life, but rather an intensive invasion of that life.

I have often wondered how to break down the barrier
between my airline seat partner and myself, after we have
received our prepackaged meals. I've wondered if I even have
the right to invade his or her privacy. *Oh, well,* I think to
myself, *the feeling of estrangement only has to be endured for a
moment. Then I can return to reading my book.* Perhaps it
would have been easier to start a conversation in stagecoach
days. At least on the jolting stagecoach, the book would have
been difficult to read and I would have had plenty of time to
break down the communication barriers.

The modern world of creature comforts is the only one
we know, and primitive areas of the world without them don't
look all that inviting. We might not even survive in that
"other" kind of world. What's more, perhaps we have left
behind more than a stagecoach and unpaved roads.

We do not necessarily need to go backward one hundred
years, but we do need to regain something we lost since that
time. That "something" is the ability to formulate words that
uncover humanity's ultimate needs, words that lead a per-

son from those needs into the dignity and potential that God envisioned when Christ shed His blood on Calvary for our redemption.

Phillips Brooks

To understand what we have lost, let us return briefly to the day of the stagecoach and the horse-drawn carriage. The subject of our visit is Phillips Brooks (1835-1893). One may ask, Why choose Phillips Brooks as an example of pastoral leadership? There certainly were other pastors of equal note in the late nineteenth century, among them Henry Ward Beecher, John Henry Jowett, and Russell Conwell. But let us consider Reverend Brooks as one good example among many from whom we can learn.

The time in which Brooks ministered was characterized by rapid change. The height of his ministerial career was at Trinity Church, Boston, in 1869-1891. American historian Arthur Schlesinger, Sr., has designated the years 1875-1900 as "a critical period in American religion." During those years, the debate over biological evolution reached a high pitch. Textual criticism of the Bible became the most controversial topic of textbook and pulpit. Comparative religion became an academic endeavor which pointed out the failures of Christianity. An effort to adapt religion to the new scientific paradigm—an endeavor commonly called "modernism"—swept through the church. Professors at established theological schools went on trial for modernism. New pseudo-Christian religions such as Theosophy and Christian Science invaded the territory of Christian orthodoxy.

The church found itself more and more removed from the working class. An immigrant population unfamiliar with American customs and religious mores invaded our shores. Labor disputes began to tear the church asunder in a society ill-equipped to deal with the Industrial Revolution. In other words, there was a technological shift, possibly more significant than the technological shift we are experiencing today.

But not only did the church survive this change; it advanced. According to Schlesinger,

> Despite the many difficulties, theological and practical, which beset the path of religion, the last two decades of the century witnessed a substantial gain in church membership. Protestant communicants increased from less than ten million to nearly eighteen; the Roman Catholic population from well over six million to more than ten; the number of Jews from less than a quarter million to approximately a million. It was a striking testimonial to the vitality of organized religion that the growth was proportionately greater than the general advance of the population.[1]

Preaching and Christian Character

No one thrived better than Phillips Brooks during this time. However, he was not a program planner, an organizer, nor an administrative innovator. He thrived as a preacher of the gospel. He believed, beyond any doubt, that the most important thing he had to offer the hundreds that crowded Trinity Church each Sunday was the Word of God, described and conveyed through human words. In John Woolverton's assessment: "If the ceremonial of candles, stained glass, vestments, incense, and solemn manual acts of consecration made the supernatural visible in Anglo-Catholic parishes, Brooks made it 'speakable.'"[2] He sought to provide understanding, hope, dignity, and aspiration so that the public might experience the transforming power of Christ's love. For Brooks, proclaiming a life-changing word was the highest endeavor to which an individual could be called. He was the living embodiment of John Killinger's ideal: "We would rejoice at paying whatever price is necessary to the accomplishment of

---

[1] Arthur M. Schlesinger, Sr., "A Critical Period in American Religion, 1875-1900," *Religion in American History: Interpretive Essays* (Englewood Cliffs, N.J.: Prentice-Hall, 1978), 312.

[2] John Woolverton, *The Education of Phillips Brooks* (Urbana, Ill.: University of Illinois Press, 1995), 109. For a brief historiography on Brooks which represents varied assessments, see Woolverton's even-handed treatment in his "Introduction."

our great aim, to set a life-saving, soul-ordering word loose in the midst of a congregation of human beings, and then to see it work!"[3]

Brooks paid the price. He used the spoken word to invade the despair, frustration, hopelessness, confusion, guilt, and apathy that have enshrouded human consciousness in every age. Biographer Alexander V.G. Allen stated, "Preaching was the exclusive object that occupied his mind; the message to be delivered and the form it should take from morning till night, in hours of leisure or apparent relaxation, on his journeys, in vacations, in social gatherings, he was thinking of subjects for sermons."[4]

Allen's comment may lead one to believe that Brooks narrowly perceived the task of sermon preparation. Not so. He knew that the character of the preacher was what needed preparation. Foremost in the formation of the preacher's character was his or her relationship with Christ. The preacher had to be a person of a certain character, moving hearers toward that certain character. A sermon that persuaded and moved people was what he strived to produce; yet he knew that its effectiveness flowed out of the pastor's identity. "According to the largeness of your own Christian life will be the power to preach that largest sermon."[5] Attention to the spiritual transformation of others could be accomplished only through the preacher's own transformation. "First of all, before a man can value the soul of other men, he must have learnt to value his own soul.... He who preaches to the inner life of others must himself have an inner life."[6] Raising the spiritual possibilities of others could be commu-

---

[3]John Killinger, *The Centrality of Preaching in the Total Task of Ministry* (Waco, Tex.: Word Books, 1969), 26.

[4]Alexander V.G. Allen, *Phillips Brooks, 1835-1893: Memories of His life with Extracts from His Letters and Note-Books* (New York, N.Y.: E.P. Dutton and Company, 1907), 279.

[5]Phillips Brooks, *Lectures on Preaching* (Grand Rapids, Mich.: Zondervan Publishing House, n.d.), 134.

[6]Brooks, 278.

nicated only through raising the preacher's own possibilities. Brooks stated in his Lyman Beecher Lectures to the students at Yale in 1877, "The personal desire to be pure and holy, the personal consciousness of power to be pure and holy through Christ, reveals the possibility of other men."[7]

Intellectual Depth

Sermon preparation was not a myopic enterprise for Brooks. He believed that the pastor who read and studied only for sermon preparation would be shallow in both thinking and speaking. Reading must be done for personal enrichment as an end in itself. Out of that enrichment would flow depth of thought and breadth of understanding. Thus, Brooks constantly had a book in his hand, especially when traveling via train or carriage. He read philosophy, history, theology, and poetry. Much of his reading followed the intellectual currents of the day, including authors who confronted and challenged the Christian message: Huxley, Darwin, and Spencer.

Brooks was capable of preaching to any congregation and, if given time, of lecturing on almost any subject. For a lecture that Brooks gave on "Milton as an Educator" in 1874 before the Massachusetts Teachers Association, his notebooks demonstrate that he delved into the writings of Locke, Bacon, Spinier, Quintillion, Montaigne, Comenius, Pestalozzi, and Basedow. Brooks referred to this willingness to pursue and understand someone else's frame of reference as "literary courage." He defined courage as the "power of being mastered and possessed with an idea."[8] He wrote:

> Read books themselves. To read a book is to make a friend; if it is worth your reading, you meet a man, you go away full of his spirit; if there is anything in you, he will quicken it.... To make young people know the souls of books, and find their own souls in knowing them, that is the only way to cultivate true literary courage.[9]

7Brooks, 278.
8Allen, 285.
9Allen, 285.

A Parish Philosophy

For Phillips Brooks, words were redemptive. They were redemptive beyond the walls of the church sanctuary and they transcended sermon form. Brooks' occupation was an almost endless, unbroken activity of speaking: the Episcopal Theological School at Cambridge, Andover Seminary, Massachusetts State Normal School, Howard University, evangelistic services at Fanuiel Hall, Johns Hopkins University, Methodist Divinity School at Boston University, Cornell University, William's College, and so on. He even filled in for Dwight L. Moody in one of his crusade services when Moody was sick. Allen stated, "When he returned to his house after an absence or journey, to find many invitations awaiting him, he followed the rule to accept them in the order in which he opened the letters, not allowing himself to choose which he would prefer. It was a principle with him never to decline an invitation to preach unless prevented by some previous engagement."[10]

Brooks' intellectual life was fortified by extended periods of reading, writing, contemplation, and travel. Many of his summers were spent in a cottage on the Atlantic seashore, commuting back and forth to Boston on Sundays. On August 3, 1878, Brooks noted, "I never had such a profoundly quiet summer as I am having now. I am here in a queer little village, on an obscure back bay of Boston Harbor, where there is nothing to do, at least where I do nothing, no sailing, no fishing, no riding, no walking. Nothing in the world but plenty of books and time and tobacco."[11] Besides the summers away from routine parish duties, there were eleven trips abroad, most of them from three months to a year in duration.

All this absence from church would certainly cause us to question Brooks' attention to administrative detail. Allen answers, "He had the gift for administration. He had his eye

---

[10]Allen, 566.

[11]Allen, 332.

on everything, knew all that was going on, and seemed to be everywhere. When anybody wanted to do anything, he would make himself master of the situation in five minutes."[12] We would also be tempted to ask if Brooks, with all of his travel and bookishness, had time for the people of his parish. Again Allen answers, "He had the capacity for mental concentration, so that the presence of others or the talk going on around him, even an interruption from a caller, were no disturbance."[13] A summary of a typical day for Brooks is insightful:

> His hours were regular. He rose at seven and from the time he was heard stirring in the morning he was singing to himself, and continued what was rather the effort at a tune until breakfast, which was at eight. Then followed a short interval of work before the crowd of callers came. He would have no office hours, nor would he refuse to see any one who called. Lunch was at one. After lunch came calls on the sick, or meetings of various kinds. He made few parochial calls. Six was the dinner hour. He sometimes found it hard to get out in the evening. Often there were callers. In the evenings when he did not go out and there were no callers, he was most delighted. At ten o'clock the house was shut, and at eleven he was in bed.[14]

So the question still plagues us: How did Phillips Brooks have so much time for both people and the life of the mind? Quite simply, he conceived the overall task of ministry much differently than we do today.

For us, ministry has evolved into a system or technique to be mastered. We generally assume that anyone, at any point in life, no matter their background, can enter pastoral ministry—even as a second or third vocation—simply by learning the scheme. The scheme is offered in the latest seminar, complete with notebook and overhead transparencies. And if anyone should think that pastoral ministry might require

---

[12]Allen, 569.
[13]Allen, 562.
[14]Allen, 563.

more than a week's preparation, seminary courses are offered via the Internet. By contrast, Brooks' preparation did not allow emotional and spiritual disengagement, but called for an intense community with the people he served and a grasp of the human condition which only a liberal education could afford. His teachers at Harvard were the likes of Asa Grey, Henry Wadsworth Longfellow, and Louis Agassiz.

> The poets of the eighteenth century and of the early nineteenth had for him a sweet charm. He read Shakespeare and books illustrating his age. He took up Lamb and Sauthey, but did not so early discover Milton, Coleridge, or Wordsworth. There was a calming influence in these writers of the eighteenth century, with their simple world, at wide remove from the desire for reforms, the agitation, the aspirations, the new interpretations of the age into which he was born. Here lay something of the preparation for his life work. He gained a picture of life in another age, which afforded a basis for comparison and criticism when he should come to the work of his own time.[15]

Transcendent Man

Brooks believed that the only way his age could be understood was to understand other ages. By learning the words that have transcended all times, Brooks would be able to speak to his own time. He would not only be representative man, he would be transcendent man. He would be able to interpret his own circumstances via a panoramic vision that would compare and contrast. His words would not be caught up in the transitory bric-a-brac of the moment but in great truth and in great duties. The destiny of human souls depended upon the transcendent truth he preached. After quoting St. Francis de Sales' statement that the knowledge of the priest was the eighth sacrament, Brooks declared that an ignorant clergy was worse than no clergy at all.

---

[15]Allen, 12-13.

> As I begin to speak to you about literary style and homiletical construction, I cannot help once more urging upon you the need of hard manly study; not simply the study of language and style itself, but study in its broader sense, the study of truth, of history, of philosophy; for no man can have a richly stored mind without its influencing the style in which he writes and speaks, making it at once thoroughly his own, and yet giving it variety and saving it from monotony.[16]

For Brooks, monotony in ministry resulted from allowing its critical identity to slip from the center to the periphery. The center of ministry was a reverence for truth, a reverence that would transform people. "Beware of hobbies," he wrote. "Fasten yourself to the centre of your ministry; not to some point on its circumference."[17] In the personal love and service of Christ, the pastor would be a great "water main attached to the everlasting reservoir of God's truth and grace and love, and streams of life by a heavenly gravitation, pour through him to refresh every weary soul."[18]

Brooks was deathly afraid that something might mitigate the flow or pollute the stream. There was always the lurking possibility that ecclesiastical machinery and organization would tyrannize the parish. He belittled association of the church's mission with schemes and systems of a programatic nature. He believed that our programs are often created by default, because we fail to fully represent Christ in word and deed.

> She degrades the dignity of her grand commission by puerile devices for raising money and frantic efforts to keep herself before the public which would befit only for the sordid ambitions of a circus troupe. You must cast all that out of the church with which you have to do, or you will make the pulpit perfectly powerless to speak of God to our wealth-ridden and pleasure loving time. You

---

[16]Brooks, 146-7.
[17]Brooks, 97.
[18]Allen, 580-1.

must show first that His Church believes in Him and trusts Him and is satisfied in Him, or you will cry in vain to men to come to Him.[19]

Trusting the Job Description

Phillips Brooks built his ministry on the twin pillars of the love of truth and the love of souls. His life was a combination of devotion to Christ, constantly digesting the thoughts of great thinkers, and spending time with ordinary people. These people included the average layperson with whom he loved to dialogue and the clergy with whom he met monthly in the "Clericus Club" to discuss theological issues of the day. With all this fraternizing, socializing, and studying, something had to yield. Indeed it did. For instance, when Trinity Church built a new facility, a magnificent Romanesque edifice, we know almost nothing about Brooks' involvement in the project. Even though he left his stamp on the architectural design and color of the church building, during the period of its construction he continued to study, speak, and travel as incessantly as ever.

Brooks' ability to turn the project of building a new church facility almost totally over to competent laymen raises a curious question. We modern ministers, who pride ourselves in the newfound discovery that all Christians are called to ministry and we can trust the laity to carry out many duties of the church, seem to be entrapped in miniscule details of administration more than ever. What pastor today would take off to Europe or leave for an extended preaching stint in the middle of a major building program, as did Brooks? Brooks was a person who knew how to trust. He trusted his people. He trusted his own perception of ministry, which required him to devote primary attention to the development of his own soul and intellect.

Brooks was a peerless prophet for the latter part of the nineteenth century. He gave himself to analyzing the prob-

[19]Brooks, 240.

lems of his day, combating both systemic and individual evil, dissecting human nature, and inspiring his hearers to dignity and nobility. He neither sought nor shunned eloquence. As the words tumbled out, they were a natural expression of his diligent preparation and the depth of his soul. He saw that his task was to bring the transcendent mysteries of the Christ-life to bear on the most common human needs. Brooks stated in his Beecher lectures, "To apprehend in all their intensity the wants and woes of men, to see the problems and dangers of this life, then to know all through us that nothing but Christ and His redemption can thoroughly satisfy these wants, that is what makes a man a preacher."[20]

Brooks Foresees Postmodernism

Sven Birkerts, in his *Gutenberg Elegies*, though he never mentions Brooks by name, decries the loss in American society of all that Brooks represented—the ability to carve out paradigms of meaning, the willingness to tolerate paradox and subtlety, the love for ideas and imagination, and the appreciation for sacred art which has been a part of all ages. Birkerts argues that finely nuanced thinking is now the privatized occupation of the intellectually elite, who are more removed from the populace than ever. Scholarly dialogue goes on within the academic guild while a sweeping electronic collectivization dumbs down discourse for the masses.

It was this dumbing down of public discourse of which Brooks prophetically forewarned: "You must count your work unsatisfactory unless you waken men's brains and stir their consciences. Let them see clearly that you value no feeling which is not the child of truth and the father of duty."[21] He who would be a child of truth must resist both popularity and sentimentality. Such resistance did not mean that the comprehension of a congregation should be held suspect. "Trust the people to whom you preach more than most min-

---

[20]Brooks, 27.
[21]Brooks, 245.

isters do. Begin your ministry by being sure that if you give
your people your best thought, it will be none too good for
them. They will take it all."[22]

Some, especially Birkerts, would question Brooks' optimism. Birkerts defines the electronic age as one that can tabu-
late figures and facts but cannot comprehend the subjective
data that has always been the stuff of art. Postmoderns communicate only in sound bytes, not for the purpose of what
Birkerts calls "duration" and "inwardness," but for the
immediate tasks of managing and marketing. The vast difference between communication in the instrumental sense
and communion in the affective, soul-oriented sense Birkerts
describes as follows:

> The gains of electronic postmodernity could be said to include,
> for individuals, (a) an increased awareness of the "big picture," a
> global perspective that admits the extraordinary complexity of
> interrelations; (b) an expanded neural capacity, an ability to ac-
> commodate a broad range of stimuli simultaneously; (c) a rela-
> tivistic comprehension of situations that promotes the erosion
> of old biases and often expresses itself as tolerance; and (d) a
> matter-of-fact and unencumbered sort of readiness, a willing-
> ness to try new situations and arrangements.
>
> In the loss column, meanwhile, are (a) a fragmented sense of time
> and a loss of the so-called duration experience, that depth phe-
> nomenon we associate with reverie; (b) a reduced attention span
> and a general impatience with sustained enquiry; (c) a shattered
> faith in institutions and in the explanatory narratives that for-
> merly gave shape to subjective experience; (d) a divorce from the
> past, from a vital sense of history as a cumulative or organic pro-
> cess; (e) an estrangement from geographic place and commu-
> nity; and (f) an absence of any strong vision of a personal or
> collective future.[23]

---

[22]Brooks, 208.

[23]Sven Birkerts, *The Gutenberg Elegies: The Fate of Reading in an Electronic Age* (Boston, Mass.: Faber and Faber, 1994), 27.

While in many ways the top half of postmodernism is not to be despised, the bottom half has created an enormous back-draft into which has entered fragmentation, alienation, materialism, restlessness, and the other ills that are plaguing us. Due to our human limitations, something must be forsaken. Birkerts envisions himself as standing at a crossroads, choosing between the information highway of the Internet and the pathway of the soul. Though not writing as a theist, Birkerts defines *soul* as "our inwardness, our self-reflectiveness and orientation to the unknown."[24] As we converse with the affable efficiency of our new technologies, we may miss the street signs that call for subtle yet critical differences of direction: inwardness rather than outwardness, intensiveness over extensiveness, reflection as opposed to manipulation, mystery rather than access, and permanence versus provisionality. Birkerts writes,

> My core fear is that we are, as a culture, as a species, becoming shallower, that we have turned from depth—from the Judeo-Christian premise of unfathomable mystery—and we are adapting ourselves to the ersatz security of a vast lateral connectedness. That we are giving up on wisdom, the struggle for which has for millennia been central to the very idea of culture, and that we are pledging instead to a faith in the web.[25]

Should not Birkerts' fear be intensified in those of us who are called to be prophet-priests? A fear that through the use of words we will no longer enable persons to purge the bacteria of their souls, no longer be able to present to them a transforming vision, no longer lay a foundation on which they can build a home, and no longer inspire them to be change-agents in a world that is being conformed to conspiratorial forces driven by economic utilitarianism? Should not the ministry of the gospel, more than any other

---

[24]Birkerts, 212.
[25]Birkerts, 228.

profession, be cautious of the cultural assumption that expediency and creature comfort are better, simply because they are more readily available? Can we still make it possible for our people to imagine a world of depth and meaning which often calls for sacrifice, patience, and endurance? Can we not give them a word that will let them know that the gods of the system cannot give life? Is there not a place to believe that a word spoken through a Spirit-filled human being can do more to effect good than the cool media of VCRs and computers? This word, according to John Killinger, "galvanizes men, upends them, probes them, haunts them, follows them into their most remote hiding places and smokes them out, drives them out coughing and sputtering and crying into the open light of new grace and new freedom and new love."[26]

Phillips Brooks had a great mind, not so much because of his innate intellect, but because he lived in a time when ideas counted. As David Wells has argued, anything that smacks of intellectualism is as suspect today as claims to being aristocratic or blue-blooded were during the American Revolution. "What shapes the modern world is not powerful minds, but powerful forces, not philosophy but urbanization, capitalism, and technology."[27]

Truly prophetic words always raise questions about the dominant culture. If that is so, the pastor of this century must beome something other than the dominant culture's type of leader—the economist, manager, strategist, psychologist, and technocrat. Who else besides the pastor will set people free from the torrents of consumerism that are sweeping us along? Is not pastoral leadership the one vocation that should be able to articulate a different course? The prophetic stance necessarily involves the ability to suggest viable alternatives to enculturation. In Bruggemann's words, "The prophet has only the means of word, spoken word and

---

[26]Killinger, 24.
[27]Wells, 61.

acted word, to contradict the presumed reality of his or her community."[28]

What was so refreshing about Phillips Brooks was his uniqueness. He was a man engaged in his times but not engulfed by his times, a man steeped in divinity yet highly aware of secular currents. He had no doubt that, in spite of a shifting societal paradigm, what people need most and what they will always need most is theological discourse that offers transcendent meaning. He stands as a sharp rebuke for those of us overwhelmed by postmodernity, who have masked our anxiety with facile and often superficial words on the latest ecclesiastical scheme. Prophets such as Brooks are called to God's wisdom, a wisdom which entails assessing the world situation from God's perspective. Brooks was a humble giant who lived in the full confidence that a divine perspective was what the world needs most. He stood in stark contrast to David Wells' observation, which unfortunately typifies much of the leadership of the contemporary church:

> What is most remarkable about modern people is that they are not in scale with the world they inhabit, informationally and psychologically. They are dwarfed and they have been emptied of their metaphysical substance; more precisely, it has been sucked out of them. There is nothing to give height or depth or perspective to anything they experience. They know more, but they are not necessarily wiser. They believe less, but they are not more substantial. They are attuned to experience and to appearances, not to thought and character.[29]

The Postmodern Irony

Critical to the pastor's task is the articulation of a different world view, which Wells refers to as having "height," "depth," and "perspective." This world view must not be articulated in a truncated, isolated, brittle, or defensive fash-

---

[28]Walter Bruggemann, *The Prophetic Imagination* (Philadelphia, Pa.: Fortress Press, 1978), 66.

[29]Wells, 52.

ion. It must be a world view that encompasses, but not necessarily embraces, all of life. The Christian world view recognizes that there is a theological and moral dimension to every idea and every event under the sun. Granted, there are many more ideas and events for us to assess than there were for Brooks. But therein lies the irony. Brooks' intellect was greater and his world smaller than ours. Our intellects are smaller and our world greater than his.

This does not mean that we need to give ourselves to sorting through every new technology, every educational theory, every artistic endeavor or legal decision that arrives on the scene. But if we are not at all conversant with bioethics, politics, the arts, the innovations of Silicon Valley and the various other enclaves of our society, then we are trying to pretend that the world does not exist. That unfortunately is the world view which many pastors adopt.

Brooks involved himself in the issues of his time through study, reflection, and dialogue with others. His religion was relevant to every phase of life. He assumed that his hearers were well read; that assumption quickened him to delve into areas beyond his "professional" interest. He appeared to be a child of his age while resisting its currents. For Brooks, no profession offered a greater opportunity to expand the powers of both mind and soul as did the pastoral ministry. "That which all men ought to remember, it behooves the minister more than all men not to forget, how closely the mental and moral natures are bound together in their characters and destinies."[30]

Yes, the contrast is vivid. Educated at Harvard, steeped in philosophy, history, and literature, Brooks not only was on a par with other professionals but at times he stood head and shoulders above them. His pattern is rarely seen among ministers today. We often confuse diplomas with a quest for learning. We are likely to hold an undergraduate degree in ministry, yet experience no deeper thought than a book writ-

---

[30]Brooks, 92.

ten by the latest ministry technique guru. We lack the ability to fashion Scripture exegetically into a form that our people can comprehend, so we offer formulaic sound bytes in the place of a comprehensive theological paradigm.

We cannot go back to the nineteenth century. But that should not stop us from asking whether we have lost something important along the way. Times were different then, as Woolverton states: "Nineteenth-century Americans went in droves to hear lectures, debates, and sermons, much as people today partake of salad bars. Educated males were expected to be able to deliver speeches, contend in forensics, and edify with disquisitions; the sermons of ministers were meant to instruct and illuminate."[31] In other words, for post-Civil War America, words were readily acceptable currency. This currency was minted "by the assumption that words and particularly religious words, corresponded to what is, that language was still trustworthy, that *logos* and *cosmos* were inseparable and that the covenant between rhetoric and reality was not yet broken."[32]

We may never again be able to fill large edifices with people who come to hear a preacher because of the persuasiveness of his argument, the powers of his logic, and the cadences of his eloquence. But that isn't the issue. The issue is whether we believe there is anything in Phillips Brooks worth emulating, or whether he is an antiquated relic of a time without airports, computer monitors, radar, and global communication. The question is whether we accept Brooks' view of preaching as the communication of truth through personality, flesh-and-blood personality. He said, "It must come through his character, his affections, his whole intellectual and moral being."[33]

Electronic technology and human personality are vastly different communications media. God chose the latter when

---

[31]Woolverton, 36.

[32]Woolverton, 99.

[33]Brooks, 8.

He set in motion the plan of redemption two thousand years ago. Brooks comprehended that the preacher's task is to continue the unfolding of this plan. "It is the Spirit who gives life; the flesh profits nothing; the words that I have spoken to you are spirit and are life" (John 6:63).

No one ever penned more inspiring words than the following. Their refreshing, profound simplicity is worth more than all the high-tech voltage of today's communications media. They signify where technology ends and the work of the prophet-priest begins:

> O little town of Bethlehem, how still we see thee lie!
> Above thy deep and dreamless sleep the silent stars go by:
> Yet in thy dark streets shineth the everlasting Light;
> The hopes and fears of all the years are met in thee tonight.
> —Phillips Brooks, 1868

Chapter 5

Priestly Ministries: Ancient and Modern

Though prophet and priest may have been nearly exclusive offices in the Old Testament, these distinctions are attenuated, if not completely erased, under the new covenant. More importantly, they are combined in Jesus Christ, the prototype for all ministry. Jesus' discipling of the Twelve clearly demonstrated His balancing of the prophetical-priestly task: He confronted and comforted, scolded and assured, warned and consoled. Jesus demonstrated that prophetical-priestly words are wise words, prudent in their time and place. As the Apostle Paul explained, such words are perceptive of propriety, fitting for the moment. "Let no unwholesome word proceed from your mouth, but only such a word as is good for edification according to the need of the moment, so that it will give grace to those who hear" (Eph. 4:29).

Even in the Old Testament the roles of the priest and the prophet sometimes overlapped. The first prophet referred to in the Scripture is Abraham (Gen. 20:7). The same text refers to Abraham's *intercession* for Abimelech, normally a function of the priestly role. Furthermore, there is evidence that the worship cult was not the exclusive domain of priests in the Old Testament periods. As Robert Wilson suggests, the numerous social and religious functions of the prophets do not fall into neat categories. The same argument could be asserted for the priests.[1]

The traditional division of labor—that is, prophets speak for God and priests speak for the people—is effaced in the person of Christ. The cross transcended humanity and its values (prophetic) while at the same time being continuous with it (priestly). The word of mercy and the word of judgment converged at the cross. The cross, the primary metonymy of Christianity, forever identified the pastor as both a prophet and priest. As Charles Bartow writes, "No preaching can be truly prophetic (even in the most sharply critical sense of that term) that is not thus pastoral, personal, and profoundly filial. Preachers do not only speak to their congregants; they speak with them on their behalf, as one of them."[2]

A Stabilizing Ministry

Ministry at times calls for maintenance and other times for disruption. Prophets interrupt and disrupt; priests stabilize, soothe, and absolve. Priests enable us to put the past in proper perspective while the prophet sharpens us for the future. In the Old Testament, the priests provided social cohesion and were essential for the well-being of the community.

---

[1]Robert Wilson, "Early Israelite Prophecy," *Interpreting the Prophets*, ed. by James Luther Mays and Paul J. Achtemeier (Philadelphia: Fortress Press, 1987).

[2]Charles L. Bartow, *God's Human Speech* (Grand Rapids: William B. Eerdmans, 1997), 114.

Priests were charged with telling the story of faith through ritualized symbols and ceremonies. These custodians of tradition transcribed and interpreted the Law. They were also responsible for its dissemination. Teaching and applying the Law was a conservative function that kept society intact.

Law maintenance and genuine spirituality are almost impossible to interface wholly. The spirit of the law often eventuates into the letter of the law and becomes legalism. Legalism is taking pride in the laws one is able to keep while ignoring weightier matters that are more complicated or demanding. Legalism serves as sublimation for guilt. Legalism often indicts others for the purpose of camouflaging one's own faults. It creates an atmosphere of self-righteousness that doesn't admit failure. Legalism sees the mote in others' eyes while ignoring the beam in one's own.

Religious institutions are at the same time life-giving and life-draining. They become ends in themselves rather than the blessedness that Christ accurately described and acted out. Christ did not come to do away with the benefits of institutional religion, but to infuse the institution with life so that it could be even more beneficial. The temple, which was defined by law, hierarchy, and greed, could become a place enlivened by passionate service and sacrifice. But like most of us, the Jewish priests preferred an ideology that proffered security and comfort rather than a gospel that would save them from themselves.

The avarice, status consciousness, oppressiveness, and legalism of the Jewish priestly class, which was constantly at odds with Christ's ministry, should not blind us to the original design regarding those whom God chose for the most important task in Israel. The priestly task was dizzying: ritual provision, donation disbursements, temple maintenance, tax assessing and collecting, judicial decisions, penalty pronouncements, Scripture reading, and worship leading. Whether they were accounting or anointing, the priests were at the center of the political establishment that found its authority in theocratic sanction. These multitudinous skills and tasks cause us to lose sight of the theological design of the priesthood, a design which Jesus had no intention of thwarting or condemning. This theological design called for the following essential tasks. To understand them is more accurately to understand both the speech of Christ and the role of the contemporary pastor. We have parsed out the priestly roles not for the sake of academic classification, but to help us comprehend and emulate them.

The Ministry of Mediation

The priests fulfilled a mediatorial role between God and humankind. The ritual sacrifice provided the mediation; Christ came to be that once-and-for-all sacrifice. Thus, Christ is the one Mediator between God and humankind (1 Tim. 2:5). But that does not do away with the ministry of mediation. The same charge and promise which God made to the Levites is applicable to pastoral leaders today:

> By those who come near Me I will be treated as holy,
> And before all the people I will be honored (Lev. 10:3).

The mediatorial function of the priestly office enables us to understand the foremost task of pastoral ministry—i.e., making God known. To make God known is not synonymous with making Him immediately accessible. It does mean to increase the people's perception that God is relevant to all facets of life. The God-relevancy index clashes with a Western world view that marginalizes religion. A theocracy in which religious leaders regulated things such as contact with the unclean, prescriptions for leprosy, proper social practices regarding the menstrual cycle, and nocturnal seminal emissions is far removed from twenty-first-century America. It seems even farther from persons living in drug-infested neighborhoods, family members victimized by senseless bombings, mothers and dads caught on the treadmill of vocational stress and domestic strain.

The question of God's location may not be as primary as the pastor's location. The priest was to bring Israel into harmony with God by being in harmony with God himself. Sacred harmony called for the priest to live in a liminal state without land, secular occupation, and preoccupation with earthly provision. The priest was divinely set apart as one who could cross the threshold between the sacred and profane, one who could define clearly the difference between the two. Only through this knowledge could God be approached and communion between God and the people established.

Today's pastor may not be willing to live in such a liminal state, separated from the prevailing culture in a way that allows the world to locate God. True, the pastor does not have to provide a buffer of protection from God as did the Old Testament priest. But pastors must not be so engulfed by the profane that they are unable to represent a holy God, who transcends our individual tastes and preferences. God is no less holy now than three thousand years ago. The truth is that many pastors represent the God of "the slick and the slack" (a term borrowed from David Wells), who are on easy terms with modernity. Today's pastor should contemplate the powerful ritual that is acted out in Exodus 29:35-36a, 45: "'Thus you shall do to Aaron and to his sons according to all that I have commanded you; you shall ordain them through seven days. Each day you shall offer a bull as a sin offering for atonement.... I will dwell among the sons of Israel and will be their God.'"

The mediatorial pulling of God and humanity together calls not only for sanctification (i.e., separation unto God) but also for fraternal solidarity with the community. It was this latter aspect of priesthood for which the religious leaders condemned Christ. "For both He who sanctifies and those who are sanctified are all from one Father; for which reason He is not ashamed to call them brethren" (Heb. 2:11). This theological assertion was more than an abstraction without practical implication. The God-man socialized with prostitutes and tax collectors. His inclusive divine empathy ran counter to the Jewish law of distinction. The Paschal Lamb reversed the meaning of the Passover rite:

> It is a Passover sacrifice to the Lord who passed over the houses of the sons of Israel in Egypt when He smote the Egyptians, but spared our homes (Ex. 12:27).

The Passover rite accented the distinction between the Israelites and the Egyptians, but the Lamb of God brought them together. Further distinctions had evolved over the course of history—male and female, light and darkness, secular and profane, Jew and Gentile—and these distinctions ordered the Jewish world. This ordered universe placed the Jew at the top of the order and produced a mentality that affirmed, *I'm better than they are.* Christ's dismantling of this Jewish order was a bitter pill for the religious establishment to swallow. They no longer had an exclusive right to God. As Paul exclaimed, "He died for all…. Therefore, we are ambassadors for Christ, as though God were making an appeal through us" (2 Cor. 5:15a, 20).

A Ministry of Spiritual Direction

Priests were at the center of Israel's spiritual and ethical direction. Their use of the *Urim* and the *Thummim* would belong today only to the most backward civilizations. But who is to say that these primitive amulets would be any more outside a rational contemporary world view than is the current fascination with astrology and horoscopes? But needless to say, pastoral counseling predicated on the social sciences (specifically, Rogerian inner-direction) has not been highly favorable to this peculiar methodology. These mechanical devices, the *Urim* and the *Thummim*, certainly cut down on time. Two *noes* meant no; two *yeses* meant yes; a yes and a no meant *come back later.* But normally there was little equivocating on such issues as tactical matters (2 Sam. 5:19), accusing and condemning the guilty (Josh. 7), and assessing the future welfare of the nation (Judg. 18:5). The primitive nature of the above should not blind pastoral leadership to the theological implications, i.e., the sincere desire to seek the will of God in matters of ethics, vocation, geographical moves, etc. Albert Vanhoye writes, "At the root of this desire, we can discern a profound religious conviction; they were persuaded that human existence could not find its proper orientation without a positive relationship with God. The manner of the consultation is a secondary aspect."[3]

The first clergy person ever chosen in the New Testament received his official start with the casting of a lot, a *kleron* (Acts 1:23-26). This charismatic process represented the divinely appointed nature of ministry. The priestly nature of pastoring is not simply that the person is under divine appointment, but it should be a constant reminder that everyone is under divine appointment. Pastoral ministry addresses the providential, vocational aspect of life. Pastoral counseling is parenthesized by: (1) What does God want in this particular situation? and (2) What does God want for your overall life? Above all, pastoral words are continuously both implicitly and explicitly reminding persons that God is in control.

In our time, the methodologies of sociology, psychology, and counseling have eroded the mystical and charismatic nature of spiritual leadership. There is a gift of wisdom that goes beyond technique and relies upon the discernment of the Spirit. This wisdom is the product of a deep abiding relationship with God. Wayne Oates states, "A person who comes to a Christian pastor for guidance in a personal difficulty usually expects that pastor to be an interpreter of the mind of Christ, 'a teacher come from God.'"[4] Or, as Karl Barth

[3] Albert Vanhoye, *Old Testament Priests and the New Priest: According to the New Testament* (Petersham, Mass.: St. Bede's Publications, 1986), 21.

[4] Thomas Chapman, ed., *A Practical Handbook for Ministry: From the Writings of Wayne Oates* (Louisville, Ky.: Westminster John Knox Press, 1992), 59.

puts it, "When they come to us for help they do not really want to learn more about living: they want to learn more about what is on the farther edge of living—God. We cut a ridiculous figure as village sages—or city sages."[5]

The individual who comes to the spiritually endowed counselor rather than the psychiatric professional is seeking viable alternatives of action. To provide such direction, the pastor must live within the spiritual paradigm of wholeness and life, taking seriously Christ's words to His disciples, "'When He, the Spirit of truth, comes, He will guide you into all the truth'" (John 16:13a). This spiritual-ethical dimension of a pastor's work should be clearly evident.

A ministry professional stood in the pulpit and related how he had purchased a book at a garage sale. When he returned home, he discovered a steamy passage with which he was not entirely comfortable. About 2:00 in the morning, he said, God woke him with the conviction that he must get rid of the book.

Okay, I'll throw it away tomorrow morning, he thought.

God impressed upon him that he must dispose of it now. He got out of bed and dropped the book in the household trash can.

God still would not let him rest. He made clear that the man must remove the book from his house. So he found himself out on the back porch, dropping the book into a garbage can.

That's not good enough, God told him. *You need to get that book off your premises. Your home is holy, your children are holy, and your wife is holy.*

About 3:00 in the morning, the man found himself pitching the book into a neighborhood dumpster.

---

[5]Karl Barth, *The Word of God and the Word of Man* (London: Hodder & Stoughton, 1928), 189.

Such interpretations of the ethical dimensions of life identify the pastor as a soul guide who can be trusted. A college student, entrapped in guilt, approached a campus administrator who lacked any formal training in counseling technique. She bluntly informed the administrator that she constantly lied. In fact, she was so obsessed by lying that she did not know when she was telling the truth or a falsehood. The counselor told her to confess and make amends to the last person to whom she had lied. Two days later, she returned to her confessor and said, "I just confessed to my twenty-eighth person and I am free." Such freedom cannot be discovered in the resources of human endeavor, but only through a humble, complete reliance upon the Holy Spirit.

Pastoral leadership often must lead the community of believers in seeking the will of God. The perception of what God wants is often *transrational*—i.e., beyond data seeking and statistical calculation. The pastor calls the community to prayer for both corporate and individual guidance. The Quakers' "sense of the meeting" is more than collective intuition; it is the confidence that Christ is in the midst of His church and that the Holy Spirit "'will guide...into all truth'" (John 16:13). No rational construct or calculated data gathering is sufficient to replace the *modus operandi* of the early church in making decisions: "'For it seemed good to the Holy Spirit and to us'" (Acts 15:28a).

The Ministry of Nurture (Spiritual Feeding)

Ezekiel's prophetic warning was focused on the priests of Israel. "'Woe, shepherds of Israel who have been feeding themselves!'" (34:2b). In return for bringing spiritual nourishment, the priests of Israel were to receive physical provision. Evidently, these priests were "on the take" without fulfilling their responsibilities. Instead of fattening the sheep, they were getting fat off the sheep. The indictment that the shepherds fed themselves "and did not feed My flock" (v. 8) was also true of the priests during Christ's earthly ministry. "'Woe to you, scribes and Pharisees, hypocrites, because you devour widows' houses, and for a pretense you make long prayers; therefore you will receive greater condemnation'" (Matt 23:14). To be "on the take" rather than fulfilling covenantal expectations is a sad commentary on the profession of ministry. The ultimate paradigm for ministry was provided by Christ, "'I am the good shepherd; the good shepherd gives His life for the sheep'" (John 10:11).

Good shepherds constantly exalt the Good Shepherd and enable the flock to eat of His flesh and drink of His blood. This takes place primarily at the eucharistic table, but it also ought to take place in all of the church's personal and corporate encounters that are symbolized by the holy feast. Christ's exhortation to feed His sheep encompasses the entire health of the sheep. The ritualistic concerns of the Levitical priesthood to provide confession, repentance, atonement, covering, reconciliation, expiation, and forgiveness are now entrusted to those Christian leaders who render spiritual oversight. "Shepherd the flock of God among you, exercising oversight not by compulsion, but voluntarily, according to the will of God; and not for sordid gain, but with eagerness; nor yet as lording it over those allotted to your charge, but proving to be examples to the flock" (1 Pet. 5:2-3).

Pastors are undershepherds who oversee the flock, offering, representing, and modeling the redemption of the Chief Shepherd. What the Old Testament priests enacted by way of ritual, the New Testament priests are to enact by the spoken and acted Word. Our words are to symbolize the Word offered by God for our redemption. Christ's blood was spilt so that justification and sanctification might come to humanity. Making persons holy was the accepted agenda of both Old Testament priests and of Christ himself and must continue to be that of contemporary pastors. While we must utilize contemporary idioms as much as possible, we must not change the priestly agenda of making persons righteous through the blood of Christ.

Feeding sheep means more than giving temporal persons what they want; it calls for giving immortal souls what they need. Words may be enticing and intriguing but barren of the vital and central themes of biblical salvation. Prophetical-priestly preaching issues a call for repentance, inspires the faith of justification, exhorts to entire sanctification, and seeks a growing identity with the mind of Christ. The prophet-priest is one who mines the theological themes of Scripture so that he or she will draw men and women to Christ. The true shepherd prays for and contemplates words that will represent adequately a magnificent Christ who offers a magnificent salvation. Priests give themselves to the enrichment of thought and speech that will produce robust Christians.

Worship whose diet does not consist of reverence, repentance, and restoration is something other than worship. Pastors are in critical need of recovering spirit-anointed language that will speak of the greatness of God and thus create a hunger for God. In John Jowett's words, "We are not going to enrich our action by the impoverishment of our thought.... You cannot drop the big themes and create great saints."[6] The peril of the church is the demise of the vision to convert words into the quest for God. The following from Jowett addresses the perfunctory character of ministry, a constant temptation from the apostles until now.

> His words were only words, they were not spirit and life; he dwelt in the outermost courts of the temple, near to all the other traffickers in holy things—he was not a servant of the holy place, not a living priest of the living God, and his peril is our peril, subtle and insistent, the peril of remoteness from central issues, the peril of making substances appear shadows, and of making the holy splendors of grace seem like immate-

[6]J.H. Jowett, *The Preacher: His Life and Work* (New York: George H. Doran Company, 1912), 97.

rial dreams. And, therefore, may we not fitly add to our private devotional an extra intercession and may it not be this, "From all cold officialism of mind and heart, from the deadliness of custom and routine, from worldliness in which there is no spirit, and from ministry in which there is no life; from all formality, unreality, and pretense, good Lord, deliver us!"[7]

A Ministry of Blessing

One of the most specific and peculiar acts entrusted to the Old Testament priesthood was the rite of blessing. Numbers 6:23-27 directs the priests to say the following:

Speak to Aaron and to his sons saying,

"Thus you shall bless the sons of Israel. You shall say to them:

'The LORD bless you, and keep you;

The LORD make his face shine on you,

And be gracious to you;

The LORD lift up His countenance on you,

And give you peace.'

So they shall invoke my name on the sons of Israel, and I then will bless them."

This invocation has become known as the Aaronic benediction. The Greek word *eulogeo* ("to bless") and the Latin word *benedicere* ("to speak well of") essentially mean the same thing. Since the noun *benediction* does not have an equivalent English verb form, the Latin verb has normally been translated *bless*. A benediction is "a blessing pronounced in favor on a person or a thing. A solemn invocation of a divine blessing especially at the end of a church service."[8]

Because this particular ritual somehow gravitated to the end of the worship service, the rite became a prayer of dismissal. Worshipers now miss what they most long to hear, a

[7]Jowett, 104.
[8]*Webster's New Twentieth Century Dictionary Unabridged*, 172.

pronouncement of cosmic inclusion, a divine affirmation from an objective frame of reference. Personhood and security of identity can be received only through affirmation of the ultimate transcendental Other. The Rogerian "autonomous self," the adult "you're okay," and even the Buberian "thou," are all insufficient to erase the doubt which continuously asks, "Do I belong?" and, "Am I worthwhile?"

Self-acceptance can be realized only from a transcendent source—the Creator of the universe. God's pronouncement of acceptance takes into account the defects of sin, defects which psychology glosses over. God's acceptance promises forgiveness and restoration, the opportunity to become somebody. In order for that to happen, God's name has to be attached to the individual's name. The pastoral blessing lets even the non-Christian know that God is willing to be identified with "*me.*" The pastoral blessing floods the auditors with the affirmation that God wants to be identified with them. This affirmation places the worship service under a beatific canopy of personal grace and provides the ultimate assessment of God's unconditional positive regard. The benediction is God calling us by name:

> But now, thus says the Lord, your Creator, O Jacob
> And He who formed you, O Israel,
> "Do not fear, for I have redeemed you;
> I have called you by name; you are Mine!" (Isa. 43:1).

The benediction represents God's positive attitude toward His creation. The church must love the world before it can redeem it. Therefore, the priestly duty of the pastor is to make this pronouncement in tandem with the prophetic condemnation of sin and the call to repentance. This superior blessing, which comes from the ultimate Superior, counters and supersedes the world's assessment that takes place in the classroom, on the athletic field, and in the workplace. Self-esteem and other-esteem always fall short of what we need. This deficiency is shored up by defense mechanisms such as emotional compensation, perfectionism, legalism, and constant striving—a damning delusion that one can present one-self good enough to impress God. The benediction is the priestly function that extends mercy to all of us when we have come up miserably short. It is the pronouncement of the full potential of human existence, as expressed in 1 Peter 2:9-10:

> But you are a chosen race, a royal priesthood, a holy nation, a people for God's own possession, so that you may proclaim the excellencies of Him who has called you out of darkness into His marvelous light; for you once were not a people, but now you are the people of God; you had not received mercy, but now you have received mercy.

The benediction offers wandering humanity a transcendent identity. As Albert Vanhoye states, "To put the name of God upon someone is to establish a personal relationship between God and that person. The benediction is therefore nothing other than effecting a lifelong relationship with God."[9] The prophet-priest's power and duty to bless, to pronounce that one is acceptable by a transcendent Source—a source which is unbiased and benevolent—is a unique responsibility that is unavailable to other professions. The prophet-priest represents a source beyond himself, the Source beyond all sources. Wayne Oates has stated, "For the pastor to relinquish or fear to use this power and refuse to think of the role of this blessing in counseling is a dear price to pay for one's own secularization."[10] The blessing (benediction) is the climax of the Christian worship service. Rather than a dismissal that communicates, "Finally, it's over," the blessing charges the congregation with embodying the gospel wherever they work and play beyond the walls of the church.

The Ministry of Intercession

The new covenant has issued an invitation for all Christians boldly and confidently to approach the throne of grace. There is no clerical monopoly on access to God. God has

---

[9]Vanhoye, 26.
[10]Chapman, 302.

raised up a kingdom, a household of priests (Rev. 5:10). The Old Testament role of the high priest has been fulfilled by Jesus, who intercedes on behalf of His brothers and sisters. This intercession of Christ is the single greatest ongoing fact of the Christian's spiritual experience.

Christ has purchased for the Christian a priestly vocation, not born of aristocracy, caste, or wealth, but of grace. The priestly role of the pastor is to enable Christians to exercise this priestly vocation wherever sovereign grace has placed them. Priestly leadership means enabling other Christians to prevail in the world through intercession. Intercession transforms the common duties and pleasures of life into spheres of ministry. The most menial workplace is transfigured via the privilege of intercessory prayer as Christians come in contact with every sort of person. Prophet-priests are continually casting a vision for their flock to stand in the gap between God and humanity. A pastor is called to enable parishioners to accept this divine appointment as strategically placed persons. Whatever the obstacles or restrictions in the work-play environment, Christians can equip themselves with an attitude of prayer as they daily go about the priestly task of drawing fellow humanity into the presence of Christ.

The most important thing Jesus did during His earthly ministry, before Calvary, was to pray. As pastors we will do no better. By precept and example, we will transform our parishioners into priestly intercessors, people who bathe life in prayer and approach the exigencies of life with the predisposition of prayer. The pastor enters into covenant with his or her people so that they will be change agents in the world through prayer. "Praying without ceasing" (1 Thess. 5:17) fulfills Paul's exhortations to pray for those in authority, pray for one another, and in particular to pray for those entrusted to one's care, especially the immediate family. The closer the concentric circle of concern, the more explicit our priestly role becomes. In the same passage where Paul reminds us there is one mediator between God and man, he exhorts,

"Therefore I want the men in every place to pray, lifting up holy hands, without wrath and dissension" (1 Tim. 2:8).

George Washington Carver was a brilliant scientist, inventor, artist, mentor, and teacher. But he did not claim any native or acquired talents. His vision to transform the impoverished soil of the South into crop-yielding farms was a direct call and promise of God. He claimed the land through persistent scientific endeavor, infused with spirituality. Often, people who went to hear Carver speak on his scientific discoveries instead heard a lecture on prayer.

Curiously, Scripture records no charge given to the Levitical priesthood to pray for the children of Israel. Yet a powerful metaphor was provided by Aaron, the high priest, who bore the burdens of Israel as he came into the presence of God:

> You shall take two onyx stones and engrave on them the names of the sons of Israel, six of their names on the one stone and the names of the remaining six on the other stone, according to their birth.... You shall put the two stones on the shoulder pieces of the ephod, as stones of memorial for the sons of Israel, and Aaron shall bear their names before the Lord upon his two shoulders for a memorial (Ex. 28:9-10, 12).

To be remembered to God by a significant other is critical to identity formation. The highest affirmation we can give others is to tell them that we have remembered them before the throne of God. The prophet-priest is right at the center of that identity formation for both individuals and the community. "'Aaron shall carry the names of the sons of Israel in the breastpiece of judgment over his heart when he enters the holy place, for a memorial before the Lord continually'" (Ex. 28:29).

The Ministry of Absolution

Old Testament priests acted as community physicians, physically and spiritually. For the various sins of the community, there were blood offerings and scapegoats. For a wide range of physical diseases, there were ritual washings, burnings, and ostracisms. "Thus you shall keep the sons of Israel separated from their uncleanness, so that they will not die in their uncleanness by their defiling My tabernacle that is among them" (Lev. 15:31). The cultic sacrifices prescribed for leprosy demonstrated how the spiritual and physical natures of humankind are inextricably bound. Physical disease and spiritual failure both necessitated a blood offering. A pronouncement of "clean" could be given by the priest only after a sacrifice had been made, blood placed on the limbs of the individual, and hygienic measures taken. "The priest shall next offer the sin offering and make atonement for the one to be cleansed from his uncleanness. Then afterward, he shall slaughter the burnt offering. The priest shall offer up the burnt offering and the grain offering on the altar. Thus the priest shall make atonement for him, and he will be clean" (Lev. 14:19-20).

The activity described more than any other regarding the Levitical priesthood is ritual sacrifice. Blood is referred to eighty-six times and sacrifice forty-five times in the book of Leviticus. Paramount to the priest's work was closing the gap between the unrighteousness of humankind and the indisputable holiness of God. Expiation was the only way to make amends for guilt. The life of an animal would have to be taken, an act of mercy on God's part to allow a vicarious offering to serve as an *atonement* (i.e., a covering for sin).

The Old Testament sacrifice foreshadowed the propitiation that would be made by Christ, the ultimate act that would reconcile humanity to God by answering the penalty of death that had been pronounced upon humankind. Kenneth Grider writes, "The death of the sinless Christ, on behalf of us sinful humans, the just for the unjust, assuages the Father's holy wrath against sin, reconciles the Father to us, making it possible for him to forgive all who repent and believe."[11] The

---

[11] J. Kenneth Grider, *A Wesleyan-Holiness Theology* (Kansas City, Mo.: Beacon Hill Press, 1994), 325.

essential difference between the animal blood and the sacrifice of Christ is that, while the former could accomplish the peace of forgiveness, only the latter could effect spiritual transformation. The writer to Hebrews states, "For if the blood of goats and bulls and the ashes of a heifer sprinkling those who have been defiled sanctify for the cleansing of the flesh, how much more will the blood of Christ, who through the eternal Spirit offered Himself without blemish to God, cleanse your conscience from dead works to serve the living God?" (Heb. 9:13-14).

Christ was to effect forgiveness not only through His actions, but through His words: "'Your sins have been forgiven'" (Luke 7:48) and "'I do not condemn you, either. Go. From now on sin no more'" (John 8:11). After His resurrection, Jesus entrusted His eleven remaining disciples with the instrument of absolution. It may have been the most mystical and most potent gift which Christ left behind. Absolution is always to be enacted within the parameters of sincerity, honesty, repentance, and commitment to the living Christ. "'If you forgive the sins of any, their sins have been forgiven them; if you retain the sins of any, they have been retained'" (John 20:23). Most of us long for someone with whom we can share the disjunctures of our imperfect lives. Christ's priests are not able to pronounce absolution unless they are willing to listen. Listening is a major part of priestly work.

Although pastors and laity cannot grant God's forgiveness, they are called to affirm His forgiveness. The sinner must hear, either explicitly or implicitly from the Christian community, "You are forgiven." There is a critical link between this word of acceptance and the sinner's inner realization. It falls under the category of what Richard Nelson calls performative speech: "It did what it said in the very act of saying it."[12] The declaration of absolution was an essential

---

[12]Richard D. Nelson, *Raising up a Faithful Priest: Community and Priesthood in Biblical Theology* (Louisville, Ky.: Westminster John Knox Press), 45.

part of the Old Testament priestly blessing and provided the meaning for the cultic ritual. Indeed, it was a call to words. Nelson writes,

> Israelite priests were therefore ministers of God's word and by no means only ministers of the altar of sacrifice. To summarize, priestly utterance fell into three categories: Revelatory speech (oracle) disclosed God's will. Institutional speech (*torah*) established and taught the distinction between clean and unclean and between holy and profane, and went on to communicate the legal and ethical implications of being Yahweh's people. Performance speech (blessing declarations) effected blessing upon Israel and validated the effectiveness of their sacrifice.[13]

There is a fine, nonetheless distinct line between validating the sacrifice and the effectiveness of the sacrifice. Only the Godhead can do the former; in other words, the sacrifice of Christ is objectively efficacious, whether anyone ever applies it or not. But there is a sense in which all of us need to hear a verbal validation of that personal application from someone else who has experienced forgiveness. An illustration of this priestly act within the spirit of apostolicity was practiced by John. "I am writing to you, little children, because your sins have been forgiven you for His name's sake" (1 John 2:12).

The inextricable relationship between physical and spiritual healing is found in the *locus classicus* text for the Christian community's healing ministry (James 5:13-18). The method here described by James directly answers an obvious question: If the power of God is available through the church to heal the sick, why wouldn't it be available for the forgiveness of sins? "And the prayer offered in faith will restore the one who is sick, and the Lord will raise him up, and if he has committed sins, they will be forgiven him. Therefore, confess your sins to one another, and pray for one another so

---

[13]Nelson, 46.

that you may be healed. The effective prayer of a righteous man can accomplish much" (5:15-16).

A pastor recently took the full implication of the James passage. Before anointing members of his congregation for healing, he invited persons to come forward to confess their sins to members of his pastoral staff as they stood at the front of the church. The response in this very large congregation was overwhelming. For more than two hours, individuals streamed forward in brokenness and contrition to confess their sins and hear the blessing of Christ's atonement proclaimed by Christ's church: "You are forgiven in the name of the Father, Son, and Holy Spirit." This corporate worship service vividly demonstrated the pastor's priestly function. It exemplified how the church transcends the scientific paradigms of psychology, sociology, and medicine. At the conclusion of the service, the pastor's seven-year-old son made the profound observation, "That was a holy thing, wasn't it, Dad?" The primary task of pastoring is conducting holy transactions in the name of a holy God.

Many years ago, a colleague of mine was attending a conference sponsored by his denomination. The longer he stayed, the more his conscience was troubled. He felt guilt-stricken by certain standards that were being presented at the conference. His spirit sank lower and lower, with little hope of relief. Upon picking up the newspaper, he learned that the missionary E. Stanley Jones was in town. This young pastor found out the whereabouts of Jones' hotel and made an appointment with him. After listening to my friend's story, Jones commented, "Young man, it is my discernment that your all is on God's altar and that your intention to serve Christ is sincere. Go in peace." My friend left Jones' hotel with the deep realization that whatever had been troubling him was completely gone.

Such incidents are living fulfillments of Christ's promise, "'Truly I say to you, whatever you bind on earth shall have been bound in heaven; and whatever you loose on earth shall have been loosed in heaven'" (Matt. 18:18).

Words of direction, blessing, and absolution are powerful instruments of ministry. Therefore, they must be used prayerfully, cautiously, and without ulterior motive. The pastor represents not himself or herself but Christ and the local community of believers. They have entrusted the pastor with the "keys to the kingdom" (cf. Matt. 16:19). There is no power in the pastor's words themselves, and hence they never should be associated with superstition, magic, or cultic manipulation. They work miracles only because they are born of the Holy Spirit and the speaker is yielded to Jesus Christ. In Dallas Willard's words, "Such rituals work as part of living in the kingdom of God and enlist the personal agency of that kingdom to achieve their ends. Hence, they are not tools by which we engineer our desired result. We are 'under authority' and not 'in control.'"[14]

Conclusion

The priestly acts of feeding, mediating, interceding, absolving, forgiving, and blessing transcend statistical analysis. They cannot be assessed via conference reports and district minutes. The people whom we honor in ministry are those who produce growing attendance, finances, and physical property. Yet our recognition of these achievements disregard the prophetical-priestly nature of pastoral care.

The essential nature of ministry is not production. Ministers are stewards of God's grace, so the essence of ministry is sacramental. No other profession defines its task primarily as dispensing grace to its clientele. Yet pastoral care does precisely that. It applies Christian grace to the potentials and ills of the human condition. The quantifiable evidence of that dispensing of grace, such as church attendance and financial giving, are collateral results and not the purpose of our work. If we focus on these by-products, our motive becomes tainted.

[14]Dallas Willard, *In Search of Guidance* (Grand Rapids: Zondervan, 1993), 145.

Pastors and their parishioners are called to dispense grace without fear or favor, regardless of the outcome. This sacramental orientation enables the pastor to avoid losing his or her identity in bureaucratic processes and institutional concerns. Enabling individuals to realize their full potential in Christ must always transcend organizational motives. The optimum question for a Christian organization always is, "What is the most gracious thing we can do?" rather than, "What is the most beneficial for the institution?"

A pastor in a city where I ministered started a healing service on Wednesday evenings. The church was small, but 50 to 150 persons attended this service each week. The pastor gave a brief teaching and distributed an appropriate leaflet at each service. Persons were then invited to come forward to kneel for anointing, and prayer. The healing service became known throughout the metropolitan area and was attended by people from a wide range of denominations. Since most of these people were already members of other churches, they did not make any financial or physical contribution to this pastor's parish. Nevertheless, he had a wide influence which only eternity will measure. Many people were spiritually blessed because this pastor practiced the stewardship of grace.

Ministry's sacramental character is the basis for all pastoral care. Sacramental speech must not be compromised for more tangible, temporal pursuits.

Chapter 6

Jeremiah:
A Priestly Prophet

Judah's most critical problem was a crisis of spiritual health, a crisis created by inept spiritual physicians. Their prophet-priests had failed at both diagnosis and prognosis.

> They heal the brokenness of the daughter of My people
>   superficially....
> Is there no balm in Gilead?
> Is there no physician there?
> Why then has not the health of the daughter of My
>   people been restored? (Jer. 8:11a, 22).

Jeremiah interpreted the political and economic disease of Judah as a collapse of the national soul, a direct result of misguided soul care. His experience demonstrates that spiritual leaders must be effective spiritual "physicians."

Today's pastor is likewise in the business of restoring physical health. The spiritual physician administers spiritual vitamins, health food, and tonic to the spiritually malnourished, the emaciated, crippled, diseased, and oppressed. The temptation is to dilute the dosage or to offer placebos. Is it possible in today's church to be an honest, accurate, insightful, sensitive healer of souls, and at the same time be free from political, economic, and ecclesiastical agendas? Probably not. On the one had, we are faced with the danger of Lone Ranger Christianity. On the other hand, there is the danger of a bloated bureaucracy more attuned to self-advancement than to authentic kingdom expression. Both dangers will beset us until Christ returns.

Jeremiah did not call for dismantling the temple and dismissing those entrusted with her welfare. He did call for reformation, especially the reformation of a priestly profession that had become distracted from its central calling. Judah needed a major upheaval of its clergy. They had become more concerned with keeping life's edges neat, maintaining status quo, living at ease, and being able to discourse on the most current topic of the day. There was only one possibility for hope—a major turning, repentance, and conversion of those entrusted with the people's spiritual welfare. At the heart of Jeremiah's message is *repentance*—a concept articulated by Jeremiah more often than by any other Old Testament prophet. J.A. Thompson states, "a glimpse of its verbal usage shows that in the book of Jeremiah there are forty-eight instances of the covenantal use of *shub* ("repent"). No other book in the Old Testament has this concentration of the verb."[1] Thompson offers further illumination: "The main emphasis seems to be with the idea of 'return' (to God), 'repent' and 'turn back' or 'repent' from evil. In many ways the root *shub* embodies the germ of Jeremiah's message."[2]

---

[1] J.A. Thompson, *The Book of Jeremiah* (Grand Rapids: Eerdmans, 1980), 77.
[2] Thompson, 80.

The national calamity which Jeremiah faced was complex and systemic. None of the priests' neat ecclesiastical prescriptions would provide healing. The complexity of the problems defied simple solutions and facile explanations. The disease was so advanced that only the most adept, knowledgeable, committed, and well-prepared physician would be able to begin the healing process. Jeremiah stood face-to-face with a patient eaten up with cancer of the soul. No soothing technique, no stimulative pill, nor simple excisions would do.

The only solution, according to Jeremiah, was a complete transformation of the nation's character. That transformation needed to begin with their spiritual leaders. Likewise today, if the church is not to crumble from devouring disease on the inside and cultural pressure on the outside, a cure must be discovered. The recovery of spiritual health will be nothing less than a supernatural miracle. Such miracles, which amount to reversals of human character, dwarf the so-called miracles of nature. The church can exist without the latter, but it will die without the former.

Jeremiah's healing work moved the people of Judah from sickness to health in several different ways. Let us examine the various facets of the healing process.

From Outward Conformity to Spiritual Inwardness

Inauthentic spiritual existence is marked by a form of godliness, disconnected from passion. The heart is not really in one's relationship with God. Pleasing God is traded for currying political, social, economic, or even religious advantage. For all of us, the spiritual life is not an either/or existence. Our religious activity may be tainted by less-than-best motives, but the job of the spiritual physician is to be constantly moving those entrusted to his or her care toward spiritual congruity and integrity. The task at times can be disheartening.

> For what purpose does frankincense come to Me from Sheba
> And the sweet cane from a distant land?

Your burnt offerings are not acceptable
And your sacrifices are not pleasing to Me (Jer. 6:20).
The diagnosis of Judah's ills was returned from the head Physician: *unacceptable worship*. God did not send this message in a vacuum. God's assessment resonated with the prophet's own observation of his people.

Doesn't the same sickness characterize many worshipers today? As I sit on the platforms of various churches that I visit, I can observe the body language, deadpan expressions, closed postures, and unenthusiastic responses of the so-called worshipers. The bride of Christ is about to go to sleep, or is at least distracted—distracted by temporal agendas, plaguing anxieties, false values, and fleeting pleasures. Too many worshipers act as though the God of the universe is not worthy of their undivided attention.

Can we get their attention? Can we shatter their false views of reality? Can our words enter their circumstances to the extent that they will come to know there is a reality of ultimate things beyond their immediate concerns? Are there words sharp enough to pierce the frailty and vulnerability of their daily existence? Only through a Jeremiad imagination that produces words faithful to God's character, though often at odds with the modalities of conventional wisdom, can we overcome the barriers. The initial response may be as disheartening as that of a patient who has been informed of a terminal disease. In Walter Bruggemann's words, "To do that requires that speech must not be conventional, reasonable, predictable, or expected. It must shock people's sensitivity, call attention to what is not usually noticed, break the routine, make statements with ambiguity so that people can redescribe things that have long since seemed settled, bear surpluses of power before routing assessments."[3]

At some point, the spiritual physician needs to inquire as to how the patient perceives his or her own spiritual con-

---

[3]Quoted in Mays and Achtemeier, 118.

dition. Do the patients believe themselves to be born of the Spirit? There is optimism in the physician's labor because it is possible for *any* person to be regenerated, to become a new creature in Christ Jesus. This does not mean that the pastor runs around, asking all members of the congregation if they have experienced the new birth. It also does not mean that the pastor should assume that everyone who comes for psychological, marital, vocational, or other counseling is devoid of spiritual life. It does mean that the pastor operates with the new birth constantly in view. It also means that the most critical direction in which the pastor can lead anyone is toward the new life found in Jesus Christ. This may not happen on the first encounter, and it will always require sensitivity to the patient's perception and readiness. But a parishioner who has placed himself or herself under a pastor's care for whatever reason—cultural, emotional, existential—has the right to know that he or she is *dead* outside of Jesus Christ.

Unfortunately, accurate diagnosis and prognosis of a person's spiritual health often are missed in pastoral conversation. A seminary student was approached with a stormy marital problem. The lady said that both she and her husband were unwilling to attend one another's church. Since neither was willing to switch to a different denomination, they were at an impasse and they did not attend church at all. In an extended conversation, the seminary student failed to make a diagnosis of the woman's spiritual condition. The following questions would have been helpful, but were absent from the conversation:

"What does God think about your situation?"

"What would God tell both of you to do?"

"What would be the best solution to your predicament?"

"Tell me about your spiritual journey. Tell me about the most significant spiritual experience of your life."

"What solution would enable you to maintain or come into a meaningful relationship with Christ?"

"What is really at stake in this disagreement with your husband?"

This practitioner-in-training neglected to ask any of these questions. He failed to realize that most pastoral conversation begins with identifying the symptoms of the problem, but should not end there. It is left to the spiritual physician to place the real spiritual issue within the patient's perception.

August Spangenberg acted as an insightful spiritual physician in the following conversation with a troubled young Anglican priest named John Wesley. Starting with Wesley's symptoms, he incisively probed the minister's spiritual crisis:

> When Wesley asked for advice concerning his work, Spangenberg instead pressed some highly personal questions. "Do you know yourself? Have you the witness within yourself? Does the Spirit of God bear witness with your spirit that you are a child of God?" Wesley was taken aback by such directness. Spangenberg was quick to spot his discomfiture, and was encouraged to multiply his inquiries. "Do you know Jesus Christ?" he asked point-blank. Wesley stalled: "I know He is Saviour of the world." But that was not good enough for this persistent surgeon of souls. "True," Spangenberg agreed, "But do you know He has saved you?" That was the vital thing. Wesley was perceptibly hesitant: "I hope He has died to save me." Still the pressure was maintained: "Do you know yourself?" Wesley weakly mumbled, "I do," to hide his embarrassment, but he confessed in his *Journal* that they were "vain words."[4]

Guiding others toward spiritual inwardness through life in Christ is not solely the work of professional ministers. Nevertheless, it ought to be a skill in which the pastor specializes. Spiritual probing cannot be set aside for psychological counseling techniques, recovery programs, or support groups. All of these may be necessary for the patient to move toward wholeness and maturity, but they must serve as

---

[4]A. Skevington Wood, *The Burning Heart: John Wesley, Evangelist* (Minneapolis, Minn.: Bethany Fellowship, Inc., 1967), 55.

supplemental activities and not replacements for the pastor's primary counseling activity. The spiritual physician works with the conviction that God usually changes persons from the inside out, not from the outside in. "I will put My law within them and on their heart will I write it; and I will be their God, and they shall be My people" (Jer. 31:33b). A change in the seeker's circumstances may enhance spiritual inwardness, but can never serve as the source. Thomas Merton made this discovery when he had gone through the severe hardships and tortuous rigors of becoming a Trappist Monk.

> . He undoubtedly found great joy in the graceful medieval ordering of his life and in the sheer physical beauty of the place daily unfolding around him. But did this claim to have found out the meaning of his life—to have resolved all his earlier problems—truly represent his feelings in his *novitiate* or were there doubts that he was repressing?... For Merton the discovery that it was not possible to live the whole of his life on a high romantic plane, came not at first by a resentment of the hardships, or by a longing for freedom, or by disappointment in his fellow monks, but by the sad little discovery that despite the outward change in his way of life, inwardly he had not changed at all.[5]

The greatest gift a prophet-priest can give parishioners is the possibility of a genuine change of character. Real change does not come via self-help kits or even through our most resolute will power. "Can the Ethiopian change his skin or the leopard his spots? Then you also can do good who are accustomed to do evil" (Jer. 13:23).

From Satisfied to Seeker

"And you will seek Me and find Me when you search for Me with all your heart" (Jer. 29:13). It is a paradox of human existence that, the more one has of God, the more one wants.

[5]Monica Furlong, *Merton: A Biography* (San Francisco: Harper and Row Publishers, 1980), 139.

Ironically, spiritual satisfaction leads to dissatisfaction. The spiritual physician has effectively signed a professional oath that states, "My first order of business is to lead those under my spiritual care in the pursuit of God as found in Jesus Christ." Often, other areas of ministry are allowed to become primary: leadership in numerical growth, leadership in structural growth, and leadership in fiscal growth. Yet the pastor is to make all growth within the church subservient to spiritual growth. *Spiritual growth* is defined as making people more Christian than they already are.

Idol Worship. There are two main obstacles to the church's becoming more Christian in character, both of which were faced by Jeremiah in his prophetic work. First is idol worship:

> As the thief is shamed when he is discovered, so the house of Israel is shamed; They, their kings, their princes and their priests, and their prophets, who say to a tree, "You are my father," and to the stone, "You gave me birth." For they have turned their back to Me, and not their face. But in the time of their trouble they will say, "Arise and save us." But where are your gods which you made for yourself? Let them arise, if they can save you in the time of your trouble, for according to the number of your cities are your gods, O Judah (Jer. 2:26-28).

The people of Judah gauged their spiritual health by false gods. Happiness was measured by what they could produce rather than by what God had given. They expected to be saved by objects of their own making. Peter Craigie points out that these gods of wood and stone represented the Jews' own powers of creativity, symbols of birth and parenthood. "Israel had as many gods as it had cities, but with every new god, it became weaker, not stronger."[6]

A spiritual physician enables the patient to focus time and energy towards becoming more like Christ. Whatever distracts the believer from this is idol worship, the sin of making God in our own image. It reverses the divine order

---

[6]Craigie, 39.

and fabricates a cosmic counterfeit. While God is attempting to make us in His image, we attempt to make God in our image. This subversion of the divine intention perverts all that is good.

Of course, the persons in our congregations will not be divided neatly into idol-worshipers and non-idol-worshipers. All of our lives are marked by activities that seemingly have little eternal significance—washing the car, cutting the grass, painting the house, etc.—all of which point to the transitory nature of life. We may refer to a stint at the hairdresser's as "getting a permanent," but we know that nothing we do is permanent.

The pastor is placed in the unenviable position of trying to enable parishioners to discern when certain uses of time, energy, and things are a spiritual distraction rather than a spiritual enhancement. Unfortunately, there is no simple prescription or do-it-yourself test for this diagnosis. However, several diagnostic questions can help us assess whether a certain pursuit is God worship or idol worship. Jeremiah raises these questions.

First, what is really going to matter to us in time of crisis such as death, sickness, or loss? The idol worshiper seeks immediate gratification, such as the temporary thrill of buying a new house, a new car, a new technology, or a new experience. The pastor is called to move parishioners from the thrill of immediacy to an appreciation of eternity. In the end, at death's door, how would I rewrite the script of my life? What kind of car, house, or computer would I have owned? How much time would I have given to surfing the Internet, to playing golf, to prayer, to Scripture, to my wife? These questions enable a person to evaluate life via an outside-life experience. Whereas Charles Dickens enabled his character Ebeneezer Scrooge to dream about how his life might end, the pastor enables individuals to catch a vision of the reality beyond their immediate world. Part of worship is a transcendent stepping outside of everyday life and viewing it as God sees it. This view from the outside may call for rearranging priorities, a necessity that may not have been perceived in the hurry and scurry of each day.

Second, does the worshiper's way of life build relationships or neglect them? Inordinate amounts of time spent on things which cannot communicate (inanimate objects that cannot reciprocate love, affection, and understanding) is idol worship. An alternative is provided by

> …the voice of joy and the voice of gladness, the voice of the bridegroom and the voice of the bride, the voice of those who say, "Give thanks to the Lord of hosts, For the Lord is good, for His lovingkindness is everlasting (Jer. 33:11a).

Here we catch a glimpse of the home of a husband and wife who are still very much in love: laughing, joking, talking, conversing, delighting in the presence of one another. Even in the marriage relationship. Sex can say, "I want to get something from you." In contrast, a loving couple's sexual relations say, "I like to spend time with you."

We can assess our devotion to others and to God, rather than to things, in measurements of time. Allotment of time indicates our assignment of significance. To be devoted to someone is to spend time with that person. The whirlwind of activity choices will require intentional scheduling if we are not to ignore God and other persons. The world, which is no friend to grace, will rob me of these life-enhancing relationships. So the spiritual leader must constantly attempt to enrich the divine-human conversation for himself or herself, as well as for parishioners.

Third, how do we pray? God exhorts His people through Jeremiah, "'Call to Me and I will answer you, and I will tell you great and mighty things, which you do not know'" (33:3). The temptation for the American pastor is to paraphrase God's promise to "give you great and mighty things *which you desire*." Instead of material prosperity, which is most often detrimental to spiritual formation, God promises wisdom. Wisdom is the ability to see life as God sees it, to attach significance to that which merits significance in His sight.

Look at what the nation of Judah could have had, if they heeded Jeremiah's call—health, healing, peace, truth, cleansing, and pardon (33:6-7). Israel's prosperity would have been to God's glory and would not have gone unnoticed by their pagan neighbors.

> It will be to Me a name of joy, praise and glory before all the nations of the earth which will hear of all the good that I do for them, and they will fear and tremble because of all the good and all the peace that I make for it (33:9).

God delights in blessing His people, and prayer serves to interpret God's blessing. The blessing is for those who are submitted to God's sovereign grace. Grace provides the trust that God is working out His redemptive purpose. Prayer is the heightened consciousness of the unseen hand and the unchanging Mover. Prayer is the worshiper's submission to God's plan, even when elements of that plan are distasteful. God allows temporary discomfort so that ultimately equity, justice, and truth with triumph. Authentic prayer is the grace-endowed human aspiration of what God wants rather than what we want.

> Therefore thus says the LORD of hosts, the God of Israel: "Behold, I am going to punish the king of Babylon and his land, just as I punished the king of Assyria. And I will bring Israel back to his pasture and he will graze on Carmel and Bashan, and his desire will be satisfied in the hill country of Ephraim and Gilead" (Jer. 50:18-19).

The church and ultimately the world needs pastors who lead them in prayer. The early church took seriously the call to intercession. The second-century Liturgy of St. James prayed for the

> ...Peace that is from above, and the love of God, and the salvation of our souls, let us make our supplication to the Lord.

For the peace of the whole world, and the unity of all the holy Churches of God.

For them that bear fruit and do good deeds in the holy Churches of God, that remember the poor, the widows and the orphans, the strangers, and them that are in need; and for them that have desired us to make mention of them in our prayers.

For them that are in old age and infirmity, the sick, the distressed, and that are vexed of unclean spirits, their speedy healing from God and salvation.

For them that live their lives in virginity, and purity, and ascenticism, and in venerable marriage, and them that carry on their struggle in the caves and dens and holes of the earth, our holy fathers and brothers.

For Christians that sail, that journey, that are strangers, and for our brethren that are in bonds and exiles, and imprisonment and bitter slavery, their peaceful return.

For the forgiveness of our sins and remission of our offences, and that we may be preserved from all affliction, wrath, danger and necessity, and the insurrection of enemies.

For good temperature of the atmosphere, peaceful showers, pleasant dews, abundance of fruits, fullness of a good season, and for the crown of the year.[7]

Such interecession was much different from our present practice of prayer. It was non-pragmatic—i.e., not aimed at immediate results. One of the purposes of prayer is to allow its participants to transcend the nagging particulars of life that normally preoccupy us. Prayer allows ordinary people to become players in much larger stakes: Washington, the United Nations, Bosnia, Afghanistan, and the totality of the world. There *is* a time for prayer to address immediate and local problems, even Uncle Larry's lumbago and Aunt Gertrude's gout. Prayer can petition God to cure many of

---

[7]*The Liturgies of SS. Mark, James, Clement, Chrysostom, and Basil, and the Church of Malabar*, J.M. Neale and R. F. Littledale, trans., seventh ed. (London: Griffith Farran & Co., Limited, n.d.), 42-43.

our aches and pains. But I suspect that what prayer really needs to do is displace our self-serving agendas with more critical concerns. I once met someone who wears a Super Bowl ring. He explained how he fervently prayed that God would help him and his teammates to win that game. I could not help but ponder the incongruity between God's listening to the NFL player and persecuted Christians behind the Iron Curtain at the same time.

The most healing ministry the pastor has to offer is prayer. As in all spiritual disciplines, prayer cannot be divorced from actual time spent and energy expended with one's parishioners. If a pastor leaves a non-praying people and moves on to greener pastures, that pastor leaves a diseased flock. When the pastor spends time with his or her people, designating hours devoted to the divine-human encounter in prayer, the church becomes the salt and leaven God has envisioned. Prayer replaces human agency with divine agency. Prayer does not eliminate our going into the world, but makes our going possible. The pastor need not turn the church into a monastery to discover a hint of Thomas Merton's monastic revelation:

> The eloquence of this liturgy was even more tremendous: and what it said was one simple, cogent, tremendous truth: the Church, the Court of the Queen of Heaven, is the real capitol of the country in which we are living. This is the center of all the vitality that is in America. This is the cause and reason why the nation is holding together. These men hidden in the anonymity of their choir and their white cowls, are doing for their land what no army, no congress, no president, could ever do as such: they are winning for it the grace and protection and the friendship of God.[8]

Merton's youthful and enthusiastic appraisal of the Roman Catholic liturgy may have been misguided in some ways, but he was not wrong in considering a prayerful community to be the chief capital of personal and national health. The

[8]Furlong, 105.

pastor who leads a congregation in the prayer disciplines will offer a strong antidote to the poisons of the soul, which seep from the sewers of America's perversions. The pastor can do no better than to encourage his or her people to trade some time of interaction with cyberspace for moments of prayer. Such an exchange will serve to dismantle Satan's superstructure of evil. Spiritual physicians realize that we do not need larger ecclesiastical organizations; we need more occupied prayer closets. God is not looking for better evangelism methods but for better people. Sincere prayer changes the one who prays before it changes the world for which one prays. In Parker Palmer's words, "In prayer we find the ultimate space in which to practice obedience to truth, the space created by that Spirit who keeps troth with us all."[9]

Arrival Theology. The second obstacle thwarting Judah's seeking of God was an "arrival theology" of spirituality. The Jews' sense of "having it made" spiritually stunted their spiritual growth. This Judean either/or concept of spirituality mitigated against Jeremiah's call for spiritual revival. Insular smugness deafened Judah to God's voice. They confused their arrival in the Promised Land with continued conquest. There was always room for spiritual growth. "What if there is no more territory to conquer?" becomes a mute and hypothetical question. There always is more!

Judah was not the only nation to fall victim to "arrival theology." In American evangelical thinking, entrance into the Christian fold is more akin to arrival than it is to the beginning of a pursuit. Once one has found an object, there is no need to seek it. If one searches for a precious stone, unearthing it results in a trip to the nearest bank vault. In contrast, if one finds a friend, the relationship is mutually progressive and revelatory. Searching for God with all of our hearts (Jer. 29:13b) designates not an ultimate possession of God, but an ongoing process of getting to know and love Him.

---

[9]Parker Palmer, *To Know As We Are Known: A Spirituality of Education* (New York: Harper and Row, 1983), 125.

In Augustine's words, what one does not know, she or he cannot love; and what one does not love, she or he cannot know.

No one is completely whole spiritually, yet the spiritual physician leads a congregation in pursuit of wholeness. Spiritual fitness is gained by degrees, as is physical fitness. Being "in shape" or "out of shape" carries little meaning as a discipline assessment.

The disciples of spiritual life attempt to beat back encroaching death. It is a day-to-day battle. The false perception that the battle is won (triumphalism) is equivalent to spiritual pride. "The arrogant will stumble and fall with no one to raise him up" (Jer. 50:32a). The only way that the company of the redeemed can keep from falling is to continue seeking spiritual robustness. It is dangerous to believe that today's spiritual stamina guarantees tomorrow's vigor. Strangling the church's health is the belief that one's past spiritual experience guarantees today's Christian vitality. Though only a few within evangelicalism's broad spectrum of theology overtly espouse eternal security, most of us have adopted it. The result is a sterile faith that knows little of the thirst that is absolutely essential to find spiritual nourishment.

Thus, the spiritual physician faces the delicate task of affirming a parishioner's spiritual security and at the same time urging that person to "press toward the goal." The order of salvation is marked by crises, a multitude of crises within a lifetime of journey. Regeneration and entire sanctification are critical crossroads on that journey, but neither experience will put one on a plateau of self-congratulatory ease. Paradoxically, when one comes face-to-face with Christ, spiritual hunger is both satisfied and intensified. The spiritual banquet table is not a place of momentous gorging, but of a moment-by-moment feast. John Wesley sounded this note in his 1770 reminder to the Methodist General Conference: "Does not talking, with proper caution, of a justified or sanctified state, tend to mislead men; most naturally leading them to trust in what was done in one moment? Whereas we are every moment pleasing or displeasing to God, according to our works; according to the whole of our present inward tempers and outward behavior."[10]

The spiritual physician is tempted to adopt a persona which masks the hurts and frustrations of parish life. Jeremiah's honesty reveals the despair and depression which at times marks the life of a prophet-priest. Note Jeremiah's radical mood swings:

> Woe to me, my mother, that you have borne me as a man of strife and a man of contention to all the land! I have neither lent, nor have men lent money to me, yet everyone curses me.... Your words were found and I ate them, and Your words became for me a joy and the delight of my heart; for I have been called by Your name, O LORD God of hosts (Jer. 15:10, 16).

The psychological, physical, and spiritual drain of a soul guide takes its toll. The shepherd needs the solace of the flock. Mutual confession leads to wholeness, which in turn leads to vitality. While pastors are spiritual leaders, they do not have to deny their own personal faults. Though the pulpit is not a place for melodrama, it can allow the pastor to confess being in need of healing grace, just like everyone else. Such disclosure will move both pastor and people toward God. The only kind of people who can move forward are those who allow their defects to be exposed to God's glorious presence. Confession is often uncomfortable, but it is the only route to spiritual health for both clergy and laity. Honesty is the only route to spiritual authenticity. Wise and candid disclosure by the prophet-priest will serve as a catalyst for parishioners to drop their defenses. It is the one posture that invites spiritual renewal.

From Illusion to Reality

None of us sees things as they really are. Our limited perception lies between us and the object of our interpretation. All of us are left with the task of identifying the psychologi-

---

[10]Wesley, 8:338.

cal defenses and perverted motives that warp our perception. The false prophets of Judah wanted to maintain their livelihood that depended on the good will of the people. The good will of the people was predicated on a prophetic message that pronounced, in essence, "All is well," and promised, "All will be well."

> They healed the brokenness of the daughter of My people superficially,
> Saying, "Peace, Peace,"
> But there is no peace (Jer. 8:11).
> We waited for peace, but no good came; for a time of healing, but behold, terror! (Jer. 8:15).
> Harvest is past, summer is ended, and we are not saved (Jer. 8:20).

Superficial health assessments are failures for the spiritual physician that could result in an eternal malpractice suit. Granted, the modern desire to "tell it like it is" has often been fulfilled in crudeness and naive simplicity that ignore the complexities of life. But far more common have been the cases when the pastor has failed to probe sufficiently in order to identify the most urgent issue. Lack of sufficient stringency characterizes a clergy who perceive they serve a God whom C.S. Lewis described as a grandfather with a long flowing white beard, who at the end of the day yawns, pronouncing that a good time was had by all. A.W. Tozer caustically described a contemporary pastor as an asexual religious mascot whose "handshake is always soft and whose head is always bobbing in a perpetual Yes of universal acquiescence."[11]

The movie *Mass Appeal*, which I show to my ministerial students each year, depicts a priest who basks in the benevolence of his congregation. His need for his flock's approval has attenuated his ability to speak truth. His ministry is defined by a fear of offending his parishioners, lest he lose them. This pathological fear of loss was conceived in his childhood

---

[11]A.W. Tozer, *Man: The Dwelling Place of God* (Harrisburg, Pa.: Christian Publications, Inc., 1966), 168.

experiences of rejection and abuse. Father Farley's mode of response is so sublimated that, when confronted by an overwhelming crisis, he exclaims, "I don't even know what truth is anymore."

In Jeremiah's time, Judah was headed for destruction. Jerusalem would be sacked, the temple razed, the women raped, and all but the weak and infirm shackled and transported as slaves to a foreign land. The last king of Judah, Zedekiah, would watch as the Chaldeans slaughtered his seventy sons, then he would have his own eyes gouged out. Judah refused to believe that there would be a day of reckoning for their idolatry and injustice. The prophets failed to service notice that the nation was headed for shame and enslavement.

> Then the LORD said to me, "The prophets are prophesying falsehood in My name. I have neither sent them nor commanded them nor spoken to them; they are prophesying to you a false vision, divination, futility and the deception of their own minds. Therefore thus says the LORD concerning the prophets who are prophesying in My name, although it is not I who sent them—yet they keep saying, 'There will be no sword or famine in this land'—by sword and famine, these prophets shall meet their end!" (Jer. 14:14-15).

Few among us would fail to notice that our American forefathers' vision of ensuring domestic tranquility seems at present less certain than ever. An eighteen-month-old child is slain in a drive-by shooting while held in his grandmother's arms. A fourteen-year-old child steps into his public school and executes two of his teachers with a hand gun. Two teenagers are killed in an argument at a high-school football game. An eleven-year-old commits suicide, while another eleven-year-old stomps his teacher to death because she criticized him. A teacher becomes pregnant by her eighth-grade student. These events were the result of perverted priorities, family fragmentation, and loss of moral authority. The public square is increasingly the battleground for cultural warfare, racial antagonism, and protected self-interest. Public institutions of education, welfare, and party politics find themselves less and less able to provide solutions. In this midst of this anarchy stands the metaphysician with his or her specialized knowledge of the human soul. The temptation is to dilute the specialty by choosing the world's tactics rather than God's remedy. God's remedy calls neither for new techniques nor new measures.

> Thus says the LORD, "Stand by the ways and see and ask for
>   the ancient paths,
> Where the good way is, and walk in it;
> And you will find rest for your souls" (Jer. 6:16).

Human agencies can treat only symptoms. The metaphysician is uniquely positioned to treat the actual disease.

> The heart is more deceitful than all else
> And is desperately sick;
> Who can understand it? (Jer. 17:9).

The spiritual physician understands how prosperity, selfish motives, greed, and restlessness obscure the perennial disease of all human beings. G.K. Chesterton referred to it as seeing oneself out of proportion to the universe. Every healthy-looking, well-clothed, and relationally astute parishioner the pastor faces every Sunday is tempted by the lust of the flesh, the lust of the eyes, and the pride of life. The pastor offers the one remedy that will prevent these universal propensities from destroying the church and its potential. The remedy is Christ living in us, and the Christian hope is that we can be progressively conformed to His way of doing and thinking.

There is a "good way," hardly any of it provided by organization or brokerage. The pastor specializes in the "good way" of mutual caring and support through intercessory prayer, affirmation, encouragement, and building up of one another. These ministries lead those who would find true self-improvement to full restoration through repentance and forgiveness. We find reconciliation with God by the means of grace such as contemplation, prayer, Scripture study, stewardship, community service, and the sacraments. The metaphysician is not called to be an expert in politics, economics, or sociology. Rather, she or he is the professional who prescribes what will mend a broken relationship with God. A confusion about this role will result in having many shepherds who

...have ruined My vineyard,
They have trampled down My field;
They have made My pleasant field
A desolate wilderness (Jer. 12:10).

The wilderness inside today's church is a much greater threat than the storm on the outside. Nurturing the vineyard so that it thrives is the pastor's first order of business. The greatest gift a metaphysician can give this world is a congregation of persons of Christian character and perception. The guide of souls equips them to integrate everything they buy, think, or do within a Christian matrix. This matrix consists of thinking and acting in a thoroughly Christian manner, free of contradiction and inconsistency. This activity moves the Christian toward reality and in turn moves the world toward wholeness. Authentic Christianity is the balm for a world reeling from the despair of disillusionment.

This disillusionment can be dispelled only if the prophet is lovingly honest. A wife was divorcing her husband in order to pursue a relationship with another man. Even though she and her husband were confessing Christians, she believed her temporary happiness held a higher priority than her vow of marital fidelity. She was even convinced that personal fulfillment (as she interpreted it) was a divine right. The pastor arranged for an encounter between the separated couple. Unable to convince them of their biblical responsibility and public witness to God, the pastor stated, "I am praying that God will do whatever it takes, including affliction or pain, in order to align you with His plan and purpose." The wife was so infuriated that she ordered the pastor to leave the house. Yet, I am convinced that the pastor spoke the truth in love.

He fervently believed what many pastors need to discover—compassion without truth is not really love. It is a failure of moral nerve.

From Despair to Hope

As long as there is physical life, the spiritual physician never has to make the pronouncement that "it's too late." God is constantly predisposed to spiritual restoration and full redemption for every individual. As Jeremiah did, we can declare with confidence God's promise,

> "For I know the plans that I have for you," declares the LORD, "plans for welfare and not for calamity to give you a future and a hope" (Jer. 29:11).

Though there was little immediate good news for the nation of Judah, God's long-range plan was one of reclamation. There would remain a believing remnant whose posterity would reinherit the Promised Land. No matter how waywardly God's children stray, God acts tendentiously to gain glory for himself. His glory is vitally connected to the welfare of His people.

The spiritual director constantly reminds individuals that God is kindly disposed toward them. This does not mean that God condones our sinful condition. I believe that God wept along with Jeremiah for Judah's life-run-amok. Jeremiah's tears were God's tears. Walter Bruggemann reminds us, "This move from guilt to healing as found in the taxonomy from Jeremiah and Leviticus affirms the reality of God's rage, God's hurt, God's ache, and God's self-giving love. The panoply of God's rage, hurt, ache, and love is an awesome dramatic reality in the life of faith."[12] God means to recover His investment in the human enterprise, an investment we have wasted because of our bad choices.

> "In those days and at that time," declares the LORD, "the sons of Israel will come, both they and the sons of Judah as well; they

---

[12]Walter Bruggemann, *Finally Comes the Poet: Daring Speech for Proclamation* (Minneapolis, Minn.: Fortress Press, 1989), 33.

will go along weeping as they go, and it will be the LORD their God they will seek. They will ask for the way to Zion, turning their faces in its direction; they will come that they may join themselves to the LORD in an everlasting covenant that will not be forgotten" (Jer. 50:4-5).

How low had Judah gone? Low enough to sacrifice their children to appease and manipulate false gods. True religion declares a God of holy love who does not act capriciously, but out of righteous character. God will be faithful, though we are faithless. No matter how dark the hour, His message is essentially positive. Even the message that God will destroy evil is positive. Unfortunately, Judah would have to endure the purgatory of exile. Only then would she truly appreciate God's offer of cleansing and forgiveness.

Christians find hope in the divine initiative of prevenient grace. God's good will toward us is forever sealed in Jesus Christ. He is the last word of every sermon, every pastoral conversation, every counseling session, every funeral, and every wedding. Sometimes the Word will be more implicit than explicit, more covert than overt. But Christ always extends to us the potential that our reality can be redefined. Obedience to the Word means "an anticipation of the restoration of personal and interpersonal life, happy families, domestic well-being, and joy, shared food, and delighted relationships."[13] No one has ever stated this promise more practically than Wesley did before a magistrate:

"But I hear," added he, "you preach to a great number of people every night and morning. Pray, what would you do with them? Whither would you lead them? What religion do you preach? What is it good for?" I replied, "I do preach to as many as desire to hear, every night and morning. You ask, what I would do with them: I would make them virtuous and happy, easy in themselves, and useful to others. Whether would I lead them? To heaven; to God the Judge, the lover of all, and to Jesus the Mediator of the new covenant. What religion do I preach? The

[13]Bruggemann, *Finally Comes the Poet*, 41.

religion of love; the law of kindness brought to light by the gospel. What is this good for? To make all who receive it enjoy God and themselves: To make them like God, lovers of all; contented in their lives; and crying out at their death, in calm assurance, 'O grave where is thy victory! Thanks be unto God, who giveth me the victory, through my Lord Jesus Christ.'"[14]

God loves the world. Although the world has *No* written on it, God intends that our *No* be consumed by His *Yes.* The pastor seeks to evoke by the power of the Holy Spirit a responsive yes that will be coupled with God's yes in every ministry situation. Thus, the motif for every ministry encounter is, "If you'll agree to it, God can work a miracle in your life." We as pastors can approach the human crisis with the certitude expressed by Karl Barth, that God deals with persons, "not with a natural *therefore*, but with a miraculous *nevertheless.*[15] There never has been a situation so dark that the positive light of grace cannot dispel the darkness. There is always hope. In poet W.H. Auden's words, "Nothing can save us that is possible. We who are about to die demand a miracle."[16]

Pop psychology promotes a self-centered philosophy of actualization without any universally acceptable standard of what an actualized person is or ought to be. This perverts the prophetic message. The message is further undermined by a philosophy of relativism that denies there is an absolute standard of truth. If there are no normative standards of rationality and communication, we ask in vain, "What is the truth?" If everyone has the truth, no one has the Truth. Everyone is supposed to be a *logos* unto himself. The only answer to this chaos is an objective frame of reference, above and beyond all feeling, sensing, and reckoning.

I know, O Lord, that a man's way is not in himself,
Nor is it in a man who walks to direct his steps (Jer. 10:23).

---

[14]Wesley, 8:8.
[15]Casalis, 104.
[16]Quoted in *Gravity and Grace*, Joseph Sittler, ed. (Minneapolis, Minn.: Augsburg Publishing House, 1986), 112.

In 1934, Richard Byrd set up an observation station in Antarctica, located 123 miles south of Little America. While he lived alone for five months in a hut, the temperature outside dropped to 75 degrees Fahrenheit below zero. Because of the cold and darkness, it was dangerous to venture outside. In order to do scientific experiments on the frozen ice and find his way back to the hut, Byrd would venture out by feeling his way along a line tied to a succession of poles. One night while making some observations and calculations, he inadvertently strayed beyond sight of the last pole. Byrd had no idea of his location, much less the whereabouts of the line leading back to his shelter. He knew he would not be able to survive the elements, so he knelt down and built a small ice beacon in the snow. He then took several paces from the beacon and returned to it. He repeatedly did this, each time changing direction by a few degrees, but never venturing beyond sight of the beacon. He repeated this maneuver until finally he came to the last pole of his constructed guideline, which led him back to safety. His life was spared because he established a frame of reference.

Jeremiah's direction was established by a sure frame of reference. Ministry in any age must be oriented to a pole star—the incarnate Word, Jesus Christ, as revealed in Scripture. Christian ministry requires checking and rechecking that point of reference in order not to become disoriented by fads, cultural mores, and expedient pragmatism. A pastor must be concerned not only about the letter of the law but the spirit of the law. The pastor daily waits before God with Bible open, asking God to illuminate and apply the Word freshly to his or her own heart and life. Everything the church does must be measured by this illumination. The pastor is called to Word assessment. This ongoing spiritual diagnosis must be done according to the character of Christ. Out of the christocentric diagnosis comes a prescription for healing.

An invitation was given at the end of an evangelistic sermon and one person responded. He wept agonizingly, almost to the point of despair. Even though he was a faithful church member, he had been in a deep depression over the past five years. He had at one time been deeply involved in pornography. The images of his former lust so constantly gripped him that he had lost confidence in both the power and love of God. A "soul physician" knelt beside him while others gathered around to pray. The minister guided the seeker through a portion of James 5: "The prayer offered in faith will restore the one who is sick, and the Lord will raise him up, and if he has committed sins, they will be forgiven him" (v. 15). This man who had come to God in the depth of despair received both forgiveness and healing.

Life *can* be different in the perennial optimism of grace. The Word applied by the Holy Spirit, in the form of human words, is the church's prescription for life's ills. May we desire to offer it as much as the sick long to receive it.

Chapter 7

Words
Of Worship

In his carefully documented book, *Doxology*, Geoffrey Wainwright argues that theology throughout the history of the Christian church has been primarily formulated in Christian worship. Often this has been for the better, as it was when Paul's christological formula in Colossians 1:13-20 was read in the early church.

Sometimes it has been for the worse, especially in America. This is precisely the point of Laurence Moore's book, *Selling God*:

> Was there any way for religious leaders to avoid a market mentality, the imperative to expand, the association of growth with innovation, the reliance upon aggressive publicity, the assumed importance of building networks that linked the local to the national, the habit of thinking in tangible exchange terms that

allowed a quick tabulation of returns, converted souls or its measurable equivalent, moral behavior for expended effort?[1]

The American context of conformity through democratic leveling, the absence of a state church, and the vast harvest of souls emphatically stated *no*. Avoidance was impossible. Moore succinctly states the downside of all this: "When religion had to shout shrilly in the marketplace, the potentially ennobling aspects of spirituality had no chance to develop."[2]

And what are those ennobling aspects of spirituality? We may possibly agree on a few: a discovery of truth about ourselves and the world about us from an objective frame of reference; a knowledge of the transcendent God revealed in Scripture; a revelation of God in His holiness that transforms human character; an exaltation of Christ and His redemption that leads to honesty, confession, and repentance; a sensitivity to the Holy Spirit that empowers and enables individuals to "do justice, love kindness, and walk humbly with your God" (Mic. 6:8). The ennobling aspects are seen in adoration of God the Father, in repentance and faith toward Jesus Christ, and in full reliance on the enabling of the Holy Spirit. Worship must be solidly rooted in the triune God.

But even for those of us who are attempting to be as Christian as possible in our worship, delicate dialectics still have to be negotiated. We want worship with wide doors and low thresholds; yet, if it does not attract spiritual giants, it should at least produce them. We want worship that is inclusive of all, but retains the exclusiveness of the gospel. We want worship that enables persons to cope with this world, while at the same time maintaining a firm grip on the world to come. We want worship that is in a contemporary idiom without being faddish, giddy, and downright trivial. We want worship that interprets life domestically, recreationally, morally, and a dozen other ways while at the same time saying

---

[1]R. Laurence Moore, *Selling God: American Religion in the Marketplace of Culture* (New York: Oxford University Press, 1994), 119.

[2]Moore, 270.

life is more—it is a transcendent vision. We want worship that creates a community of the gospel without being reduced to an ideology of intimacy that is cliquish and clannish.

The above is further compounded by the various "worship camps" vying for their market share of worship trends in the evangelical world. The Reformed camp calls for worship to be cerebral and creedal; conversion takes place primarily in the mind. The Charismatic camp calls for worship to be spontaneous and live; conversion takes place primarily in the emotions. The Pietistic/Holiness camp calls for humble and obedient worship; conversion takes place primarily in the affections. The Liturgical Renewal worship camp calls for worship to take place in a symbolic encounter; conversion takes place primarily in the psychosomatic realm. Certainly, this is a simplistic taxonomy because the above categories often overlap. In some denominations, all four are vying for attention.

All of these groups need to be on friendly terms. If they are not, worship lobotomy occurs. However, because of socio-economic and cultural influences, worship will more often be of one style than the others. So be it; that isn't our real problem here. Our problem as preachers is that we are in danger of being shipwrecked on the rocks of banality or eviscerated to the point of theological meaninglessness. William Fore[3] and Quentin Schultze[4] have helped us to understand that television is not a replacement for but an extension of worship in the local church. Both local and television worship services are often pragmatic, utilitarian, and Manichean; both often operate on the American success ethic. Worship is more attuned to erasing the perplexities and complexities of life than exalting the mysteries of life.

---

[3]William F. Fore, *Television and Religion: The Shaping of Faith, Values and Culture* (Minneapolis, Minn.: Augsburg Publishing House, 1987).

[4]Quentin Schultze, "Keeping the Faith: American Evangelicals and the Media," *American Evangelicals and the Mass Media*, ed. Quentin Schultze (Grand Rapids, Mich.: Zondervan, 1990).

In 1985, Neil Postman traced in his *Amusing Ourselves to Death* how the history of photography was replacing lexicology. He explained that rationality had been replaced by photographic images (often backed by rhythmic beats that appeal to primal urges). Postman went on to point out in an excellent essay, "Shuffling Off to Bethlehem," that since worship can now be piped into our recreation rooms while we eat popcorn and drink Mountain Dew, sacred space and time have eroded. Postman made the theological connection between the death of words and our modern inability to worship. Israel was forbidden to worship idols because God was not to be reduced to an image. "We may hazard a guess that a people who are being asked to embrace an abstract, universal deity would be rendered unfit to do so by the habit of drawing pictures or making statues or depicting their ideas in any concrete iconographic forms," Postman wrote. "The God of the Jews was to exist in the Word and through the Word, an unprecedented conception requiring the highest order of abstract thinking."[5]

While I would not want Postman's use of the word *abstract* to limit the personhood of God, his point is well-taken. The failure of contemporary worship in America is the failure to think in language that takes the biblical concept of God seriously. I have the opportunity to visit fifteen to twenty worship settings a year, other than my home church. These worship services are often quite varied, but most would exhibit the following characteristics.

A. They are highly subjective; there is little focus on a sovereign, transcendent God. In fact, there is little objective description of God at all. If someone were to attempt to gain a comprehension of God from much of contemporary worship's content, it would be well-nigh impossible. This worship calls for little engagement of the mind at all.

---

[5]Neil Postman, *Amusing Ourselves to Death: Public Discourse in the Age of Show Business* (Binghamton, N.Y.: Viking, 1986), 9.

B. They are non-creedal and unscripted. The divine drama does not formulate the structure of the worship service. A theological script provided by the Apostle's Creed and hymns that are theologically narrated, such as "Arise My Soul, Arise," are often completely absent. The trinitarian formula which provides a direction for the worship ("Father, Son, Holy Spirit" or "Praise, Confession, and Mission") is bypassed for an aimless concoction.

C. There is no interaction with the world. If I had attended these worship services blindfolded on different planets, I would not have been able to discern simply through listening which planet I was visiting. Seldom does the language of worship indicate that the worshipers live on the planet of Bosnia, Liberia, or the Israeli-Palestinian conflict. The unitiated worshiper in most evangelical worship services would interpret God, not as One who loves the world, but One who intervenes on behalf of quite privatized agendas. God has been domesticated to the point of being totally preoccupied with the crisis of the moment. Rarely do these crises possess anything of a global nature, but are regulated to immediate self-interests of a pragmatic, utilitarian kind.

For Americans, God is highly accessible. In fact, we access God somewhat in the manner of maid service of an expensive hotel. This "amenities theology" normally does not pause long enough to be staggered by the psalmist's query,

What is man, that You take thought of him,
And the son of man that You care for him? (Ps. 8:4).

Allow me to give one example of a culturally induced transition within worship. Most Sunday morning worship services in my denomination utilize a time of "open altar." Worshipers are invited to pray regarding the stresses and strains of their lives. God will provide both intervention and interpretation to those who assess circumstances in recent days to have fallen on the unfortunate side of the ledger. Life is tough and it is hoped that God can make it more palatable. I do not recall the "open altar" being described as a place to pray for Rwanda or even our hometown of Kansas City. Thus, worship is not a place where the worshiper embraces the world, but a place where one asks God to alleviate one's personal pain.

D. They are often generic. This means most worship services are non-Wesleyan, non-Reformed, non-anything. There is no discernible historical rootage that would provide theological identity or mission to the outside world. It is "universal cliché"[6] worship, keyed by Bill Gaither's "Let's Just Praise the Lord." In other words, let's just grin, stroke one another, and gather around the piano.

E. They are often casual. A sign advertising a Saturday evening worship service posted in front of a church reads, "Casual Contemporary Worship." Are we dealing with an oxymoron here? Dare we use the word *casual* in connection with the holy Creator of the universe? Dare we just drop in on God, kick off our shoes, and stay awhile? The root meaning of the word *casual* is "chance"—that is, nonchalant, accidental, random, or showing little concern. We need a holy reverential fear, so our language does not reduce God to a benign deity who demands little consideration of the propriety due the divine-human encounter.

Prophet-priests can give propriety to the language of worship. Since language will dictate both bodily posture and inner attitude, we are in desperate need to recover worship language. We can begin with language that is both theological and biblical. Instead of the pallid and banal, "Good morning," we would begin the worship service with, "Bless the Lord, the One who is to be blessed," "The Lord is risen," "Holy, holy, holy is the Lord God Almighty," or some other ascription. The various salutations of Paul in his letters to the churches could serve as words of welcome and greeting. "Grace to you and peace from God our Father and the Lord Jesus Christ" (Phil. 1:2).

---

[6]A term borrowed from David Wells.

We could cut out the small talk that accents the trivialities and non-consequential events of the moment. Many worship services could lead one to believe that God is a cosmic caterer. The pastor is expected to lace the service with comments such as, "Suzy won the 4-H pumpkin contest"; "Jack is home from college"; or, "The Smiths are off for vacation to the Caribbean this week." Even worse is the infusion of humorous quips as if God were a court jester. True, God does have a sense of humor, but it is more subtle than most worship leaders imply. While much of our worship leading may leave our people chuckling, it probably leaves God weeping.

While prophet-priests have always been entrusted with God-language, we have an urgent need for that language heretofore unparalleled in church history. As the Wesleyan renewal counteracted rationalism, as the American frontier revival embraced the migratory masses, as crusade evangelism invaded the urban metropolis, might not the prophetical-priestly office now renew the accurate use of words which are both civil and christocentric in worship? Journalists decry the death of civility. Language has been degraded by the entertainment industry. A language that knows no anathema has invaded the classroom and is no respecter of age or gender. Several weeks ago, a fifth grader made an insulting remark to my wife, a public school teacher, that would have been unheard of when I was of grade-school age. Rudeness, disrespect, and discourtesy are the norms; kindness, deference, and reverence are absent. Much of this demise may be traced to a loss of God-language, the religious paradigm that once provided the hegemony for the American identity. We again need to hear the message of Micah 2:7: "For the lips of a priest should preserve knowledge, and men should seek instruction from his mouth; for he is the messenger of the LORD of hosts."

Of the following six prophetical-priestly functions, the first three are mostly priestly and the second three are mostly prophetic. Each aspect is determined by what Thomas Oden calls the "bold intention of Christianity to combine the ministry of word and sacrament, the prophetic and priestly ministries, into a single ordained public office in which one person serves both the priestly office of conducting public worship and the prophetic office of providing insight, instruction, exegesis, and proclamation of the word."[7]

Providing Words of Reverence

Gothic exteriors, stark interiors, high ceilings, and towering steeples in medieval Europe all indicated the grandeur, complexity, and beauty of God. Even in colonial America, clapboard churches boasted of steeples that rose above all other town buildings. Because these steeples could be seen for miles, they were a means by which a traveler could find a town. But even more telling was the location of the church at the center of town. All of life revolved around God. This absolute frame of reverence signified that God was to be worshiped. The very essence of worship in America was reverence. Thus, the Puritans were direct descendants, at least ideologically, of the Hebrews. The Hebrews understood worship as prostrating oneself before God in total subservience. Neither the Hebrew tabernacle nor the Puritan meeting house were places of triteness and levity.

Any architectural promotions of God's *tremendum mysterium* have long passed off the American scene. Even the grand and ornate St. Patrick's Cathedral in New York City is dwarfed by the surrounding skyscrapers. Megachurches are now building worship centers, which are not a theological attempt to centralize God. These new edifices indicate little of the traditional God symbolism that has marked worship structures of the past. Rather, they are multifunctional facilities equipped with the latest technology capable of expediting entertainment and informational events. In fact, the electronic gadgetry may serve to blend these events together

---

[7]Thomas Oden, *Pastoral Theology: Essentials of Ministry* (San Francisco, Calif.: Harper and Row, 1983), 87.

in a fashion that diffuses their purpose. The religious nov-
ice, whom these user-friendly events target, is introduced to
a God who serves rather than a God who is to be served. At
most, God is to be applauded (as was the spotlighted, resurrected Jesus figure in the latest Passion play I attended). The
Hebrews did many things to indicate that they were paying
homage to their Maker and Redeemer, but they never applauded. Neither did the Puritans. "Just a cultural transition,"
some would say. Is it not time to notice that some transi-
tions, even in proposed houses of worship, may detract from
rather than exalt God?

The primary order of business for the priest is to preserve God's identity. Hallowing God's name is serious business. Slighting God is a serious blunder. Worship talk that
leaves the worshiper with the impression that God is bent on
our happiness, that God's main preoccupation is with our
material prosperity, that God is an American icon, or that
God is to be identified with the will of the people is the sin
of priests enmeshed in American culture. James Hunter
charges that the current accommodation of American Christianity

> allows for a forum in which religious one-upmanship can take place
> smoothly, maintaining, not so much that Evangelical Christianity
> is more true than other faiths, but that Evangelical Christianity is
> superior to other faiths because of the superior (i.e., inner-worldly)
> benefits it provides: inner peace, true joy and happiness, depend-
> able fellowship, and a source of strength in times of need, all in
> addition to an eternal life in heaven.[8]

Of all that we do in the public gathering of God's people,
exaltation most exemplifies worship. In the absence of reverential, submissive, surrendering, praising adoration, worship
is something other than worship. Perhaps it could be called a
religious rally or collective therapy, but not worship! The

---

[8]James Davidson Hunter, *American Evangelicalism: Conservative Religion and the Quandry of Modernity* (New Brunswick, N.J.: Rutgers University Press, 1983), 91.

primary posture for biblical worship is bowing in humble servitude. Words fail, thoughts grope for expression, and emotions are mixed. Worshipers delight in God's presence, but are stripped of all the preoccupations that normally carry them through the day. The priest begins corporate exaltation by recognizing God's majesty and His preeminence above all other existence. Thus, the congregation enters into the highest human endeavor.

> I will bless the LORD at all times;
> His praise shall continually be in my mouth.
> My soul shall make its boast in the LORD;
> The humble shall hear it and rejoice.
> O magnify the LORD with me,
> And let us exalt His name together (Ps. 34:1-3).

Providing Words of Provision

The nineteenth-century theologian Samuel Hopkins, as well as his contemporaries, believed that disinterested benevolence is a state of grace attainable in this life. This meant that God could so free a person from self-interest that the individual would love God regardless of the return of that love. Whether Samuel Hopkins ever made that claim for himself, I do not know. The truth is, most of us covet God's blessing. The difficulty lies interpreting what God has in mind when blessing us.

The priest is not concerned with positioning people so they may receive future blessings at the hand of God. Rather, priests heighten the awareness of all that they already are within the flow of God's blessing. Conversion for the purpose of positioning oneself for the benevolent stream that cascades from God's throne is less than conversion. It is a self-interested currying of God's favor. Most of us have been used by so-called friends, but God in His infinite grace forgives our ulterior motives.

The priest reminds his or her congregants that the very fact that we are gathered together in Christ's name demonstrates God's favor. We are recipients of life, strength, mobility, family, and friends. There is an infinite supply of God's grace. The priest is to bring each worshiper to the affirmation, "Christ prays for me. My name is written on His hands. My identity is secured in Him. My significance is not located in my own strivings but in Christ's infinite love." Few priests could have stated it as eloquently as John Newton:

> See, the streams of living waters,
> Springing from eternal Love,
> Well supply thy sons and daughters,
> And all fear of want remove.
> Who can faint while such a river
> Ever flows their thirst assuage?
> Grace which, like the Lord, the Giver,
> Never fails from age to age![9]

Of course, some people in every congregation feel that life has dealt them a bad blow. They perceive that God is the inflicter of their misfortune. They desperately need the God of hope. Hell is the place or state where there is no more hope. Priests are the purveyors of hope. Out of tragedy comes the triumph of life and the clear and certain witness that God sustains and sanctifies us. The priest is

> …to grant those who mourn in Zion,
> Giving them a garland instead of ashes,
> The oil of gladness instead of mourning,
> The mantle of praise instead of a spirit of fainting.
> So they will be called oaks of righteousness,
> The planting of the LORD, that He may be glorified (Isa. 61:3).

In no way would I contend that a priest's words are magic or that Scripture can be disseminated as a panacea for all ills. On the contrary, biblical words may be even more painful than joyful when first heard. Nevertheless, they move us toward reality in Christ. Salvation is offered in Christ, not as a coping mechanism for life's setbacks, but as a process toward

---

[9]John Newton, "Glorious Things of Thee Are Spoken," *Sing to the Lord* (Kansas City, Mo.: Lillenas Publishing Company, 1993), no. 670.

full potential in this life and ultimate triumph in the next. Because we have placed our hope firmly in Christ, God is honing and shaping us for divine glory. Peter reminds us, "Beloved, do not be surprised at the fiery ordeal among you, which comes upon you for your testing, as though some strange thing were happening to you; but to the degree that you share the sufferings of Christ, keep on rejoicing, so that also at the revelation of His glory you may rejoice with exultation" (1 Pet. 4:12-13).

Priestly words of provision are superintended by the Holy Spirit. There is a dynamic that goes beyond being able to plan and deliver them. Solvency for the tragedies of life does not rest on the minister's verbal ingenuity. Both preparation and spontaneity must be submitted to God's sovereign grace. Public prayer is not for the purpose of exhibiting one's fluency or even prompting God to bring to fruitition one's intentions, no matter how lofty they may be. The priestly prayer is to ask God to take planned words for corporate worship and use them beyond our intentions to bring word, event, and setting together in ways we have not even imagined. Thus, the minister must confess that human wisdom is inadequate and planning is myopic.

The priest works in faith that God can inspire worship participants because his or her words have been inspired by God's grace. Grace connects the worship event and preparation for that event. One's human foresight is not capable of bringing the planning and the event together so that redemption will take place. Redemptive words must be bathed in prayer and surrendered to God's supernatural application. At times there is a trans-rational, even mysterious quality to prophetical-priestly words. A Scottish lady, after listening to Reinhold Niebuhr speak at Edinburgh, commented, "I dinna understand a word ye say when ye preach, but somehow I ken that you're makin' God great."[10]

---

[10]Richard Wightman Fox, *Reinhold Niebuhr: A Biography* (New York: Harper and Row, 1987), 188.

I once served as an associate pastor at a large church in Portland, Oregon. When the pastor left town, he would often ask me to fill the pulpit. Fortunately, he would give me plenty of lead time. Unfortunately, when he was preaching through a particular book of the Bible, he would assign to me the portion of Scripture on which he would have preached had he been there. Thus, six weeks ahead of time, he assigned to me Genesis 49. I had no idea what Genesis 49 was about until I stepped into my office and opened to the reference. Aha! The blessing of Jacob to his twelve sons. Even though I believe all Scripture is equally inspired, I don't believe it is all equally inspiring. In fact, I remember asking Dr. Dennis Kinlaw, whom I consider to be one of the greatest Old Testament preachers, about Genesis 49. He too noted that there didn't seem to be any rhyme or reason to the patriarch's blessing. Why was Benjamin to be slaughtered, Levi to become priest, Judah to be a progenitor of Christ, and so on? The blessing didn't make sense.

However, within five minutes of looking at the passage, I had sketched out the three-point outline which I would preach six weeks later. The title, "It Doesn't Make Sense." The outline:

A. God brings logic out of the illogical.

B. God brings worth out of the worthless.

C. God brings redemption out of the unredeemable.

Over the next several weeks, flesh was put on the skeleton of that outline and the message took form. I went to bed in anticipation of arising to preach to approximately eight hundred people the next morning. At 12:20 A.M., the phone rang. The pastor's wife was calling to tell me that at 4:30 the previous afternoon, Rod and Christine Kagey had been killed. These members of the congregation were 26 and 24 years of age. I sat on the side of my bed in dismay. My mind raced over the last few months and days. Rod was handsome, gracious, and soft-spoken. His highly courteous deportment did not curtail the effectiveness of his 6'4" frame on the basketball court. Christine was gifted, charming, and beautiful. She had won the talent portion of the Miss Idaho contest, which would have led to the Miss America contest.

The most important characteristic about Rod and Christine was their commitment to Christ. Some months before, I had asked Rod to join me in evangelism visitation each Thursday evening. He prayed about it and responded with a yes. Rod participated in the weekly training and without fail was available for home visitation and sharing the gospel.

Two weeks before they were killed, Rod and Christine had approached me and asked if I would be willing to accompany them to call on a young woman with whom Christine had been working. Diana, who had been raised a Mormon, had demonstrated an interest in the claims of Christ. We set up an appointment for Thursday evening of that week. A couple of days before we visited Diana, I asked Rod if he would be willing to share the gospel with her during the visit. He had been on many evangelistic visits with me, but had never personally shared the plan of salvation on our appointments. That Thursday evening, Diana eagerly accepted what Rod said as he clearly enunciated the claims of the gospel. Today, Diana is married to a Christian and living overseas with her family.

Now Rod and Christine were dead. I arrived at Rod's parents' home at about 1:30 A.M. and found them grieving, but not as those who have no hope. There was a tranquility about the parents, even though they had lost their only son. A few hours later, I stood before a grieving congregation and preached a sermon, the embryo of which I had prepared six weeks before: "It Doesn't Make Sense." Event and word had come together, far beyond my humble attempts at planning. God had spoken, not I. May it ever be so!

Offering Words of Invitation

The approach to God in Old Testament times was complicated by ritual and restriction. Only the high priest had the right to approach the mercy seat, and that through elaborate ritual reserved for one day a year. But now the veil of the temple has been torn in two, which not only means that humankind is inside the holy of holies with God, but that God is outside with us. No group of people—whether by race or profession or any other criterion—has exclusive right to God's ear. Our universal right to approach God has been recorded in the doctrine of the Christian church as the "priesthood of believers." Church architecture which depicts a separation between laity and clergy or which circumscribes an inner sanctum for a chosen few is theologically amiss.

Nevertheless, there remains a task which is the particular responsibility of the priest, i.e., to make sure that all people understand that God is approachable. All laity and clergy have the right to issue an invitation to approach God. It is the responsibility of the priest to proclaim this invitation in public. Scripture abounds in these invitations. Our public worship gatherings should abound in them. Within the Bible is found the substance of the invitation, which accurately depicts God and His mercy. Scripture does not describe our approach to God as something trite, sentimental, or casual. It preserves a demarcation between God's being freely and even courageously approached, and God's being accessed in a utilitarian manner, rather like we call up information via the Internet from some distant computer file. The biblical invitation reflects nothing of the casualness and impersonalization of today's world. Above all, persons never close the gap between themselves and God via right, guarantee, or personal privilege. The code words of America's technological and economic system weaken, if not completely undermine, the theological foundation on which God must be approached.

Allow me to call your attention to two Old Testament invitations and two New Testament invitations that ought to echo from within our sanctuary walls:

"Come now, let us reason together,"
Says the LORD,

"Though your sins are as scarlet,
They will be white as snow;
Though they are red like crimson,
They will be like wool" (Isa. 1:18).

Seek the LORD while He may be found;
Call upon Him while He is near.
Let the wicked forsake his way
And the unrighteous man his thoughts;
And let him return to the LORD,
And He will have compassion on him,
And to our God,
For He will abundantly pardon.
"For My thoughts are not your thoughts,
Nor are your ways My ways," declares the LORD.
"For as the heavens are higher than the earth,
So are My ways higher than your ways
And My thoughts than your thoughts" (Isa. 55:6-9).

Come to Me, all who are weary and heavy-laden, and I will give
you rest. Take My yoke upon you and learn from Me, for I am
gentle and humble in heart; and you will find rest for your souls.
For my yoke is easy and My burden is light (Matt. 11:28-30).

Since we have a great high priest who has passed through the
heavens, Jesus the Son of God, let us hold fast our confession. For
we do not have a high priest who cannot sympathize with our
weaknesses, but One who has been tempted in all things as we
are, yet without sin. Therefore let us draw near with confidence
to the throne of grace, so that we may receive mercy and find
grace to help in time of need (Heb. 4:14-16).

The foremost reason to use biblical invitations in worship is that they make accurate statements about God.
Worshipers deserve to know to whom they are being invited. God is available, but only to those who come in
repentance. He is not accessed as perfunctorally as dialing
911, even though prevenient grace often prompts the unre-

pentant to call on Him in an emergency. God is ready to demonstrate compassion to those who come to Him in contrition; but that compassion may not be readily comprehended because God may not interpret life on our terms. The very thing we consider a curse may be a blessing. God may not rid us of the circumstances that we count as ill, but is more than willing to bear the burden for us. The prophet-priest exhorts all people to cast their cares upon God. We come in confidence that God exercises infallible empathy and precise insight about the most complicated of circumstances.

For some strange reason, many of the worship services I attend seem bereft of messages that lend dignity to the name of God. God does not need our validation, but persons in our hearing need words that dignify God's character. Contemporary priests are often given to chit-chat about the weather, community events, personal trivia, and other items that bear little eternal significance. The worship leader often quips and jokes in the manner of a pep-rally M.C., as if to stimulate benumbed spectators who are often bewildered about the purpose of the gathering. Pulpit levity belies an empty worship storehouse that should be stocked with Scripture, hymns, poetry, and historical liturgy. These resources need to inundate worship, and at least some of them need to be committed to memory.

> Lift up your heads, O gates,
> and be lifted up, O ancient doors,
> That the King of glory may come in!
> Who is the King of glory?
> The LORD strong and mighty,
> The LORD mighty in battle.
> Lift up your heads, O gates,
> And lift them up, O ancient doors,
> That the King of glory may come in!
> Who is this King of glory?
> The LORD of hosts,
> He is the King of glory (Ps. 24:7-10).

One of my favorite worship texts was written by Joachim Neander in 1680:

> Praise to the Lord, the Almighty, the King of creation!
> O my soul, praise Him, for He is thy health and salvation!
> All ye who hear,
> Now to His temple draw near;
> Join me in glad adoration![11]

The priests of various denominations issue invations through different methodologies and symbols. My denominational ritual utilizes an altar call, usually at the end of the service. People respond quite often out of the exigencies of life—crumbling marriages, breached relationships, depleted finances—the list is endless. Whatever the methodology, a biblical priest offers certitude that God does not minimize the stuff out of which life is made. He desires to bring healing to the particulars of our existence. Every proclamation of God's Word in corporate worship must proffer an invitation. To proclaim God's adequate provision but not allow worshipers to partake is a scandal of the lowest order.

The invitation needs to be delicately nuanced so that God will not be misrepresented. This means that affirming the divine resources often entails spiritual direction. A man who had a severely retarded adopted son came to the altar to pray for his son's healing. The pastor knelt to pray for him. The pastor prayed that there would be resolution of the man's doubt and increased certitude that God would work in behalf of the badly deformed boy. The son had demonstrated mental and physical progress over the past several years, but was still far from normal. As the pastor continued to pray for and counsel his parishioner, they seemed to be getting nowhere. The father expressed his overwhelming frustration. From his perspective, God had simply not delivered on His promises.

The pastor broke through this emotional and spiritual stalemate with the following question: "Has God healed *you*?"

---

[11]"Praise to the Lord, the Almighty," *Sing to the Lord*, no. 20.

The quiet and incisive question was disruptive, even jarring, to the father's conscience. Until this time, he had been unable to come to grips with reality or accept the present situation. This was the primary issue, rather than the issue of God's healing. The lesser miracle of God is to restore a perfect world; the greater miracle is for God to give us a perfect attitude in an imperfect world. Unbelief, the primal sin, states that God's resources are insufficient for the demands of life, life as it is.

Though God is concerned about our concerns, His ultimate concern is that our concerns be conformed to His concerns. His ultimate concern is that we be conformed to the character of Christ. The invitation of the gospel is always for the purpose of transformation. The priest serves as a beacon of mercy, attracting persons to the realization of the gospel promise: "And although you were formerly alienated and hostile in mind, engaged in evil deeds, yet He has not reconciled you in His fleshly body through death, in order to present you before Him holy and blameless and beyond reproach" (Col. 1:21-22).

In our present self-oriented society, the priest needs to ensure that those who are invited find not simply a measure of emotional satisfaction, but that they receive the grace to deal with life as defined in the person of Christ. My parents, who attended Holiness churches, experienced anxiety, despair, depression, and at times exhaustion—but they were rarely invited to come forward and pray about those emotions. They *were* invited to repentance, restitution, and cleansing from guilt. Conviction (the gap between our performance and God's expectations) was their primary motivator. One altar call deals with subjective adjustment, and the other with objective transformation. My parents did not have the time to reflect on their exhausted, stressed-out state, yet worship was not the place where they expected to acquire an emotional tune-up. The altar call, the foremost sacrament in our church, was a sacred spot of radical encounter with a God who was expected to cremate, not to caress their sin problems.

God's cremating process is His loving plan. This priestly announcement is that God loves us. Of course, God's love is evidence in unexpected places and ways. The priest's invitation is to receive whatever comes from God's hand, the hand from which all good things come. Paul declared, "All things belong to you, and you belong to Christ; and Christ belongs to God" (1 Cor. 3:22b-23). This promise is not so much one of gracious reception as it is of gracious perception. In the words of Ralph Waldo Emerson, "Thou shall have the whole land for thy park and manor, the sea for thy bath and navigation, without tax and without envy, the woods and the rivers thou shalt own, and thou shalt possess that wherein others are only tenants and boarders."[12]

Providing Words of Vision

As we have argued previously in dealing with Jeremiah, word pictures have always been the prophet's stock in trade. They are especially relevant in post-Enlightenment America. The irony is that modern pastors are less inclined or less capaable of using them. Visions inspire; they convict; they quicken; they prompt; they motivate. Above all, visions encounter us; they stop us in our tracks. They may not do all of the above at the same time. But sooner or later, visions should convey the transcendent truths that run rampant through worship: God is holy; humanity is proud; material things are enticing; grace is free; and all that is in the world is the lust of the flesh, the lust of the eyes, and the pride of life (1 John 2:16).

Worship calls for speech of visual vignettes: vignettes of life that has been, life as it is, and life in the age to come. These vignettes awaken hunger, clarify values, proffer grace, affirm belonging, intensify guilt, and heighten hope. Life can be something more than mere existence. It can be lived-in-

---

[12]Ralph Waldo Emerson, "The Poet," *The Norton Anthology of American Literature* (New York, N.Y.: W.W. Norton and Company, 1986), 403.

God consciousness. Persons should know that God can extend their influence beyond mere physical existence. Elisha asked for a double portion of the spirit that was upon his mentor. What a great text that offers us a powerful vignette: "And when the man touched the bones of Elisha he revived and stood up on his feet" (2 Kings 13:21c). Life's influence can be extended long after the body's biodegradable content has been devoured.

Our worlds are small, our consciences are dormant, and our visions are shortsighted. "Eye has not seen and ear has not heard..." (1 Cor. 2:9), but it is the preacher's job to change all that. Vivid word pictures, produced by sanctified imaginations, confront slumbering congregations and, if not startle, at least annoy them. As was said about one preacher who used powerful metaphors derived from his careful reading of the Scripture, "He comes in through the back door!" Every parishioner deserves to expect that his or her pastor will come into everyday life through *some* door during the present worship service. The parishioner just doesn't know which one.

Truly effective preaching is often traded for flattened-out discourses. Preaching which seeks to suit everyone's taste is quickly forgotten. Heart-rending, mind-expanding, character-challenging preaching is often done off the beaten path, to people who hunger to have their souls stretched to their eternal limits. A Baylor University survey recently noted "the most effective preachers" in the English-speaking world. In the words of Thomas Long, who was included in the list of the top twelve, "You can find [effective preaching] round the corner and down the street by pastors who articulate the church's mission to these people in this place."[13]

Such was the case for Lawrence Hicks, a man who served most of his ministerial life in a small denomination in Ashland, Kentucky, not exactly the crossroads of the world. Though he was far from a household name, he was beloved

---

[13]Kenneth L. Woodward, "Heard Any Good Sermons Lately?" *Newsweek* (March 4, 1996), 51.

by his denomination and would swell the crowds at whatever church or camp where he preached. He was a master of word pictures and created spiritual hunger through vivid descriptions of both this world and the next. The following demonstrates how Hicks reached the totality of his congregation's personality through graphic imagery.

> Three men were riding along with me from Chattanooga, and just as the radio faded on, a Negro quartet from Atlanta was singing. I don't know where they got the song, I wish I had it now. But one of them was singing in a high tenor falsetto away out in front of the rest of them, and they sounded like houds after the fox, trailing behind him. The three were humming in the background, trailing off into a deep bass; and that Negro was singing, "There must be a heaven, somewhere!" The rest of them were humming it in the background. The Holy Spirit paid a visit to my automobile, and we got blessed! As we rolled down a Georgia road, with a mellow southern sun, and a southern Negro, singing, "There must be a heaven, somewhere!" I thought of the cotton fields of Mississippi and Alabama in days of slavery. I thought of the old stories that my grandmother told me. I thought of the longing as they looked up and sang, "There must be a heaven, somewhere." I thought of all the bitter dregs and the disappointments, I thought of all the dying babies down in the "Quarters." I thought of all the old black mammies lifting up their heads, when their children went into slavery, and saying with a broken heart, "There must be a heaven, somewhere, with streets of gold and sparkling walls where healing waters run down glorious hillsides, where everything will be made right, and I'll have my darling back in my arms again! There must be a heaven somewhere."[14]

True, Hicks sometimes went to extremes. His oratory was overly affective and sentimental. But ministers have such a generalized fear of the affective that pulpit speech has been flattened into platitudes or "how-to" instructions, which are

---

[14]Lawrence B. Hicks, *There Must Be a Heaven Somewhere* (Louisville, Ky.: Pentecostal Publishing Company, n.d.), 26-27.

about as heart-grabbing as a refrigerator manual. The anointed vision that causes people to weep, shout, hope, laugh, or even say "amen" is almost absent. Such sterility leaves congregations unchanged. Such visionless prattle knows little of the Word of God as "living and active and sharper than any two-edged sword, and piercing as far as the division of soul and spirit, of both joints and marrow, and able to judge the thoughts and intentions of the heart" (Heb. 4:12). Every parishioner ought to demand of their prophet, "Read my nature. Expose my gods. Awe my affections. Stir my imagination. Convict my conscience. Quicken my step. Wound my pride. Free my mind. Lift my spirit. Give me a vision. Make me fall in love. If not, I am going to perish."

Providing Words of Decision

Pictorial images represent the quintessential moods, desires, and struggles of life. They provide the archetypes that define life and enable the individual to name the demons that comprise lust, hate, fear, anxiety, revenge, and other maladies of the spirit. Giving these diseases a name, often by identifying their graphic features, is the first step toward cure. This is not accomplished by reciting a laundry list of ills that plague humankind. It is certainly not done by accusing certain kinds of people with having certain kinds of sin. It is best realized by the prophet's ability to symbolize life via stories and universal images from which none of us is exempt.

Leo Tolstoy told the story of a peasant farmer named Pahom who sacrificed and saved to buy his own forty acres. He then learned from a traveler that he could sell the forty acres, which he had carefully developed, and buy a much larger tract of land located beyond the Volga River. After several years of tilling his land and even renting additional land, he grew dissatisfied. *If it were all my land,* Pahom reasoned, *I could be independent, and there would not be all this unpleasantness.* He then heard how an individual had purchased 13,000 acres for 1,000 rubles. Upon traveling to the country of the Bashkirs, he inquired of the chief about the price of their land. "Our price is always the same: 1,000 rubles a day." Then came the explanation: "You can have as much land as you can get around in one day for the price of 1,000 rubles. There is only one condition. If you don't return on the same day to the spot where you started, your money is lost."

Pahom started early the next morning, envisioning that he could cover thirty-five miles. The chief placed his fox-fur cap at the starting spot. Pahom placed his 1,000 rubles in the cap. He then headed in a single direction until late in the morning. Wet with sweat and very thirsty, he turned sharply to his left, pausing to take a drink from his flask. In the afternoon, it was terribly hot, but one thought drove him on: *An hour to suffer; a lifetime to live!* Often his journey was extended to include a piece of ground it would be "a pity to leave out." By the time he had defined the angle that would lead him back to the starting point, it was late in the day and he was exhausted. As the sun was setting, he began running, throwing away almost everything that was slowing his pace: coat, boots, flask. *What shall I do?* he wondered. *I have grasped too much and ruined the whole affair. I can't get there before the sun sets.* It looked as if he would not make it, but he would give the effort every ounce of energy he had. Running back toward his starting poiont, marked by the cap and the 1,000 rubles, Pahom's lungs heaved. His muscles ached and his legs seemed detached from his body. He was seized with terror to think that he had lost everything.

Just as the sun dropped below the horizon, Pahom fell to the ground on top of the cap. He had finished the circuit and earned much land. His servant tried to revive him, but Pahom was dead. Blood oozed from his lifeless form. "His servant picked up the spade and dug a grave long enough for Pahom to lie in and buried him in it. Six feet from his head to his heels was all he needed."[15]

---

[15]From "How Much Land Does a Man Need?" in *Leo Tolstoy Short Stories*, ed. by Ernest J. Simmons (New York, N.Y.: Random House, 1965), 2:199.

Tolstoy possessed what Henry James refers to as a "sense of reality," a sense of the existential angst, the universal condition. No group of people exhibited a keener insight about the human plight than the Hebrew prophets. After the Hebrews arrived in the Promised Land, God enacted justice by fairly dividing the land among the tribes and in turn among their families. Everyone had been given (in today's terms) his Ford Escort and his three-bedroom flat with all the amenities, at least enough to make life comfortable. Comfort and equity would continue through a willingness to work and close attention to the precautionary measures which God employed to insure civil harmony: laws for Sabbath keeping, principles of soil conservation, regulations for jubilee celebrating, proscriptions against usury, and many others. These were not legalisms meant to restrict, but principles that would serve as foundations for peace with neighbors and satisfaction in the midst of God's plenteous provisions.

It's hard to believe, but God's provision was not good enough for these people. They were inflicted with the existential angst of life. One-upsmanship and idolatry served to enslave both self and others. More land, more money would provide a bigger flat with nicer amenities, they thought. The Ford Escort with a stereo and air conditioning could be replaced with a Lexus—or a pair of them! God's laws were being interpreted, not as preventing the destruction of self, others, and the good earth, but as depreciating the world's benefits to self. We have no evidence that the Hebrews ever kept God's injunctions of allowing the land to stand fallow every seventh year, or of forgiving debts and returning land to its original owners every fiftieth year.

Both Tolstoy and the Hebrew prophets attempted to cast a vision that challenged the prevailing view. While the Law cannot portray an alternate world view, the Holy Spirit can. Joel prophesied,

> *Contentment*: "And you will have plenty to eat and be satisfied"
> (2:26a).

Equity. "I will pour out My Spirit on all mankind" (2:28b).
Generativity: "And your sons and daughters will prophesy" (2:28c).
Hope: "Your old men will dream dreams,
Your young men will see visions" (2:28d).
Equality: "And even on the male and female servants I will pour out My Spirit in those days" (2:29).

Joel's words served as the biblical text for the Day of Pentecost. The words were applied by the Holy Spirit and took effect in the early church.

Hope: "This Jesus God raised up again" (Acts 2:32a).
Generativity: "For the promise is for you and your children" (2:39a).
Equity: "They began selling their property and possessions and were sharing them with all, as anyone might have need" (2:45).
Equality: "…Continuing with one mind in the temple, and breaking bread from house to house" (2:46a).
Contentment: "…They were taking their meals together with gladness and sincerity of heart" (2:46b).

True, such liberation was not found by everyone; but for those who did, life became a new adventure. "Joseph, a Levite of Cyrian birth, who was also called Barnabas by the apostles (which translated means son of Encouragement), and who owned a tract of land, sold it and brought the money and laid it at the apostles' feet" (Acts 4:36-37). The collective mood of early Christian worship is one of freedom, freedom to make God-ordained decisions about life. These decisions are the radical evidence of transformed character.

The prophet calls worshipers into question. Matters of loyalty, fidelity, and commitment are addressed. Modalities of justice, mercy, and forgiveness are offered. The prophet's questions demand a change of heart and a change of action. The prophet does not assume that his or her people are on the highway of holiness. More than likely, if they are Americans, they are on the highway of personal security and creature comforts. But life can take on new meaning and even American Christians can

> Come with joyful shouting to Zion,
> With everlasting joy upon their heads (Isa. 35:10a).

Prophetic preaching arrests persons on the highway of complacency, selfishness, and perverted ambition. Their pious posturing will break down, so that the prophet cannot allow ritual to replace true reformation. She or he refuses to allow routine to prevail. In Annie Dillard's words,

> I often think of the set pieces of liturgy as certain words which people have successfully addressed to God without their getting killed. In high church they saunter through the liturgy like Mohawks along a strand of scaffolding who have long since forgotten their danger. If God were to blast such a service to bits, the congregation would be, I believe, genuinely shocked.[16]

The prophet is tempted to substitute metaphors and images with vows of resolution. But resolutions are inadequate; they fall short of transformation. The congregation's only hope is in God's breaking in with sovereign grace. The decision to take a new direction is itself enabled by grace. Only God can enable the right choice when we stand at a crossroads of life, wanting to go in both directions. The prophet empathizes with that dilemma. In fact, it never really is ultimately solved this side of eternity. In the David Lean movie, *Lawrence of Arabia*, a despondent T.E. Lawrence is reminded by his Arab friend that he once said, "A man can do whatever he wants to do." To which Lawrence responds, "Yes, but a man cannot want what he wants to do." Wanting what we want to do—i.e., what we ought to do—comes only through a miraculous event at the core of our nature.

Before the prophet points the way, he must reveal the hearer's heart. As Elizabeth Fry reflected on her conversion

---

[16]Annie Dillard, *Holy the Firm* (New York, N.Y.: Harper and Row, 1997), 59.

experience under the ministry of the itinerant Quaker preacher William Savery, she wrote, "I'll never forget the impression he made upon my mind. How well he hit the state I was in. I thank God that He sent a glimmer of light into my soul."

The prophet presents alternatives for fuller and deeper dimensions of living. She or he is a special person sent to a special people with a special message. Every preachment is a shaft of light that both exposes and expects, by the power of the Spirit, that persons can be different. C.S. Lewis said the real proof of the gospel is not so much that evil men can become good, but that good men can become better. The vision of the prophet awakens our deepest longings and encourages us to believe that these deepest longings can be fulfilled. But there must be change. One parishioner, after hearing his pastor preach, immediately started a sequence of actions that would change his vocation and uproot his family. The result? The peace and contentment of spreading the kingdom. God's Word had effected human surrender.

Every vision of the prophet becomes a personal summons to make the ultimate decision of life: "Not my will but thine be done" (Mark 14:36).

Providing Words of Mission

The persons whom the prophet addresses are often bored because their lives are detached from the divine plan. The jobs and responsibilities to which they attend are ends in themselves, rather than a means to extend God's work. Unless they perceive themselves as part of a much larger order than production and consumption, life becomes a task to be endured. The prophet proclaims that life is more than repetition. It is a mission full of unexpected surprises.

Perhaps not everyone in your congregation will become an agent of major social change, as did Elizabeth Fry, who reformed the prison system of England. But each individual must be addressed with the questions, "Who will go?" and,

"Who will be sent to a hurting world?" Every worship service should become a commissioning service, applying the words of Christ, "You did not choose Me but I chose you, and appointed you that you would go and bear fruit, and that your fruit would remain, so that whatever you ask of the Father in My name He may give to you" (John 15:16).

The ability to persuade people that they are *sent by God* is based on a theological world view. God is in control of the world and there are no neglected spots of that control, though His control is often not apparent. True, God's activity does not always seem fair, and God works out His purposes in ways that do not legitimate our claims to happiness. But nevertheless, God is alive and active in the classroom, office, and assembly plant. If parishioners are not convinced of this, they set out on Mission Impossible and their energy quickly dissipates. Only if persons are convinced that they are divinely placed, only then can they see the grandeur of life's vocation. The operational phrase for this vocation is, "I'm part of a much bigger picture than my immediate surroundings indicate."

Worship has been truncated if it does not issue marching orders, if it does not inspire and equip a person to become a change agent. Parishioners should never be dismissed from the presence of God. They are to be charged with carrying God's glory with them. Because "the Most High does not dwell in houses made by human hands" (Acts 7:48), life is lived by the power of the invading and permeating Holy Spirit. Houses of flesh becomes temples of the Holy Spirit and conduits of God's glory. God and church are not to be left behind at Sunday noon. Every worship service is climaxed with the assurance, if not the exact words of Christ: "All authority has been given to Me in heaven and on earth. Go therefore.... I am with you always, even to the end of the age" (Matt. 28:18-20).

To be sent by God means to adopt a different ideology, a different frame of mind from that of the secular culture. Satisfaction is defined at a different level from prevailing notions of blessedness. All activity for every day is submitted to God's sovereign grace. This grace is omnipresent. The psalmist could say, "If I make my bed in hell, behold, thou art there" (Psa. 139:8b, KJV). The promise of Pentecost is that "you know Him because He abides with you and will be in you" (John 14:17b). Upon this fact is established the belief that worship can be integrated into the whole of life. The priest is the steward of grace and has invited worshipers to receive grace; now the prophet commissions them to distribute that grace. One of my favorite benedictions is, "And God is able to make all grace abound toward you; that ye, always having all sufficiency in all things, may abound to every good work" (2 Cor. 9:8, KJV). Prophetical-priestly worship authorizes the Christian to abound in the world for which Christ died.

Conclusion

The prophetical-priestly words of worship express delicate tensions: freedom of expression defined by dignity of order; reverence for a holy God who extends inviting grace; enthusiastic participation that includes the most timid and introverted among us; a scope that is evangelistic while realizing that worship should move everyone along the order of salvation; worship that transforms individuals without being legalistic and manipulative; worship that offers salvation to the sinner and sanctification to the believer; worship that is rational and yet transrational. These tensions are so delicate that they deserve our most critical thinking and deepest spiritual aspiration. Ad-libbing our way to God will not suffice. Nothing is more nauseating both to God and worshiper than an unprepared worship leader. In no place do words matter more.

Chapter 8

Domestic Words

R ichard Baxter, in his classic book, *The Reformed Pastor*, described a remarkable pastoral method from his personal experience: "Before we undertood this work, our hands were full, and now we are engaged to set apart two days every week from morning to night.... It will be as much as we shall be able to do, to go over the parish once a year (being about 800 families."[1]

According to Baxter, the public aspect of ministry (preaching and administering the sacraments) will be undermined if not coupled with private nurture of the home. "You are not likely to see any general reformation until you procure family reformation. Some little religion there may be here and there; but while it is confined to single persons,

---

[1]Richard Baxter, *The Reformed Pastor*, ed. by William Brown (Carlisle, Pa.: The Banner of Truth Trust, 1983), 183-184.

and is not promoted in families, it will not prosper, nor promise much future increase."[2] Baxter believed the pastor must have a direct hand in the promotion of family religion by asking the master of the family whether he prays with them and reads the Scripture, "advising them to use a form of prayer," seeing that there are "some useful moving books besides the Bible.... Direct them how to spend the Lord's day; how to dispatch their worldly business, so as to prevent encumbrances and distractions; and when they have been at church, how to spend the time in their families."[3]

The systematic contact between the pastor and the family that Baxter described would be almost unheard of today. Many are quick to point out the time constraints of today's pastor. However, we need to remember that the pastor's duties in Baxter's culture were multi-faceted (settling estates, reconciling legal disputes, and prescribing medical remedies), far more so than the responsibilities of a contemporary pastor. Another distinct difference rests in the authority of a seventeenth-century parish pastor as opposed to the pastor's position in the eyes of the church-hopping congregants today. But Baxter was well aware that his own parishioners had similar attitudes:

> They commonly think that a minister hath no more to do with them but to preach to them and administer the sacraments to them and visit them in sickness; and that, if they hear him and receive the sacraments from him, they owe him no further obedience, nor can he require any more at their hands.... They consider not that all souls in the congregation are bound, for their own safety to have personal recourse to him for the resolving of their doubts, and for help against their sins, and for direction in duty and for increase of knowledge and all saving grace; and that ministers are purposely settled in congregations to this end, to be still ready to advise and help the flock.[4]

---

[2]Baxter, 102.
[3]Baxter, 100-1.
[4]Baxter, 180-1.

In short, Richard Baxter based clergy-family connectedness on spiritual-biblical convictions. The American pastor's responsibility to visit the family for the purpose of conducting spiritual conversation remained a staple of pastoral activity until the twentieth century. With the arrival of psychology as a science and the identifying of pastoral care with counseling, pastoral responsibilities were radically redefined. Pastoral care was no longer conducted in the home; it transpired in the church office, in the form of crisis counseling. Pastoral care was no longer proactive in terms of spiritual nurture; it was reactive in terms of unraveling the problems of Americans who had been awakened to the hypothesis that there were unsettled accounts in their unconscious minds which "old-time religion" was ill-equipped to address. Brooks Holifield has meticulously traced the evolution of pastoral care in America as a mastery of mental techniques and scientific insight into the general organization of the mind, especially into the "particular characteristics of the child, the young mind, and the mature mind."[5] The following description of a rector in Northampton, Massachusetts, was far removed from Baxter's systematic understanding of family spirituality.

> He began each session by asking his client to be seated in a comfortable chair before a fire and practice rhythmic breathing, muscular relaxation, and visual imagery. He then led the client into the silence of the quiet mind by offering tranquilizing suggestions, followed by healing suggestions often interrupted with readings from the Bible or even a short sermon.[6]

The psychological paradigm enabled pastors to undermine their own authority further by adopting the cultural consensus that authority was no longer grounded in the church, government, or other traditional structures, but in the self.

---

[5] E. Brooks Holifield, *A History of Pastoral Care in America: From Salvation to Self-Realization* (Nashville, Tenn.: Abingdon Press, 1983), 226.

[6] Holifield, 205.

Freedom was contrasted to dogmatic religion. Religion became a private affair, in keeping with America's newly accented mind-your-own-business mentality. The boundaries between church and home were rigidly defined. American Christianity became preoccupied with a God who fulfilled the self rather than a God who ordered the home. Holifield succinctly summarizes the pastoral care transition: "As changes have come in the social order, changes have come in pastoral care...from self-denial to self-love, from self-love to self-culture, from self-culture to self-mastery, and from self-mastery to self-realization."[7]

The economic boom in post-World War II America combined with self-actualization psychology to thrust Americans into an all-out pursuit of mental and material satisfaction. The mad rush to obtain modern appliances and automobiles induced dad and mom both to work outside the home, leaving little time to enjoy those things, much less to give their children the quality time they needed. Even if parents did have the time, where would they find the expertise? Dr. Benjamin Spock taught us that raising children was a specialized business that demanded intricate knowledge of developmental processes. Spock was only the most visible tip of the iceberg. Below the surface were the previously accepted child-centered approaches of Jean Jacques Rousseau, Jean Piaget, and others. Child-centered education shed rigid parental discipline and encouraged the child to dictate his or her own developmental pace, rather than confronting the child with clear moral values. This overly indulgent attitude toward children has led William Damon to characterize the American web of societal problems as "demoralization," a loss of moral standards and a debilitating lack of moral spirit.[8] This web of problems includes a 124-percent increase of murders among children aged fourteen to seventeen from

---

[7]Holifield, 351.

[8]William Damon, *Greater Expectations: Overcoming the Culture of Indulgence in America's Homes and Schools* (New York, N.Y.: Free Press, 1995), xiv.

the late 1980s to the early 1990s, one million teenage pregnancies per year, and an increased amount of time devoted to pleasure-oriented diversions, such as watching television for up to five hours a day.

Churches, schools, and social agencies are all aware that we have these problems, but disagree over what is the best solution. These disagreements have produced what Damon refers to as false oppositions, "competing visions about the proper relationships between children and adults."[9] These include polarities between child-centered and adult-centered inclinations, such as experience vs. memorization, passive vs. active learning, external vs. internal motivation, and self-esteem vs. social interaction. In the face of these conflicting ideas, "discipline in the home has become a vexing dilemma rather than an act that comes naturally to parents. It has become, in fact, a lost art."[10]

The Youth Director

The parents in post-World War II evangelical churches were as bewildered as everyone else. In the face of parents' lack of time and expertise at child-rearing, the church created a specialized order of ministry called the "youth director." This suborder of pastoral care was the tangible evidence that the church had embraced the child-adult polarization that the rest of society accepted. This mind-set assumed that youth are a highly defined segment of the human species who are expected to listen to weird music, maintain blitzkrieged private bedrooms, swing on the refrigerator door every fifteen seconds, assume hairstyles that defy sexual identity, and speak a lingo indecipherable to anyone above the age of thirty. This polarization was most commonly referred to as "the generation gap." Christian parents believed the youth director would enable both the institutional church and the parents to cross this gap, and this would restore order to the universe.

---

[9]Damon, 99.

[10]Damon, 115.

But instead of bridging the gap between parents and youth, this new order of ministry only widened it. The youth director was a surrogate parent, paid to provide activities which the biological parents did not have time to provide. Evangelicals bought into the false notion that a paid specialist could provide family leadership which they could not, could communicate in a language they did not know, and could provide spiritual nurture they had no training to provide. The traditional means of grace provided by the body of Christ were no longer thought to be sufficient. Youth required their own specialized means, which served to separate them from both church and family.

This led to a truncated application of pastoral care. Rebelliousness, loneliness, promiscuity, and general adolescent maladjustment were not viewed as systemic problems to be confronted by the sanctifying ministries of both church and famiily. Youth could be isolated and treated by the youth director much of the time, without ever talking with the senior pastor or the rest of the church. The old saying that "it takes a village to raise a child" had been lost on the church. Now it was assumed that the work could be done by a youth director. The pastor was no longer an intimate part of the home, enabling the family to perceive how the growth of the individual family members was inextricably bound to one another. The prophetical-priestly role was relegated to sanctuaries filled with families who no longer sat togeter, much less sought God together.

Community Covenants

An essential prophetical-priestly task of the church is to enable parents to assume, within the context of church life, authority for giving spiritual guidance to their children. The pastor should enable families to develop covenants, unwritten community consensuses about the behavior and goals toward which the family should be guided. Just because they are unwritten does not mean they cannot be clearly communicated and adopted. Family behavior addresses fairness, justice, responsibility, self-respect, and mutual concern for the welfare of both individuals and the family unit. These principles are not proclaimed *ex cathedra* by the family member who has the most power and money. They are adopted through loving participation in work, play, and worship. In the absence of this participation, ethical obligations appear to be capricious moral mandates. Unfortunately, the church has often failed to encourage the kind of participation and communication that would allow its families to discover a biblically informed consensus of values.

The prophetical-priestly role of pastoral care means enabling families to build infrastructures of Christian values and subsequent action. The family members need to become Christian toward one another before they can become Christian to the outside world. John Henry Newman wrote, "The best preparation for loving the world at large, and loving it duly and wisely, is to cultivate an intimate friendship and affection towards those who are immediately about us."[11] This intimate friendship and affection begins in the home. Only once in the New Testament are we commanded to imitate God (Eph 5:1). The specific application of this command occurs in Ephesians 5:25-27: "Husbands, love your wives, just as Christ also loved the church and gave Himself up for her, so that He might sanctify her, having cleansed her by the washing of water with the word, and that He might present to Himself the church in all her glory, having no spot or wrinkle or any such thing, but that she would be holy and blameless."

The goal of the prophetical-priestly ministry is to make those around us holy. One of the measurements of being made holy in Christ is the ability to enable through the power of the Spirit those around us to be holy. Holy words and deeds enable those around us to become better people. The tempta-

---

[11]C.S. Dessain, *The Spirituality of John Henry Newman* (Minneapolis, Minn.: Winston Press, 1977), 51.

tion, at times for apparent reasons, is to neglect those who know us best. I was recently intrigued by Sonya Tolstoy's commentary on her husband, novelist Leo Tolstoy. His quest for Christian perfection consisted of giving up hunting, smoking, drinking, and eating meat, as well as forsaking the flesh through vows of chastity. Since his wife became pregnant sixteen times, the chastity must have lasted for only brief periods.

> There is so little genuine warmth about him; his kindness does not come from his heart, but merely from his principles. His biographies will tell of how he developed the laborers to carry buckets of water, but no one will ever know that he never gave his wife a rest and never—in all these thirty-two years—gave his child a drink of water or spent five minutes by his bedside to give me a chance to rest a little from all my labors.[12]

Grace-Giving Words

The passage that precedes the Ephesians 5 exhortation for husbands to sanctify their wives has much to say about the use of words. Those who put on "the new self, which in the likeness of God has been created in righteousness and holiness of the truth" (Eph. 4:24) are exhorted to lay "aside falsehood, speak truth each one of you with his neighbor, for we are members of one another. Be angry and yet do not sin, do not let the sun go down on your anger" (4:25-26). As one continues through the passage, there is a distinct holy word texture: *wholesome, edifying, gracious, kind, tenderhearted, forgiving, spiritual, melodious,* and *thankful.* These are contrasted to words such as *unwholesome, bitter, wrathful, angry, filthy, silly,* and *coarse.* Some positive words will be deliberate, while others will be spontaneous "according to the moment, so that it will give grace to those who hear" (4:29b).

America's homes are desperately in need of graceful words. One evening, I stepped into my daughter's room where

---

[12]Philip Yancey, "Be Perfect More or Less: Tolstoy, Dostoevsky, and the Impossible Sermon on the Mount," *Christianity Today*, July 17, 1995.

she was diligently studying. She had had a bad day. As any concerned father, I began to give her words of encouragement and affirmation. In fact, it seemed that Heidi had had a lot of bad days in high school, both academically and athletically. There had been many moments of frustration and failure. Evenutally, she became co-valedictorian of a large high-school class and an all-conference athlete. Here achievements were secondary, however, to her character of fortitude, perseverance, and trust. I believe God used my prophetical-priestly words as a means of grace to help her.

My words to Heidi that night were spontaneous, in the sense that they were unplanned and unexpected. On the other hand, they were deliberate within the intention of daily communication of a dad with his daughter. True, I have often failed in that intention; but my prophetical-priestly ministry as a father will not happen outside of the intention. Such a prophetical-priestly role in the home must be communicated and modeled by the pastor. Turning his or her parishioners into prophet-priests is a primary objective of soul care.

The kingdom of God will not come to Earth until it comes to the home. It will not come to the home without loving, planned, personal communication. This communication cannot be provided by the surrogate parents of technology and materialism. While our technology has gotten better, the family situation has become worse. While the percentage of adults who are college graduates is four times what it was in 1945, and while households with television sets have increased to 98 percent, the percentage of children born out of wedlock grew eightfold in the same period. Robert J. Samuelson states, in his *The Good Life and Its Discontents: The American Dream in the Age of Entitlement, 1945-1995,* "Too much was expected of prosperity as a cure for social ills. Money cannot transform human nature, nor neutralize all social upheavals."[13]

---

[13]Robert J. Samuelson, "Great Expectations," *Newsweek* (January 8, 1996), 24-33.

The need for prophetical-priestly ministry in the home is greater than ever, especially for families who don't eat together, work together, or do much of anything together. Our current lifestyles and communication methods are building walls of impersonalization. A sense of personhood has been diminished by the lack of face-to-face communication and consequential interaction. If we are not careful, the communication revolution of the Internet will only increase the communication gap between family members. This gap can be closed only through person-to-person interchange, which requires keeping my body in the presence of my family's bodies for extensive periods of time. Prophetical-priestly language cannot take place outside of smiles, frowns, tears, laughter, anguish, warmth, and all kinds of body language. Remote family control simply will not work. The following are prophetical-priestly acts that take place in the form of family interpersonal encounters.

Closure on the Past

Closure involves an assessment of the past. One cannot become an ethically responsible person without remembering. A prophet will encourage familiy members to assume accountability for their past actions. A preistly response by family members may involve forgiveness, absolution, or healing acceptance. Quite often an action of the past was neither morally right nor wrong, but hindsight reveals that the action could have been more Christian or socially responsible. Closure is not merely the process of judging or correcting someone. It can be a communal act of covering the past with healing grace. If a family never looks back, they accumulate the emotional and relational baggage of misunderstanding, miscommunication, and grievance. The work of clearing out the family's interpersonal "attic" may take place at the end of the week, at the end of the school year, at particular holidays, or whenever. It needs to take place at regular intervals.

One family established the custom of sitting down together to assess the previous school year. The assessment reviewed both the high and the low moments. When it was time for the son to disclose his low moment of the year, he did so with great difficulty. Unbeknown to his parents, he had been paddled (in his assessment, unfairly) by his teacher. These parents could have simply assumed the teacher had been fair, or they could have exonerated the child by laying all blame at the feet of the teacher. Instead, they discussed the event thoroughly with both their son and the teacher. They knew that such a discussion would promote reconciliation, the only route properly to encounter and alleviate their son's guilt.

One of the most disturbing trends in our society is a parental protectiveness that defends and excuses the moral maladjustment of children. Parents' constantly coming to the defense of their children's disruptive behavior has made the job of teaching in the public school systems almost impossible. Niether parents nor children are willing to accept clearly defined parameters of speech and behavior. Classroom freedom has fragmented to the point of anarchy, an entitlement to act out one's whims at the expense of others. It would be better to confront children with their personal accountability. Perhaps then the trend cited by William Damon could be curbed:

> A well-designed study of parents' and teachers' observations over time was conducted between 1976 and 1989 and published in November 1993. The reults showed behavioral declines for children of all ages and both sexes during the study's thirteen-year period. In 1989, according to parents and teachers, children were far more likely to "destroy things belonging to others," to "hang around" with others who get into trouble, to do poorly on their schoolwork, to be "underactive," "whining," "sullen," "stubborn," and "irritable." More children were lying and stealing; more were being held back a year in school; more were friendless; and more had chronic though minor physical problems such as frequent stomachaches. Fewer children were participating in sports or other healthy outdoor activities, and fewer had found any activity in life that truly engaged them, including their education.[14]

---

[14]Damon, 13.

Betty attended our church along with her three children. Frank, the father and husband, never accompanied her. Betty made a pastoral appointment with me to discuss Johnny, their fourth-grader, who was getting into fights on the school playground. The constant skirmishes had come to the attention of the teacher and then the principal. Now the principal had contacted the parents. Betty was concerned enough to seek counseling help. I could have theorized that there was aggression in the home which Johnny was acting out on the playground. Perhaps Johnny was not receiving the attention he desperately craved; thus, he was seeking it through unacceptable behavior. But I resisted the temptation of making an snap judgment. Instead, I asked Betty if Frank would be willing to accompany her for a time of discussion with me.

Almost to my surprise, Frank agreed to a counseling session in my office. As the three of us sat together, we talked about the importance of family commitments, shared responsibility, spiritual leadership, recreational time, and many other ingredients that are critical to a family's health. As they drove home, Frank commented to Betty, "I thought he was going to talk to us about Johnny, but instead he talked only about us!"

Betty later said, "Frank doesn't realize that Johnny's problem *is* us."

I visited Frank several times in his home and talked with him about his relationship to Christ. He was one of the best bowlers in our large metropolitan area, with several trophies to prove it. This father and husband could skillfully roll a polyurethane ball across a wooden floor to knock down plastic pins, but for whatever reason, he did not have the desire or skill to communicate meaningfully with his own family.

Frequent, open communication is vital to the family's health. When a parent directs a child to reflect on the events of the past week or past year, the child hears an important message: "I am interested in your welfare. I want to bear with you any burden that needs to be borne. I want to help you untangle anything that needs to be untangled, and tear down any barriers that we have inadvertently erected between us." Tracing the past may be the only way to maintain reconciliation in a family. Forgiveness is not a once-and-for-all events. It is an ongoing process that addresses misunderstandings and allows children to state their grievances. This atmosphere of open expression without fear of reprisal provides the candor for correction and healing. Families who retrace their steps are the only ones who can be freed from the past. Those who try to bury the past through denial and suppression are risking a future of haunting memories and unresolved conflicts. Our mental "attic," the unconscious mind, is always unforgiving if left unattended. Closure is the task of keeping it ordered and cleaned out, on an ongoing basis.

Values for the Present

Priestly words attach family time and energy to ultimate things. Prophetic words warn family members concerning undue attachment to penultimate things. The first activity culminates in worship of God as revealed in Jesus Christ. The second attempts to eliminate everything from our lives that is not in keeping with the worship of the One who embodied and displayed all true virtue. The very act of leading a family in worship demonstrates that there is a value that transcends our temporal and transient concerns.

Every waking moment, all of us go through a process of value formation in both the private and the public sector. An N.F.L. team has just lost a play-off game in their hometown to a team they were supposed to beat. This happened in front of eighty thousand rabid fans, some of whom had slept outside in the freezing cold just to buy a ticket. The mayor said, "I feel as if someone I care about has died. It's that kind of trauma." A store owner stated, "I had one employee who was so sickened by the loss that he spent the night vomiting." One father's kids put signs on all the doors to their house saying, "Dad, when you come in, don't break anything because the

Chiefs lost." A sociologist commented, "The way we live to-day is very isolated—our lives and jobs aren't really connected so we have very little in common with each other. And, if at most times our lives are dull and predictable, at least during football season there is an added sense of excitement and purpose. And so when our teams lose they've taken away our future. If we can't win at football, what can we win at?"[15]

Americans don't have much to live for, or at least don't know that they do. Allow me to disavow any kind of pious posturing about the previous example. My heart raced and my adrenaline rushed when that football game was on the line. Many times, I thought the world stood still when my own child was at home plate or the foul line, especially when her performance was crucial to the game's outcome. I was completely consumed by my emotional attachment to her, disproportionate to any related consequence.

Also, I believe there is value in a community's pulling together for a sports team. There is also value in my child's having an opportunity to bring years of diligent practice to fruition. There is solidarity in depending on the success of others while they in turn depend on your success. However, in our society, this solidarity does not normally take place within the context of Christian pursuits, but rather in the context of athletic or academic competition.

None of us is exempt from the urge to stamp our identity on the world, to secure a legacy of achievement and adulation. A socially acceptable way of becoming a "significant other" in the eyes of the world is through athletics. For the really pious among us, there are always the more "acceptable" lusts of good grades and artistic perfection. Because these lusts are so subtle, we have all the more reason to reflect upon them and clarify our motives in pursuing them. Robert Roberts makes this attempt as he contrasts kingdom principles with what he refers to as the "philosophy of beak and claw":

[15]Glen Rice and Matthew Schofield, "Bummed Beyond Belief," *Kansas City Star* (January 9, 1996), A1, A10.

Christianity on the other hand sides with the retarded philosophy of life which says we are all in this together. It says that we are
all heroes and heroines not because we are victors on the world's
terms, but because we are created in God's image and are his
daughters and sons; we are to be princes and princesses in his
kingdom. We gain this prize not by besting each other, but through
God's grace and the pursuit of his kingdom goals. There is no
limit to the number who can be "winners" in this sense. To be
"somebody" is not to be at the top of a pecking order, but to serve
faithfully in the cause of the kingdom, and that may be done as
well at the "bottom" as at the "top." This means that the matters
in terms of which competitions are set up—how beautiful,
wealthy, or clever you are, how much influence you have over
others, how fast you can run, how beautifully you can play the
piano or how brilliantly you can argue and write books, and so
on—are all of decidedly secondary importance by kingdom standards.[16]

Prophet-priests are constantly engaged in stating and
clarifying kingdom standards. This can be done only with
Bible in hand, focusing on the One who clearly demarcated,
in both deed and word, primary from secondary values. Consider these words, which merit constant application: "Do not
store up for yourselves treasures on earth, where moth and
rust destroy, and where thieves break in and steal. But store
up for yourselves treasures in haven, where neither moth nor
rust destroys, and where thieves do not break in or steal; for
where your treasure is, there your heart will be also" (Matt.
6:19-21). Homes and families with fluctuating values are filled
with fluctuating moods, attitudes, and emotions. Predicat-
ing life on the variables of loss-gain, win-lose, succeed-fail,
possess-have not, is a frustrating roller-coaster ride. The hectic obsession with getting and gaining is often at the risk of
emotional and spiritual depreciation, not to mention destroyed relationships.

---

[16]Robert Roberts, *Taking the Word to Heart: Self and Other in an Age of Therapies* (Grand
Rapids, Mich.: William B. Eerdmans Publishing, 1993), 161.

There is one overriding assumption in modern America: The increase of possessions assures the increase of happiness. David Walsh argues in his *Selling Out America's Children*, "We need to spend twice as much time with our kids and half as much money on them."[17] The marketplace messages that enable corporations to sell millions of dollars' worth of gadgets and games to American families at the expense of tripling credit-card debt between 1980 and 1990 are: "Happiness is found in having things." "Get all you can for yourself." "Get it all as quickly as you can." "Win at all costs." "Violence is entertaining." "Always seek pleasure and avoid boredom." And, "Always be dissatisfied with what you have."

Answers to the following questions indicate a family's seriousness (or lack thereof) about confronting the world's values: When was the last time we turned the TV off because the content was too violent? When was the last time we decided not to purchase something because it would not be in keeping with Christian stewardship? How long has it been since we decided not to participate in an activity, even though everyone else seems to be doing it? Has our family recently tried to decide on a Christian alternative of action when several alternatives could have been taken? The last time a crisis took place, did we attempt to find a Christian response as a family? When a family member was treated unfairly, did we discuss what response would be most in keeping with being a Christian? Have we recently discussed what it means to be affluent Americans while much of the world goes without?

Without the conversation that ensues from asking such questions, Christian value-building in the home is unlikely. Persons will act ethically only insofar as they ethically understand their situation.

A couple of the above questions relate to the family's stewardship responsibilities. The Old Testament priests were accountable for administering the temple collections. At the

[17]David Allen Walsh, *Selling Out America's Children: How America Puts Profits before Values—and What Parents Can Do* (Minneapolis, Minn.: Fairview Press, 1995), 123.

same time, prophets were responsible to let the people know when enough was not being collected. "Will a man rob God? Yet you are robbing Me! But you say, 'How have we robbed Thee?' In tithes and offerings" (Mal. 3:8). Malachi's indictment indicates an overall philosophy that needs to be discussed and adopted by the entire Christian family. What is the family's commitment of giving to the church? to missions? to individuals in need? to local causes? The family's stewardship philsophy not only entails money, but also time given to service organizations or community projects. Such contributions can become projects owned by the entire family. Nothing should be more rewarding to a father than to hear his twenty-two-year-old daughter inform him that she is going to give her tax refund to the local city rescue mission. What better family outing than a Saturday night visit to that same mission? All of these acts and discussions attempt to define what it means to be *blessed*—i.e., enabled to give out of God's unmerited favor. They are attempts at what Rodney Clapp refers to as "priestly stewardship." Clapp states, "We are chosen of God to declare and exemplify the will of God to creation, and in turn to represent the needs and praise of all creation to God—the core description for priests."[18]

If Christ-centered values are not gained at home, they are unlikely to be learned in other institutions. Our "Christian" colleges are using the same marketing techniques as their secular competitors. Recruiters say, "Our degree will enable you to get ahead, climb the corporate ladder, get a better job, make more money, realize self-fulfillment, and survive in an age of rapidly changing technology." The underlying message is, "Though we claim to be Christian, there won't be any required courses in our curriculum that focus on taking servanthood jobs, surviving on less money, bucking America's cultural trends, or making your family different from almost everyone else's." If these courses were in the curriculum, they would be muted by the institution's overt behavior. In short,

---

[18]Rodney Clapp, "Why the Devil Takes Visa," *Christianity Today* (October 7, 1996), 32.

the family cannot expect other institutions to establish the model for kingdom living. The family is the kingdom of God in microcosm. That is where value consistency must be taught.

Focus on the Future

Both prophets and priests deal in the future, but not in ways of which they are often accused. The prophetical-priestly ministry enables persons to make decisions based on reason, righteousness, and confidence that God desires the best for His children. This confidence consists of trust in the sovereign grace of God. "And we know that God causes all things to work together for good to those who love God, to those who are called according to His purpose" (Rom. 8:28).

The greatest insurance for discovering the will of God is right character. Right character is doing God's will today. Doing God's will today takes care of doing God's will tomorrow. God's will cannot be discovered outside of dwelling within the written Word, and applying that Word as it reveals the living Word to our lives. Doing God's will consists of being conformed to the image of Christ. It compares our image to God's image. The discovery of our image is facilitated by asking and trusting the Holy Spirit to apply Scripture to our lives. In James' analogy, the Word is a mirror that enables us not to forget what kind of persons we are (James 1:22-25). An ongoing measurement of ourselves via the Word, which examines our motives, desires, and values, is the only way our future can be faithfully charted. This process safeguards us against illusory impressions, feelings, and perceptions that may emerge from our own vantage point or emotional state. J.I. Packer has written,

> The fundamental guidance which God gives to shape our lives—the instilling, that is, of the basic convictions, attitudes, ideals, and value-judgments, in terms of which we are to live—is not a matter of inward promptings apart from the Word but of the pressure on our consciences of the portrayal of God's character

and will in the Word, which the Spirit enlightens us to understand and apply to ourselves.[19]

Applying prophetical-priestly words withing the family does not consist primarily of advice-giving, though children and spouses may at times need our advice. Again, the prophetical-priestly role consists of applying complementary words: The priest will lead the family in seeking God's will through prayer, while the prophet will lead the family in understanding and applying the Word. Prophetical and priestly ministries are not mutually exclusive. The tasks convert for the purpose of seeking both corporate and individual wisdom.

Wise people act prudently withing a sound paradigm of assumptions, values, and commitments. Unless these are in place, we can make no good decisions. People with vacuous theologies and philosophies make vacuous choices. Wise actions take into account both the temporal and eternal welfare of all who will be affected by those actions. Wise choices will be attuned to the holiness, justice, and love of God. The prophet-priest's first business of enabling others to make right choices is to introduce them to God. In other words, I began to help my daughter choose her husband and her life vocation when I first read a Bible story to her and prayed at her bedside.

Scripture describes the covenant relationship between God and His people. This relationship consists of our trusting obedience that responds to God's offer of grace and guidance. The provision of God's guidance falls within the context of His other provisions—health, food, and abundant opportunities for service. God has validated His promises with His practice. He has been good and will continue to be good toward us.

A parent enables his or her child to look forward by looking backward. It was this two-way perspective that Moses

---

[19]J.I. Packer, *Knowing God* (Downers Grove, Ill.: InterVarsity Press, 1973), 214.

provided as he and the nation stood on the brink of the Promised Land.

> "For I proclaim the name of the LORD;
> Ascribe greatness to our God!
> The Rock! His work is perfect,
> For all His ways are just;
> A God of faithfulness and without injustice,
> Righteous and upright is He" (Deut. 32:3-4).

> "Like an eagle that stirs up its nest,
> That hovers over its young,
> He spread His wings and caught them,
> He carried them on His pinions.
> The LORD alone guided him" (Deut. 32:11-12a).

The archetypal Exodus journey is played out in every family as they learn a faith that takes the next step, a faith that prevents stockpiling the world's goods, a faith that draws strength from the community of believers known as the family. The journey of Israel would have been impossible without the journey of the family. It was the father who gathered the family together to remind them of why they had left Egypt and where they were headed. Without this continuous reminder, their nomadic lifestyle just did not make sense. Prophetical-priestly words connect yesterday with today, and today with tomorrow. Without this connectedness, life is an impulse without overall design and purpose.

The prophetical-priestly role of the parent is a delicate task that embraces life while resisting enculturation. Children need to experience both the joys and disappointments that are part of the school classroom, athletic team, summer camp, neighborhood play, and the fullness of life with all its surprises. Focusing on the future is not so much showing children the quickest way to get from point "A" to point "B." It is providing them experiences, education, and above all spiritual truth that enable them to negotiate the turns and potholes of life. A young person's decision of where to go to college will have been largely determined because of previous discussions of educational experiences. The decisions about whom to marry will have been mostly determined because of previous discussions of right relationships. Surrounding the issues and events of life with reflection and discussion is far more rewarding than surrounding individuals with material things and pleasures.

Prophets and priests are craftspersons of Christian character. The greatest gift that any of us will give the world is children who embody Christianity as it was portrayed and taught by Christ. Only as our words are incarnated can they save the world. J.I. Packer writes, "Truth in the Bible is a quality of persons primarily, and a proposition only secondarily: it means stability, reliability, firmness, trustworthiness, the quality of a person who is entirely self-consistent, sincere, realistic, and undeceived."[20]

Teaching the Family to Pray

The past, present, and future all are encompassed by prayer. Prayer addresses both the limitations of time and the eternal dimensions of God's grace. It affirms each family member, regardless of achievement, and expresses praise *that they are* rather than *for what they are.* The very act of naming family members before the throne of God, in their presence, enhances identity formation and releases courage for the formidable tasks of life. Prayer lifts family members beyond themselves and enables them to see others from God's vantage point, whether the other is a sibling or a stranger. Prayer enables transcendence, a life beyond the petty squabbles and self-centeredness that plague most families. Without transcendence, life is shortsighted, always grappling with the immediacy of the moment. Myopia drowns in its own petty concerns. It is like the sailor on Columbus' ship who could not wait to return to Spain in order to inherit the dying shoemaker's job in his native village. Many families never catch the big picture.

---

[20]Packer, 102.

The difference between families that pray together and those that don't is one person. This is the prophet-priest who calls the family together for prayer. Prophet-priests reserve sacred space in time which blocks out TV, phone calls, and other distractions. There is no perfect time for prayer. A regular family "time out" will have to be arranged in view of family rhythms and schedules, which is jealously guarded and protected. Nothing will test the prophet-priest's spiritual nerve more than calling the family together for a spiritual retreat. Culture is against it; Satan is against it. Thus, it is all the more vital. Family corporate prayer is the indispensible option for spiritual sustenance.

As family members each take their turns in audible prayer, values are formulated, desires are articulated, anxieties revealed, grievances cleared, and reconciliation actualized. Prayer releases grace, which consumes the misgivings and misunderstandings of the previous days and hours. It is amazing how the family's collective mood is almost always improved after a time of prayer. The pressure is lifted from asserting our own worth and justifying our own failures. Family prayer is the activity which best promotes candor and honesty. There is always the temptation to cover up our faults, especially be those of us who claim to be spiritual directors. Motivating family prayer is the love of God, which covers a multitude of sins.

As the family priest leads the family in worship, the home becomes a habitat of praise and thanksgiving. Without prayer, life is circumstantial and the circumstances are never right. As in the game of baseball, prayer can field the bad hops and even admit an error on the ball that was easily playable. Prayer confesses in the company of those closest to us, "I muffed it." Whether the fault is our doing or someone else's, we will allow God to use it for His glory. Prayer is the family's opportunity to embrace life with all of its ups and downs, triumphs, and disappointments. In Dag Hammarskjöld's words,

"Night is drawing nigh."
For all that has been—Thanks!
To all that shall be—Yes![21]

If parents could give their children any gift, let it be the disposition to pray. This is the disposition that all of life can be hallowed by God's grace—the walking, talking, eating, working, and playing. The outcome is up to God, a fact which lifts a tremendous burden. The family is not the master of its fate. The very posture of praying celebrates our dependency on a God who cares, though His interpretation of and intervention at life's critical junctures may be beyond our understanding.

An elderly man stood in the doorway of a church I pastored. As we conversed, he pointed to the house just across the street, where he had been raised. "My dad used to lead us in family devotions each evening," he said. "One day, as a young lad, I arrived home late and the family was already kneeling in the living room. I knew it was such a holy moment that, rather than disturbing them, I knelt on the front porch until they were through praying." No greater gift could a prophet-priest give his or her family than reverence for a holy God. Such a disposition is a result of honest, dependent, confessional, grateful, worshipful, collective prayer.

---

[21]Dag Hammarskjöld, *Markings* (New York, N.Y.: Ballantine Books, 1964), 74.

Chapter 9

Conclusion: Making Our Way Back

Prophet-priests specialize in diseases of the soul: sin, despair, depression, loneliness, alienation, anger, hostility, pride, greed, avarice, addiction, and fear. The list is almost endless. Of course, these sicknesses eventuate in the systemic evils of ethnocentricity, nationalism, exploitation, oppression, and racism. Prophet-priests do not draw a sharp demarcation between individual and corporate evil, but work on the assumption that they are inextricably bound. To neglect one is to neglect the other, and to treat one is to treat the other. The prophet-priest's words are for the purpose of sensitizing parishioners to both, and in turn to shift the balance of power between good and evil.

This monumental task requires God-given perception—seeing, hearing, and thinking of the highest order. On one hand, the thought processes of a deluded world must be critically engaged. On the other hand, they must be transcended by the disciplines of abstinence, solitude, reflection, contemplation, prayer, and biblical study. Reading the prevalent spirit of the times is necessary. But even more important is continuing the task of Christ, described by Simeon, "that thoughts from many hearts may be revealed" (Luke 2:35b). The most important vision that any individual will ever have is the vision of himself or herself illuminated by the living Word. Opening the eyes of the spiritually blind and the ears of the spiritually dumb is foremost on the pastoral agenda.

The primary metaphors for understanding in both the Old and New Testament are *seeing* and *hearing*. Nowhere is this more dramatic or even humorous than when Jesus healed the man born blind by placing clay upon his eyes. "The man answered and said unto [the Pharisees], 'Well, here is the amazing thing, that you do not know where He is from, and yet He opened my eyes" (John 9:30). Seeing is contrasted to spiritual lostness and darkness, a condition to which Jesus often referred. "For the Son of Man has come to save that which was lost" (Matt. 18:11). Lostness is a state of disorientation, alienation, and bewilderment.

In February of 1996, veteran outdoorsman Mike Goodell parked his canoe on Billy's Island at the edge of Okefenokee Swamp in Georgia to begin a several-hour nature hike. A couple of hours later, Goodell found himself in foliage so think he was completely disoriented. Though Billy's Island is only eight miles square, Goodell emerged forty-one days later. Meals of bugs, leaves, and berries, washed down with swamp water, had enabled him to survive though he lost fifty pounds during the ordeal. Swamp experts knew his general location, but they were not able to track him down, even with the most sophisticated equipment. One can only wonder how many times Goodell must have longed for a dime-store compass.

The human plight encountered by the contemporary prophet-priest is the pervasive malady of lostness. The optimism that human beings can order their world via technology and sheer striving turns into disillusionment. The alarm signals of stress, guilt, fragmentation, and broken relationships indicate that our world is out of control. We need a reordering. That reordering must start from within.

Prophet-priests enable that reordering. If they are caught up in the same hurried pace and hectic schedule as the rest of the world, they will be rendered impotent. Even the juggling of holy objects can fail to deliver people from their hellish existence. The ecclesiastical whirlpool can be dizzying. Prophet-priests who have lost their perspective are not able to give perspective, which is what parishioners most need.

If one is to comprehend the universe, one must give careful attention to one's immediate surroundings. There is no better example of this than Annie Dillard's journal, *Pilgrim at Tinker Creek*. Her painstakingly careful observations of nature as it unfolds in the mountains of western North Carolina provide a macroscopic understanding of the world through microscopic inspection of her environment. As we accompany her, we learn how to stalk life in order to learn the clues of existence. "Stalking is a pure form of skill," she says, which calls for patient waiting and motionless observation. What is observed is a small part of a much greater order, a counterpart to the rest of the world. An aphid lays a million eggs, a winter rye grass plant grows 378 miles of roots and fourteen billion root hairs in four months, and in one season a large elm produces as many as six million leaves. Obviously, Dillard had help with her arithmetic, but the calculations do not detract from her firsthand experience of Earth's fecundity and intricacy.

All plant life is constantly attacked by bean beetles, borers, weevils, bulb flies, cutworms, stink bugs, screw-worms, sawflies, poultry lice, cheese mites, cluster flies, puss caterpillars, itch mites, and long-tailed mealy bugs. "What if you were an inventor and you made ten percent of your inventions in such a way that they could only work by harassing, disfiguring, or totally destroying the other ninety percent?"[1] Then there are creatures which don't destroy other species but routinely devour their own. The female praying mantis bites off and digests the male's head during the act of sexual intercourse. Dillard describes her observation:

> I lay on the hill this way and that, my knees in thorns and my cheeks in clay, trying to see as well as I could. I poked near the female's head with a grass; she was clearly undisturbed, so I settled my nose an inch from that pulsing abdomen. It puffed like a concertina, it throbbed like a bellows; it roved, pumping, over the glistening, clabbered surface of the egg case testing and patting, thrusting and smoothing.[2]

Annie Dillard envisions herself as a prophet, one who lives in the "gaps, the clefts in the rock." She urges us, "Squeak into a gap in the soil, turn and unlock—more than a maple— a universe."[3] The secrets of the universe yield glimpses of divinity and the incomprehensible secrets that God has locked into the world, which are accessible to those who will knock, seek, and ask. But there is a price to pay. One must be separated from the world, as were the Hebrew prophets who became distinctive people, consecrated to see things that others could not see. "I am a fugitive and a vagabond, a sojourner seeking signs," Dillard writes.[4] "The secret of seeing, then, is the pearl of great price. If I thought he could teach me to find it and keep it forever, I would stagger barefoot across a hundred deserts after any lunatic at all."[5]

Whatever biblical prophet-priests were, they were unique. They were called to see what others could not, discern what others could not, go where others would not, touch those whom others would not, and say what others dare not. Thus, the priests'

---

[1]Annie Dillard, *Pilgrim at Tinker Creek* (New York, N.Y.: Harper and Row, 1974), 229.
[2]Dillard, 57.
[3]Dillard, 269.
[4]Dillard, 267.
[5]Dillard, 33.

seven days of ordination consisted of washing, clothing, anointing, sprinking, pouring, slaying, burning, offering, mixing, waving, and boiling. The identity of Aaron and his sons was unmistakably sealed: "Moses and Aaron went into the tent of meeting. When they came out and blessed the people, the glory of the LORD appeared to all the people. Then fire came out from before the LORD and consumed the burnt offering and the portions of fat on the altar; and when all the people saw it, they shouted and fell on their faces" (Lev. 9:23-24).

We must ask, "Will the recovery of this unique and even strange identity be a deterrent to the church's role as an evangelistic community?" "Will officialism undermine universality, inclusiveness, and empathy?" This is possible, but not probable. The American church did not lose its potency because its prophet-priests were overly unique. The church lost its power because the prophet-priest's role became perfunctory. They lost the passion for enabling the Christian community to see what the world could not. The prophet-priests became as blind as everyone else, unable to discern the hand of God. They became like Eli, who thought that Hannah's fervent intercession out of a pining, depressed soul was the result of alcoholic consumption.

No, a lowering and blurring of the pastor's office will not do. Only a holy consecration, a recognition and awareness of distinctiveness and separation will allow for God-hearing, God-seeing, God-talking, and God-following people. We desperately need the isolation of Tinker Creek. Only on that basis can the prophet-priest say, "Come with me, discover what I have discovered. I have no corner on God and God's truth; God is as accessible to you as to me. If I can enable you to catch a glimpse of God, I am truly rewarded. But I must tell you there is a price to pay. You may have to spend your time differently than others. You may have to reorder your life. You may have to reverse your values. You may have to downsize. You may have to be still. If you don't, you may someday realize that life has been misspent."

The bottom line of the prophetical-priestly ministry is enabling individuals to make the right investment of their lives. We cannot all go to Tinker Creek and sit for hours waiting for an elusive muskrat to climb on the bank to sun himself. Neither can we sit on a pole as did Simon Stylites for over thirty years, nor live in a cave as did Elijah. But we all can find a closet, as Jesus suggested. People who spend time in a prayer closet often gain a perspective on life that others do not have. They come to value what God values, rather than what the world values. They live in the same world, yet in a different world from everyone else.

The prophet-priest is called to picture and describe God's world. God's world is the world that is and the world that is to come. The prophet-priest's articulation of this world is fiercely honest about the present and optimistically hopeful about the future. In spite of a ravaging parasitic amorality that constantly must be beaten back, all of life's inherent contradictions will be replaced one day by fertile ground and blossoming roses. Until then, the prophet-priest is called on to do what only she or he can, to encompass all of life with God's grace and wisdom. There will be plenty to keep us from triumphantly pontificating. There will always be a sense of failure. We too will at times be left chillingly numb, as was the Episcopal priest who was asked to infuse meaning into the senseless slaying of a teacher and sixteen children at an elementary school in Dunblane, Scotland. We had better be accustomed to living in the cleft of the rock and under the shadow of the Almighty, or we will have no word to speak. And the people of this world must have a word—the Word— or else the universe becomes a silent, empty tomb.

Not that the word of a pastor always will be more accurate or empathetic than someone else's. Often it will simply be more representative. The community of believers, both local and catholic, has designated this person as their representative. Thus, the pastor assumes greater dimensions than himself or herself. The pastor carries the portfolio of apostolicy, a role conferred upon those throughout the history of the church who have taken the oath of full-time commitment to the healing of souls. The pastor is expected to have a competence and connectedness that brings reassurance of immeasurable magnitude to the most forlorn of circumstances. It is not unlike the summons of the family physician which Sherwin Nuland describes: "The mere knowledge that someone had gone to the drugstore to call the doctor and the word that he was on the way, changed the atmosphere in our small apartment from terrified helplessness to a secure sense that somehow the dreadful situation could be made right."[6]

Just as the family physician once represented a transformative body of knowledge and expertise, so the pastor represents a body of transcendent truths. The church has been the foremost custodian of those transcendent truths. We are convinced that the things in life that change least are the things most worth knowing. The earth revolves around the sun. God has revealed himself in the flesh. Persons are given to defending their own egos. These are universal truths. Priests are custodians of these truths and prophets are the proclaimers of them. To have a firm grasp on and keep perception of a rightly formed understanding of the world is their task. Not that their understanding never changes—adjustments are perfectly in order. The fact that they are keepers of the understanding (i.e., the interpreters of life) is the essential paradigm of ministry. The essence of this paradigm is the purveyance of the saving knowledge of Jesus Christ.

Wisdom regulates life in a way that transcends time and culture. The wisdom of the ages orders life whatever the circumstances or crises at hand. For the Christian, this wisdom has been deposited in the Scriptures and incarnated in Christ. Prophet-priests are protectors and providers of this grand depositum, as assuredly as the Levitical priesthood

---

[6]Sherwin B. Nuland, *How We Die: Reflections on Life's Final Chapter* (New York, N.Y.: A.A. Knopf, 1994), 247.

mainatined the ark of the covenant. Holy words, spoken and acted, are now the critical elements of that covenant rather than a staff, manna, and tablets of stone. Prophet-priests live under the divine mandate that the covenant of grace be not lost to mankind. Words that accurately represent the covenant are the currency of pastoral ministry.

To be sure, these covenant words will be culturally influenced. Thus, God does not expect the prophet-priest to be an obscurantist, cut off from society. The pastor speaks God's truth in the language of the people, making sure that nothing is lost in the translation. What a delicate task! So the portfolio carried by prophet-priests is also that of kingdom interpreter. Interpreters enable hearing, understanding, and the subsequent bearing of fruit. They have been granted to know the mysteries of the kingdom of God. No greater responsibility ever will be given to human beings.

We must know the reward of following God's command, "Cease striving and know that I am God" (Psa. 46:10a). We invite whoever will come to the quest. Anything less is trivial pursuit.

Thanks be to the Father, the Son, and the Holy Spirit for the call to pastoral ministry. "How will they hear without a preacher? How will they preach unless they are sent? Just as it is written, 'How beautiful are the feet of those who bring glad news of good things!'" (Rom. 10:14c-15).

Index of Scripture References

Index of Subjects
and Proper Names

U

Urim and *Thummim* 70–71.

V

values
  Christian 149
  family 155–159
Vanhoye, Albert 71
visions 132–135
visitation, pastoral 143, 145
vocation 141

W

Wainwright, Geoffrey 38, 113
Wells, David 43–44, 59
Wesley, John 92, 101–102, 108–109
Whitefield, George 39
Willard, Dallas 85
Wilson, Robert 66
wisdom 97, 161, 173–174
  gift of 71
Woolverton, John 48–49, 62

world view, Christianity as an
  alternate 137–138
worship 113–138
  contemporary, deficiencies of
    116–117
  early Christian 138
  humorous language in 119
  language of 118–119
  modern inability to 116
  preaching in 35
  spirit of 75–76
  televised services 115
  theology formulated in 113
  unacceptable 89–90
  utilitarian emphasis of 115

Y

youth director
  specialized order of ministry
    147–148

Z

Zedekiah, King 104